The author was born in England in 1912, when his parents
were in Europe for two years; at six months he was taken back
to Australia where his father owned a sheep station. When he
was thirteen Patrick White was sent to school in England, to
Cheltenham, 'where, it was understood, the climate would be
temperate and a colonial acceptable'. Neither proved true, and
after four rather miserable years there he went to King's
College, Cambridge, where he specialized in languages. After
leaving the university he settled in London, determined to
become a writer. His novel *Happy Valley* was published in
1939; *The Living and the Dead* in 1941. During the war he was
an R.A.F. Intelligence Officer in the Middle East and Greece.
After the war he returned to Australia and is currently living
in Sydney.

His other novels are *The Tree of Man* (1956), *Voss* (1957), *Riders
in the Chariot* (1961), *The Solid Mandala* (1966), *The Vivisector*
(1970), *The Eye of the Storm* (1973), *A Fringe of Leaves* (1976)
and *The Twyborn Affair* (1979). In addition he has published
two collections of short stories, *The Burnt Ones* (1964) and *The
Cockatoos* (1974), which incorporates several short novels, and
his autobiography, *Flaws in the Glass* (1981). In 1973 he was
awarded the Nobel Prize for Literature.

PATRICK WHITE

THE AUNT'S STORY

PENGUIN BOOKS

Penguin Books Ltd, Harmondsworth, Middlesex, England
Penguin Books, 625 Madison Avenue, New York, New York 10022, U.S.A.
Penguin Books Australia Ltd, Ringwood, Victoria, Australia
Penguin Books Canada Ltd, 2801 John Street, Markham, Ontario, Canada L3R 1B4
Penguin Books (N.Z.) Ltd, 182–190 Wairau Road, Auckland 10, New Zealand

—

First published by Eyre & Spottiswoode 1948
Published in Penguin Books 1963
Reprinted 1969, 1971, 1974, 1976, 1977, 1982

—

—

Made and printed in Great Britain by
Hazell Watson & Viney Ltd,
Aylesbury, Bucks
Set in Linotype Granjon

For

BETTY WITHYCOMBE

CONTENTS

Part One MEROË

She thought of the narrowness of the limits within which a human soul may speak and be understood by its nearest of mental kin, of how soon it reaches that solitary land of the individual experience, in which no fellow footfall is ever heard.

OLIVE SCHREINER

I

But old Mrs Goodman did die at last.

Theodora went into the room where the coffin lay. She moved one hairbrush three inches to the left, and smoothed the antimacassar on a little Empire prie-dieu that her mother had brought from Europe. She did all this with some surprise, as if divorced from her own hands, as if they were related to the objects beneath them only in the way that two flies, blowing and blundering in space, are related to a china and mahogany world. It was all very surprising, the accomplished as opposed to the contemplated fact. It had altered the silence of the house. It had altered the room. This was no longer the bedroom of her mother. It was a waiting room, which housed the shiny box that contained a waxwork.

Theodora had told them to close the box before the arrival of Fanny and Frank, who were not expected till the afternoon. So the box was closed, even at the expense of what Fanny would say. She would talk about Last Glimpses, and cry. She had not lived with Mrs Goodman in her latter years. From her own house she wrote and spoke of Dear Mother, making her an idea, just as people will talk of Democracy or Religion, at a moral distance. But Theodora was the spinster. She had lived with her mother, and helped her into her clothes. She came when the voice called.

At moments she still heard this in the relinquished room. Her own name spilt stiff and hollow out of the dusty horn of an old phonograph, into the breathless house. So that her mouth trembled, and her hand, rigid as protesting wood, on the coffin's yellow lid.

From the church across the bay a sound of bells groped through a coppery afternoon, snoozed in the smooth leaves of the Moreton Bay fig, and touched the cheek. The blood began to flow. I am free now, said Theodora Goodman. She had said this many times since the moment she had suspected her mother's silence and realized that old Mrs Goodman had died in her sleep. If she left the prospect of freedom unexplored, it was less from a sense of remorse than from not knowing what to do. It was a state that she had never learned to enjoy. Anything more concrete she would have wrapped in paper and laid in a drawer, knowing at the back of her mind it was hers, it was there, something to possess for life. But now freedom, the antithesis of stuff or glass, possessed Theodora Goodman to the detriment of grief. She could not mourn like Fanny, who would cry for the dead until she had appeased the world and exhausted what she understood to be sorrow. Fanny understood most things. The emotions were either black or white. For Theodora, who was less certain, the white of love was sometimes smudged by hate. So she could not mourn. Her feelings were knotted tight.

Now waiting for Fanny in the yellow afternoon, the thick light prepared a greater state of uncertainty. The chair backs loomed. The back of the little, ordinarily graceful prie-dieu was solid as a tombstone. If gestures were completed, it was according to a law of motion, which takes over from the will, and which now guided Theodora Goodman's black. Black had yellowed her skin. She was dry, and leathery, and yellow. A woman of fifty, or not yet, whose eyes burned still, under the black hair, which she still frizzed above the forehead in little puffs. You could not have noticed Theodora Goodman. Her expression did not tell. Nor did she love her own face. Her eyes were shy of mirrors. Her eyes fell, except in moments of necessity, frizzing out the little puffs of hair, when she outstared, with a somewhat forced detachment, her own reflection. This thing a spinster, she sometimes mused, considering her set mouth; this thing a spinster which, at best, becomes that institution an aunt.

Viewed this way the situation was more tolerable. There were times when the morning sang with bulbuls encaged in palms, their throats throbbing from behind green slats, and yes, it was very tolerable. She became lighter now, too. Her arrested black flowed through the afternoon. Even a mahogany tombstone dissolved. She was at most, but also at least, an aunt. She swam down the passage, out of her mother's room, away from the influence of the coffin, and in the suave silence she saw across the bay the pepper trees tossed into green balls by a wind starting, that raked the sea until all the little white boats jumped and fretted and pulled at their moorings to be away.

Oh yes, in other circumstances, this could have been an afternoon on which children came, when they would run and pull at her, their hot laughter, and their chocolate hands, after they had been stuffed with tea. Then it was something to be an aunt, of importance, dashing, almost rakish. Tell us something, Aunt Theo, they cried. Yes, yes, she said; but first I must find my breath. Where; they said; is it under the bunya-bunya tree? Because it was a joke. It was huge. Let us stroke Aunt Theo, said the boys; we shall stroke her moustache.

That was no longer so very terrible when the boys said it. Affection can blunt words, and with affection she responded to their hands. But it was not so much the boys she loved. They were round and hard and fierce as furry animals. It was Lou, whose eyes could read a silence, and whose thin, yellow face was sometimes quick as conscience, and as clear as mirrors. Theodora loved Lou. *My niece.* It was too intimate, physical, to express. Lou had no obvious connection either with Frank or Fanny. She was like some dark and secret place in one's own body. And quite suddenly Theodora longed for them to bring the children, but more especially Lou, when they came to town for the funeral. Since her mother's death, she could not say with conviction: I am I. But the touch of hands restores the lost identity. The children would ratify her freedom.

When the doorbell rang the whole house shook and recovered.

This must be Fanny and Frank, said Theodora, but she waited for them to be brought in and decently arranged in the drawing-room.

She would have waited longer, if the silence had not begun to gape open. So she went down. And it was really down. Certain encounters took her to the depths.

She opened the door and found the uneasy group, Fanny and Frank, not only, yes also, the two boys and Lou. But how, felt Theodora, it is unlike Fanny to consider simple requests, let alone answer unmade prayers.

There was no time to investigate.

'Theo, Theo,' cried Fanny in rising gusts, 'how terrible it is! And for you, Theo, on your own.'

Her kiss was wet and spasmodic on Theodora's cheek.

'Poor dear Mother,' Fanny cried.

'It was not very terrible,' said Theodora. 'She died in her sleep. I went in. It was like any morning. After the man had pushed the paper under the door. It was like that.'

But Theodora was insensitive.

Fanny cried. Once she had been plump and pretty. Now she was red and fat. She cried because it was expected, and because her clothes were tight, and because it was easier to cry, and because she increased in importance by crying for the dead. She also remembered vaguely a piece of pink coconut ice offered by her mother's hand. So Fanny cried.

Frank mumbled. It was not so much in sympathy as protest. Here was something to be held off. But there were also greetings to be made. Never very articulate, except in talking sheep, he now damped his few words as a measure of respect. Theodora touched his hand, which was rough and hard. The backs of his hands were covered with red hairs.

'Sit down, Frank,' said Theodora. 'And how is everyone else?'

To thaw the children, who sat stiff with solemnity round their parents, where they had been placed. Now they murmured. They hung their heads. They were still strangers. But they began to fight the situation and come alive.

'It is not the sort of occasion,' Fanny said, blowing her nose. 'But I took the opportunity. The boys must have overcoats. They grow so ... fast.'

Her last word slipped out quite shockingly, beyond control, and she put her face inside her handkerchief and cried. But now it was not so much her mother's death as the tragedy of domesticity, that avalanche of overcoats and boots.

'Steady on, Fanny,' said Frank, who had not experienced the exaltation of grief.

He looked sideways, at no one, and tapped with his yellow boot.

'George got a cinder in his eye,' said young Frank.

'Shut up, Frank,' said George, and blushed.

'You did! You did! He put out his head near Mittagong, and it flew in. Mum made a thing with a handkerchief and fished it out.'

'Shut up,' cried George. 'You dope! I'll kick you in the stomach if you don't shut up.'

'Boys!' said Fanny, only just. 'You've no idea, Theo, what I endure.'

But it was good. Theodora looked at the boys, their hard knees, on which the cuts had healed. The bodies of the boys denied the myth of putrefaction. So that she drew breath quickly, severely, through her nose, as if her contempt and disgust for a tasteless practical joke had been finally justified. She was whole. She was free. And Lou came and sat beside her. Lou did not speak, but she could feel very positively the thin bone of an arm pressed close against her waist.

'May one go up?' asked Fanny, her eyebrows sewn together by pain.

'Yes,' said Theodora, 'if you want. Only there is nothing to see. Only the coffin, that is.'

'Poor dear Mother,' said Fanny. 'I would have given so much for a last glimpse.'

Her husband sucked his teeth. It was not regret, but a vastly irritating fragment of ham from a sandwich eaten in the train.

'I said to Frank,' said Fanny, 'as soon as we got your wire, I said, I cannot believe that Mother has passed over without saying good-bye. Didn't I, Frank?' she said, because he needed drawing in.

Frank Parrott sat. He was watching his wife prepare to perform some act. His mind lumbered to the club, to the talk of wool clips and stud rams. Now he sat glassily among the women. His hands were heavy on his thighs. The mature Frank Parrott often reminded Theodora of a stuffed ram, once functional within his limits, now fixed and glassy for the rest of time. He was what they call a practical man, a success, but he had not survived.

'Hold hard, Fanny,' said Frank, 'I'm coming too.'

He got himself heavily out of his chair, manipulating his heavy thighs. He would go, not to patronize a coffin, but to pass time in the lavatory. Besides, Theodora made him sidle. To sit with her alone in the same room. Her ugly mug, that was always about to ask something that you could not answer.

So Frank Parrott followed his wife out.

Now the drawing-room was smooth. Bells swam on its surface from across the bay, and the voices of the boys, their shall-and-shan't, passing and repassing, jostling like wooden boats on summer water.

'May we play with the brass ball?' asked Lou.

The brass ball was unfailing.

'Yes, yes. Please!' cried young Frank.

So they took the filigree ball and rolled it over the carpet. It was something that Grandmother Goodman had brought from India once, and which, she said, the Indians fill with fire and roll downhill. And although its hollow sphere was now distorted and its metal green, when rolled across the drawing-room carpet the filigree ball still filled with a subtle fire.

'What do the Indians do it for,' said young Frank.

'Yes, why?' asked George. 'Aunt Theo, why do they fill the ball with fire?'

But Lou did not ask. She patted the ball.

'I have no idea,' said Theodora. 'I have forgotten. Or perhaps I never knew.'

'It's silly,' said George. Suddenly he wanted to kick it.

'It's not,' said Lou.

Her hands protected not only the Indian ball, but many secret moments of reflected fire. Above her the legs of the boys sprang straight and menacing as concrete towers. George would be a farmer like his father, and young Frank said that he would build bridges. But Lou, who continued to roll the filigree ball, flowed, in which direction you could not tell, and for this Theodora trembled. The boys you could have piled into two heaps of stones. But Lou was as unpredictable as water. Theodora sensed this. The shape of her own life had not been fixed.

Then Fanny had begun to impose herself again. She was already steaming in the passage. Fanny came.

'Lou,' she said through her swollen nose, 'you have torn your pants. Oh dear, oh dear. And crawling about on the carpet. You'll dirty your knees. Theo,' she said, 'where is Frank? I am exhausted. It is the air. The air of Sydney makes blotting paper of me.'

'But it will improve now. There is a breeze,' said Theodora, as she had heard other people say.

With the same slightly incredible conviction Frank Parrott was closing the door. She watched his veins, and the way he composed his mouth to resist judgement, whether this was aimed or not. Theodora did not aim at Frank. At most she considered with detached regret the process by which bronze can melt to fat. But he winced under what he believed to be forgiveness.

'I suppose she made a will, Theo,' said Frank, to stamp the situation with authority.

'Yes,' she said, 'she told me.'

'Yes, yes,' said Fanny. 'But it is always safer to *see*. These old people, and Mother of course was old. George, Frank, behave yourselves, and put away that brass ball.'

'We shall see,' said Theodora. 'The will is with Mr Clarkson. But, as you know, there was very little to leave. And what there is, she told me, she intended I should have.'

'Of course,' Fanny said.

In the wind from the bay the leaves of the Moreton Bay fig were less smooth. The bell from the distant church tolled through tossed trees.

'No one can deny you deserve it, Theo,' said Fanny.

No one, that is, but Fanny, in her heart. Her life was a life of full cupboards. She kept them locked. She made inventories of her possessions. She did quick sums on the backs of envelopes, and was both amazed and afraid at the answers that she got. She was afraid that the plenty might diminish, just a little; this made her lie awake at night.

'And what are your plans, Theo?' asked Frank.

'I shall probably go away.'

'Good heavens,' said Fanny, 'where?'

Freedom was still a blunt weapon. Theodora did not answer, because she did not know.

'Anywhere. Or everywhere,' she said at last. 'Except that the world is large.'

Theodora, blushed Fanny, is quite, quite mad.

'It is very awkward for me,' she complained, 'when people ask me your plans.'

'But that is nobody's business,' Theodora said.

She wiped her mouth with her handkerchief. Strength had at last made her weak. And now, for a moment also, she touched with the ball of the handkerchief the humiliating fringe of her moustache. Perhaps, after all, she would remain the victim of family approval and her upper lip.

'Theo is quite right,' she heard the thick voice of Frank.

She was surprised, and grateful, but controlled, as if treading on a doubtful plank.

'She may even find a husband,' the voice continued. 'At her age. With her money. In Europe,' it said.

He looked at her for the first time since coming into the house, so that she felt the weight of it. His resentment was colossal. She saw the lips above the brown teeth, and she heard the laughter that did not come, but which should have burst thick and obscene, like the laughter of men that breaks through the frosted partition in a public house.

'Don't be a fool, Frank,' said Fanny, disposing of her husband. And then in the appropriate key of sorrow, 'What time is the funeral?' she asked.

'At ten o'clock in the morning,' said Theodora.

Now Frank yawned, and stretched, to show by physical pantomime that he had not lost face. He would look up Bags Browne at the club. And dear, dear, remembered Fanny, there were the overcoats for the boys, before the shops shut.

'I don't want an overcoat,' said George.

'You'll get a whipping, my man,' his father said.

Afterwards, young Frank hoped, they would buy ice creams, and he would choose a sundae with marshmallow and chopped nuts, which last time made him sick, but it was good.

'I shall stay with Aunt Theo,' Lou said.

It was too unimportant for even Fanny to object, or maybe it was that Fanny, aiming her displeasure at vaster targets, was exhausted. Anyway, she ignored an opportunity. She looked at Lou and agreed, deciding at the same time that she was yellow, scraggy, and unattractive. She had been christened Marie Louise, but circumstances and the child herself had conspired.

Then they had all gone, and the light became merciful.

'There was an old woman in the train,' said Lou, 'had her things tied up in a leopard skin. She had a photo of her married daughter, and three cold mutton chops. Her daughter's name is Mavis Forbes.'

'It is possible,' said her Aunt Theodora Goodman.

So that a great deal remained remote, and upstairs a hideously shiny wooden box endeavoured to contain a mystery.

'Did Grannie Goodman want to die?' asked Lou.

And again Theodora could feel the thin bone of an arm pressed against her waist.

'I expect she felt it was time,' she said. 'There was nothing left to do.'

'I don't want to die,' said Lou.

'There is no reason why you shall.'

But Theodora, talking of reason, drew in her mouth for her own oracular glibness, suddenly taking it upon herself to dispose of life and death, as if they were presents wrapped in tissue paper. She looked at the child's face. How far it was deceived she could not discover. It was a still, dark pool that for the moment did not reflect.

'Tell me about something,' said Lou, the words warm in Theodora's shoulder. 'Tell me about Meroë.'

'Meroë?' said Theodora. 'But my darling, you have heard it, and there is very little to tell.'

She had told the story of Meroë, an old house, in which nothing remarkable had taken place, but where music had been played, and roses had fallen from their stems, and the human body had disguised its actual mission of love and hate. But to tell the story of Meroë was to listen also to her own blood, and, rather than hear it quicken and fail again, Theodora smoothed with her toe the light on the carpet, and said, 'But, my darling, there is very little to tell.'

2

IT was flat as a biscuit or a child's construction of blocks, and it had a kind of flat biscuit colour that stared surprised out of the landscape down at the road. It was an honest house, because it had been put up at a time when the object of building was to make a house, a roof with walls, and the predominant quality in those who made it was honesty of purpose. This is something that gets overlaid by civilization, in houses by gable and portico, in man by the social hypocrisies, but sometimes it survives in the faces in old photographs, beside the palm, and it was present too in Meroë, which was what someone had called the house before the Goodmans came.

Someone had called it this, and no one in the district remembered why. It had been accepted along with the other exotic names, Gloucester, Saumarez, Boscobel, Havilah, Richmond, and Martindale, that have eaten into the gnarled and aboriginal landscape and become a part of it. It was the same with Meroë. No one ever debated why their flat daily prose burst into sudden dark verse with Meroë in their mouths. *Meroë*, they said, in their flat and dusty local accents. Although the word smouldered, they were speaking of something as unequivocal as the hills. Only the hills round Meroë had conspired with the name, to darken, or to split deeper open their black rock, or to frown with a fiercer, Ethiopian intensity. The hills were Meroë, and Meroë was the black volcanic hills.

Up towards the house the flat swept, the tussocks grey in winter, in summer yellow, that the black snakes threaded, twining and slippery, and the little unreliable creek, whose brown water became in summer white mud. The house looked over the flat from a slight rise, from against a background of skeleton trees. But there was no melancholy about the dead trees of Meroë. They were too far removed, they were the abstractions of trees, with their roots in Ethiopia. On the north side of the house there were also live trees. There was a solid majority of soughing pines, which poured into the rooms the remnants of a dark green light, and sometimes in winter white splinters, and always a stirring and murmuring and brooding and vague discontent.

This was the north side of the house, but on the south side there were roses, an artificial rose garden so untidy that it looked indigenous, and which was made because Mrs Goodman wanted one. She said from her sofa, let there be roses, and there were, in clay carted specially from a very great distance. For a moment it gave Mrs Goodman a feeling of power to put the roses there. But the roses remained as a power and an influence in themselves long after Mrs Goodman's feeling had gone.

Theodora, lying in her bed, could sense the roses. There was a reflection on the wall that was a rose-red sun coming out of the earth, flushing her face and her arms as she stretched. She stretched with her feet to touch the depths of the bed, which she did not yet fill. She felt very close to the roses the other side of the wall.

'Theo,' they called, 'it is time. It is time you washed your neck. It is time you went to the piano and practised scales.'

'Yes,' she answered, 'I'm coming.'

But she lay in the warm bed, remembering sleep, and drifted in the roselight that the garden shed.

These years had the roselight of morning, but there were also the afternoons, in which the serious full white roses hung heavy, and the lemon-coloured roses made their cool pools in a shade of moss. There were the evenings when red roses congealed in great scented clots, deepening in the undergrowth.

'Where are you going, Theo?' they asked.

'Nowhere,' she said.

She ran, slowed, walking now alone, where she could hear a golden murmur of roses. Above her she could see the red thorns, and sometimes she reached, to touch. She felt on her cheek the smooth flesh of roses. This was smoother than faces. And more compelling. The roses drowsed and drifted under her skin.

'Theodora, I forbid you to touch the roses,' said Mrs Goodman.

'I'm not,' cried Theodora. 'Or only a little. Some of them are bad.'

And they were. There was a small pale grub curled in the heart of the rose. She could not look too long at the grub-thing stirring as she opened the petals to the light.

'Horrid, beastly grub,' said Fanny, who was as pretty and as pink as roses.

Theodora had not yet learnt to dispute the apparently indisputable. But she could not condemn her pale and touching grub. She could not subtract it from the sum total of the garden. So, without arguing, she closed the rose.

Altogether this was an epoch of roselight. Morning was bigger than the afternoon, and round, and veined like the skin inside an unhatched egg, in which she curled safe still, but smiling for them to wake her, to touch her cheek with a finger and say: I believe Theodora is asleep. Then she would scream: I am not, I am not, and throw open her eyes to see who. Usually it was Father.

Or else you waited for Father to come out from behind his door. It was a solemn and emotional event. Your father is not to be disturbed, said Mother, which gave to his door a certain degree of awfulness. But Father himself was not awful. He was serious. He sighed a lot, and looked at you as if he were about to let you into a secret, only not now, the next time. Instead, and perhaps as compensation for the secret that had been postponed, he took you by the hand, about to lead you somewhere, only in the end you could feel, inside the hand, that you were guiding Father.

The room where Father sat was the side the pines were. It was plain as a white box, but filled with a dark murmuring of boughs, and the light was green and shifting that fell through pines. There was a little lamp that stood on Father's table. It had a thick green-glass shade and a shiny brass stand. It was a reading lamp. Your father is a one for books, sighed Gertie Stepper, as the flour crept up her arms and her face grew red from squeezing so much dough. The tone of Gertie Stepper's voice made it something sad and incurable, almost as if it were an illness, what Father did with books. And old books, foreign books, Gertie sighed; in this house it is always books, your mother too, only it is different in a lady. So you walked past Father's door with a sense of awfulness, especially as it was that

22

side of the house, where sometimes the pines, when the wind blew, flung themselves at the windows in throaty spasms.

If you went inside, Father was sitting with his chin on his chest, looking at books. He would sit like this for many hours, only his breath lifting his beard, as steady as a tree. Really Father was not unlike a tree, thick and greyish-black, which you sat beside, and which was there and not. Your thoughts drifted through the branches, or followed the up and down of the breathing that lifted Father's beard. He had grey eyes. Above the heavy grey-black thicket of the beard the eyes were light and clear. But they did not always look.

'You must come in, Theodora,' Father said finally. 'You must come in whenever you like, and take to books.'

'Better a girl than a man,' said Gertie Stepper. 'No one never lived off gingerbread.'

Which of course was silly. Gertie Stepper could talk rubbish, although she also Understood Life, and had been in seven situations since a girl. When Father asked you into his room and invited you to take down books, it was something to make you feel solemn.

If you could not understand the words of books, the names, the names sang, and you could touch the brown, damp paper with your hands. There were the foreign books too, which Father, Gertie said, used to read all the time. There were Herodotus and Homer. You asked, and Father said. He told you something funny. It was the bird that sat in the crocodile's throat. Fanning his larynx, Father said. Herodotus wrote this in a book. It was both funny and strange. And the crocodile lay in a river called the Nile, which flowed not far from Meroë.

'But at Meroë there is only a creek,' Theodora said.

'There is another Meroë,' said Father, 'a dead place, in the black country of Ethiopia.'

Her hands were cold on the old spotted paper of the complicated books, because she could not, she did not wish to, believe in the second Meroë. She could not set down on the black grass of the country that was called Ethiopia their own yellow stone. In this dead place that Father had described the roses were as brown as paper bags, the curtains were ashy on their rings, the eyes of the house had closed.

'I shall go outside now,' Theodora said.

Because she wanted to escape from this dead place with the suffocating cinder breath. She looked with caution at the yellow face of the house, at the white shells in its placid, pocked stone. Even in sunlight the hills surrounding Meroë were black. Her own shadow was rather a suspicious rag. So that from what she saw and sensed, the legendary landscape became a fact, and she could not break loose from an expanding terror.

Only in time the second Meroë became a dim and accepted apprehension lying quietly at the back of her mind. She was free to love the first. It was something to touch. She rubbed her cheek against the golden stone, pricked by the familiar fans and spirals of the embedded shells. It was Our Place. Possession was a peaceful mystery.

At Our Place, wrote Theodora Goodman on a blank page, *there is an old apricot tree which does not have fruit, and here the cows stand when it is hot, before they are milked, or underneath the pear trees in the old orchard where the cottage has tumbled down. I see all these things when I ride about Our Place, with my Father. Our Place is a decent size, not so big as Parrotts' or Trevelyans', but my Father says big enough for peace of mind.*

'Fetch your pony, too, Theo,' Father called, 'and we shall ride round the place.'

So you did, riding just above the yellow grass, under the skeleton trees. Theodora sat straight, riding round Our Place with Father. She listened to the clinking of the stirrups, and the horses blowing out their nostrils, and the heavy, slow, lazy streams of sound that fell from the coarse hair of their swishing tails. Theodora looked at the land that was theirs. There was peace of mind enough on Meroë. You could feel it, whatever it was, and you were not certain, but in your bones. It was in the clothes-line on which the sheets drooped, in the big pink and yellow cows cooling their heels in creek mud, in magpie's speckled egg, and the disappearing snake. It was even in the fences, grey with age and yellow with lichen, that tumbled down and lay round Meroë. The fences were the last word in peace of mind.

Things were always tumbling down. Some things were done

24

up again with wire. But mostly they just lay.

And in this connection Theodora Goodman discovered that Our Place was not beginning and end. She met for the first time the detached eye.

'Meroë?' said Mr Parrott. 'Rack-an'-Ruin Hollow.'

Which Theodora heard. She was waiting for Father, in town, under the long balcony of the Imperial Hotel. She hung around, waiting, and there were men there. She could smell their cloth, and the smell of drying horse sweat that left their leggings. The men stood in the shade of the Imperial Hotel. They spread their legs apart because they were important. They owned cattle and land. There was Mr Parrott, and old Mr Trevelyan, and Alby Poynter, and Ken Searle.

Goodman was a decent fellow, said old Mr Trevelyan, and he shook his head, though it usually shook, it was like that. Yes, said old Mr Trevelyan. It was bad. And the fences fallin' down.

'All this gadding off to foreign places,' said Mr Parrott. 'Sell-in' off a paddock here and a paddock there. George Goodman has no sense of responsibility to his own land.'

This was awful. It made your stomach sick, to hear of Father, this, that you could not quite understand, but it was bad enough.

Then Father came out. He was wearing the old Panama hat. He was laughing at something good that had happened inside the Imperial Hotel. It was so good that Father had come to the surface, and his eyes saw. And she wanted to laugh too, but she could not. Her stomach was sick with the sense of responsibility that Father, they said, did not have.

'So long, Ted, Alby,' Father called, nodding and laughing to the men. 'Theo, where are you?'

'So long, George. So long, Mr Goodman,' replied the men, as if nothing had been said.

It was all smiles. But Theodora Goodman was thin and yellow with shame.

'Here I am, Father,' she said. 'I waited here in the shade. The buggy is round the side.'

They drove home high in the buggy, between the black wheels, listening to the stones that they lashed up. Theodora sat with knotted hands. She was oppressed by a weight of sadness, that nobody would lift, because nobody would ever know that she was shouldering it. Least of all Father, who was thick and mysterious as a tree, but also hollow, by judgement of the men beneath the balcony. Now she linked together what they said with remarks that Gertie Stepper made. I been all my life with practical people, Gertie said, punching at the dough.

The wheels of the buggy on the road from town thrashed the stones, and Father said, 'Nothing to say, Theo?'

'Why,' she said, 'no.'

There was nothing to say. His nearness and the flashing of his Panama hat were hard enough to bear.

It was true what the men said, it was quite true. They had sold Long Acre, and Nissen's Selection, and Bald Hill.

'I refuse to vegetate,' said Mrs Goodman. 'Let us go somewhere. Before we die.'

Her voice struck the dining-room door, beyond which lamps had just been lit, and the big hambone still glittered, and the apple peel Fanny had thrown across her shoulder lay coiled on the carpet.

'It's reckless, Julia,' Father said.

'Then let us be reckless,' said Mother, and, the other side of the dining-room door, she must have tightened her mouth.

'Let us be reckless,' she said. 'And die. We can sell a paddock. Let us go to the Indies.'

Mother's voice burned the quiet air. It was stifling as an afternoon of fire.

Father laughed. 'I suppose we can sell Long Acre,' he said. 'Old Trevelyan's willing to buy.'

Then they were both silent, as if consumed by Mother's fire.

'The Indies,' Mother breathed.

That was Long Acre. But there had been the other trips, to Europe twice, and to India, from which many things were brought back, in silk and glass and mahogany, as well as a brass filigree ball that the Indians used to fill with fire. When Father and Mother had gone, and the rooms of the house were shut, there was this to look forward to, the things that would be brought back. Sometimes the rooms were shut for a long time, and it was like living outside a house, into which you looked occasionally through a window at the frozen furniture. The shut

26

rooms sound like music boxes that have stopped playing. You hold your ear against the sides, which contain a creaking, of music waiting to burst out as soon as somebody touches the spring. It was like this too with the closed rooms, waiting for someone to walk in and coax life from the furniture.

'You must be good children,' Mother said thoughtfully. 'And behave. And brush your teeth. And practise your scales.'

She said it through her green veil, moistening her lips slightly with her tongue. The boxes had been locked that morning and sent to town in the spring cart. And now she sat putting in time, waiting for the buggy to come round. She turned her head this way and that. She touched the bow on Fanny's hair. Mother did not kiss. Or not much. And then only Fanny. *My pretty little parakeet*. Mother liked better to arrange things, the ornaments in cabinets, or on little tables in the drawing-room, then to sit and watch what she had done.

Once there were the new dresses that were put on for Mother's sake.

'Oh,' she cried, 'Fanny, my roses, my roses, you are very pretty.'

Because Fanny was as pink and white as roses in the new dress.

'And Theo,' she said, 'all dressed up. Well, well. But I don't think we'll let you wear yellow again, because it doesn't suit, even in a sash. It turns you sallow,' Mother said.

So that the mirrors began to throw up the sallow Theodora Goodman, which meant who was too yellow. Like her own sash. She went and stood in the mirror at the end of the passage, near the sewing room which was full of threads, and the old mirror was like a green sea in which she swam, patched and spotted with gold light. Light and the ghostly water in the old glass dissolved her bones. The big straw hat with the little yellow buds and the trailing ribbons floated. But the face was the long, thin, yellow face of Theodora Goodman, who they said was sallow. She turned and destroyed the reflection, more especially the reflection of the eyes, by walking away. They sank into the green water and were lost.

There were many bitter days at Meroë when the roselight hardened and blackened. The earth was hollow with black frost, and the grass lanced the air with silver spears. Then the hands stuck to the music, beating out the icy bars of a nocturne, which were stiff and blunt when they should have sailed out as smooth and continuous as a wedge of swans. Not this nocturne that beat its little glass hammer at Meroë.

Mother's voice crackled at the fire. She warmed her rings. Her small head was as bright and as hard as a garnet beside the fire.

'No, no, Theodora,' crackled Mother. 'Not that way. Where is your feeling?' she said. 'This horrible up and down. Can't you feel it flow? Here, give it to me.'

As if it were a thing. But Mother sat down. She played the music as it should have been played. She took possession of the piano, she possessed Chopin, they were hers while she wanted them, until she was ready to put them down. Only, watching the hands of Mother, which always did what they wanted to, Theodora was not moved. The music had lost its meaning, even the meaning that lay in the stiff up and down, the agonizing angularity that Chopin had never meant to be, but which was part of some inner intention of her own.

'The piano is not for Theodora,' Mother sighed. 'Fanny is the musical one.'

Fanny could play a piece, and it was a whole bright, tight bunch of artificial flowers surrounded by a paper frill. Fanny played her piece. And when she had played it, it was finished. She jumped up, and laughed, and was content.

Outside though, beyond the fire and the carpets and the last notes of Fanny's completed piece, there was the long, black, bitter sweep of the hills. Theodora walked in the garden of dead roses. One of the hills, they said, which was now dead, had once run with fire, its black cone streaming, but now it brooded black against the white sky. Only if you walked on the side of the hill there was a last flicker of gold from the wattles, of which the bark oozed a deeper golden gum, so that the rock gave up some of its blackness, the hill melted and flamed still.

Down the road from the direction of the hills the Syrian came from time to time. He came into sight at the bend in the road, where his wheels thrashed, splashing through the brown water of the ford. From a good distance you could see the dirty canvas swaying and toppling above the cart, and there was time to shout a warning, to call, 'The Syrian! Here comes the Syr-i-urn!'

This made everyone run out of the house, everyone from the back of the house – that is, Gertie Stepper, and Pearl Brawne, and Tom Wilcocks, and Fanny, and any old man who was being given tea. Everyone ran out. It made quite a scattering of fowls.

Gertie said the Syrian sold trash, but everybody liked to buy, and Gertie even, to touch and choose. It was exciting as the cart grated through the yard. Turkeys gobbled. Dogs barked. The day was changed, which once had been flat as a pastry board. Now it was full of talk, and laughing, and the whining of the Syrian's mangy dog, and the jingled harness of his old blue horse. Now there was no question of work, now that the Syrian had come.

The Syrian himself was dry and brown, with blue tattoo marks on his hands. The eyes were deep and dark in the bones of his face. But they did not tell much, nor did his voice, in the language that he talked. When the Syrian became intelligible, he spoke in shillings, or with his brown hands. He uncovered his brown teeth in a clockwork smile. Out of the cart, from under the old tarpaulin, he brought the openwork stockings, the ribbons, the shawls, the mouth-organs, the safety-pins, and the pen-knives that he sold.

Once there was a silver shawl. Horiental, said Gertie Stepper. He tossed it out for everyone to see. How it blew in the winter wind! It streamed like a fall of silver water from the Syrian's hand.

'Oooooh!' everybody cried.

And, 'Oo-*er*,' said Pearl Brawne.

But Gertie Stepper, she got red, all except her pinched-up mushroom nose, and she hit at the brown knuckles with an iron spoon.

'Hey, you,' said Gertie. 'You no good. No good shawl. You think I no see, eh?'

And now it was a fact. The splendid shawl that everyone had pushed to see was a poor, ragged, flapping thing that fell. It lay exposed on the hard ruts. The Eastern shawl had a hole in the corner, which the Syrian had held hidden in his hand.

'Cheap. Very cheap.' He smiled and pointed.

'Yairs, yairs,' said Gertie. 'That may be, Mr Ali Baba. You can keep that to tell in court.'

Then everybody laughed, even Gertie Stepper, almost, from behind her tin-rimmed spectacles that were mended with a piece of string.

Once when the Syrian left, Theodora went with him some of the way. In the white-lit winter evening her legs grew longer with the strides she took. Her hair flew. She had increased. She walked outside a distinct world, on which the grass quivered with a clear moisture, and the earth rang. In this state, in which rocks might at any moment open, or words convey meaning, she stood and watched the Syrian go. His silence slipped past. The hills settled into shapelessness. She was left with the trembling of her knees.

Afterwards, trailing through the shrunk yard, there was no external evidence that the Syrian had been. The meat-safe still creaked on its wire hook, and the kitchen window's yellow square denied the immensity of shapelessness. Even Theodora Goodman's hair hung meekly in damp tails.

'Wherevervyoubeen, Theo?' asked Gertie Stepper.

'I walked some way with the Syrian.'

'That dirty Syrian hawker man! Don't you never do that again!'

'Oo-*er*,' said Pearl Brawne, and she giggled into tea.

The kitchen was bright, white. It's warmth nuzzled, like fur.

'Theo, fancy,' Fanny said. 'And it's dark too. I'd be afraid.'

Fanny was often afraid. She sat up in bed and screamed when the nightlight sank in the saucer. But in the mornings Fanny shone. In the mornings Fanny took her basket, after she had practised scales, which were always so smooth and pleasing to Mother. She sat and rocked on the veranda, under the hanging maidenhair. She pursed up her mouth, to amuse, and said, 'Now I shall do my broidery.'

She stitched a man in a cocked hat, and a train with smoke in its funnel, and a border of morning glories. And in the middle of it all she stitched:

FANNY GOODMAN

1899

'There, Theodora. Look at your sister,' said Mother.

'Oh, leave me alone,' Theodora cried. 'I am all right.'

Because she felt her own awkwardness. After she had hidden in the garden, she looked at her hands, that were never moved to do the things that Fanny did. But her hands touched, her hands became the shape of rose, she knew it in its utmost intimacy. Or she played the nocturne, as it was never meant, expressing some angular agony that she knew. She knew the extinct hills and the life they had once lived.

'Let us play at houses,' Fanny said. 'I shall have a house with twenty rooms. In one room there will be ivory, and in another gold, and another amethyst. I am going to dust the ornaments with a feather duster. I have children too, but they will not be allowed in these rooms, in case they are boisterous and knock over my things. You are my husband, Theo, but you will be out most of the day, riding round the place. You have many sheep, and you will make a great deal of money, and buy me diamonds and lovely furs. In the whole district there is no one as rich as us. Listen, Theo, look! How can you play if you don't listen?'

'Yes? Tell me,' Theodora said.

And she returned. She stood to learn the rules of the game that she must play.

Fanny made many rules. She thought of many clever games, which were like the swift, smooth music that she played, or the morning glories that she stitched. There they were. Mother was proud.

'Fanny is the *artistic* one, Mrs Parrott,' Mother said.

'But Theodora,' said Father, 'has great understanding.'

'Of course,' said Mrs Parrott, who looked frightened, as if it were the first time she had been given this to eat.

'Theodora,' she said, 'is a good, bright girl. She is always very polite.'

Mrs Parrott had a weak voice. To assist it she had to suck a lozenge, of which she kept a supply in a little silver box. Her bag was full of rich things, but she was a thin and sandy woman, pale, like her voice, and the pale things she said.

'Children are funny little things,' said Mrs Parrott.

Whenever she came to the house, Father usually left. Father

said, 'Come on, Theo. You and I shall go out and shoot.'

She had a small rifle which she took on these occasions, and which was the cause of many arguments. Because Mother hated and despised Theodora's rifle. She said it was unseemly for a girl to traipse about the country with a gun. But Father stood firm. This was something, he said, that Mother would not understand. It was wrong and unreasonable, Mother said. It was something, said Father, that he could not very well explain. Anyway, Theodora kept her rifle.

Because of the many words that it had caused, she never mentioned it. She took it down in silence from the rack on the wall outside Father's door, and the weight of the rifle, and the smoothness of its wood, and the coldness of its dark, keen metal, together with other circumstances, added solemnity to her act. On afternoons when she went shooting she let herself out by the side door to avoid the heat of argument. The side door opened on to the pines, and for many years Theodora connected the hush of dead needles and the sound of living pines with the smooth, clean, oily smell of her little rifle.

It hung rather too heavy from her bony shoulder, as she made her legs keep pace with Father. Her joints appeared excessively loose. Theo should have been a boy, they said, the more obliging ones, hoping to make the best. But she herself had never considered what could not have been such a different state. Life was divided, rather, into the kinder moments and the cruel, which on the whole are not conditioned by sex.

Anyway, carrying the rifle, she was free. They walked through the paddocks, through the yellow tussocks, where the sloughed snakeskin chafed and chattered, through the grey, abstracted, skeleton trees, and past the big black boulders that the hills had tossed out before they cooled. Father did not speak. He respected silence, and besides, whether it was summer or winter, the landscape was more communicative than people talking. It was close, as close as your own thought, which was sometimes heavy and painful as stone, sometimes ran lighter than a wagtail, or spurted like a peewit into the air.

From the rise above the swamp Father would aim at a rabbit scut. Theodora aimed too. She was everything in imitation, and because of this the importance of what she did was intense. The rifle kicked her shoulder lovingly. She loved, too, the smell of shooting, its serious pungency, which the wind puffed back into her nose, and which afterwards remained, sharp and flinty, on her hands. She took her hands to tea unwashed, with a sense that this was something the others could not share.

'Perhaps after all pretty futile,' Father once said, breaking open his gun over the carcass of a rabbit.

The voice did not immediately convey. She had bent to touch the body of the still-warm rabbit. The killing did not move her after a time, as it did at first, the blood beating in her own heart. In time, behind the rifle, she became as clear and white as air, exalted for an act of fate and beauty that would soon take place, of which her finger had very little control, it was an instrument.

Then Father's voice bore in. 'A pretty kind of idiocy,' it said. 'A man goes walking with a gun, and presents his vanity with the dead body of a rabbit.'

After the moment of exaltation, and the warm shining fur, she was puzzled, and it hurt. Father was moody, Gertie said, he had had more education than was good. So perhaps that explained.

'It must have died quickly,' she said.

Barely offering the words.

'Yes,' laughed Father. 'But death lasts for a long time.'

And then, by the sound of his voice, she knew that they should be going.

After this, Theodora sometimes walked in the paddocks alone. Once the hawk flew down, straight and sure, out of the skeleton forest. He was a little hawk, with a reddish-golden eye, that looked at her as he stood on the sheep's carcass, and coldly tore through the dead wool. The little hawk tore and paused, tore and paused. Soon he would tear through the wool and the maggots and reach the offal in the belly of the sheep. Theodora looked at the hawk. She could not judge his act, because her eye had contracted, it was reddish-gold, and her curved face cut the wind. Death, said Father, lasts for a long time. Like the bones of the sheep that would lie, and dry, and whiten and clatter under horses. But the act of the hawk, which she watched, hawk-like, was a moment of shrill beauty that rose above the endlessness of bones. The red eye spoke of worlds that were brief and fierce.

Theodora Goodman's face often burned with what could not

be expressed. She felt the sweat on the palms of her hands.

'You've got a fever,' said Gertie Stepper, her own dry, wondering hand on a forehead.

'No,' said Theodora. 'Leave me.'

The face of Gertie Stepper was perpetually wondering, behind the tin-rimmed spectacles, under the distracted hair. She groaned beneath the weight of practical things. On her upturned hands she held the roof of Meroë. She waited for something unfortunate to happen. As it had, it did, and would. As it had happened to the late Mr Ernie Stepper, coal miner, of Newcastle, in an accident in a mine. Under marble they put Ernie Stepper, and the marble said: *The bowels of the earth revolted and claimed him for their own.* This saying was made up by a Mr Barney Halloran, bookmaker's clerk, poet, and friend.

'Yes, it's terrible what happens,' Gertie Stepper used to say.

It happened, or something, to Pearl Brawne.

Pearl Brawne helped Gertie Stepper in the house. She was that Mrs Brawne's eldest girl. That Mrs Brawne did washing, and got drunk, and Mr Brawne had gone. Pearl was about sixteen, and big. Theodora and Fanny used to look and look at Pearl, at the overflowing mystery of a big girl.

'You will find life slow at Meroë,' said Mrs Goodman. 'But it is up to you, Pearl, to see what you can make of it.'

'Yes, Mrs Goodman,' said Pearl.

She looked down.

In spite of her age, Pearl Brawne looked down a lot, because she was still shy, and you looked up through Pearl, and it was like looking through a golden forest in which the sun shone. Pearl was beautiful. Pearl was big and gold. Her hair was thick heavy stuff, as coarse as a mare's plaited tail. It hung and swung, golden and heavy, when she let it down.

'Oh, Pearl,' they sometimes said, 'let us swing on your long fair hair.'

'Go on!' giggled Pearl. 'Yous!'

She laughed and reddened. In Pearl the blood ran close to the surface and often flooded under the skin. But when she was undisturbed, Pearl was white, and especially her neck, in the opening of her blouse. Pearl swelled inside her blouse, and was white and big. She rose and overflowed. There was no containing Pearl

34

in common bounds. She was meant to swell, and ripen, and burst. And it distracted Gertie Stepper's forehead, who always looked for the end before it came.

About this time Tom Wilcocks was working on the place. Tom Wilcocks milked the cows. He fed the pigs and fowls. On Saturday he drove the spring cart into town. Tom Wilcocks smelt of milk. He was a boy from another district. From another state, they said. He had come looking for work, and the clothes that he wore were a size too big. But Tom Wilcocks knew how to carve things out of wood. He could carve a rose and a crown on the lid of a box, and Jesus Christ in mahogany.

'It is beautiful,' Fanny said. 'I shall keep it, may I? Among my things? Look, Pearl, what Tom has done.'

Because Pearl was always near. Now she scrabbled in water the potatoes that she scraped for dinner. Her red hands plunged, and glistened, and plunged.

'Pffh! I'm busy,' said Pearl. 'Mrs Stepper 'n' me, we got the dinner. All these showin' off things! I haven't time.'

She shook her heavy head of hair.

'It's time as Tom took hisself off. Always standin' round the kitchen door.'

Her voice scraped like the potato knife, which was blunt and black. It was unlike Pearl. She held her head on one side, and scraped. Or she bit her mouth, and screwed out an eye, out of the potato's face.

'What sort of things you got time for, Pearl?' asked Tom.

He lounged and laughed, in the old green coat that hung. Tom Wilcocks was rough as bags. His neck was red and strong. The pollard had caked hard on his hard hands.

'Eh, Pearl?' laughed Tom.

'You run off, Mr Cocky,' tossed Pearl.

It had begun to be a game that you watched, the game between Pearl and Tom, and it was fun, to watch for who might drop the ball, the red, glistening hand of Pearl, or Tom Wilcocks, whose dark face was laughing up.

' 'S none of your business,' Pearl said.

'Won't you tell us, eh, Pearl?'

She was thick and gold above the angry knife.

'What killed the cat?' she asked.

35

'Bet it was Pearl Brawne.'

'Tom is *funny*!' screamed Fanny.

And he was. You laughed, you laughed. But not Pearl.

'You run along, Mr Clever,' she said. ' 'S none of your business. Anyways.'

'What ain't?'

'Nothink,' said Pearl.

And then it was strange. Pearl's face swelled. It was red and bursting. It was going to cry. This made it different, now that it was a matter of sides. There was no second thought on the kitchen steps, you were on the side of the Pearl.

Tom Wilcocks pulled an ugly, winking face.

Ah well, he said, he would go and clean the harness now.

His feet slopped loose inside his big boots.

'Why did you cry, Pearl?' asked Fanny.

Pearl slapped the water in the tin basin.

'Stop tormentin' me,' she said. ' 'S none of your business. That's why.'

Such things were important and mysterious. They happened, and you had to accept. The face of Pearl that just could not be read. Her thick face swelled and cried. She chewed the corner of her handkerchief, on damp afternoons, when windows sweated, and the dogs crouched in the yard, their thin tails tucked between their naked legs.

Oh, they were long, the long wet afternoons. They did not close till five, when Tom Wilcocks brought the pails of milk. He walked across the yard, and the rain had wet his hair. It was plastered black.

'Let us go down to the flat and pick mushrooms,' it is the weather,' Theodora said on a day of rain.

'Yes, yes,' cried Fanny.

It was the weather, it was the time, when the long, sharp golden sword sliced the watery sky, and steam rose from cow dung. The air was heavy and gentle as the breath of cows. Their blue tongues licked, slapped at the brown rocks of salt.

'Let us go behind the cow bails,' Fanny said. 'That is a place we have not thought of before. And there are sure to be mushrooms. It is just what they like.'

Behind the bails where the nettles were, which the rain had

feathered, there was not so much a smell of cows as of nettles and of crushed earth. It was still and green behind the bails. Also a little frightening. The air began to choke the throat. The drops on the nettles hung suspended. And Tom Wilcocks and Pearl Brawne.

'What do you want?' asked Pearl.

Or she hissed. She hissed like a white and golden goose disturbed on its eggs beside the creek.

'We are looking for mushrooms,' said Theodora, right into Pearl's hissing face.

Sticks broke. Under Tom's feet. He was thinking where to put his hands.

'You run along,' said Pearl. 'There ain't no mushrooms here.'

And now you could see some strange and palpitating thing had taken place, unknown, or by accident, in Pearl's blouse. Pearl had burst, pinker than any split mushroom, white-cleft. Pearl's front was open. It was terrible and strange. And the terror and strangeness mounted. It took you. You had to laugh.

'Oooh,' said Fanny's voice.

You began to point, you began to sing.

'Tom Wilcocks and Pearl Brawne! Tom Wilcocks and Pearl Brawne!' the voices of the Goodmans sang, but thin, and changed, and metallic.

Tom Wilcocks laughed through his nose. He turned his face aside and spat.

'You're a pair of bold little girls,' cried Pearl. 'I hate you.'

You could see now that she really did. Hate was in the upstanding heads of nettles, and the wet, black, crushed earth.

It was time to go.

What had happened was put away, turned over, and left. Only once, Fanny had begun to giggle.

'What is it?' Theodora asked.

'Pearl Brawne lost her buttons,' Fanny giggled and sang. 'In the nettles. In the nettles.'

But Theodora did not wish to pursue this theme. She walked away. She would not think, or only a little. For the group behind the cow bails had a great spreading shadow, which grew and grew, it was difficult to ignore. On the lustier, gustier days, cloud and hill and the sinuous movement of the creek reminded. Tom and Pearl were astride the world. Tom's laugh was thick and thoughtful, in the yard, behind the twisted hawthorn, or holding in his hands blunt eels that he had pulled struggling out of the creek. Tom's laugh would not come right out of his mouth, it lay just behind his lips, and his eyes were half closed. Sometimes Theodora saw Tom's face very clearly, right down to the dark, glistening hairs that sprouted from his nose. Or the face of Pearl, recoiling in disgust from young birds, that Theodora brought to touch. But Pearl stroked the swallows' eggs, and where her blouse dipped down there were two little speckles like the speckles on an egg.

Cloud bred cloud on heavy afternoons, where Theodora walked. The water in the creek was brown and warm. Frogs brooded, and magpies flew low. Light yawned out of the hills, and from the yellow thickets of the gorse, Theodora stood and let the water lip her legs. She could just hear. Now light and water lay smoothly together. She took off her clothes. She would lie in the water. And soon her thin brown body was the shallow, browner water. She would not think. She would drift. As still as a stick. And as thin. But on the water circles widen and cut. If Pearl Brawne took off her clothes, Theodora said, and lay in the water, the hills would move, she is fine as a big white rose, and I am a stick. If it is good to be a stick, said Theodora, it is better to be a big white rose.

Not long after this what happened, happened.

It was Sunday in the dining-room. The table blazed. And Father was carving mutton with the big knife. Sunday always filled the dining-room, and the dining-table never looked so shiny, nor so round. Week days were thin days, by comparison, thinly scattered with cold meat. Watching Father carve the mutton it was like somebody with music, someone with a 'cello in his hands. Father loved to carve the joint. It was his pride. Sunday was like this. It continued all along.

'Take the joint to the kitchen, Pearl,' said Father, 'and keep it warm for you girls.'

'Yes, Mr Goodman,' Pearl said.

But this was where it happened. Pearl fell down. Between the table and the door Pearl Brawne fell, and there never was such a harvest, such a falling gold. Pearl lay on the carpet with the leg of mutton, and gravy on her face. What had happened was immense.

'Pearl, Pearl,' cried Fanny. 'Dear Pearl! What has happened? Pearl is dead!'

And then Father was helping Pearl, who still had spots of gravy on her face.

'It is nothing,' said Mother. 'Fanny, sit in your place. Do not fuss over Pearl. It is nothing,' she repeated.

Mother was very calm and straight, even though Sunday lay in pieces in the dining-room. And when Pearl had gone to the kitchen, she looked at Father and said, 'I thought as much.'

And her rings flashed.

You knew that Mother had decided, what Gertie Stepper would have called, the fate of Pearl. But it was deeper than this. Now whole mirrors rippled and walls stirred. There was a general throbbing. You could put in your hand and touch the heart.

So Pearl Brawne was to leave. She cried. She looked lumpy in her hat. She said, 'Yous would never understand.'

Tom Wilcocks had already gone.

'Where is Tom?' Fanny asked.

'Tom has gone,' said Gertie Stepper.

'Why?' asked Fanny.

But Gertie only said, 'Because.'

Soon it was all over, even the last gust of Pearl in the kitchen before she left. She cried enough to burst her seams, and outside, the cart waited with her things.

Afterwards the house continued to stir with the great mystery that had taken place. There was always a great deal that never got explained.

'I would like to know,' said Theodora, 'I would like to know everything.'

Steam rose from the sheets, for it was ironing time.

'There's a lot that isn't for little girls,' said Gertie Stepper.

She held the iron off her red cheek, which was even redder than it should have been.

'But when I am old,' Theodora said. 'Everything and everything.'

'Ah, when you are old,' said Gertie, pressing heavy on the hot sheet. 'When I am old all I shall want is a cup of tea, and die.'

It made Theodora laugh. As if it could ever happen this way.

'I once knew an old man,' said Gertie, 'who learned the Gospel of St Matthew off by heart. He was a storekeeper in Muswell-brook. And he died of intemperance, that old man.'

'I shall know everything,' Theodora said.

To wrap it up and put it in a box. This is the property of Theodora Goodman. But until this time, things floated out of reach. She put out her hand, they bobbed and were gone. She listened to the voices that murmured the other side of the wall. Or she followed the Syrian as darkness fell, and the Syrian's brown silence did not break, the sky just failed to flow through.

'How can you know? It's silly,' said Fanny. 'I shall have a blue silk dress, and a necklace of pearls, and a handsome husband, and six children, and I shall go visiting in the houses of my friends.'

Father once said to Mother that Fanny would always ask the questions that have answers.

And Mother was annoyed and said, 'Turn your toes out, Theodora. And run and do your hair. You look a fright.'

It was not surprising.

Theodora Goodman was altogether unsurprised. On her twelfth birthday the big oak in front was struck by lightning, and from three hundred yards Theodora was thrown to the ground. Gertie said it was an act of God. But Theodora picked herself up, out of the event, it was one of the things that happened, and which it was still not possible to explain, like Pearl Brawne, and Mother's moods, and the Syrian. So Theodora picked herself up and gave a rather pale laugh, because naturally she had been frightened, and went to look at a calf that had just been born.

It was this same day too, the day of the lightning, that a man came who had been Father's friend once, when Father had been prospecting, it seems. The man was sitting on the veranda, late in the morning, when Theodora walked round.

'I came to see your father,' the man said.

He had a beard, like a prophet, greyer than Father's, thick and big.

'Did you?' said Theodora.

'Yes,' said the man. 'You had a bit of a storm. That's a bad bit of business.'

He pointed to the tree.

'That is an act of God,' said Theodora. 'I was three hundred yards away, but I survived.'

'It is sometimes like that,' the man said.

And now Theodora decided to sit down, because something warm and close had been established with the man.

'Perhaps they will ask you to stay to dinner,' she mused, almost as if she did not belong.

'I dunno,' said the man. 'Sometimes it's different when they settle down.'

He sounded melancholy. And suddenly the lightning trembled in Theodora, that she had not felt, the lightning that had struck the oak.

'What's up?' the man asked.

'Nothing,' said Theodora.

But she continued to tremble.

'Or if they don't give you dinner, perhaps they will give you some money.'

'You know a thing or two,' the man said.

'I know very little,' Theodora replied.

She looked at the man who had come to see Father and knew that he must know a great deal.

'What do you do?' she asked.

'I look for gold.'

'Why?'

'Because,' he said, 'it is as good a way of passing your life as any other.'

This sounded funny. It made the walls dissolve, the stone walls of Meroë, as flat as water, so that the people sitting inside were now exposed, treadling a sewing machine, baking a loaf, or adding up accounts. But the man walked on the dissolved walls, and his beard blew.

'You must be rich,' said Theodora.

'Why?' asked the man.

Now, in fact, it was his turn.

'Well,' she said, 'looking for gold.'

'But I haven't found very much.'

She would have pitied him, but his eyes, she saw, were pleased. The man laughed. Altogether he was unlike the other people who came to the house, or anyone in the house, except a little like Father.

'You are poor then?' she said, looking curiously at the fact, to which the man's laughter gave a beautiful clarity.

'That's the obvious deduction,' he said.

Behind them they could hear the safe sounds of the house.

'Poor,' said the man, 'and hoping that your Father, for sentimental reasons, will tell them to dish me up some dinner. My belly's hollow,' he added. 'And you Father's taking a hell of a time.'

Theodora went inside to see what was happening, and the man continued to sit and kick his rather worn heels.

'You are a romantic, George,' Mother was saying. '*Romantic* and *ridiculous*, they both begin with *r*.'

'It's a pity,' said Father in a tight way, 'that you never realized this before.'

'As if I didn't,' said Mother. 'As if I didn't! I very quickly learned to spell. But, of course, I am tarred a little with the same brush.'

Then she looked at him and laughed, as if it were the least funny thing that had ever happened.

'Julia,' Father said quickly.

He could not quite find what it was he wanted to say. He took a step forward. You felt that he would have gone farther if it had been anyone else but Mother.

Mother sat on the sofa. She twisted her rings round. She rolled her hands in a tight ball and said, 'It is no use, George. I refuse to sit down to table with every tramp that comes along. I will not. I will not.'

Then you knew that Mother had won, in spite of Father breathing hard. It was terrible, the strength of Mother. All your own weakness came flowing back. Mother was more terrible than lightning that had struck the tree.

'But we can give him his dinner,' Theodora dared. 'We can give it him on the closed veranda. Round the side. Gertie can hand it through the window of the spare room.'

Short of turning her face, to avoid what she could not avoid, what she had just seen, she had to say something, and she said this.

'Oh, it's you,' said Mother sharply. 'I did not see you were there. Yes,' she said, 'Theodora seems to have solved the problem. Let him have it on the closed veranda. Round the side.'

'Let Gertie hand it through the spare-room window. To the leper,' Father said.

Then he left the room.

But the man who came was given his dinner.

'You eat an awful lot,' said Fanny.

'Because my belly's empty,' the man said, as he continued to put into his mouth boiled beef, dumplings, carrots, cabbage, squares of bread, and draughts of tea.

'I'm hungry,' he said. 'And I like eating.'

'I like meringues best,' said Fanny.

'And you?' said the man to Theodora.

'I don't know,' she said.

Under cover of the conversation between Fanny and the Man who was Given his Dinner, Theodora had withdrawn, and now she felt shy. She would have preferred the man's silence, or else the cracking of his jaws as he chewed and swallowed the boiled beef. She could not see him eat too much, because his act covered their shame.

'You're more like your father,' the man said to her. 'More like your father used to be. We was mates. We went prospecting down Kiandra way. I remember once we got lost, one Easter, in the mountains, when the snow came. There was the ghost of a man in the mountains, they said, who got lost in a snowdrift driving his sheep. We sat all night, your father and I, under the shelter of a big dead tree, listening to the dingoes howl, waiting for the ghost. Cripes, it was cold up there. We had a fire each side. But it was cold. We sat with our arms round each other, and then your father fell asleep.'

'Did you see the ghost? Did you? I would hate to,' Fanny said.

But the man said, after a little, after he felt like speaking again, 'Why, no, I didn't see the ghost. And in the morning

43

your father woke up, and we laughed. The sun was up, and we was sitting on the edge of the blasted track.'

The Man who was Given his Dinner laughed now. He brushed his beard with the back of his hand. Sun fell through the shaggy tree, and things were good to touch.

'I could tell you a lot of things,' said the man.

He said it, Theodora knew, to her, in spite of Fanny, and Gertie Stepper, who stood at the spare-room window holding the crumbs.

'Why don't you stay and tell us?' asked Fanny.

But looking at Theodora, the man's mouth opened and closed, as if it was mouthing a great potato. Then at last it closed on words. 'I got to be making tracks,' he said.

He put on his felt hat, which had blackened round the crown with sweat.

'You'll be wanting to thank the boss and the missus, said Gertie Stepper out of the window.

'No,' said the man. 'I'll just slip along.'

Gertie Stepper went quite red. 'Well,' she said, 'at your age, you know best.'

'And we shall come,' cried Fanny. 'We'll walk at least as far as the bridge. So that you can tell us things.'

But the man had stopped talking. He looked at his boots as he walked, and he sucked the beef out of his teeth. Till Fanny had to shake his arm.

'Tell us something,' cried Fanny. 'Why don't you speak?' she said. 'Soon we shall have gone.'

But inside the man's silence, Theodora could feel his closeness. The sleeve of his coat touched her cheek. The sleeve of his coat smelt of dust, and mutton fat, and sweat, but it stroked her, and she bit her tongue.

'Yes,' said the man, 'it's as good a way of passing your life. So long as it passes. Put it in a house and it stops, it stands still. That's why some take to the mountains, and the others say they're crazy.'

By this time they had come to the bridge just below Meroë, and this year there was quite a lot of water in the creek, there under the bridge it flowed fast. And for a moment they hung over the rails and looked at the water which flowed under, and they felt good, the man from his full belly, and the children from the solemnity of what they scarcely understood.

'They say they're crazy,' yawned the man. 'And perhaps they're right. Though who's crazy and who isn't? Can you tell me that, young Theodora Goodman? I bet you couldn't.'

He looked at her with a fierce eye, of which the fierceness was not for her.

'I would come if I could,' said Theodora.

'Yes,' said the man. 'You would.'

'Don't be silly,' said Fanny. 'You're a girl.'

'I would come,' said Theodora.

Her voice was so heavy she could hardly lift it. Her voice tolled like a leaden bell.

'You'll see a lot of funny things, Theodora Goodman. You'll see them because you've eyes to see. And they'll break you. But perhaps you'll survive. No girl that was thrown down by lightning on her twelfth birthday, and then got up again, is going to be swallowed easy by rivers of fire.'

And now Theodora began to think that perhaps the man was a little bit mad, but she loved him for his madness even, for it made her warm.

'Now I must be going,' said the man. 'And you young ladies walk off home.'

'Good-bye,' said Fanny, shaking hands. 'Perhaps you will feel hungry and come again.'

'I'm inclined to say I'd eat my hat, but perhaps for your sakes, perhaps,' said the man.

'When?' asked Fanny.

'August seventeenth, next year,' said the man.

'Good-bye,' said Theodora.

'Good-bye,' he said.

When he had gone Theodora realized that he had not looked at her again, but somehow this did not seem to matter. They sat beneath the shaggy tree in the night of snow, and the snow as it fell melted, on entering the circle of their warmth. She rose and fell on the breathing of the tree.

'What did he mean,' said Fanny, 'by August seventeenth next year? Do you suppose he will come again?'

'That is what he said,' said Theodora.

But she knew already that he would not come. In all that she did not know there was this certainty. She began to feel that knowing this might be the answer to many of the mysteries. And she felt afraid for what was prepared. The magpies sang cold in the warm air of Meroë.

3

WHEN they were older girls they were sent to Spofforths', so that the Miss Spofforths might finish what Mother had begun. For Mother sometimes lost her patience and threw the book on the floor. It was an event to leave Meroë and go to board at Spofforths'. Even though it was close enough to drive home on Saturday, it remained a terrible event. Like being forced into a room full of people, and the door locked behind. You could not turn and beat on the door, and tell them to open from the other side, because of the stareful and hushed people sitting in the room. You had simply to face the faces. And this was very awful. Goodmans' pair of brumbies, they used to say in town.

Anyway, Theodora and Fanny Goodman went to Spofforths', and the door closed.

It was a pale grey house, with a drive up to it, with privet hedges either side, and white windows that could not contain the music that flowed perpetually into the garden, the complicated pieces played by older girls. The garden was full of broken music. There were pauses as well as music. The fuchsias tumbled like detached notes waiting to bridge the gap between bars.

Inside, the house smelt of linoleum and boiled rice. It hummed and vibrated with voices, most of the rooms, except the rooms of the Miss Spofforths, where silence hung in limp leaves of dark, sponged plants, stared with the faces of Old Girls from photographs, and rumbled flatulently after lunch. These were the rooms of the Miss Spofforths. Nobody would ever beat the gong.

All the time this dark green shiny silence was very noticeable beside the golden humming in the other rooms. But this too was frightening, everything was frightening, at first. That first afternoon Theodora Goodman wondered whether she would ever fit into a pattern so elaborate and so refined.

Then a coppery girl with white skin came out on to the landing and said, 'Hello, Theo, Fanny. It is fun to think we have been put in the same room.'

It was Grace Parrott, who was a familiar face at least. Theodora remembered her mother's handbag, and the lozenges in the little box that came to Mrs Parrott's rescue when her pale voice could not find the words. And now Grace Parrott was a copper-coloured lozenge which they seized with relief on the landing at Spofforths' and were comforted.

'We also have Una Russell,' said Grace. 'She has come from Sydney, for her health. Her father is a jeweller. He is very rich.'

'Is she all right?' asked Fanny.

'Why shouldn't she be?' inquired Grace.

But Fanny did not know, or why she had said, except that in desperation she had.

The beds looked very white with their white quilts. Outside the window there was a hawthorn tree. This, decided Theodora, shall be my tree. Screened by its thick quilted white, the words were blurred that the girls rolled into balls with their stockings and put away in drawers.

Una Russell whose father was a jeweller, had a set of silver hairbrushes with irises embossed on the back. Her belt buckle was solid silver, and she wore a turquoise ring.

'Are there races in this town?' asked Una Russell.

'There are picnic races at Sorrel Vale,' said Fanny.

'I'm mad about races,' said Una. 'Because there's always the chance you may meet someone interesting.'

'We know all the people in this district,' sighed Grace Parrott.

'Perhaps,' said Una. 'But some people start to be interesting all of a sudden.'

The hands of Una Russell had an air of experience, arranging the silver brushes on top of the chest of drawers, that you could not help watch, the pale hands with the turquoise ring.

'How I hate school,' complained Una. 'I would like to get married. I read a lovely book about a girl who got married while she was at school, secretly, you see, to a French count.'

'Are you allowed to read about love?' asked Fanny.

But Una did not hear, and immediately Fanny was glad.

'Aren't you unpacking, Theo?' asked Grace Parrott.

Because Theodora sat on the quilt in her big straw hat, and

her face was half a brown shadow, the way the brim cut across. The impression was rather strange.

'You haven't even taken off your hat,' said Una.

She looked at Theodora, sensing something that she would not understand, and possibly something from which she must defend herself, or even hate.

'No,' said Theodora, quickly wreaking her brown shadow.

Her feet began to move about the room, allowing her to perform the various simple acts of arrival.

'What shall we be expected to do?' she asked.

'Nothing today,' said Grace. 'It is the first afternoon.'

Una Russell continued to look at Theodora, out of her experience, which could find no possible explanation.

'You'll get used to Theo,' laughed Fanny. 'She has her ways.'

Life very soon became a ringing of bells, unlike the silent drowsing days at Meroë, where time just slid along the yellow stone, rested, slid, with the lizards and the sun. Because nothing ever happened at Meroë, you could watch the passage of time, devote a whole morning to the falling of a rose. But at Spofforths' time jerked and jangled. Time was a bell. The hours were Music and Sewing and Geography and French. Only at evening, time would ease up; the bell was still, and you could hear an apple thump the earth somewhere in the long grass at the back. Then the world would begin to revolve again, like the great sphere that it is, not a coloured papier mâché thing that jerked and squeaked under Miss Emmy's hand. But the days mostly wore the papier mâché face. They were masked by the Improvement that the three Miss Spofforths dispensed.

'And now Theodora Goodman will explain habeas corpus to us,' Miss Emmy smiled.

It was a horror, but a bright horror, in Miss Emmy's voice, because Miss Emmy smiled and smiled. Miss Emmy's smile filtered through her face, out of her pleated mouth, her spectacles, and her crumpled skin. It was a smile that had lost its direction long ago. Miss Emmy would have smiled at death.

It was better with Miss Belle. Several girls, sitting in the evening at the open window, soft with the kindness of dusk, said that Miss Belle was lovely. They sighed and peeled grapes.

It was as if life had stood still on the threshold of experience. Whether lovely or not, Miss Belle was lovelier. She wore brown velvet ribbons and a cameo. Her hands, though freckled, lingered emotionally over music. She could not leave a chord. When Miss Belle sat beside the lamp and sewed, it was good to sit beside her, to smell verbena, and to borrow her scissors in the shape of a stork. Her hair was rather vague, it strayed, as she talked about the galleries of Florence and Rome, to which she had had the good fortune to accompany a cousin of her mother's. Once a girl called Lottie Littlejohn had pressed some lily of the valley in a Bible, and in the holidays she had sent the lily of the valley with a letter to Miss Belle. Miss Belle put it in a rosewood box in her quiet room, with the other pressed flowers, the pansies and violets and mignonette, she had received from other girls.

There was the crumpled Miss Emmy, who smiled, and plaited leather for a hobby, and the drifting, musical, travelled Miss Belle. There was also Miss Spofforth, who was the eldest, the headmistress, and the name.

'Tell me about Miss Spofforth,' said Mrs Goodman. 'About Miss Spofforth you never speak.'

'We don't see her very much,' said Theodora. 'It is difficult to tell.'

'She seems a most superior woman,' Mrs Goodman said.

'She is horrid,' said Fanny.

'Why?'

'She is so ugly. And so strange.'

Mis Spofforth was an opaque square. Her hair was dark grey, and her skin was thick and brown. The headmistress read prayers, and signed letters, and asked questions about individual welfare if the opportunity occurred.

'Theodora,' she said, 'are you quite happy here?'

It was on the stairs.

'Yes, thank you,' said Theodora. 'I am well enough.'

If she had answered a question in a sermon she could not have felt more unwise.

Miss Spofforth was murmuring. She had not discovered the secret of unlocking other people, because she herself had never really opened.

'You must come and talk to me,' Miss Spofforth said. 'If there is ever anything you want to know.'

To walk inside one of the dark rooms in which Miss Spofforth lived, to sit among the dark, sponged plants, to say : If I could give expression to something that is in me, but which I have not yet hunted down. This is what Miss Spofforth invited, although it was not possible to accept.

Theodora waited for her to go. The meeting on the stairs, which should have been transitory, had stuck. The headmistress was fumbling with a thought that she could not bring out. So that Theodora felt hot, and looked away to hide her own guilt.

Then Miss Spofforth decided, it seemed, to give up, to move. The moments had begun to flow again. And the square dark face looked down and said, 'They must not put so much polish on the stairs. Somebody will slip.'

Theodora listened to the strong boots of Miss Spofforth squeak away across the polished floor. The distance increased, but it had been great upon the stairs. Sometimes the distance is very great.

I shall never overcome the distances, felt Theodora. And because she was like this, she found consolation in the deal mirror in the room for four. When she was alone she spoke to the face that had now begun to form, its bone. Since she had come to Spofforths' Theodora Goodman had begun to take shape, for what, if anything, she had not yet discovered, and for this reason she could sometimes suffocate. Her breath dimmed the mirror-face, the dark eyes asking the unanswerable questions. Because it was the face to which nothing had yet happened, it could not take its final shape. It was a vessel waiting for experience to fill it, and then the face finally would show.

'For goodness' sake, looking in the mirror!' said Una Russell, coming in.

Una Russell hated Theodora. She could not understand her silences.

'Yes,' said Theodora. 'I do not like my face.'

'But you look,' said Una.

'I sometimes wonder.'

'My mother once knew a very ugly woman who married an Englishman. He had a large house in the country. She did very well.'

'I don't want to marry,' said Theodora.

'Why ever not? There is nothing else to do.'

'I want to do nothing yet. I want to see.'

'If you are not careful you will miss the bus,' said Una Russell, not that it really mattered if Theodora Goodman should become what she would become.

Una Russell went out of the room, and her bangles expressed her contempt.

Theodora had begun to accept both the contempt and the distances. Because there were also the moments of insight, whether with Father, or the Man who was Given his Dinner, or even with the Syrian. And sometimes the hawthorn tree invaded the room. Its greenish light lay on the boards, and the room was lit with boughs. This made it more than tolerable.

Evenings, the others went out into the garden, where the dusk was full of hot laughter, and the fuchsias smouldered. The girls strolled through the long grass, coiled, and knit together by their words and arms, and the solid swirl of their skirts mowing the grass. But Theodora remained behind on the steps, a finger thoughtful on her mouth. She would go down soon, not now, but later. And it was not unpleasant on the steps, to smell summer at a distance, with perhaps Miss Belle playing Schumann through an open window.

One evening Theodora saw the girl who was called Violet Adams slip through the trees. She saw her blouse amongst the apple trees, and she had sometimes noticed that Violet Adams stayed alone. In the darkness her blouse would dwindle, or suddenly stand out, farther, and then closer, like some note that Miss Belle could not bear to let escape into the darker background of the music. So the white blouse recurred. And finally there was Violet Adams' face.

'What,' said Violet, 'you still there, Theodora?'

Because she had been thinking of other things, of some importance and intensity, her voice was condescending and remote. She could not believe in the presence of anything so remote as Theodora Goodman. But she was not unkind.

'I might say the same,' said Theodora. 'I watched you for a long time.'

'I went there to be by myself,' Violet said. 'I felt sad. But it was lovely. I was reading poetry upstairs. I was reading Tennyson,' she said.

And suddenly the voice and the presence of Violet Adams, if not her rather insipid words, but her white blouse in the apple trees, with the fragments of music that fell from Miss Belle's hands, swept over Theodora, and she wanted to take, and touch, and join together all these sensations and make them palpable and whole.

But instead she put her arm round Violet's waist and said, 'Shall we walk a little more?'

'Why not?' Violet sighed.

Theodora could feel Violet's sigh break against her shoulder, out of the warm blouse, which was adrift again among the apple trees. Only now there was a second white note which the dark mouth of the music just failed to swallow down.

'Do you write poetry?' asked Violet Adams.

'I never have,' said Theodora.

'I do. I write love poetry,' Violet said.

'Have you ever been in love?'

'No, but it isn't necessary,' said Violet. 'Not if you have the feeling.'

Violet's face was white. She smelt of scented soap. Her eyes were like grey moths that had escaped out of the apple trees. Theodora could feel her own humility, round Violet's thin waist her apologizing arm.

'I would like to write a poem,' said Theodora. But her mouth closed. She could not describe its immensity.

'Yes?' asked Violet quickly, because she wanted to talk about herself.

'I would write a poem about rocks,' said Theodora. Her voice beat her cruelly.

'About *rocks*!' said Violet. 'Why ever rocks?'

'And fire. A river of fire. And a burning house. Or a bush fire,' Theodora said.

Violet Adams extracted herself cautiously from Theodora's arm. 'It would be a queer sort of poem,' Violet said.

'But I shall not write it,' said Theodora. 'I doubt whether I shall ever write a poem.'

Violet Adams picked bark. She felt that she wanted to drift back into thinking about herself. But she warmed herself on Theodora, even on what she did not understand.

'Shall we be friends, Theodora?' she said, picking at the bark of the apple tree. 'And have secrets and things?'

'I would like to,' said Theodora.

'All right. Let's,' Violet said.

She came and put her arm round Theodora, and the darkness was warm and close and secretive again. They were one body walking through the trees. Their voices rose and stroked at each other like grey birds. Violet Adams was one mystery which it was possible to touch.

Later, when it was time to go in, to say prayers and brush the teeth, she became a tall pale girl, with a rather flat face, pale gold hair, and a tendency to catarrh. But Theodora loved her out of gratitude.

For Theodora Goodman the pulse of existence quickened. She hesitated less in doorways. She ran into the receiving sun. She sat at the yellow desk, which was no longer hateful, nor the trade winds which Miss Emmy blew, because now Geography was crossed by folded notes and glances behind hands.

Smoothing the electric paper, Theodora read:

I have found something *most* important I must see you in the break! Violet A.
P.S. *Don't forget!!*

Theodora did not. They went behind the oleander.

'It is a poem,' said Violet. 'In a book that I borrowed from Miss Belle's bookcase.'

'Oh,' said Theodora.

She had not expected, quite. She sensed some reason for distaste, as she looked at the bursting, wadded covers and the brass hasps of Miss Belle's purple book, while Violet Adams was preparing to read.

'Are you ready?' Violet said.

> *One of us two must sometimes face existence*
> *Alone with memories that but sharpen pain,*

54

> *And these sweet days shall shine back in the distance,*
> *Like dreams of summer dawns, in nights of rain.*

Theodora saw how very awkward at times her own feet were in their thick, black shoes.

'Are you listening?' Violet asked. She lifted her upper lip and, with the same reverence and a slight tremor, continued to read:

> *One of us two with tortured heart half broken,*
> *Shall read long-treasured letters through salt tears,*
> *Shall kiss with anguished lips each cherished token*
> *That speaks of these love-crowned, delicious years.*
>
> *One of us two shall find all light, all beauty,*
> *All joy on earth, a tale for ever done;*
> *Shall know henceforth that life means only duty,*
> *Oh God! Oh God! have pity on that one.*

'How lovely it is! But how sad!' Violet said, wiping her catarrhal nose.

Theodora said, 'Yes.'

But although she loved Violet Adams, she did not think that this was altogether her poem, and was glad when she heard the bell go for French.

Theodora Goodman and Violet Adams, their names became linked.

'Where are Theodora and Violet?' people used to call.

When they lagged beyond the last warning of a bell, when they dragged round the hill, lost in the trees, detached from the wave of girls that flowed on Sundays across the paddocks towards the church, Theodora Goodman and Violet Adams. On Sundays the trees smelt of sleep, and smoke, and crushed ants, and the thin grey, distilled smell that is the smell of trees that have stood a long time in sun. Theodora Goodman and Violet Adams yawned churchward together through the trees. Or they ducked with one head when magpies slashed at their boaters with savage beaks.

'Theodora, Violet, you must keep up,' panted Miss Emmy, propped for breath on an anthill that she did not much like. 'Step out, girls. Please! We shall be late.'

Sometimes they were, poured into the throat of the Te Deum,

and the narrow, dusty church. Then they praised the Lord in giggles from the wrong page. They emptied their lungs in terrifying spasms, which strangled the harmonium and filled the church with echoing brass.

On the side against which the girls from Spofforths' sat there was a window with St George. He was mild and smooth as yellow soap, but he had crushed the Dragon. Out of the Dragon's belly had burst peculiar bunches of crimson grapes. This window sanctified the light, which poured rich and bland and purple, even when the shingles were cracking with heat. Theodora washed her hands in purple. She listened coolly to the words that did not touch. Her own mystery offered subtler variations. Her fears were not possessive. She had not yet had occasion to summon God, who remained a bearded benevolence, or a blue and golden scroll above the altar window.

Once Theodora found beneath the pew a crow that had closed its wings and died, stiffer and blacker than old umbrellas. She touched it in the silence between the prayers. The crow was folded as neatly and as decently as a soul should be, the prayer suggested. About her own soul Theodora was not so sure. Mother, for instance, who sat ahead, a firm small outline in bottle green, would give up without hesitation when it was time, a neatly folded soul, because for Mother, you were sure, things existed in hard shapes. Mother had not dissolved at dusk under the apple trees. But sometimes, and even in a strait pew, Theodora's own soul opened and flamed with the light that burst through the Dragon's wounds.

So now she rejected the crow, gently, with her heel. She looked across at Violet Adams, from whom she had been separated on coming into the church. Theodora looked, over the heads of Lottie and Grace, and saw she had left Violet Adams behind. It was less melancholy than inevitable. She did not love Violet less. They could still walk linked through the long grass at dusk, and hate the intruder, but Theodora knew she would also prefer sometimes to risk the darkness and walk alone.

Violet looked at Theodora, through the hymn, over the heads of Grace and Lottie. She smiled the mysterious smile of someone who reads poetry and shares secrets, and Theodora smiled also, because it was true, but that was not all.

Waiting for the hymn to stop, and the voices of girls that praised the Lord in pink and blue, she watched the light blaze through the glass Dragon and gild the nape of Frank Parrott's neck, which was already gold. He sat ahead, a reddish gold.

Afterwards everyone stood about outside the church, and families picked out their own girls, to talk or to take to dinner. The girls were suddenly sheepish then, to find their lives divided into two.

'You should ask your Violet Adams out to Meroë,' said Mother, waiting for Father to bring round the horses from where they had been nosing chaff behind the church.

'Not today,' Theodora shrugged.

Because she did not feel there was much connection between Violet Adams and Meroë. She looked at Violet, who was talking hard to Una Russell and pretending not to see. There was no connection at all.

'No,' Theodora said. 'Another time.'

And she stepped back, bumping, with a thump that was heard, the hard body of Frank Parrott.

'Hello, Theo,' laughed Frank. 'It's a long time. You must get Grace to bring you over. You and Fanny. We must have a picnic.'

Frank, who had harnessed the horses to the sociable the Parrotts used for church, spoke and looked aside. Frank was uneasy in his Sunday clothes, but still a transparent gold that Sunday had not touched. Theodora wanted and wanted not to look. She remembered a red and clumsy boy, and a wart on a hard knee. Now Frank was fine and straight in his wrinkled Sunday pants, and what there was of his moustache was gold.

'That would be nice. Yes, Frank. We shall speak with Grace,' Theodora said.

Then backed, to escape any possibility of further encounter with Frank Parrott, whose Adam's-apple moved up and down. At the same time she had the impulse to give to someone something, whereas there was nothing, only her hymn book that she held too tightly in her glove. She could not feel her hand.

When Theodora returned, her face still bright, when it was evening, Violet's skin was thick and pale.

'Well,' Violet said.

57

'Oh, it is you,' said Theodora.

It was inevitable.

'Where did you get to?' Violet said.

'When?' Theodora asked. She was still dazed.

'Why, after church,' Violet said.

'Nowhere. There was such a crush.'

'I had something to tell you,' said Violet.

'What?'

'Aha,' said Violet, with a kind of pale secrecy that would not be read.

But it did not greatly matter what it was that Violet had to tell. And Violet knew. Violet was being a goose, but Theodora could have kissed her, in spite of the goosishness, and the rather shameful voice in which she had read the poem, and the steady seeping of her catarrhal nose. Theodora loved Violet dearly. She could afford to. She was strong.

Theodora waited many days for something to happen, but it did not. Often it does not happen. Theodora often looked at Grace Parrott, who was unperturbed, to see what Grace expected, but Grace did not.

So Theodora said to Grace, in tea, 'Frank spoke about a picnic.'

'Oh,' said Grace, disliking a prune. 'Frank will talk his head off.'

'I thought,' said Theodora, 'we might combine. Gertie would make the cakes.'

'But Frank,' said Grace, 'is going to Muswellbrook on Friday. He will work on the Thompsons' place. For experience,' she said.

So it was like that, as wrinkled as a prune.

'Theodora,' Violet Adams said, 'I want to see you afterwards. It is most important. I have had some news.'

Violet took Theodora into a corner of the big, dark schoolroom, not outside, which was unusual, but it was unusual news that Violet hinted at. Over the prunes she had tried to make it dark, and now to keep it so, in the deserted schoolroom, into which the light fell only a little way from the glass door, marking the boards for a space, but not the desks, these remained shapes.

Theodora felt, and would feel, blank, whatever Violet might now say. It was only a bare suggestion that Frank Parrott had made, and as a bare suggestion Grace had disposed of it. Theodora sat and waited for Violet to speak. She sat on a bench beside the big blackboard, on which there was still the figure of a problem, an isosceles triangle it was, that somebody had solved and left. It looked both frightfully simple and frightfully complex. Theodora sat. She felt the chalk dust settle on her. She waited for Violet to say something, to create a fresh figure, and present a similar problem for which a solution would have to be found. These were endless.

'Well, won't you guess?' Violet asked.

'I am going to bed soon,' said Theodora. 'I have a headache.'

Violet laughed. Caught in her own drama, she could not really believe in headaches. Besides, her news had given her an importance that Theodora lacked. She would speak, but the secret could never be equally theirs.

'I am leaving at the end of the term,' Violet said.

Theodora stirred. The blank that one gesture had rubbed was widened by Violet's words.

'I am going home,' said Violet. 'Mother considers I have had enough of school. I shall help with the housekeeping and do the flowers.'

The settled nature of it all made Violet's voice flat and matter of fact. But of course it would happen like this. The answer could have been found at the back of the book.

'But we shall write to each other, Theo.'

As if, perhaps, she had felt the coldness of her triumph, which now she wanted to warm. Theodora felt on her shoulder Violet's face.

'And I shall leave soon too,' Theodora said.

Not that this lessened the distance. Violet was already a prisoner in a house, arranging flowers in a cut-glass bowl.

'Will you be sorry, a little, that I am going?' Violet asked.

She had to probe the darkness, for one or two wounds received.

'Violet,' said Theodora, 'you ask me to say such difficult things.'

'What are you two doing in here?'

It was Una Russell, peering from the doorway.

'We were talking,' Violet said.

'Well I never!' said Una Russell.

Theodora went upstairs. She undressed. She lay face down so that she would find a thicker darkness, and lose all expression in the pillow.

Theodora cried, for what she did not ask herself, but it seemed immeasurable, the slow darkness and the days which jerked past. It was as if time were a magic lantern in which it was never omitted to change the slide. So Violet Adams came downstairs in her gloves, after the concert and the cakes, and laughed, and kissed, and cried, and went. So there were berries on the hawthorn tree and frost on the rut. So the lamb was born with two heads in the hollow, and they put it in a jar, in a cupboard at Meroë, to be shown to the curious until its wonder was forgotten.

At Meroë Theodora asked, 'When shall I be coming home?'

Father said there was no hurry, she would find, there was no hurry for anything.

'But at Meroë I shall be free,' Theodora said.

'Free?' said Father. 'Free from what?'

Handing it back it was a plate of air.

Father's beard smiled and said she had a lot to learn.

Theodora went out. She walked up the black hill, that winter had blackened further, the black cone of Ethiopia that had once flowed fire. Near the summit there stood a wooden house, or what remained of it, a narrow lantern that was somebody's folly. He had lived there with his madness and his dogs until he died, and now there were tins and bones. Theodora sat on a stone which had been part of the foundations of the madman's folly. Nobody knew what his intention had been. Only that he had built this house and lived and died.

It was both desolate and soothing to sit on the black hill. There are certain landscapes in which you can see the bones of the earth. And this was one. You could touch your own bones, which is to come a little closer to truth. After the secrets and quotations, the whispers in the orchard at Spofforths'. Now the ghost of Violet Adams had begun to be expelled. She could not endure the bones and stones. Though Theodora bowed her head. It is still possible to love the ghost that has been exorcised. There remains the need.

On the whole Theodora felt older. At Spofforths' she felt older anyway, and particularly when the letter from Violet came.

Violet had found time between keeping house and doing the flowers.

Violet had a talent for writing. She could compose.

Dearest Theodora,

I wonder how you all are, but you especially, I do sincerely wonder! That will remain, I know, the *happiest time of my life*, that I shall cherish and remember! Not that my present existence hasn't its own interesting side. I feel that I am making my own small contribution in helping dear Mother. But it lacks the finer things, dear Theodora, that I found with you. It is without *aspiration*! When I walk beside our big river, which runs some two hundred yds from the house, and which is now in flood, I like to remember our conversations. It is curious the connection between nature and life, and how one sustains the other!

I still contrive to read in an endeavour to improve myself.

I read poetry, and I am studying painting. I have even ventured to paint our river, but in gentler mood, before it was in flood, and friends have congratulated me on the veracity of my rendering. But I am not deceived! I wonder if you will ever write the poem, Theodora, you once said you would like to write. Do you know that very often you seemed to me a *closed book*! I wonder what you will do!

Now I must stop because the men are coming in from work and will expect their tea. They eat like wolves! We have three jackeroos at present, one of them a Charlie Simpson, who is a second cousin of Lottie Littlejohn! He is a cheery fellow, full of fun, and *excuse me this frivolity*, he is excellent in a waltz!

Please do give my love to Fanny, and Grace, and Una, and Lottie, and, in fact, everyone at Spofforths', but you of course, dear Theodora, will always retain the major portion of the affections

Of your sincere friend
Violet Adams

'Theodora has a letter,' said Una Russell.

'It is from Violet Adams,' said Theodora. 'She sends you all her love.'

She held the corner on the candle. She watched the paper curl.

'Won't you give it us to read?' cried Una.

'There is no need,' said Theodora.

She watched the paper curl and flame, and it was for the burning of flesh that she winced.

'Oh, it was one of those letters,' said Una Russell, and she shook her bangles, because she hated Theodora still, she hated what was unexplained.

'Violet Adams was a little insipid poor thing,' Una Russell said.

She could not watch Theodora enough, whose face was as yellow as a candle, but candlelight does not reveal.

Theodora burned the letter because it was both like and unlike Violet Adams. It was after all the letter that you would expect Violet to write, telling nothing at all. I wonder what it was, said Theodora, after the candles had been snuffed, what it was that I saw in Violet Adams. She decided that she would not think about the letter, but it kept recurring, like something she had done herself.

'I wonder what you will do?' Violet Adams had said.

And again, 'You will be leaving soon, Theodora. I wonder if you have thought about the future,' Miss Spofforth asked.

Theodora had gone into Miss Spofforth's dark room, the Study it was called, to take the book for which Miss Spofforth had sent. She had not bargained for this. Now she was caught in the wide spaces between the bookcase and the fire, becalmed in her own silence and uncertainty. Fire fell from the logs into the winter afternoon, but did not warm. A cold laurel pressed against the window out of the winter wind.

'Have you thought how you can live most profitably?' Miss Spofforth asked.

And the dark square of her face struggled to open. She very much wanted to communicate.

'No,' said Theodora. 'I shall go home, for the present. I shall live – well, as I have always lived.'

Because living was still something that happened in spite of yourself. She did not really believe, as apparently Miss Spofforth did, that you could turn living to profit.

'There is a great deal that happens,' she said.

'I am sure,' Miss Spofforth agreed.

She watched Theodora's hands move as if they were about to reach out and touch something.

'And provided one is happy, it does not much matter where,' Miss Spofforth said.

Miss Spofforth had made her own happiness, solid and unmoved as mahogany, and Miss Spofforth was unpleased. She listened to the rooms of the house around her, which was her solidly founded, profitable happiness, but the rooms did not communicate. And outside, the leaf of the cold laurel was stroking space. But this is ridiculous, Miss Spofforth said.

'I expect you will also marry,' she said, with the bright smile she offered to parents of backward or headstrong children. 'Most of the girls do.'

'I had not thought about it,' Theodora said.

She did not want this thrust at her. She did not believe in it very strongly, nor in Miss Spofforth's bright smile, which did not fit her face.

'That may be. You are not that kind of girl,' Miss Spofforth said.

And she sighed. Because she would have offered this girl her wisdom and her kindness, of which really Miss Spofforth had much. She would have touched her hand and said: Theodora, I shall tell you the truth. Probably you will never marry. We are not the kind. You will not say the things they want to hear, flattering their vanity and their strength, because you will not know how, instinctively, and because it would not flatter *you*. But there is much that you will experience. You will see clearly, beyond the bone. You will grow up probably ugly, and walk through life in sensible shoes. Because you are honest, and because you are barren, you will be both honoured and despised. You will never make a statue, nor write a poem. Although you will be torn by all the agonies of music, you are not creative. You have not the artist's vanity, which is moved finally to express itself in its objects. But there will be moments of passing affection, through which the opaque world will become transparent, and of such a moment you will be able to say – my dear child.

All these things would have been said by Miss Spofforth if they had struggled out of her squat body and her heavy face. Instead she opened the book and murmured, 'Well, that will be all, Theodora.'

'Thank you, Miss Spofforth,' Theodora said.

There was no reason to remain, except to extract the most from a sense of warmth. The fire had settled now, she noticed. She looked curiously at the face above the open book, and left.

4

WHEN Theodora returned home, and Fanny followed, after a term or two, this was the beginning of a fresh phase at Meroë. It became the home of the Goodman girls, and people spoke of it in this sense. It was no longer a low, flat, sprawling yellow house, seen against dead trees, a mass of stone that the past had heaved up, much as the hills round Meroë had heaved out their black volcanic rock, and closed, and the rock remained, dead, suggestive but dead. This was no longer Meroë. When the Goodman girls returned home, at once the place had a future, you felt. People looked at the house from the road, from their drays, carts, sulkies, buggies, and sociables, going to town. People looked to see whether the chairs were filled or not with morning gowns, or whether a group in the rose garden at the side might be credited with an interesting situation. Actually the house at Meroë, even now, did not give many clues, but this did not discourage the sideways glance. To see whether the Goodman girls. Or Miss Fanny, rather. It amounted to Miss Fanny. Though Miss Theo has a good heart, Mrs Stepper said. But sort of sawny. So it amounted to Miss Fanny Goodman, who bought a ribbon at Spurgeon's and said: I am at my wit's end, whether to take the shell-pink or the rose, you, Mr Spurgeon, must help me choose. It kind of made you feel you revolved. And Meroë, to which they turned their eyes from the road, from their drays, carts, sulkies, buggies, and sociables, this was the centre, because it had Fanny Goodman in it.

'Oh, Theo, it is lovely to be home, to be free,' Fanny said.

'Yes,' said Theodora, 'it is lovely.'

And they looked out, the Goodman girls, linked at the window by the moment of discovery, of the bald hills for the first time, and the winding creek. Their cheeks touched as they made this similar voyage. They shivered with their pleasure, and their blood ran together. Fanny is a rose, felt Theodora, but I am a lesser rose on the same stem. And it soothed, it soothed, the flesh of the rose that lay along your cheek.

Actually life at Meroë was not much different when the Goodman girls came home. Father still sat beside the pines, at least in body, or he rode round the place and looked at the fences that had fallen down. And the cows wound into the yard at evening to be milked. And Gertie Stepper punched the dough. Only the sea-green mirror at the end of the passage near the sewing room gave up different shapes, the mysterious elongated forms of young women in long dresses.

'Now that you girls are home,' said Mother, 'there's a lot that you'll be able to take off my hands.'

Not that Mother ever had very much on her hands, not that you would notice. She sat on her sofa, like a marble statue wearing silk, and read Hérédia and Leconte de Lisle. To Mrs Goodman everything had a form, like bronze or marble. She saw clearly, but not far. She saw the cattle going down to drink. She saw the sunlight as it lay among the brushes on her dressing table. She heard the passage of her own silk.

The mother of Mrs Goodman had been French, they said, or Austrian, or Portuguese, anyway foreign, which made Mrs Goodman somehow foreign and strange who could speak languages and read them, somebody said even Russian. She was an educated, a clever woman. And pretty when she was young, small and bright. Her hands were small and bright with rings. But hard as a diamond. She had a temper, Julia Goodman. The time she took her riding crop and beat the window in the dining-room because the horses were not brought round, beat the window with the handle of her riding crop, and the glass shivered, and she beat, she beat the jags that were left in the frame. Well, everybody said, this is what George Goodman has taken on.

To those who could not remember, Julia Goodman mostly sat on her sofa and was small and still. She rolled her hands into a tight small ivory ball, studded with diamond or emerald or garnet, just according, but her hands were always hard with rings.

'. . . to take off my hands,' Mrs Goodman said when the girls came home. 'Now that I am the mother of two young women, I can enjoy the luxury of growing old.'

65

And her sigh prepared for the softening of age, only it did not come, or not much, apart from a slight slackening of the skin. Watching her girls, Fanny who was pretty and the disappointing Theodora, her eyes were bright inside the bone, they could still shiver glass.

Sometimes Theodora, now that some of the pieces of the puzzle had begun to slide into place, wondered at the unaccountability of human nature, why Father should have married Mother, or Mother Father. They sat in their own rooms, and there was more than the house between; or they met at the round mahogany table, where their words bobbed and sank, bobbed and sank, in the shiny silences. They were the words spoken by two people to describe the business of living together in the same house, in which a chimney sometimes smoked, or a window stuck, and outside, the property, where a cow calved or apples were destroyed by moth. All this continued because it had been begun. It continued because they had stopped seeing what had happened. Acceptance becomes a long sleep. And if Julia Goodman took a knife and turned it in her husband's side to watch the expression on his face and scent the warm blood that flowed, George Goodman stirred in his sleep and changed position to another dream, of mortgages perhaps, or drought, or fire.

More actual even than the dream of actuality was the perpetual odyssey on which George Goodman was embarked, on which the purple water swelled beneath the keel, rising and falling like the wind of pines on the blue shore of Ithaca. George Goodman sat with his beard spread above the book. The words in his mouth were as smooth and hard and round and tangible and bright as pebbles that the sea has made to glisten. And the names. When Theodora came into the room, into the green, cold soughing of the pines, his eyes, she saw, had not returned.

'It is cold in here,' she said, and stooped.

She raked the coals to sparks and threw on another knot of wood.

'Have you ever thought, Theodora,' Father said, 'about Nausicaä, the name? It is as smooth and straight and tough as an arrow.'

She put a rug across his shoulders, because it was cold in the room at that time of year. In the middle of the day the white light would splinter through the pines.

'An arrow,' she said, 'tipped with white. A swan's feather.'

Because this was something in which they indulged, sometimes casually over the shoulder, to throw to Father the bright, coloured ball. So now she laughed and threw it as she moved towards the door, her brown face, her black hair, glistening under a beaver skin.

'I am going,' she laughed, caught still in this last mood, 'I am going to walk down towards the bridge. Because my feet have died.'

'There will be another black frost,' said George Goodman, returning out of the distance.

He said it with an air of surprise, as if it were too sudden, to find himself again in the dream of actuality. His eyes were almost feverish above the grey thicket of his beard. He is old now, she sighed. She has grown, he said, straight as a brown arrow. And as she left, he smiled.

Theodora took down a gun from the rack in the passage. She took down one of Father's guns, because in time the little rifle had become a polished toy. She let herself out by the side door, under the pines, into the blast of frost, in which her brittle body soon trumpeted its own silver. Consoled by the weight of the gun on her arm, she walked fast on the ringing frost. She walked among the tussocks with the long strides that made them say as Theo Goodman was some bloke in skirts.

How white the skies were at Meroë, wintertime. For years she remembered the winter skies, the pale watered silk. And sound coming from a long way, a calf, or horse's feet. A horse's feet, in winter, came up the road and over the bridge as steady as drums.

'Hey, Theo!' called the man's voice.

She stopped to look, through her tears that the frost had made, at a face she could not see.

'You won't catch much today,' called the man. 'They're all frozen stiff.'

That, she saw then, as he bent down towards her over the pommel, was Frank Parrott in a full moustache. His eyes were blue and watery with the cold.

'Oh,' she said, 'it's you.'

'Yes,' he said, 'it's me. I'll take you on one day,' he said. 'I'll bring a gun. I'll put you through your paces.'

'There was also to be a picnic,' she said.

He looked at her out of his blank blue eyes. 'What picnic?' he asked.

She drew down the corners of her mouth and said that it did not matter.

'What picnic?' said Frank.

'Are you here for long?' she asked.

'It all depends.'

But with no indication how. He stared down out of his mystified blue eyes, which reminded her, she laughed, of the eyes of a young bull.

'Yes,' said Frank, 'I shall come down and take you on.'

And his horse danced. A horse always danced under Frank Parrott. Whenever he rode there was a fine piece of bravura, a jingling of metal.

'I shall wait,' she called, watching him.

Now, now that she could watch him with calm eyes, she did so with pleasure, but sceptically, the red, arched neck of the young bull that she would have loved to touch, to put her hand on his poll. Frank made her feel experienced, but when he cantered off, her smile dropped. She was not quite sure.

Anyway, this time Frank did as he promised. Frank came. He rode through the laurels in a jingling of metal, jumped down with a great report, and there he stood, a reddish gold, against the yellow stone of Meroë. Theodora said : Oh, well.

'And I shall come,' said Fanny as they took their guns, 'even though I don't shoot. To see Theo make a fool of Frank.'

Fanny pursed her mouth and held her head on one side in order to show the savages she was whimsically superior. Fanny's face bloomed in the frost beside Frank's red gold. Why, God, am I this? Theodora asked, knowing that expectation and the temperature had turned her skin a deeper yellow. Now the weight of her gun would not console.

They walked round the side of the hills, the black cone, and, springing from its side, the little, blunter knob. There was a

68

cleft between, from which some ragged trees sprang, instead of smoke. And soon they began to see the ruins of the madman's folly higher up on the cone.

'Don't let's go up there,' said Fanny, pulling in her neck.

'Why,' asked Frank.

'It gives me the creeps. That side of the hill. Do you remember old Mr Lestrange, how mad? I went up there once, a long time ago, and he was chewing a piece of bacon rind. Quite mad. And bristles on him, like a red pig.'

Fanny's face became with her adventure exquisitely funny, in its disgust and fear delicately pink. She pulled at a piece of grass and giggled. Frank laughed too. He could not look at her enough.

'A rum old cove,' said Frank. 'But I can't remember.'

'Nor can Fanny,' said Theodora. 'Mr Lestrange died when she was two.'

'But I can, I can!' cried Fanny. 'You are quite wrong, Theodora. I can remember his red bristles.'

'Mr Lestrange,' said Theodora, 'was black.'

'Anyway,' said Fanny, she shook her head, 'it gives me the creeps up there. How are we going to shoot at something when nothing ever comes?'

She looked about, a little too keen, confident that her failure would not detract. She could feel his eyes. He would swallow down any little prettiness she might perpetrate. She could hear Theodora kicking at a piece of stone.

'Look,' cried Fanny, 'there are rabbits. Now,' she said, 'you can shoot.'

She gave it to them, but not without contempt, brushing it off her hands.

Frank shot. He missed. There was no subtraction from the scrambling of the rabbit scuts. Theodora took aim. Then they watched the tumbling uncontrol of fur. For a moment time had been put off its course. The fur subsided on the earth. The silence trembled, ticked, ran. It had begun again.

'One to you,' said Frank.

His face was redder than from cold. He slapped the butt of his gun with a large hand.

'I told you,' said Fanny, 'that Theo would thrash you.'

But she touched his arm to soften the blow, and her glance excluded Theodora.

They began to walk again. Near the warrens the other side of the hill there were many rabbits, scuttering or still. There was shooting enough. Altogether, in the afternoon, Frank Parrott shot six rabbits. He began to hum. He told them about the time he swam the Barwon River in flood.

'Come on now, Theo,' Frank said, 'you're not up to form.'

Because, after the first shot, Theodora had not shot another.

'It's your day,' she said.

She walked, and thought: He is like a big balloon that I hold at the end of a string, tightly when I shot the rabbit, but then he soared, as I let him out, giving him the string, the sky. Because the rest of the afternoon she had aimed a little to the right. She had wanted to. She had wanted to feel his child's pleasure soar, and say this is mine.

'It's all very stupid.' Fanny yawned. 'I shall drink gallons of tea.'

Theodora heard Frank's breathing. She did not altogether like her power. So she listened to his breathing dominate her silence, and this was better.

Until the little hawk floated, on his upstretched wings, out of the drained sky, to fold himself, to settle on a white bough.

'We'll have a smack at that,' said Frank, already at his shoulder.

'No,' said Theodora, 'not the little hawk.'

Because she remembered the red eye, and for a moment she quivered, and the whole hillside, in some other upheaval of mythical origin. She knew the white air, closer than a sheath, and the whole cold world was a red eye.

But she said quietly enough, 'Not the hawk. Please.'

But Frank had fired.

And they watched the hawk unfold his wings, drawn upward off his branch, stream out into long and lovely distances. Because Frank had missed.

'Good enough,' Frank said.

Theodora had begun to laugh. She knew with some fear and pleasure that she had lost control. This, she said, is the red eye.

And her vision tore at the air, as if it were old wool on a dead sheep. She was as sure as the bones of a hawk in flight.

Now she took her gun. She took aim, and it was like aiming at her own red eye. She could feel the blood-beat the other side of the membrane. And she fired. And it fell. It was an old broken umbrella tumbling off a shoulder.

'There,' laughed Theodora, 'it is done.'

When they were silent, Frank picked up the body of the hawk and hung it on the wire fence. Then Theodora saw that it was, in fact, a little hawk, and that it had a red eye which was half closed. She felt exhausted, but there was no longer any pain. She was as negative as air.

'Sometimes, Theo,' Fanny said, 'you behave as if you are quite mad.'

But Frank did not speak. He bit his moustache. His mind could not lumber further. He was bemused.

They walked on, and their feet made long slurring noises through the cold grass.

After that Theodora often thought of the little hawk she had so deliberately shot. I was wrong, she said, but I shall continue to destroy myself, right down to the last of my several lives. Once she walked past the spot where the hawk hung on the fence, blowing stiffly in the wind. It was her aspiration. In a sense she had succeeded, but at the same time she had failed. If Frank had not understood the extent or exact nature of her failure, it was because he could not. His eyes would remain the same glazed blue.

After the shooting and before the ball, Frank Parrott spoke perhaps half a dozen words to Theodora Goodman. She made him uncomfortable. He would have hated her for the incident of the hawk, hated her out of his vanity, but because there was something that he did not understand, he remained instead uneasy, almost a little bit afraid.

Then there was the ball at Parrotts'.

'I always like to see young people having a good time,' Mrs Parrott said.

Nobody ever listened when Mrs Parrott made remarks, because they were thin and colourless, but because she was also rich, other people often acted on the spirit of her word. So that now they began to make trifles, and jellies, and pink meringues, and it was agreed that Mr Spurgeon would play the violin, bringing a second fiddle from the livery stable at Sorrel Vale, and a Miss O'Rourke, a teacher, would manage the piano. So it was all fixed, tied up in tulle and satin, and stiff with expectation.

Fanny Goodman was afraid that the lilies of the valley that she wore would die of her excitement. Flowers did die on Fanny when she got hot. But Theodora was momentarily cool. She looked over the wheel as they drove to the ball, and she could not have felt more detached. She watched the last shapes in the paddocks, tree or sheep or matchwood fence, that the darkness still had to swallow down.

Mrs Parrott was all gladness in kid gloves. She was so glad for everything. And Grace Parrott ran forward, and kissed Fanny, and hugged her tight, almost melting with her into the one pink. They could not exchange affection enough, there on the verge of what was still to happen. Their cheeks were rubbed by the warming violins.

'Evenin', Theodora,' said Mr Parrott. 'You'll know everybody. Make yourself at home.'

This also made it easy for Mr Parrott. He dismissed himself, because for the life of him he never knew what to say to Goodman's eldest girl.

Theodora walked about the rooms where the people that she knew laughed and prepared to loose their excitement in the dance. And now it began to stir her too, but also an uneasiness. She stood upright and alone amongst the furniture that had been pushed back along the edges or into corners of the room, abandoning its normal functions. In one corner of one room there was a statue, holding her hands in a position of ugly and unnatural modesty, and this was all wrong. Theodora wondered where she could put her own hands, but she could not think. Wherever she put them, these too were ugly and unnatural.

But Mr Spurgeon the storekeeper, and the second fiddle from the livery stable, and the rather freckled Miss O'Rourke began to toss out music into the house. They played 'The Quaker Girl'. And as the music swooped, it caught up the pink tulle and the white satin, and the coloured bundles rose and fell on the wave, shook and giggled with the little twiddles that Miss O'Rourke's hands so cleverly made. But it was above all the sea on which Fanny Goodman sailed. Her words and her laughter were the spray that would whip the dancers into a consciousness of eternity. Fanny always said she could die, she could die in the arms of a waltz.

'*Come let us go to the ball,*' sang Mrs Dinwiddie, and she tapped with her fan.

She was the bank manager's wife, and she had a fine contralto, and played the harmonium at church.

'*Music and merriment call,*' Mrs Dinwiddie sang.

She would break off, and sing, and break off, and look round.

'*Gallant young lovers and laughing gels,*' she sang.

Because Mrs Dinwiddie could have done things so much better and suspected that, all the evening, she would be asked to do nothing at all. So her contralto brooded in the trough left by the violins.

Mrs Parrott looked at Mrs Dinwiddie and almost dared to frown. It was not according to plan, singing by Mrs Dinwiddie. Mrs Parrott wet her lips and looked round. She looked at Theodora Goodman, who was standing there, not having a good time. I must find a man, said Mrs Parrott. For the evening, at least, men had become commodities for Mrs Parrott. But by the time she had found ten minutes' worth of old Mr Trevelyan, which for the moment was the best commodity that Mrs Parrott could provide, she saw that Theodora had gone. There was only the pushed-back furniture.

Theodora had gone out on to the veranda. Quite suddenly she had felt that she would have to live all her life in one evening. And her life was endless. She pushed back her hair. Outside the house stars spread. It was less constrained. Men or animals watched from the outer darkness, then the dog that came forward, fawned, a young and angular collie, put out his paw. Giving the affection for which she was asked, it seemed very simple to give.

'What are you doing out here, Theodora?' Father asked.

Now she could smell his cigar.

'And what are you?' she said.

Though there was no need to ask, and she could feel that he firmly intended not to tell.

'You should go back inside,' Father said. 'You look nice. As nice,' he said, 'as anyone.'

She laughed. Because there was no deception. But she went back, and some remembered tenderness made her bright, either a word in the darkness, or the touch of a dog's paw. She was dark and upright in her bright striped dress, the red, the yellow, and the black. Her eyes burned the eyes.

Theodora danced with three young men who were brought to her: Sam Irving, who was from that district, a Charlie King from Singleton, and a Ben McKechnie from Victoria. They talked to her, or rather, she gave them things to say, and altogether it was not so bad as they expected. Theodora was not so bad. She sat with her proud-coloured dress spread out, and sometimes she laughed, out of her face that was dark and thin.

All of a sudden her life had become as elaborate as a figure in the lancers. But as quickly finished, as significant.

Then they were eating the trifles and the cakes. It seemed that all the young men had already arranged to eat their trifles and cakes in equally fragile company. Laughter broke on the tables like meringues.

'Who is the *tall* girl, alone?' squinted a short-sighted woman from Goulburn, a second cousin of Mrs Dinwiddie's.

'The long, dark, slommacky thing in the striped dress? That is Theodora Goodman.'

And Mrs Dinwiddie crumbled her meringue. Perhaps while the music recuperated they might ask her to play, but until then she was without charity.

It could not cut. Theodora ate her supper. The crueller things, she knew, were unspoken. She could not bear Mrs Dinwiddie any grudge. People were grouped in the arbitrary positions of statues. If they also spoke ugliness their words were equally arbitrary. But sometimes a silence or a presence seemed to emanate a will of its own, and this was what she resented. The militant will in an intake of breath. Then she could hate the cut of a nostril, the droop of an eyelid above an eye.

But none of this halted the inevitable.

'They've got to eat,' Frank said. 'Where's Charlie? He can play. Charlie could rock a shearers' ball. Come on, Charlie, give us a tune while the music's eating sandwiches.'

So Charlie King, who was a wizard on the keys, began to play smooth mad music, which Fanny Goodman caught in her skirt, the water falling through the outspread tulle, she had to, dancing by herself outside the sound of glasses, in the middle of the empty floor. Fanny Goodman flowed through the blue water, because, of course, by this time it was 'The Blue Danube' that Charlie King always played. His hands rippled like a pair of kid gloves. They had no bones. Pouring the suave water that Fanny's tulle skirt caught.

'*La la le-le lasa,*' sang Fanny Goodman, tossing her head to the swans.

And by this time some of the men had come and stood on the edge. They were strong and important now with food and drink.

'By Jove, Fanny,' called Ben McKechnie, 'I'll join you.'

He swam out to her, after her. She floated away, but he swam and touched her laughter, the bright glistening of Fanny Goodman. She did not resist or swim against the current. It carried them, the two, held together by the music, their eyes staring intently into each other's, but ready also at the first sign to navigate treacherous water.

'And how about Theo?' Frank said.

She thought that probably Frank had been drinking. His eye was a fiery china, and he bent forward a little as if he were about to touch some small precise object.

'Shall we, Theo? What do you say? Eh?' said Frank.

His words lumbered. But he was a blaze of fiery gold she had never seen, and Theodora was burnt.

She touched his arm, and they danced. She was close to his breathing, close to his fire, to the short fierce hairs on his close neck. And the music took them and flung them, the cool and relentless music that they entered, to lose control, that they did not question. Inside the dictatorial stream they were pressed into a dependence on each other that was important.

'Theo!' called Fanny. 'Look at Theo!'

75

And well she might, because the proud striped skirt of Theodora streamed with fire. Her body bent to the music. Her face was thin with music, down to the bone. She was both released from her own body and imprisoned in the molten gold of Frank Parrott. So that Fanny and Ben McKechnie stopped, and the others that had come out of the supper room looked, and it was something strange and wonderful that they saw, also shameful, because they did not understand.

It was Theo Goodman making an exhibition of herself, Mrs Dinwiddie said.

'There,' said Theodora, and her voice came down like two pieces of wood together. 'We shall stop now, Frank,' she said.

Although there was still music. Although he still stared out of his own surprise and the motion of what had been her body.

'I shall go out into the cool,' said Theodora.

Now he was following her like a bemused calf whom she had fed at intervals with skim milk and won to her in this way.

'Just as you like, Theo,' he said.

They went out into the silence of stars and sleeping animals. Her hand picked a leaf and smelled it. It was cold with dew.

'Jove, Theo, you put me through my paces.'

She laughed. Winding out of the heights, she could not think what turn conversation might take. Whichever way, it hardly mattered.

'These damn shoes of mine pinch,' he said.

Because he had to make some motion to hold up the darkness that was pressing down. It was too big. When Frank Parrott was on the road, droving, or for some reason overtaken by darkness, he could not scrape together a few sticks quickly enough, to make a little fire, to sit against.

'Your forget,' he said. 'It's so long between dances you forget to buy a new pair of shoes. I remember at Singleton, in the autumn, there was a ball, an' these damn shoes pinched so bad I took them off after supper and danced on my feet.'

Frank Parrott laughed. He laughed at the vision of himself. He had lit his little fire.

'Hey,' he said. 'Where've you got to, Theo? What are you thinking about?'

'Oh,' she said, 'I was thinking of how I used to go down to the creek, and take off my clothes, and float in the water like a stick. It's good sometimes to be a stick.'

Of course she was mad, and you could never really forget it was Theo Goodman. Inside they were playing 'Daisy Bell'. The music had come back.

'We ought to go in,' said Frank. 'Mother'll come out and tell us we're wasting the music.'

And now, instead, she followed him along the meeker paths. She watched the shape of his back in the doorway. It was flat and black. After all, she said, it is true, it is mostly flat and black. Even though the music travelled into other worlds.

When it was all over Theodora Goodman touched Mrs Parrott's kid glove and said it had been a lovely dance.

Yes, yawned Fanny against Father's shoulder, on the way home. It had been the loveliest dance. And Theo, what did Theo think she was doing, almost throwing Frank Parrott off his feet?

But it was over and done with, the dance that Theodora had waited for and dreaded, the way you can sometimes grasp experience before it is undergone. There was the night, for instance, somewhere early in the summer, when she woke in bed and found that she was not beneath the tree. She had put out her hand to touch the face before the lightning struck, but not the tree. She was holding the faceless body that she had not yet recognized, and the lightning struck deep. Breaking her dream, the house was full of the breathing of people asleep and the pressure of furniture. She got up. It was hot in the passage. It was as suffocating as death. A stale cry came out of the mirror in the passage, choked, as if it just could not scream, even in its agony.

'What is it, Theodora?' Father asked, coming out of his room, which was close to the mirror.

'Nothing, nothing, nothing,' she almost cried.

She did not want to look at his face.

'I was just dreaming,' she said.

'It's broken now,' Father said. 'Go back to sleep.'

'Yes,' she said, 'it's broken.'

But this did not obliterate the dream. Although she could

not see its shape, it continued to live its life in a state of vague misgiving in her mind.

'And you?' she said.

'It's thundery. I couldn't sleep.'

'Do you remember,' she said, 'it was my twelfth birthday, and I was thrown down when lightning struck the tree?'

'I had forgotten,' Father said.

'And the man came. We gave him his dinner round at the side. He said he would come again, but he didn't.'

'I had forgotten all about that. Go back to sleep, Theodora.'

Father was going back into his room, and she wanted to stop him, because all the sadness of the world was in the house. There was the possibility that when the door closed, he would suffer the fate of the Man who was Given his Dinner, she might never see him again. But there are occasions on which you cannot stop the closing of the door. It closed. It closed on Father. She was alone in the passage. It would happen. It would be like this in time.

Summer closed in. It was hot and palpable, gathering in the passages, even under the trees, where the cows stood, sculptural in the evening, after they had been milked.

'I saw that Tom Wilcocks who used to milk the cows,' Fanny said, taking off her hat. 'I wonder what happened to Pearl.'

But nobody knew what had happened to Pearl. She had left the district. She had gone to Sydney perhaps. And Fanny stuck the pins in her hat, and laughed, and reddened.

'Tom Wilcocks waved to me,' she said. 'He was in that paddock across from Bloomfields'. He was lying in a patch of buttercups. He was wearing blue dungarees.'

'And what did you do?' asked Theodora through her pins, for she was fixing a hem on a petticoat.

'Nothing, of course,' Fanny said. 'They say that Tom is no good. And you know what happened to Pearl.'

'I liked him,' said Theodora slowly. 'I liked his hands.'

'Really, Theodora!' Fanny said.

She picked at her hair in the mirror. Theodora had made her quite red. Or the drive from town. It was hot. It was stifling already, at that time of year. That evening Mrs Goodman sat about and fanned herself with the leaf of a palm. You could hear the dry motion of the palm, which only accentuated heat, and dry, dry, like Mrs Goodman's lips.

Only under the apricot tree it was cool, the old apricot tree at the back, which was now beyond the age for bearing, but which stood deep in grass and docks and still produced shade. Sometimes, and tonight, Theodora went and sat beneath the apricot tree. She took a book that she would not read. She marked her page with a dock and sat. And as she sat, there seemed to be no beginning or end. Meroë was eternity, and she was the keeper of it.

Before Mother broke in, 'Theodora, Theodora, where is my little silver paper-knife?'

Mother's voice made the hot air quiver.

'What should I do with it?' Theodora called back over her shoulder. 'I haven't seen your paper-knife.'

But Mother's voice implied that she had. The little silver paper-knife still rapped knuckles playing a scale. Mother was afraid she was no longer Mother. It gave her indigestion, not to find a proof, as she sat and fanned herself with a palm on a hot evening at Meroë.

That night it was hotter, it was the hottest, the evening of the silver paper-knife. There were little insects in the air. And the moon was red. It hung in the branches of the apricot tree, big, and swollen red, close, you could almost touch its veins.

'It must surely rain soon in this country,' the voice of Mrs Goodman complained.

But it seemed unlikely. On hot evenings all the extremes of unlikelihood conspired, felt Theodora Goodman, and for that reason you waited, you waited for the red moon to crash like a thunderous gong through the leaves. The intermediate minutes were so many flying ants, their suggestion of motion, that the hand brushed the cheek.

Then the drum beat down across the flat. You heard the horse's feet, beating the planks of the bridge. They beat deep, and more metallic, scattered and sauntered on the road, dropped and gathered, dropped and gathered, spurted as you heard the horse shy at a shadow. You could hear the fear protesting from his nose.

Theodora Goodman sat beneath the apricot tree and listened

to the horse approach. Now it was close. She could hear it acting flash in the darkness, tossing its metal; that she knew could only be Frank Parrott, yes, it could only be.

'Who's that?' he called as the horse quivered.

But she would not answer. Because for Frank Parrott it was always easy, and sometimes it should be different.

'Fanny, is it?' said Frank. 'Come up, blast you!' He kicked bitterly at the belly of the horse.

And now the darkness in the neighbourhood of the tree was drenched with the smell of horse's sweat.

'No,' she said, 'it's not Fanny.'

'Thought it was some ghost.' He laughed. 'Christ,' he said, 'it's hot.'

Frank Parrott dropped from the horse and lay beside her, with some suggestion of light along his flash Sunday boots. She listened to him settle himself, as the grass streamed out that the horse tore, his bridle trailing through the dark grass. There was an air of permanence about the position of Frank Parrott, which was at the same time false, she did not trust.

'Thought I'd come over and have a talk,' he said, his voice broken into careless bits. 'I was at a loose end. It's hot. A cove can't think in such heat. What's a cove to do?'

She drew down the corners of her mouth in the darkness.

'Soon it will rain,' she said. 'There will be a downpour, and then, Frank, you will be able to think.'

She looked through the branches at the close red moon which, in spite of its closeness, wore an expression of unlikelihood.

'What do you think about, Frank?' she asked.

She smoothed her skirt.

'Oh, I dunno,' he yawned. 'Things. The future. I want to get out of this. I'm sick of cows. I want to go in for sheep in a big way. There's more money in sheep.'

She began to feel old and oracular listening to Frank Parrott's voice, as if she didn't belong. There was this on one side, the life of men keeping sheep and making money, and on the other, herself and Meroë. She was as remote as stone from the figures in the first landscape of which Frank Parrott spoke.

'I am content,' she said. 'I would like to die at Meroë.'

'Yes,' said Frank, 'but you are you.'

He spoke thoughtfully now, not with the criticism that other people's voices had for Theodora Goodman. So that she wanted him to speak more. The blood in her stone hands ran a little quicker, perhaps from fear also, that stone will crumble. Not even Father could hold up the walls of Meroë when it was time. So now she waited for Frank to speak.

'You know, Theo,' Frank said, 'I find I like to talk to you.'

The horse with the trailing bridle had drifted far now. Only faint swathes of grass fell to his teeth.

'Why?' asked Theodora dully.

She had begun to suffocate. She could feel the pressure of the red moon.

'Because you are all right. Because, I suppose, you are honest,' he said.

His voice groped. It had great difficulty in choosing words to express what, anyway, had no shape.

'I never thought about myself as being honest or dishonest,' said Theodora. 'I never thought about being anything in particular. One lives, and that is all.'

She said all this stiffly enough, because it was her way, but inside her she was touched. She unbent inside and stroked him as if he had been a dog's head offering itself out of the darkness. Her hand passed and repassed over the coat of the red dog. And altogether Frank was not unlike a dog, animal and unconscious, with bursts of nice affection.

'I could tell you,' Frank began.

'What could you tell?' she asked.

'Nothing,' he said.

He stirred uneasily in the grass. And again the moon pressed through the branches of the old trees. He rolled over and looked at the house. And now he was different, the way the light struck his sharp spurs and glittered in the sockets of his eyes. He was no longer the nice affectionate dog. If she had touched him, touched his hands, the bones of her fingers would have wrestled with the bones in the palm of his hand.

'There will be such a downpour,' she said thickly, biting a blade of grass.

He said that it was time the dam filled, looking still at the lighted house.

Oh, God, she would have said, go, go, or stay, let us throw aside words. Now she felt that only the hands tell. To take in her lap the palpitating moon.

She heard spurs.

'I must go in and see the others,' Frank was saying.

But awkwardly, as if he would not leave her, as if he needed help, and she could only sit straight and impotent as the tree.

'Very well,' she said. 'You will find them. I shall stay a little longer. Until it rains.'

She heard his spurs disappear slowly through the grass and into the house. Then a bird flew through the air. Then a dog barked. Then it was Frank's horse completing a circle as he cropped closer. But it was all motion subtracted from motive. Even when the rain fell, the heavy, spreading drops, covering her forehead and her hair.

'This is what we have been waiting for,' she said: 'The rain.'

But it did not convince.

'You see, Theo?' Frank called. 'The rain!'

He had come out of the house and was taking his horse. His voice was very loud through the soft, fleshy splashing of the big rain.

'So long, Theo,' he called. 'It's a soaker.'

And now he was a long streak of metal down the road.

Theodora went inside, under the sound of rain on the roof. She began to unstick her hair from her forehead, when Fanny came through the lamplight into the room.

'Theo, darling,' Fanny said. 'I have something to tell you, Theo. Frank Parrott has asked me to marry him, and I have said yes.'

Fanny sat on the edge of the bed.

'Oh, yes, Fanny dear,' said Theodora. 'Frank asked. Why, yes.'

No gong could have beat louder.

'We shall take our time,' Fanny said. 'I don't dislike long engagements.'

Theodora Goodman puffed out her hair that the rain had wet. In her left temple, in the rather yellow skin, there was a long blue vein. She had to look at this vein. For the moment it was the most significant detail of geography. She could not stare enough. If only not at her own eyes.

'Long engagements,' said Theodora, 'give one an opportunity to collect.'

'Of course,' said Fanny.

She was very lovely, soft, and thoughtful. You remembered the flesh of early roses, but under the skin you could read arithmetic.

'Mother is very pleased,' said Fanny. 'Because it is really quite an event. Something for the district, I mean.'

'Why, here,' said Theodora, 'is Mother's little silver paper-knife.'

And it was. On the dressing table.

'I'm sorry,' she said, as she took it in her hand to say good night. 'You see. You were right.'

'Yes,' said Mother, 'I was right.'

She looked up. There was never any question. It could not have been otherwise. It was like this between mother and daughter. Mrs Goodman took up the paper-knife in her small hand on which the garnets shone.

'I would be very sorry to lose that little paper-knife,' she said thoughtfully.

Theodora waited. She waited to see if there was anything else she would be expected to give. She had come for this purpose. To her mother.

'Fanny told you?' asked Mrs Goodman.

'Yes,' said Theodora, 'she told me.'

'I am glad. It is an excellent match,' said Mrs Goodman. 'Our Fanny Parrott. You will have to keep my spirits up, Theo dear.'

Her lips were dry on Theodora's cheek.

Frank Parrott went away after that, to Victoria, to buy a bull. But it did not matter whether he stayed or went, after the accomplished fact, because Fanny had much to think about, to enjoy. Sitting late in her morning gown, she was big with the future, you would have said, she already felt its shape. So that Frank Parrott, the man who was responsible, was no longer so very significant. He was allowed to lapse after the act. Fanny wrote to Victoria, but it was not so much a letter to Frank Parrott as a kind of automatic writing which the future inspired.

'Theodora,' Mrs Goodman said, 'has grown thin and yellow.'

'Yes,' said Theodora, 'it has been a trying summer.'

The hills were burnt yellow. Thin yellow scurf lay on the black skin of the hills, which had worn into black pockmarks where the eruptions had taken place. And now the trees were more than ever like white bones. Out of all this exhaustion formed the clear expectant weather of autumn, smelling of chrysanthemums and first frost. Theodora filled the house with the gold chrysanthemums. Their stalks snapped and ran strong sap in her hands.

Father sat against the windowful of pines, with a plaid across his shoulders for the cold that had not yet arrived.

'Theodora,' he said, 'in the end I never saw Greece, because your mother would not come. She said it was a primitive country, full of bugs and damp sheets and dysentery. So we went to Vienna.'

Father's voice complaining was the voice of an old man, and, of course, because Father was old, his beard was white. Even so, it had just happened.

'I have been nowhere,' Theodora said.

She bent and kissed him. She was kissing, she felt, not Father, but an old man. An old man complaining in a Greek play. And she felt sad. She was sad for Meroë. Because it was coming to an end. The play would finish, after the blaze of gold.

Soon, in fact, the house was full of the smell of dead chrysanthemums, which are more than dead flowers, they are the smell of death. Only statues can resist the smell of dead chrysanthemums.

So that when Theodora woke in the night she heard that it was happening. Her heart was cold. Heavy skeins of smoke fell from the lit candle. The folds of her nightgown fell from her like folds of falling wax, from which her hair streamed. She was walking in the passages of Meroë, a reflection walking through mirrors, towards the door which had always been more mirror than door, and at which she was now afraid to look.

Inside the room, of which the windows were open, Father lay on the couch. He was close, closer than her own thought, and at the same time distant, like someone in a public house. This was also George Goodman, a decent cove, educated, but weak and lazy, said the men in the street outside the Hotel Imperial.

Now this George Goodman looked at her a little bit puzzled. But her own close thought spoke to her from his mouth and said, 'I am glad that you have come, Theodora. I thought that you would. Because I know I am going to die.'

She streamed out beside him on the carpet, kneeling, touching his knees. Her breath was hoarse. 'No,' she said. 'Not yet, Father. No.'

His voice was as pale as the grey light that now sucked and whispered at the pines.

'But there is no reason, my dear Theodora, why I should go on living. I have finished.'

'No,' she said, 'not yet.'

She would throw her strength against this stone that he kept rolling on her mouth.

'And we are close,' he said. 'It is not possible for us to come any closer.'

But it was for this that she buried her face in his knees. Time spread out before his almost extinguished voice, a great shiny metal funnel on which her hands slipped.

'In the end,' his voice said, out of the pines, 'I did not see it.'

Then Theodora, with her face upon his knees, realized that she was touching the body of George Goodman, grazier, who had died that morning.

She walked out through the passages, through the sleep of other people. She was thin as grey light, as if she had just died. She would not wake the others. It was still too terrible to tell, too private an experience. As if she were to go into the room and say: Mother, I am dead, I am dead, Meroë has crumbled. So she went outside where the grey light was as thin as water and Meroë had in fact, dissolved. Cocks were crowing the legend of day, but only the legend. Meroë was grey water, grey ash. Then Theodora Goodman cried.

5

My dear Violet,

I am filled with remorse when I think that it is many months since I received your kind letter, but you will forgive me, I hope, knowing that so much has happened. Since we moved from Meroë to Sydney, we have been fitting ourselves into a whole new life, and it has not been altogether easy. If it were only myself, it would be a different matter but Mother is set in her ways and finds it difficult to adapt herself.

However, I must not let our dull existence detract from your good news. I was interested and delighted to hear that you had married Charlie Simpson, who, if I remember, was excellent in a waltz. Violet, I hope you will be happy. *Of course you will.* While we are still on the subject of marriages, I must tell you that Fanny married Frank Parrott quietly, from the Parrotts' house, just before Mother and I moved here. It was agreed that there was no reason why any sadness should postpone the wedding, and Fanny herself was anxious to avoid coming here for a month or two before returning to Frank and Sorrel Vale, so the event took place. Fanny was disappointed, to be sure, that it was not the smart function with bridesmaids for which she had hoped, and for which she had planned the dresses, but now she is happy in her new house, on one of the small farms adjoining Mr Parrott's, which a tenant had vacated at an opportune moment. Of course this is only temporary. Frank is looking about him. He is anxious to go in for sheep.

As for ourselves, we are living in a medium house above the bay. How to describe it I don't know, for it is not a very distinguished house, thin and red, one of a row. There is a garden in the front and a garden at the back, *thin* gardens, but places in which to breathe the air, and from upstairs we have a view across the bay, which is full of delightful dancing boats. We brought with us enough furniture to furnish our smaller house. The rest we sold with Meroë.

This, Violet, was terrible. May you never experience a sale in your own house. Mr Parrott and Frank were very kind, all through, helping with the business of settling our affairs, which would have been terrifying otherwise, for my father, poor darling, was careless. However, we have enough to live on, Mother and I, in comfort. I do not want to tell you much about the end of Meroë. Enough to say the land was bought by Mr Parrott, all except the home paddock and the house, which went for a summer place to a Mr MacKenzie, who married that Una Russell from Spofforths'. Mr MacKenzie is a common sort of man with a great deal of money that he made out of beer. I did not see Una, and confess that I was glad. I could not have borne her face peering into private corners, and her bangles jangling at Meroë.

Now you almost have my story. Can you see my life? It is so mild as to be easily imaginable. At first I thought I could not live anywhere but at Meroë, and that Meroë was my bones and breath, but now I begin to suspect that any place is habitable, depending, of course, on the unimportance of one's life.

Now I must leave you, Violet. Mother is calling for her tea. Naturally she has been distressed by the loss of so many of her possessions, but I do not doubt that time and quiet will restore her.

Again I thank you for your kindness in our troubles, and send you my sincere wishes for your own happiness.

                                        Theodora Goodman

'Where have you been, Theodora?' asked Mrs Goodman.

'I was writing a letter to Violet Adams,' Theodora said.

'Violet Adams? A flat, pale girl. I remember. Outside the church. I always thought her rather an insipid friend.'

'No doubt Violet is all that you say,' Theodora said. 'But it appears that she is also kind.'

'Oh, *kindness*,' said Mrs Goodman's voice trailing into a piece of bread and butter.

The flat, pale kindness of Violet Adams, or Simpson, was like an ointment. It soothed. Theodora Goodman thought about her own letter, which she had written in reply, and which was also kind and flat, flat as its envelope, and yet she was neither kind nor flat. She wondered a little about Violet Adams waltzing with Charlie Simpson beside the great river she had once described in flood. The descriptive letters never did describe. And the writing tables of women, the useless women, must be littered with these lies. The polite, kind letters written in the code of friendship.

'I do like my tea,' Mrs Goodman sighed.

If Mrs Goodman softened, it was in moments of small nostalgia such as these, for her own physical well being. Mother is very physical, Theodora thought. She watched the rings encrusting Mrs Goodman's tea-cup. They were the same rings. And the face was the same. In age it had not softened. It had been carved a little deeper, like a stone that the artist could not bear to leave, as if the next touch might give it immortality, not destroy its soul. So Mrs Goodman sat, perfect within her limits, but, like marble, she did not expand.

'Tea,' she sighed, 'is a most civilized drink.'

And then, 'I wonder what they are up to. At Meroë. That brewer man with the watch and chain.'

Because the stomach of Mr MacKenzie had rustled with gold, and a greenstone tomahawk, and a ruby star, as Mr Parrott stood with the sun in his eyes on the yellow steps at Meroë and passed him off.

'Theo, this is Mr MacKenzie, who is going to buy the house,' Mr Parrott said.

'Miss Goodman, eh? Heard about you. You and the missus were schoolmates. So Mrs MacKenzie says.'

'We were at school together, yes,' Theodora replied.

But Mr MacKenzie was on his way to the yard, to see where he could stable motor cars. Because, of course, he had bought a motor car, in which his wife used to sit looking expensive, with a little detachable parasol.

So that Theodora did not expect there was much more to be said for Meroë. It was swallowed by Mr MacKenzie, and the mouths of the people at the general sale, the red, round, and greedy, or the brown, hatchety, suspicious faces, that gobbled or snapped at LOTS. Because objects had lost their identity and become numbers. It was doubtful whether, even with the ticket soaked off, identity would ever be restored.

When her knees began to tremble, Theodora said, 'I was not born, unfortunately, with mahogany legs.'

'Sit down, Theo. There's no need to stand about. So sit down,' said Frank Parrott.

He spoke with the accent of kindness with which people address the surface of one another's lives.

'You'll get a tidy price for this stuff of yours,' he said. 'Cockies and storekeepers like to lay their hands on something good. If they think it's got class, they're prepared to pay.'

But Frank looked sideways at Theodora. It was becoming a

habit, as if he blamed her for his own guilt, or else her ugliness, or both. Theodora accepted this approach. There were no ripples on the pool. It was flat and smooth. My brother-in-law, Frank Parrott, she said. There were moments when Theodora was as smooth as glass.

'Yes,' said Mrs Goodman, between mouthfuls, 'I wonder what they are up to at Meroë.'

She exhaled, as if the tea she had tasted had been bitter. Her eyes rounded in the stream, which might give up, she hoped, some vision of vulgarity.

'But there you are,' she said.

'What is?' Theodora asked.

The straw from the packing cases still twitched at her skirt. The sea of pines swelled, hinting at some odyssey from which there was no return.

'It is just a manner of speaking,' Mrs Goodman exclaimed. 'Really, Theodora, how tiresome you can be.'

But Mother had not embarked. Her world had always been enclosed by walls, her Ithaca, and here she would have kept the suitors at bay, not through love and patience, but with suitable conversation and a stick. Mother would have said in the end: Oh, here you are, and about time too, I was bored. What, you have seen witches and killed giants? Ah, but Ianthe, a good cook, though a horrid girl, has beaten an octopus a hundred and forty times on a stone and simmered it for eight hours in wine, and I have offered a calf to Aphrodite if she will produce six yards of purple out of the air.

Instead of all this, the more carnal Mrs Goodman said, 'I shall read. I shall read this library book that has been forced on me by Connie Ewart. Though why? Why Connie thinks I should read the latest dirty book.'

'It is not necessary, Mother,' said Theodora. 'There are plenty of clean ones in the house.'

'No. I shall read it. I shall read the book that Connie so inexcusably brought. It is dirty. It is quite foul. But it is interesting as a commentary on modern life.'

Mrs Goodman read many books. This was her life, with tea, and bezique, and conversation. Her years piled up, finically, like matchsticks on the knottier logs of time, while outside the

89

novels from the library, history was telling a story, only faintly at first, but growing in importance and alarm, until they had begun to put it in the morning paper, in serial form.

'What do you think?' people asked. 'Will it be bad? What does Theodora think?'

'Why should Theodora think?' said Mrs Goodman. 'Theodora is only a girl. She has had no experience. My solicitor tells me it is most serious. I remember once seeing the Kaiser in Berlin. Theodora, I asked you to leave the window open, and you shut it.' 'You asked me to shut it, Mother.'

'You always misinterpret what I say. Yes, as I was saying. In Berlin. And I shuddered then. Ah, but you don't know Berlin. It is full of chariots with rearing horses. And the men shave their heads.'

Now, for Mrs Goodman, the chariots moved, the horses reared higher, out of the moment in which they had been sculptured, the shaven heads were set in motion, as she sat in her room remembering her personal distaste. It was always largely personal. The horrors of war touched her in theory. She knew what expression to wear on her face. But it was for something that would remain outside her experience, in Europe, where her age and income precluded her admission. She was glad. I am old, she said, as if she had bought her way out of any further responsibility.

But Theodora walked in the streets. There were flags in the streets. There was crying. There was crying on the wharves, and in the upper rooms, where the bed ached, under the electric light which had been forgotten. Its bright bulb made little headway against the general shapelessness that was taking possession.

Once under a lamp-post there was a drunk sitting, whose face was a green lozenge, who called to Theodora from the kerb, and said, 'You are walkin', sis, as if you didn't expect no end.'

'I was thinking,' Theodora answered from the darkness.

'That is the trouble,' said the man, 'if you'll excuse me, missus, is it? Thinkin' leads to all this perpendicular emotion. You must listen to your belly and the soles of your feet. That's what I been doin', sis. An' my bloody stomach tells me there'll be a bloody end.'

'I hope you are right,' said Theodora Goodman.

'It stands ter nature. You can fill a man up, sis. Up to a point. But 'e'll spew it out. An' then 'e'll be right as rain.'

She began to be tired of the man's face, and not altogether convinced by philosophy. She began to move, because she did not know what else to do.

'You goin'?' he said. 'Thought we was havin' a talk.'

'Good night,' she called. 'I shall think about what you said.'

'Cripes, no,' said the man. 'It don't bear it. Buy yourself a drink on Bert Kelly.'

The long green shape of his face sprouted from the kerb, yearning outwards, after some unseen rain.

'Oh, mummy, mummy,' sighed the man, 'I feel as sick as sin.'

The next day Theodora Goodman got herself a job in a canteen. Whether she listened to them or not, the soles of her feet ached, which was preferable to the aching of darkness. She stood under the girders, amongst the urns, and sometimes a face searched her for more than change, the clear faces with the bronze eyelids, or thick white drooping faces with secretive, porous skins. Under the girders the urns exhausted themselves in steam. The air was as poignant as the air of railway stations. There was, of course, the same coming and going, the same solitariness even in a crowd. One man showed her a picture he had taken from a Hun. It was a photograph of two girls, two sisters, of whom the elder was wearing a locket. Staring and smiling out of the cracks of the soldier's hand, the faces of the girls expressed a belief in continuity, at least up to the moment when the photographer had squeezed the bulb. Theodora remembered the picture, and sometimes wondered at what point the illusion of individual will had succumbed to the universal dream.

'Theodora is wearing herself to a shadow,' confided Mrs Goodman.

There was not so much pity in her voice as a horrid suspicion that a shadow might escape. This kept Mrs Goodman breathless with anxiety. She would sit. She would sit and think, and listen for Theodora's key, and her long step, which would make her irritable. She sat and longed to be made irritable again.

'It is all very well,' Mrs Goodman said. 'But at this hour, I thought something must have happened.'

'A ship arrived,' Theodora said.

She had begun to hate their thin house. You could open the compartments of the house and know, according to the hour, exactly what to find, an old woman grumbling at her combinations or laying out a patience, a young woman offering objects of appeasement, or looking out of the window, or switching off the light. It was better in darkness. Theodora was less conscious of her mother's eyes. Because when there was nothing left to say, Mrs Goodman could still look.

This is my daughter Theodora, Mrs Goodman did not say, but looked, my daughter Theodora, who is unlike me either in behaviour or in body, and who at best was an odd, sallow child in that yellow dress which was such a mistake. If it were Fanny, ah, Fanny is different, who wore pink, and married well, and is a bright young woman. I remember a morning when she pricked her finger, embroidering a sampler, and I sucked the blood oozing from her little finger. Fanny was my child. But Theodora ran away and hid, or sulked about the country with that rifle, which made us all ridiculous. Theodora hides still, in the darker corners of the house, amongst the furniture, or she hides her face in a silence and thinks I cannot see. Now that her sense of duty to the world sends her to work in a canteen, she hopes that this may absolve her from duty to her mother. But I think and hope that she will not be so heartless. If I could be certain. Life would be simpler, neater, more consoling, if we could take the hearts of those who do not quite love us and lock them in a little box, something appropriate in mother-o'-pearl. Then I would say: Theodora, now that you are hollow, my words will beat on your soul for ever so that it answers regularly as an African drum, in words dictated by myself, of duty and affection. As it is, you are a hard, plain, egotistical young woman who will never interpret the meaning of love.

Instead Mrs Goodman complained, in words, into the darkness. 'Theodora, why must we sit without the light?' Her words were soft, and old, and hurt.

'Because it is more soothing,' said the voice of Theodora. 'I was tired.'

'Just as you think,' said the old soft voice of Mrs Goodman. 'I wonder where Fanny is,' it sighed.

'Where should she be?' said Theodora. 'With her husband.'

'There is no need to snap at me, dear.'

But now Mrs Goodman was consoled, now that she had been handed a photographic group. This was what she had been waiting for. Frank and Fanny Parrott on the steps. Frank had not enlisted of course. He had family obligations. He was buying a place. He would own many sheep and become a figure in the country. It was decided from the start that time would not stand still for Frank and Fanny Parrott.

Dearest Theodora (Fanny Parrott wrote in time),

It is just a week since we took possession at Audley, and everything is still so topsy-turvy I can scarcely collect my thoughts to write. There are packing cases in the hall, builders in the kitchen quarters, and shavings everywhere! But I must do my best to describe our place, I am so excited, it so far exceeds all that Frank had said. By this I mean the house, and not the land, because land is just land, and Frank says he is pleased with the stock, so I suppose he is. But the house, Theo, is so lovely, a new shiny brick, you would say quite new, with little balconies and gables, and shiny turrets like a medieval castle, and some of the windows are divided up by lead into those little lozenges. I feel I am in *Europe*! There is a fine gravel drive leading up to the porch, which gives a house an unusual air in the country, and there are neat rose-beds, really beautifully laid out, not like our higgledy-piggledy old rose garden at Meroë.

Inside there are several big and magnificent rooms which we shall not use, except when we entertain, and a study for Frank, and a little room which I shall call my boudoir and live in mostly. It was a stroke of fortune, such a house, with what Frank says is the right land, but sometimes it does give me the shivers, when I go through the rooms where they found Mr Buchanan, but they say he was always unstable, and once as a boy had opened his veins with a razor, now this tragedy with a pistol. They say he had a mistress, quite a common woman, who used to take baths in milk, like some empress, wasn't it!

I forgot to say there are five spare rooms, and one room we shall use for a nursery – when! Dear Theodora, it will be such a joy, but of course there is plenty of time, and I am determined to enjoy my life, because you never know, and this *sad* war, we might have gone to Europe.

Now, what about you, Theo? Some time I mean to have a straight talk, because we both feel it is time you married, someone quiet and steady, not necessarily exciting, because this would not be the right kind of man, I mean the kind you like. So I am going to rack my brains, and then I shall insist.

Darling, I wonder if you would do something for me. I wonder if you would buy six yards of blue velvet to match the enclosed pattern of silk, if you can find it. This *dreadful*, ravaging war! The poor Hetheringtons have lost their second son. So sad.

Frank says I must get you to stay as our first visitor and ask over at the same time some good-looking young man.

My love to dearest Mother, I hope she is not bored, and to you, of course, Theodora, lots.

Your loving
Fanny

p.s. I saw that Una MacKenzie (Russell that was). She was quite green when she heard about my house, and that vulgar husband, they say he is on the *booze*!

p.p.s. Daisy Ritchie has had the Vice-Regals to stay. I am puzzling my head where she put them, it is such a very miserable house, with only recently a W.C., and the door of that doesn't lock.

Reading the letter from Fanny, Theodora sat again on the bed. They were darning stockings, in midsummer, at Meroë, and Fanny was eighteen. This had remained her age. Fanny loved the glossy things, to take up by handfuls, and hold, and keep. Theodora touched the little square of pale blue silk, for matching which she would receive a husband. If Fanny did not forget, between altering the kitchen quarters and entertaining in the magnificent, ordinarily closed rooms. Although Fanny's face was closed to her own reality, there were times when Theodora loved her, the child of eighteen, smooth and pretty as a square of pale blue silk. It is these little tangible moments, she felt, that make the blood relationships almost congruous.

'What is that you have got, Theodora?' Mrs Goodman asked.

'It is a letter from Fanny.'

'My girl doesn't write to me any more,' Mrs Goodman complained.

'But it is the same thing. You may read it.'

'I thought perhaps there might be something you did not want me to see.'

She took the letter that she would read once, twice, from her daughter Fanny Parrott, who spoke to her in words. Mrs Goodman read with pleased indifference of Fanny Parrott's magnificence. Because her own day for this was done, she could not altogether believe that magnificence existed still. Though it would suit Fanny, when it would never have done for Theodora. Theodora, she said, is an old maid. And the sheet of paper tittered in her hand over Fanny's nonsense about husbands. Men came to the house sometimes even now, and Theodora sat with them, but without the brilliance and deception they expect and need. Mrs Goodman listened to them take their hats and go, and she knew from their feet on the carpet they would go home undisturbed to bed.

But on the evenings when no one came, Mrs Goodman said, 'Theodora, fetch the cards. Let us try a hand or two.'

Then Mrs Goodman would make marriages with Spanish pomp. She would tingle with hate and love in anticipation of the little kiss.

'This fine lady,' she muttered, 'is waiting to be kissed. If he can get through. No, no, he won't. He can't!'

She held her cards in a firm fan.

Sometimes Theodora could feel the hatred in her mother's hand. She could feel the pressure of the rings. Sometimes the mirrors swelled into the room, and the chandelier prepared its avalanche of glass. But mostly Theodora did not care.

'Look, it is your game,' she said.

'It is no fun,' said Mrs Goodman, 'when one's opponent does not try.'

Sometimes on these occasions she was like a one-eyed queen squinting for weaknesses.

'I shall read till I feel sleepy,' Mrs Goodman said.

But from the cover of her book her hand peered, diamond-eyed. She waited to snap the covers and say : You are caught, I saw you quail, I saw your soul gape open like a wound. It was the great tragedy of Mrs Goodman's life that she had never done a murder. Her husband had escaped into the ground, and Theodora into silences. So that she still had to kill, and there were moments when she could have killed herself.

The day Theodora threw down her hat and said, 'They say it is over, Mother. We shall have peace.'

'Peace?' Mrs Goodman murmured, studying its implications. 'Then you won't have to work in that canteen. You shall stay at home and rest.'

Her rings scraped on each other. She was the one-eyed queen, scanning a situation in which lay her last hope.

Theodora saw this, but more often than not it went on like a distant and rather wooden charade. She cultivated a vision of distance. The whole landscape became a distance, even when she walked close, under fire from scarlet salvia.

Summertime the whole air burned scarlet with salvia. She closed her eyes, let it become her smile, and in this airy disintegration there was some peace. To trail like the path of a hornet through the tasselled pepper trees. To mingle the glow of her scarlet parasol on the asphalt hill. Scarlet lit her face. It ran like blood beneath her brown skin. So that people stopped to look, sensing something strange, mopping their heads on the hot hill. But Theodora Goodman walked slowly through their glances, into the sound of the thin steeple, of the little spiky church, that stood protesting in the glow of summer.

In Theodora's world a wet finger could have pressed the cardboard church, and pressed, until the smoking sky showed through. Sometimes an iron tram careered quite dangerously along the spine of a hill. People mopping their heads wondered uneasily into what they sank in Theodora Goodman's eyes. People casually looking were sucked in by some disturbance that was dark and strange.

It was after the war some time, a year or two perhaps, that people began to talk about the tragedy of Jack Frost. Frost was a pastrycook. He kept a shop in George Street to which people went, the people who had names and good addresses, but Jack Frost himself lived in a street in Clovelly which was just a street. One Sunday Jack Frost cut the throats of his wife and three little girls. Just like that. Then, when he had locked his house, he walked to Central Station, where he was taken, asking for a ticket to a place of which he had forgotten the name.

The Jack Frost case caused quite a stir. People talked. They saw the shop. It was painted a dark green. And inside the window cakes stood on stiff stands, puffs blowing clouds of cream, and tarts high with black cherries, with paper doilies underneath. When the Jack Frost tragedy occurred, people were reminded of themselves in the shop, buying the murderer's cakes, and passing the time of day. But it was horrible. Always so decent and polite, under it all Frost was mad, to kill his wife and three little girls. Unhinged by the war, of course. He had served, the papers said, in France. And *Truth*, which people began to buy, not from their newsagents, but over the garden fence, *Truth* had a full account, with photographs. It had a letter which Jack Frost wrote in his madness before he did the deed.

Dear All (wrote Jack Frost),
    It come to this. I come home this evening, I seen your faces Winnie, Evelyn, Thelma, and Zoë, I see us all sitting round the table buttering our scones for Sunday tea. I saw as you didn't know what was in the next room. Then I say to meself I will put up them smiles so as we can all walk out, though maybe the Judge won't agree.
    Dear All, you will forgive me, yes I know, because it is already done, and now, my dears, we shall see.
                                    Your ever loving dad and husband,
                                                        Jack Frost

It was terrible, they said, and indecent, to print madness for the public to read. People were moved far more deeply than they were by the bodies of lumpy girls, which appear so monotonously and anonymously on wasteland in the suburbs. The Frost case was worse, they said. They felt his cakes in their stomachs. They saw the dark hairs on his wrist as he handed back the change. The Frost case was very close, and for that reason they felt sick, and could not understand.

They were discussing it in the drawing-room, Mother, and Mrs Ewart, and a Miss Stevenson with a gold tooth, who had been brought for the first time. There was also Mr Clarkson, who had been recommended to Mrs Goodman by the Parrotts as solicitor.

Miss Stevenson with the gold tooth shuddered, and fingered the top of her glove. She always avoided murders, she said. There were so many nice things in the world.

'But to think,' said Mrs Ewart. 'Those three little girls. They looked such nice little girls. The three. If only it had been one. Or even two.'

'That, Connie,' said Mrs Goodman, 'is irrelevant detail. We were discussing the ethics of the case.'

Mr Clarkson said the whole incident had been distorted out of its true proportion, and the room listened, because he was a man. The Jack Frost murders had struck a chord of mass hysteria, which was always waiting to sound, and now particularly, since the war, since people had been left high and dry by other horrors. Now the individual was free to take the centre of the stage again and dramatize himself.

'Don't you agree, Miss Goodman?' asked Mr Clarkson.

He was a bald man, with strong, clean hands.

'Partly,' said Theodora. 'It is very personal. I find it difficult. Quite honestly. Difficult to discuss. I have thought about it. And it is still so close. Like something one has done oneself.'

Mrs Goodman cleared some phlegm from her throat in an exasperated, throaty spasm.

'Theodora, Mr Clarkson, sometimes has pretensions to be unusual,' Mrs Goodman said.

'It is understandable that Miss Goodman should feel as she does,' said Mr Clarkson.

And he straightened a pearl that pinned his tie.

Theodora did not hear this, as she had gone out on to the balcony. In the room she had been disturbed, by its various undertones, and Mr Clarkson, he was the most disturbing of all, because kindness wears an expression that expects truth. Now she stood by herself on the cramped lower balcony, from which it was barely possible to see the bay. The landscape at which she looked was quite devoid of complexity. There was a smooth breeze in the big Moreton Bay fig. The afternoon was, in fact, as settled as the voices of middle age that murmured through the glass door, except that Theodora continued to see Jack Frost's irreproachable façade, through which Frost himself had finally dared to pitch the stone.

Then Mr Clarkson came outside. Miss Goodman, he could see, was in a state of nerves. Her skin jumped.

'I came out here to get the air,' she said.

Her silence added that she hoped she would be left. But Mr Clarkson, who had the smooth texture and the smoky smell of rich, thick-set men of forty, did not hear silences.

'I like your view, Miss Goodman,' Mr Clarkson said. 'It is my view reversed. If I stand on my balcony I can see yours. There, you see, the yellow house, beside the church.'

And he pointed at a square of stone, in a blur of trees, on the ridge that formed the opposite arm of the bay.

'You must come one day and see for yourself.'

'Thank you,' she said. 'I go out very little.'

'All the more reason then.'

His voice compelled her to make the balcony her universe, outside which the sound of trees swam, words in the room, and the ripple of a dove. It would be very easy, she felt, to allow the kindness, the affluence, the smoky voice of Mr Clarkson to engulf. But because of this she resisted. She could feel her neck, under its lace frill, stiffen into bone. She hoped, with both her hands, to take refuge in her ugliness. Now she summoned it up from all the reflections that had ever faced her in the glass.

'You will not find me very good company, Mr Clarkson,' said Theodora Goodman's mouth.

That she turned on him, her dark lips, that made a thin seam in the yellow skin. There were moments, said Huntly Clarkson, when Theodora Goodman was no longer scraggy, her head a strange dark flower on its long stem, but defensive, with a strange dark smell, like a lily that folds its lips secretively on a fly.

'This question of company,' he said, 'is something for me to decide. The people who love us have a habit of sticking on labels that are never acceptable, and very seldom correct.'

'Oh, and this is my daughter Theodora,' Mrs Goodman had said. 'Of course, you will know my younger girl, Fanny Parrott. At her mother-in-law's. Fanny is a great favourite. With everyone.'

Mrs Goodman had let all this escape through her veil, in a last gasp of breath, the first morning, after the stairs. She wanted, she said, advice on many little things, none of them important, but still, it is always comforting to know that there is somebody to ask. Mrs Parrott had suggested, implied Mrs Goodman, that Mr Clarkson would offer that comfort and advice. Mr Clarkson agreed, amiably, above his desk, which was prosperous and broad, and at which he could already feel the tyranny of Mrs Goodman aimed. He noticed that she was a small, neat, hateful woman, with small, neat, buckled shoes, and many rings. She sat in the light and kept her ankles crossed. But her daughter sat in shadow, and drew with her parasol on the floor characters that he could not read. The daughter's face was shadow under her large and timeless hat. Her clothes were quiescent and formalized as stone.

'Then we shall see something of each other,' Mrs Goodman commanded. 'I shall expect you at our house.'

So it had come to that. On the balcony. In the afternoon.

'He is my solicitor,' said Mrs Goodman to Mrs Ewart and the gold-toothed Miss Stevenson. 'He is Dolly Armstrong's nephew. He is rich. He is a widower. Yes, I believe it was sad. Quite young. But there you are. He has everything else in life. His house is full of exquisite things.'

'Tell us, Julia, now,' asked Mrs Ewart, 'is Theo interested at all? Poor Theo. It would be nice.'

'I am too discreet to ask,' Mrs Goodman said. 'But Theodora is a fool. She is a stick with men.'

Miss Stevenson tweaked at the top of her glove. Her position had grown delicate.

'I only thought,' said Mrs Ewart, 'it would be so nice.'

'But what would Mr Clarkson want with Theodora?' Mrs Goodman asked.

'If you would come,' said Mr Clarkson, 'I would show you my fox terriers. I would ask you to lunch.'

Doves drowsed in the afternoon, in the sea glaze. This, felt Theodora, should be delightful if one knew how.

'You are very kind, Mr Clarkson,' she said. 'Shall we go inside?'

And they did. They walked back into the conversation of the old women, behind which Theodora hid her indecisions. Then, saying something about a handkerchief, she went to her room, and stayed while voices combined in the hall, dawdled, and diminished.

The door banged twice, the permanently loose letter-box, before Mrs Goodman called, 'Theo, where are you? Going off like that. Everyone wondered if you were ill. You are a strange girl.'

In her mind Mrs Goodman had already roughed out several

landscapes, in which a younger, more exquisite version of herself stood in the foreground, holding Huntly Clarkson's arm, whereas, in fact, she sat on her drawing-room sofa and thoughtfully moistened her lips. Reality struggled with her fantasy. She was consumed.

'I went up to my room,' Theodora said, 'because I was bored.'

'If that is the case, it was rude,' said Mrs Goodman.

But because she did not believe, she burned.

'An odd impression it will make on Mr Clarkson.'

'Mr Clarkson asked me to lunch.'

'You will go of course,' said Mrs Goodman.

She could not wait for the answer, to feel her anger or contempt.

'I don't know yet,' said Theodora, 'whether I shall go or not.'

She would have liked to repay his kindness with a frank gesture of acceptance, the kind of gesture that Huntly Clarkson would expect, and get, from some woman of complexion, shadowless in a blue dress. The kind of woman who would receive a diamond brooch in a velvet box without a performance of gaucherie, who would press the hand that gave. Theodora remembered Huntly Clarkson's hands, which were large and clean. The hands had rested on the stucco balustrade, waiting to give. But she could not, she thought, take, and regret rushed at her, so that she had to write:

Dear Mr Clarkson,

If you will forgive my failure to accept, I would like to come when you suggest.

Theodora Goodman

In this way Theodora Goodman went to the house of Huntly Clarkson, which stood in a blaze of laurels, a rich house, full of the glare of mahogany and lustre. The floors shone. There was an air of ease that disguised the industry which achieved this state. The servants were silent and well oiled. If they did not speak, it was because they had learnt their functions too well. They had a kind of silent contempt for anyone who did not understand what these functions were. So the servants of Huntly Clarkson looked at the shoulders of this woman helping herself to a cutlet, and condemned her as she tried to thank. Her glance was indication of her income and her status. She was a woman of no account, whose clothes were not of this or any fashion, whose face was ageless in appearance, though they would have put her somewhere in the thirties.

'I did not ask anyone else,' said Huntly Clarkson, 'because you didn't suggest you wanted them.'

'How not suggest?' she said, dazed by the noises the silver made on the table. 'At the time I was a blank. You have read things off me that were never there. Really. I assure you.'

But there was a kind of ease between them. She began to think that it might be a pleasant thing, a friendship with Huntly Clarkson, if she could resist his house, his servants, and his furniture. These were all magnificently assured. They fixed time in the present. Even the old things inherited from grand-fathers and aunts, even these pandered to Huntly Clarkson and the present, as if they began and ended as part of his upholstery. She looked at the rich, shining, well-covered body of Huntly Clarkson and wondered if he would exist without his padding.

'When you are not the solicitor I know, what do you do?' she asked.

'I enjoy myself,' he said. 'It would be tempting to do this all the time. If one hadn't a kind of puritan misgiving. But outside this I succeed very well. I eat rich food. I smoke cigars. I go on an average of once a week to the races. I give dinner parties, which are sometimes boring, but there is always the spectacle of smart women with bare shoulders and diamonds.'

'I have never done any of these things,' said Theodora. 'I wonder why you have asked me?'

'That is why,' Huntly Clarkson said.

He laughed, but as if he were a little puzzled by his clever-ness. As if he had thought that he knew, and then discovered he did not.

'I collect,' he said, 'unusual objects. I have the signatures of four English kings. I have the breviary of Maximilian of Mexico and a ball of hair that was cut out of the stomach of a cat.'

Then she laughed, too, because he made her warm and dash-ing, almost as if her shoulders were bare, and she flashed like a spray of diamonds.

'I see,' she laughed, 'there is very little you haven't got.'

'Yes,' he agreed. 'And the odd part of it is, I am perfectly happy.'

He bent forward to confide, so that she looked into his well-shaved skin, and smelled the smell of rich, urbane men, which was new to her. Huntly Clarkson described happiness, and it was something you could touch. She drew back a little, almost afraid he might expect her to. But it was very delightful, and afterwards, sitting on the veranda, in a lull of wine, when the little fox terriers came, jumping, flirting, flashing, worrying, and prancing on their thin white wooden legs.

'I hope you will come often,' Huntly Clarkson said. 'I would like you to meet my friends.'

It brushed cold along her skin. To sit alone in the drawing-room surrounded by the bare, diamond women.

'I would never be very good at these things,' said Theodora Goodman.

'Just as you think,' he said.

But she was sad, because she could feel that he had sat back.

And he had. He felt that he had eaten too much. He was bored by dogs, and the prospect of the office, and Theodora Goodman. Why had he asked Theodora Goodman to his house? If it was out of pity it was praiseworthy. He often did praiseworthy things. But he was tired of himself. He wanted to loll right back and listen to something extraordinary as he fell asleep.

'Have you ever seen a volcano?' she asked. 'I would like to sail past in a ship, preferably at night.'

He opened his eyes.

'Why, yes,' he said. 'I have seen Vesuvius and Etna. And Stromboli. That from a ship. They were not so very extraordinary. None of them,' he said.

The green blaze of laurels crackled. Now she knew that she would go. It was easier to escape than she expected, from where she had never belonged.

But it settled down into being one of those relationships it is difficult to explain, a kind of groove in which minds fit, though not visible from outside. This persisted for some years.

'Theo and Mr Clarkson see quite a lot of each other,' hesitated Mrs Ewart hopefully.

'Theodora and Mr Clarkson,' said Mrs Goodman, 'are friends.

Though why, it is difficult to say. Theo is an admirable girl, although I am her mother, but not of Huntly Clarkson's world.'

Oh, no. Mrs Goodman, even at her age, sat erect. She sat perpetually at a dinner table. She could have acted so many lives so much better than the actors. For this reason she resented the voice of Huntly Clarkson asking for Theodora on the telephone.

If reasons were not within the grasp of Mrs Ewart or Mrs Goodman, nor were they altogether apparent to Huntly Clarkson or Theodora Goodman themselves. I suppose, said Theodora, if I responded to clothes it would be something the same. All the rich and sinuous sensations of silk and sables would not have been unlike the hours spent with Huntly Clarkson, which smelled of cigars, and brilliantine, and leather. The sensations that Huntly Clarkson gave were no less voluptuous for being masculine.

'Theodora,' Huntly Clarkson said, 'let us go to the races, let us lunch at a hotel.'

She watched them stand champagne in silver buckets.

'I believe you are not impressed,' said Huntly Clarkson.

'No,' she said. 'I am the soul of shabbiness.'

But her mouth denied what sometimes she would have accepted. The world was plated, after all.

If Huntly Clarkson invited Theodora again, and often he said he would not, that it gave no return, he invited her because of some indefinable uneasiness and discontent, a sense of something that he had not yet achieved. This was in no way connected with what the eager and the innocent would call love. Shaving himself in his undervest on those clear, fine aggressive mornings, when the flesh feels firmer, less fat, Huntly Clarkson laughed. It was not love. Huntly Clarkson had loved as far as he was capable, and finished. Love and Theodora Goodman were, besides, grotesque, unless you were prepared to explore subtler variations of emotion than he personally would care for. Standing in his well-planned bathroom, he shaved his face thoughtfully. He listened to the rasp of the razor on the surface of his skin and admired the clean passage it made through the soap.

Huntly Clarkson did not go to church. He collected pictures, for their value. Sometimes he listened to music, but as a logical stage in developing the evening after dinner. If he experienced malaise, he usually put it down to physical condition. He took things for it. But when, in the midst of his well-planned bathroom, on a clear, clean, sharp morning, shouting with nickel taps, his mind pursued the foggy paths, out of the sun, in all elusiveness, he did not turn to bottles. He chose the telephone. I shall go when I have shaved, he said, and subject myself once more to Theodora Goodman. I shall catch on to the dry thread of her voice, that does not compensate. I shall subject myself, he said, that is the word. But if he felt less complacent, he also felt relieved.

Sometimes on the telephone he still attempted even to buy her with brilliance.

'And by the way,' said Huntly Clarkson, 'you will come on Tuesday, To dinner. To help with Moraïtis.'

From behind her diffidence Theodora said she would. It was touching and amusing, though unconvincing, to be reminded one is indispensable. But this, she said, is the convention in which Huntly lives. The same voice would speak the same words to Marion Neville and Elsa Boileau, summoning them to some imaginary rescue, and this was commonly called charm. So Theodora armed herself with irony. She would go. She would sit just outside the blaze of diamonds, assisting at a social function, the dinner for Moraïtis, who would give a series of four concerts, to which Marion Neville and Elsa Boileau, who *loved* music, would go. Theodora probably would not. She had entered a stretch of years in which she chose flatness.

When she arrived at the house, in which all the lights had been lit, so that it was quite hollow, she knew that the dinner would take place in spite of Moraïtis. He was a small dark man, opaque, bald, and physical, who smiled the propitiating smiles for words only half understood. Already Moraïtis had begun to hope that it would soon be over.

Marion Neville had a cousin, she said, who had been on a cruise to Greece, and had brought back some very beautiful embroidery from one of those islands, she forgot which, where the sanitation was quite appalling, and everyone got tummy troubles, though Esmé was fortunately provided with some indispensable pills, she forgot what.

Greece was a primitive country, said Moraïtis.

But he made it a sad virtue. He was a Greek with sad eyes. He waited for the women to talk about music, because women, a certain kind, do talk about music, and these were they. He looked in rather a tired, dispassionate way at the body of Elsa Boileau, which was passive, and brown, and almost fully exposed. Moraïtis waited for what she was bound to say.

'Of course we are all looking forward to your concerts,' Mrs Boileau said. 'Because we get very little that is good. So seldom the real artistes. We had D'Alvarez, of course. Most striking. She changed her dress I don't know how many times during the performance. By the way, Marion, Sybil *is* wearing what I said she was. Madeleine's model, which isn't. Such a scream.'

Paul Boileau listened to his wife with the apologetic-dog expression of a man who suspects his wife is a bitch, only he is just not sure. He had to pull himself out of her words, to remind himself he had something to tell, and this was from the stock exchange. He would take Huntly and Ralph Neville into a corner. Ralph especially liked to be in on things. He spent a great deal of his time getting *in*. Consequently he dropped his voice frequently when speaking, whether it was some story of political graft or just the price of eggs.

Oh, dear, said Marion Neville, if only I could remember if it is a violin or a 'cello the wretched little fellow plays, oh, dear, these dagoes have funny eyes. But she would ask him to her house and get him to autograph a celebrity tablecloth.

Huntly's table was smouldering with red roses, the roselight that Theodora remembered now, of Meroë. She swam through the sea of roses towards that other Ithaca. On that side there were the pines, and on this side Moraïtis. His hand begged for mercy, fingering a crumb. And Theodora granted it. They did not speak much.

Except once when his voice swam up, as if remembering, and said, 'The roses ...' turning to her to offer his discovery.

'We lived once in an old yellowstone house,' she said. 'Old for here, that is. And one side was a thicket of roses. A tangle. I tell myself I can remember roses reflected on the ceiling, in the early morning, when I was a child. Do you think this can be a fact, or just absurd?'

'Yes?' he said doubtfully.

But although he did not understand, she knew that there was much that he would. In the eyes of Moraïtis there were many familiar objects. He held things with humility, his glass, or knife. Altogether there was little correspondence between Moraïtis and what was going on now round Huntly Clarkson's table. He stood in the reflected roselight.

At the end of the dinner they brought with the dessert some very expensive crystallized fruits, which were no longer fruit but precious stones, hard, and their sweetness had a glitter. This was the apotheosis of the meal, in which the light brandished swords. You forgot the flat words in the glitter of glass and diamonds, the big crystallized stones that hung from Marion Neville's body, and the angelic straps on Elsa Boileau's brown shoulders. The whole of Huntly Clarkson's life lay there on the table, crystallized, in front of Theodora Goodman, and she knew at such moments that there was nothing more to know.

Theodora, felt Huntly Clarkson, is an upright chair, a Spanish leather, in which an Inquisitor has sat, a shabby rag of skin passing judgement on souls. For a few moments he hated Theodora. The way you can hate something that is untouchable.

But the evening of the dinner for Moraïtis the shallower moments prevailed. The two diamond women took out the rag-bag of conversation, their coloured snippets flew. And Paul Boileau watched his wife. He tried to read the answer to his own suspicions in the inclinations of her body, in the intonations of her voice. He looked at the Greek as much as to say: Are you the one who will provide the clue? Because the Greek happened to offer himself at the moment, a concrete object of suspicion.

The Greek suddenly walked, as if he had made up his mind, and sat beside Theodora Goodman.

'They have put me in a room,' he said, 'where I cannot practise.'

The words that he suddenly found he took out with precision. He smiled to see.

'It is all furniture,' he said. 'I cannot live in such a room. I require naked rooms.'

'Bare,' said Theodora Goodman.

'Bare?' said the Greek. 'Naked is the word for women.'

'Naked can be the word,' said Theodora.

'Bare,' smiled Moraïtis, for a fresh discovery. 'Greece, you see, is a bare country. It is all bones.'

'Like Meroë,' said Theodora.

'Please?' said Moraïtis.

'I too come from a country of bones.'

'That is good,' said Moraïtis solemnly. 'It is easier to see.'

He sat forward with his legs apart, his body crouched, his small muscular Greek hands clasped between taut knees. Theodora looked at his thinking hands.

'You see, I am a peasant,' said Moraïtis. 'I am very conscious of the shape of the country. I come from the Peloponnese. It is rich, fat, purple country, but underneath you can feel the bones. Many people were killed there. Greeks die often,' he said.

All the time he was thinking with his hands, feeling his way from object to object, and his hands struggled together to contain the mystery of death.

'Greeks are happiest dying,' smiled Moraïtis. 'Their memorials do not reflect this fatality. All the Greek monuments suggest a continuity of life. The theatre at Epidauros, you have seen it, and Sounion? Pure life. But the Greeks are born to die.'

'I have not seen it,' said Theodora. 'I have seen nothing.'

'It is not necessary to see things,' said Moraïtis. 'If you know.'

But now he had left her. He had begun to take some fresh path. He pursued it, upright now, drumming and humming, sometimes looking out this way and that through the thicket of other people's conversation, seeing and surprised.

Marion Neville looked at a little wristwatch set with small diamonds and rubies and said that they must go.

So it was time.

'Good-bye, Miss Goodman,' said Moraïtis. 'I shall remember we are compatriots in the country of the bones.'

'What is all this?' asked Huntly Clarkson.

'Nothing,' said Theodora. 'We were indulging in a flight.'

Huntly knew then that the door had closed. This, perhaps, was the extent of his relationship with Theodora Goodman. She closed doors, and he was left standing on his handsome mahogany interior, which was external, fatally external, outside Theodora Goodman's closed door. Huntly Clarkson stood and wanted to overcome his humiliation, which he could not pay anyone to take.

The dinner for the Greek 'cellist was on the Friday. On the Tuesday there took place the first of the four concerts that Moraïtis would give, and this was variously described as brilliant, as a magnificent tapestry of sound and colour woven by a master hand, and as a feast for all music lovers. So that it was smart to talk about the Moraïtis recitals, and to learn the names of the pieces that he played.

Theodora had not been. She very much doubted whether she would go. Because, in thinking, she had become obsessed with Moraïtis, his words, his hands. It is not necessary to see things, said Moraïtis, if you know. It is like this, she said. And yet, for the pure abstract pleasure of knowing, there was a price paid. She remembered the Man who was Given his Dinner, the moment on the bridge, which was the same pure abstraction of knowing. But the exaltation was cold without the touch of hands, the breathing and stirring and waking of the tree in the snow.

Anyway, Theodora Goodman did not go to any one of the Moraïtis recitals. She waited, rather, to hear that they had passed, and that Moraïtis, whom she would not see, had gone. And like this, they were over. On the walls and hoardings the bills were already covered over by other wonders. She breathed. She felt exhausted, thin, after a long summer. Only Moraïtis did not go. He would remain, the papers wrote, for one more concert, as a guest artist, he would play the Such-and-Such Concerto.

Then, if that is how it is to be, decided Theodora Goodman.

'Enjoy yourself,' Mrs Goodman said, as if she were half afraid she might.

She remembered as a consolation that Fanny had been the musical one, whereas Theodora had often played an angular music that did not exist. Her thin, dark, struggling arms had filled Mrs Goodman with distaste.

At the concert, as at all concerts, everyone was rounded and well fed. Music filled out the lines and emphasized banality. It is not possible to listen to music without the body becoming a hump on a chair. Over the hall a great grey dumb organ hung and brooded, as it had over other similarly irrelevant occasions, of civic pomposity, or the paper folly of charity balls. Now an orchestra, playing an overture by a Russian, made the dust dance dimly on the organ's face, stirred the dinners in stomachs on the chairs. Some of the chairs were still empty, the chairs of smarter people, who ate longer, later dinners, and who would arrive only in time for the name of Moraïtis.

Theodora Goodman sat close, but to one side, in such a position that she was an oblique assistant to the strings. But she could not listen much. She heard the slabs of music piled one upon the other. She waited for the heap to be made, till Moraïtis should come. And her bones were sick and brittle, her hands burned. Good-bye, Miss Goodman, Moraïtis had said, I shall remember we are compatriots. Taking it for granted there would be no reunion, but why, unless Moraïtis accepted the distances, in which case there was no need. Now she wondered about him, in the wilderness of preliminary music, where he stood, perhaps in a small brown, bare room with two large gilt mirrors of an unfashionable century, in which he stared at his blue chin, working together his muscular hands. Through the rain of distant music, in a comb of corridors, Moraïtis stood in the perspective of the brown room, which tried to contain him, but which failed, defeating its own purpose in reflections of reflections, endlessly. Just as Moraïtis himself defeated his own inadequate face, overflowing through the cavities, or thought eludes the skeleton of words. Theodora saw the reflection of Moraïtis suddenly pick up a tumbler of water from a tin tray, and all the reflections swallowed. Then the reflections gave a quick glance at their teeth. Each of these solemn acts was repeated by the mirror, and isolated, and magnified, without detracting from its privacy. Because Moraïtis was protected by some detachment of unconcern. He accepted the isolation. He retied his bow. The eyelids were contemptuous on the eyes.

At that moment people had begun to clap, and she knew that he had come. He stepped out on to the stage in the isolation which he had brought with him from the mirrors. His bald head shone like a bone. Moraïtis sat down and put his 'cello between his legs, and now you could see that his isolation fitted him closely, aptly, like an armour, which would protect in him some moments that were too delicate to expose. Theodora watched. He saw and did not see. Now she was closer. It was no longer a matter of intervening heads and chairs. She was herself the first few harsh notes that he struck out of his instrument against the tuning violins.

Then the silence crackled. The concerto had begun. The violins made a suave forest through which Moraïtis stepped. The passage of the 'cello was difficult at first, struggling to achieve its own existence in spite of the pressure of the blander violins. Moraïtis sat upright. He was prim. He was pure. I am a peasant, he said. And he saw with the purity of primitive vision, whether the bones of the hills or the shape of a cup. Now the music that he played was full of touching, simple shapes, but because of their simplicity and their purity they bordered on the dark and tragic, and were threatened with destruction by the violins. But Moraïtis closed his eyes as if he did not see, as if his faith would not allow. He believed in the integrity of his first tentative, now more constant, theme. And Theodora, inside her, was torn by his threatened innocence, by all she knew there was to come. She watched him take the 'cello between his knees and wring from its body a more apparent, a thwarted, a passionate music, which had been thrust on him by the violins.

The 'cello rocked, she saw. She could read the music underneath his flesh. She was close. He could breathe into her mouth. He filled her mouth with long aching silences, between the deeper notes that reached down deep into her body. She felt the heavy eyelids on her eyes. The bones of her hands, folded like discreet fans on her dress, were no indication of exaltation or distress, as the music fought and struggled under a low roof, the air thick with cold ash, and sleep, and desolation.

But in the last movement Moraïtis rose again above the flesh. You were not untouched. There were moments of laceration, which made you dig your nails in your hands. The 'cello's voice was one long barely subjugated cry under the savage lashes of the violins. But Moraïtis walked slowly into the open. He wore the expression of sleep and solitary mirrors. The sun was in his eyes, the sky had passed between his bones.

Theodora went as soon as it was over, out of the applause,

into the trams. She walked some distance, the other side of the screeching trams, without seeing much. Her hollow body vibrated still with all she had experienced. Now it was as empty as hollow wood.

'Did you spend an enjoyable evening?' Mrs Goodman asked, glancing with apprehension over the covers of her book.

'It was more than enjoyable,' said Theodora, taking off her gloves.

Mrs Goodman would have said something hard and destructive, only she saw that Theodora was now strong, and for this reason she did not dare. Theodora was removed. She had the strength of absence, Mrs Goodman saw. This made her very strong. It was also rather immoral, the strange, withdrawn mood that one could not share. In her failure to find words Mrs Goodman's old, soft-fed stomach grizzled and complained.

'I am not feeling very well. I think I shall go to bed. It is something I have eaten.'

But the absence of Theodora persisted, and in the morning. Many mornings trumpeted across the bay their strong hibiscus notes. The mornings smelled of nasturtium, crushed by the bodies of lovers on a piece of wasteland at night. Theodora sat sometimes to remember the music she had heard. At these times she sat and looked at the piece of wasteland which was between their thin house and the bay. And the music which Moraïtis had played was more tactile than the hot words of lovers spoken on a wild nasturtium bed, the violins had arms. This thing which had happened between Moraïtis and herself she held close, like a woman holding her belly. She smiled. If I were an artist, she said, I would create something that would answer him. Or if I were meant to be a mother, it would soon smile in my face. But although she was neither of these, her contentment filled the morning, the heavy, round, golden morning, sounding its red hibiscus note. She had waited sometimes for something to happen. Now existence justified itself.

About this time Fanny wrote to say it was going to happen at last. When I was so afraid, dear Theodora, Fanny wrote. But Fanny had made of fear a fussy trimming. Emotions as deep as fear could not exist in the Parrotts' elegant country house, in spite of the fact that Mr Buchanan's brains had once littered the floor. Fanny's fear was seldom more than misgiving. If I were barren, Fanny had said. But there remained all the material advantages, blue velvet curtains in the boudoir, and kidneys in the silver chafing dish. Although her plump pout often protested, her predicament was not a frightening one. Then it happened at last. I am going to have a baby, Fanny said. She felt that perhaps she ought to cry, and she did. She relaxed, and thought with tenderness of the tyranny she would exercise.

'I must take care of myself,' she said. 'Perhaps I shall send for Theodora, to help about the house.'

So Theodora went to Audley, into a wilderness of parquet and balustrades. There was very little privacy. Even in her wardrobe the contemptuous laughter of maids hung in the folds of her skirts.

'God, Theodora is ugly,' said Frank. 'These days she certainly looks a fright.'

The servants knew, and took up his contempt. Miss Goodman, an old maid, they said, a scarecrow in a mushroom hat. She wore long shapeless dresses of striped voile, which made her look an oblong with a head and legs.

Fanny heard laughter, she heard Frank, but she did not speak, because she did not care enough, in her condition, in a boudoir cap. She looked at her fair plump face and wiped the sweat from a wrinkle with a pink puff. She made little grimaces for her figure, but only as a matter of course. Because her figure, like her self-importance, had momentarily swelled.

Sometimes Fanny talked to Theodora about My Baby.

'You've no idea, Theo,' she used to say. 'It's most solemn. As a sensation, I mean.'

'I don't doubt,' said Theodora.

She pushed her needle through the flannel. She sat with her head bent, so that you could not see, and really, Fanny said, she sometimes wondered why she had sent for Theodora, she was less than human, she was no advantage at all.

Fanny Parrott finally had her child. It was a girl, whom they called Marie Louise.

'Sounds fancy,' Frank said, out of his slow, red face.

'It's most distinguished,' Fanny replied.

Theodora took the baby outside, where the landscape was less pink, and the baby learned to stare at her with solemn eyes. The baby's head trembled like a flower. It was reminiscent of the tender unprotected moments of her own retrospective awkwardness. So Theodora loved the child. Theodora became beautiful as stone, in her stone arms the gothic child.

'She is sweet,' said Fanny. 'Ugly, of course. But sweet. Give her to me, Theo. My baby. My little sweet.'

And at once Theodora was ugly as stone, awkwardness in her empty hands. But the child swelled round and pink on the mother's pink breast, and had all the banality of wax.

Before she had finished, Fanny Parrott had three children. They were her husband's also, but his achievement was secondary. Fanny spoke about Your Father to her children, giving an official status, but scarcely raising an image of love. Fanny was safe now, she had children and possessions, she could dispense with love.

'When you are good little children I am the happiest of women,' she used to say, though it was doubtful who was taken in.

'Is Aunt Theo happy?' asked Lou.

'Why ever not?'

'Aunt Theo hasn't any children,' said Lou.

'Aunt Theo,' said George, 'has a moustache. I felt it. It was soft.'

'I forbid you to speak like that!' said Fanny.

Sometimes she smacked her children for the truth.

'You must respect your aunt,' she said.

Respect became something written in a book for children to learn, just as Theodora Goodman became the Respected Aunt. She could make a dancer with a handkerchief. She could tell about Meroë. And, falling asleep, they raised their hands, but respectfully, to touch the moustache that was black and soft, and warm and kind as dogs.

She was the Respected Aunt. She was also the Respected Friend. All these years the lives of Theodora Goodman and Huntly Clarkson had not diverged, or only incidentally. They looked for and discovered in each other a respect that overcame aversion. Though often he was dubious. Theodora remained obscure. He could not read her. And she made him conscious of this illiteracy, amongst his other limitations.

If he experienced aversion it was because she broke the corners off his self-esteem, the most brittle of his valuable possessions, and continually failed to repair the damage. I shall subject myself to Theodora Goodman, he had said, but for some reason she refused to take command.

'Theodora,' he said, making a further effort, 'we shall take the steamer.'

They took the steamer to where, under the pines, they ate big whiskered prawns, and the revolving horses flared their scarlet nostrils, and the figure in pink tights beat with her little hammer on the bell. Theodora was delighted with the merry-go-round, because she did not expect much. But Huntly Clarkson, who expected more, though what, trod the empty prawn shells into the sand and trodden grass and tried to ease his neck out of his collar.

Huntly was glad when the little steamer rushed them back through the green night, full of the rushing of the green water, that smelled of salt and oil. He sat with his hat in his lap and about his head a recklessness of cooling sweat. These are the moments, he felt, when the tongue can take command, without the assistance of drink, when the body is no longer ridiculous, when it is possible to talk of poetry, and God, and love, without belittling or destroying. He wanted to speak to Theodora. He wanted to admit his inadequacy, which, for once, had become almost a virtue, like a thick hawser trailing in a white wake.

Theodora began to sense, through the engine's oily agony, that soon it would be said. The darkness was green and close and moist. She preferred, and she turned in her mind to, the wooden horses prancing in unequivocal sunlight.

'I shall take you to dinner,' Huntly said.

Because there remained his inadequacy. Whenever he failed, she noticed, his instinct was to give.

'You have already given me lunch,' she said.

The green light made her gentle. Words were blown out of the mouth, blurred, and tossed back towards the luminous wake of the ship. At such moments of obliteration I can almost accept the illusion, she felt.

'You give me so much, Huntly,' she said.

'You are a most difficult woman, Theodora.'

'To myself I am fatally simple,' she said. 'But let us talk instead about the prawns.'

Time slipped past them with the water. Huntly Clarkson was surprised to hear his voice, astonishingly level, legal, and unsurprised.

'If I were to suggest marriage, Theodora,' apparently he said.

It flew back in the wake of other lost phrases. And now it was unwise.

'It would be a supreme act of kindness,' she said. 'Even for you.'

Rationalized, his gesture was a little feeble. Huntly Clarkson was not pleased. But Theodora Goodman was grateful. The farce had not screamed.

'I am forty-three,' she said.

'It is not a question of age,' he replied. 'I am older.'

But it was not a question that he was able to explain.

'I am ugly,' she said. 'I have never done things well.'

But Huntly Clarkson could not explain, least of all his own greater humility and discontent.

Theodora Goodman listened to the intense and varied activity of the sturdy steamer, and smiled for an incident that probably had not occurred.

Then she looked out and said, 'Look, Huntly, here is the quay already.'

'I am stubborn,' he said, but more to hold his own.

He was also tired. The streaming of the water had made him ponderous with age.

Lights floated in the sea-green darkness. Fantastic lake dwellings sprang from an electric swamp on glistening piles. The little boxed-in landing stage shuddered and braced.

'You are avoiding answers, Theodora,' said Huntly Clarkson as they walked through the crowd.

She walked stiffly past the pale faces of the sleepwalkers that the darkness lapped. Pushing to reclaim proximity, he would have touched her arm, to emphasize, but Theodora drifted in the crowd, and he heard his now ponderous breath, and the creaking of his starched collar and his gold-linked cuffs. An enormous distance of sleep stretched between himself and Theodora. He could not part the drifting bodies of the crowd.

'I thought I had lost you,' Theodora said.

As she turned and allowed him to return, his face, violet in a patch of light, had a strained kind of individuality, of waking in the crowd sleep.

'I was just behind you,' he said briefly.

They walked together into a labyrinth of tramlines and converging trams.

Huntly Clarkson did not altogether believe that Theodora Goodman would reject the yellow façade and the laurel blaze of his great stone house. Admitting at times that stone will crumble, at others he recovered his faith in its continuity and strength. He offered all this in return for some small mental service that he could not very well define, because, after all, perhaps it was not small, but great. Either way it was invisible and strange.

'It is very strange indeed, Elsa Boileau said, 'this hold that Theodora has over Huntly, a man who could go anywhere at all.'

To Elsa Boileau anywhere at all meant Government House, Romano's, and the Golf Club.

'But the point is, will she catch him?'

'That is not the point at all,' said Marion Neville, who was less physical and more detached. 'The point is, will Huntly catch Theodora? That is what it amounts to, which makes it far more strange.'

Anyway, they went all of them that Easter to the Agricultural Show. Theodora wore a long, an oblong dress of striped brown silk. Her attitudes were those of carved wood, while the powdered, silky, instinctively insinuating bodies of Elsa Boileau and Marion Neville flowed. Their laughter flowed wonderfully over the shoulders of Theodora Goodman. Huntly Clarkson appeared undeterred. He wore a little scarlet parrot's feather in the black band of his grey hat, which gave him a nonchalance, which made Elsa Boileau narrow her eyes, which she did when weighing up the physical possibilities. But Huntly Clarkson laughed, and talked to Ralph Neville and Paul Boileau, and seemed pleased and undeterred. As if this were his world, the world of chestnut bulls with mattress rumps, and jet trotters, and towers of golden corn. There were many faces that Huntly knew. They spoke with an eager deference.

But Huntly turned to Theodora and said, 'You must tell me if you are tired or bored.'

And at once he had lost some of his strength that deference gave him, and the stud bulls.

'You must not bother about me,' she said.

'But I do,' he said. 'You know.'

And at once the presence of the others was a pressure.

'There is no reason why I should be anything but happy,' said Theodora.

'Really?' he said, trying to be pleased.

But Theodora was happy. The glare had half closed her eyes. She wandered half alone in the tune her sun-thinned lips hummed, in the smell of the crowd, and the bellowing of bulls. There are times when the crowd and the sun make the individual solitude stronger and less assailable than bronze.

Soon after this Ralph Neville discovered the little shooting gallery, presided over by the female clownface, where the clay ducks jerked on the leather stream, and the kewpies and the chocolates gathered flies. Ralph Neville began to jingle the coins in his pocket, and to gather his audience excitedly, for what febrile exhibition he could not quite suggest, but it had to take place, some primitive, dimly apprehended tail-spreading by the red cock.

'Come on, Paul, Huntly,' Ralph called.

His neck was bursting in his collar, rich red. His hands gathered them in, and his eyes, watery blue from many bars.

The clowness yawned, preening, out of her white cloud, saying it was sixpence a pot, and high-class prizes for the winners, kewpie dolls for the ladies, wristlet watches, and boxes of lovely chocs.

Huntly, Paul, and Ralph took the little toy rifles to shoot at the jerking clay ducks, jerking on their leather stream to bob behind a painted waterfall. But Elsa and Marion were bored. They stroked their expensive clothes. With their beautiful-smelling useless fingers they smoothed their pasted lips. And all the time the emotional, hysterical, canvas-tearing voice of the little toy rifles as the men missed the clay ducks.

'You men wouldn't earn your living as cowboys,' Marion said.

The clowness dusted a kewpie. She was a cloud, but fleshy, big, white, smelling of warm flesh and the hot flinty barrels of the rifles she handed back.

'Ladies care to try their luck?' the clowness asked. 'Come on, girls, show the gents how.'

'No, *thank* you!' Elsa laughed. Now she had begun to be annoyed. She bit her purple upper lip.

'I shall try,' Theodora said.

'Have you been hiding your talents, Theodora?' Marion asked.

But Theodora took the rifle, closing her eyes to the glare. She stood already in the canvas landscape against which the ducks jerked, her canvas arms animated by some emotion that was scarcely hers. Because the canvas moments will come to life of their own accord, whether it is watching the water flow beneath a bridge, or listening to hands strike music out of wood. The Man who was Given his Dinner, and Moraïtis, for some, had already shown her this. Now she stood in the smell of flint and powdered flesh, from which the world of Huntly Clarkson had receded, and she took aim at the clay heads of the jerking ducks. She took aim, and the dead, white, discarded moment fell shattered, the duck bobbed headless.

'Good for Theodora,' Ralph said.

They all gathered, watched, spoke, but they were speaking now at a door that had closed tight, leaving them embarrassed and surprised. They did not know what any of this might signify. They watched the clay ducks shatter each time Theodora fired, and it was as if each time a secret life was shattered, of which they had not been aware, and probably never would have, but they resented the possibility removed. It was something mysterious, shameful, and grotesque. What can we say now? they felt.

'The lady appears to be a crack shot,' the clowness said. 'Care for a kewpie, dear? Or chocs?'

But Theodora did not hear. Huntly Clarkson's face was smiling, but grey.

'Let us go on somewhere else,' Theodora said.

They walked over the grass that feet had trampled dead green. At Meroë also, she remembered, the grass was dead, whether among the tussocks on the flat or along the flanks of the black volcanic hills; and she remembered, too, the swift moment of the hawk, when her eye had not quivered. It is curious, she felt, and now, that my flesh does not flap. She was quite distinct. She was as taut as leather, or even bronze. And somewhere behind, the others trailed in uneasy silences of best clothes. Huntly, who walked almost beside her, had become big and soft, with a band of sweat beginning to show through the broad band round his smart grey hat. An abject and sorry deference had begun to make Huntly soft. He was all acceptance, like a big grey emasculated cat, waiting to accept the saucer of milk that would or would not be given. Only Huntly had begun to know that it would not. In the circumstances, or any way at the moment, you could not say that he was sad, because it had to be like this, from the beginning. Behind them the others walked, half knowing, in their silence, ever since Theodora had shot the clay heads off the ducks, that she was separated from them for ever by something that their smooth minds would not grope towards, preferring sofas to a hard bench.

Only some way farther on Huntly turned to Theodora and said, 'You realize we forgot to collect your prize?'

She looked at him and regretted his smile. It was like the last smile of someone on a railway platform, to whom one should have spoken while there was still time.

'Yes,' she said, 'I realized.'

So they walked on, and later in the evening they went out of the gates.

'Did you enjoy yourself?' asked Mrs Goodman, half in fear.

'Yes,' said Theodora. 'I had a mild success at a shooting range.'

Mrs Goodman turned her face, as if she were hiding a scar,

and her breath some quick stab. She hated her daughter painfully. She hated her feet, which had always seemed to move over the earth without touching, and the ridiculous rifle she had carried, which still blackened her brown hands.

'In front of all those people?' Mrs Goodman said.

'Why ever not? They applauded me,' said Theodora dryly. 'I won a kewpie in a feather skirt.'

Mrs Goodman stared at one of her rings that she had never seen before.

'You must have looked a sight,' said Mrs Goodman, 'carrying a vulgar doll through the crowd.'

In her hate she would have hewn down this great wooden idol with the grotesque doll in its arms.

'I spared your sensibility,' Theodora said. 'I did not take my prize.'

'I cannot believe that I played even an indirect part in the incident,' said Mrs Goodman.

'Mother, must you destroy?'

'Destroy?' asked Mrs Goodman.

'Yes,' said Theodora. 'I believe you were born with an axe in your hand.'

'I do not understand what you mean. Axes? I have sat here all the afternoon. I am suffering from heartburn.'

At night Theodora Goodman would bring her mother cups of hot milk, which she drank with little soft complaining noises, and the milk skin hung from her lower lip. She was old and soft. Then it is I, said Theodora, I have a core of evil in me that is altogether hateful. But she could not overcome her repugnance for the skin that swung from her mother's lip, giving her the appearance of an old white goat.

Mrs Goodman rumbled and sighed. 'Give me my slippers. Give me my glasses, Theodora. It is time I took my drops. It is cold. It is hot. I am an old woman, and nobody understands the tragedy of age, unless they have experienced it themselves. You, Theodora, will experience a double hell, because you have rejected life.'

'Go to sleep, Mother,' Theodora would say.

'Sleep! How can I sleep?'

Horses clattered through the grey light.

'Why won't you take him?' Mrs Goodman said.

'Why must I take, take? It is not possible to possess things with one's hands.'

'I remember the other evening he rode across the bridge. Well,' said Mrs Goodman, 'Fanny has been happy. It was different when one waited for the sound of horses' feet.'

Horses clattered through the grey world that was Mrs Goodman's sleep, and the morning when Theodora, for some inexorable reason, had got up and gone to look at her mother. Theodora breathed low. Her hair hung over her mother's bed, just not sweeping the face. Neither the softening of sleep nor the callous demolition of age could conceal Mrs Goodman's hatefulness. If there had been only the old soft body, Theodora could have pitied, as if it had been some discarded object in white kid. But she did not pity. At times she could still love, because her mother sat at the end of the passage of roselight, upright on her scroll-back sofa, reading from mahogany lips the little hard poems of Hérédia, which she let fall like pebbles from the past, and the roselight closed and opened. Faces swam at Mrs Goodman's will, the drowning faces of the lost or dead, Father, and Gertie Stepper, and the Syrian, and Pearl Brawne. You see all these faces that I command, said Mother, it is they who give me my significance, they are why I can smile, and you will answer it with love.

It was like this, to Theodora, watching her mother's face in the grey light of morning, through which cold hoofs clattered, and the milkman's bucket. But she could also hate. Love and hate, felt Theodora, are alternate breaths falling from the same breast. And now her own breath was choking and knotting inside her.

If I were to open my mouth, she said, as wide as it will go, and scream from the bottom of my stomach to the top of my voice. Aaahhhhhhhhhhh!

But she did not do it. She trembled for the idea.

She began to walk about the house to avoid her thoughts, but it is not possible to avoid thought, it will not be cut.

She went into the kitchen. Outside there was a wind sawing and rasping, a thin gritty wind of morning, blowing off concrete and damp brick. The light was so thin in the kitchen that it was not quite moonlight, not quite morning. It glittered on the zinc. The skins of the onion rustled.

Theodora took up the thin knife, very thin and impervious, from where it lay in the zinc light. Now she remembered most distinctly the last counsel Jack Frost had held with the meat-knife in the kitchen. She remembered him standing by the dresser. She could see the black hairs on his wrist as he weighed the pros instead of biscuits.

But this, she trembled, does not cut the knot. She threw back the thin knife, which fell and clattered on the zinc, where it had been put originally to be washed. There was the cup too, which the knife nosed, the empty cup which Mrs Goodman held to her chin and its trembling beard of white skin.

It has been close, felt Theodora, I have put out my hand and almost touched death. She could see its eyelashes, pale as a goat's, and the tongue clapping like a bell.

Bells rang across the bay for morning. Theodora Goodman went upstairs. She paused on the landing, halted by the wave of her mother's unarrested sleep. Light slashed the face of Theodora Goodman to the bone. I am guilty of a murder that has not been done, she said, it is the same thing, blood is only an accompaniment. She went on to her own room, away from the act she had not committed, while her mother continued to sleep.

'Theodora, you look as if you have seen a murder,' said Mrs Goodman when she woke.

'I did not sleep, Mother. I shall take an aspirin.'

'Ah, where would we be without aspirin!' Mrs Goodman said.

When we have drained the last emotional drops from a relationship, we contemplate the cup, which is all that is left, and the shape of that is dubious. So neither Mrs Goodman nor Huntly Clarkson had survived in more than shape.

'I seldom see you now, Theodora,' Huntly said.

'If I had anything further to give you, then you would see me,' said Theodora. 'But we have both survived a phase.'

'Surely you are making your necessity mine?'

By this time he was able to laugh.

'Let us call the necessity a common one,' she said.

Though her defence of it was firm, and even brutal, she had not yet discovered what this necessity was. Her days were endless. But at least I am an aunt, said Theodora, when her hands trembled in the grey light, waiting for bells. It had both a close and a distant sound like the letter from Lou:

Dear Aunt Theo,

I wish you were here. Blossom had a calf among the buttercups, I saw her lick it with her blue tongue. The calf is mine, and the boys have theirs. If you would like a calf and will come, I would like to give you mine. I have called her Plum. George got a boil. They put on bread poultices and it made him scream. I hope that I never get a boil. I draw a lot. I will send the pictures that I drew to you and Grannie Goodman when I have got tired of them. I have drawn a house where seven children live. I have drawn a yellow thunderstorm. When you come I will play you my piece, it is the Snow Queen, I am not very good, and Mummy says the piano is not for me. Sometimes I get my nuckles rapped, and it hurts when there is frost. Frank has learnt to make some new faces. They are awfully funny. He will make them when you come. See then what a lot you will get, I shall be surprised if you do not find it tempting.

With love from
Lou

'If you would like to go, Theodora,' Mrs Goodman said, 'there is no reason why you should not. I have the utmost faith in Dr Gilsom, and I can always call in Connie Ewart if anything should happen.'

So the relationship between Lou Parrott and Theodora Goodman remained both close and distant. Paper, from long holding, becomes warm in the hand. This way Theodora was warmed. She carried the letter from Lou, she carried it even in the street, secretly, in her glove.

In the streets in which Theodora walked at dusk the sky was restless. Its fever fluctuated. The violet welts and crimson wounds showed. The trams gushed sparks. All along the streets the hour was fusing even the fragments of unrelated lives, almost of Theodora Goodman. The faces clotting at corners were not so very obscure in this light. The veins were throbbing with the same purple. It was about this time that Theodora noticed the big white flower, glittering and quivering with pollen, grow slowly from the pavement, sway and bend, offering its thick arum skin.

Theodora felt the warm gusts of the white woman. She felt her eyes. She saw the wet lips that many nights had pulped. Such a glittering progress, that was both lovely and obscene, turned her own skin to bark under her brown clothes.

> *How did you feel*
> *When you captured your ideel?*

the woman sang.

Her teeth were gold, and her voice as thick as blotting paper, that you began to read, the yellow writing in reverse. Theodora held the woman's voice before the mirror, and the glass was hung with golden plaits, heavy as harvest on the dining-room carpet. Out of the past Pearl fell.

'Pearl!' said Theodora. 'It is surely Pearl!'

'Pearl?' said the white woman, as if doubting an echo.

She held her head on one side against the screaming of the trams.

'Yes,' said Theodora, 'yes. Pearl.'

She came closer to touch the woman's hand, to confirm that what was fat and white had once been cold and red, from washing in the yard.

'But of course,' said Theodora, 'even I am forty-five.'

'If a day,' said the woman coldly.

Because now she suspected a plant, some new game the johns were trying on. Her face hardened to resist.

'But you have lasted, Pearl,' said Theodora. 'How beautiful you are still.'

'I'm no bloody corpse,' the woman said. 'So they tell me anyways. But who are you, with your Pearl, Pearl?'

Now it was not so much a plant that her voice feared, as somebody trying to open a cupboard of which she had thrown away the key.

'Come on,' she urged, her white forehead cracking in a black frown. 'I ain't got all night. I got an appointment with a friend.'

Then her face began to open up. It was as clear as morning. Pearl Brawne stood trembling in the yard.

'Christ, strike a bloody light! Let us see,' said Pearl. 'It makes you feel sick. It makes you feel queer. Theo Goodman, eh?' she said. 'How about a drop to buck us up? Just one before they close.'

Theodora Goodman went with Pearl Brawne into the public house. It was no longer odd. She followed Pearl beyond the rasping of the frosted glass.

Pearl said two ports. She said it would warm the cockles.

Though the air was already suffocation hot. It swirled grey. At the bar a man with a mulberry nose had a talent for eating glass. He was munching slowly at his tumbler. It did not seem odd, though somebody screamed.

'Makes you think they was loopy,' Pearl said.

Theodora did not see why.

Because object or motive had achieved a lovely, a logical simplicity. She had found Pearl. She touched the stem of her frail glass. Things were as plain as the notes of a five-finger exercise played in the frost.

'Well, Theo, tell,' said Pearl, arranging her big white hands in front of her bust.

'There is nothing to tell,' said Theodora.

'Go on, Theo,' Pearl said, 'there is always everything to tell.'

'I am forty-five,' said Theodora, 'and very little has happened.'

'Keep that under your lid, love. It is something to forget,' said Pearl, knitting her hands.

'I am an aunt,' said Theodora. 'I suppose there is at least that.'

'I could have guessed it,' said Pearl.

'Why?'

'Now you are asking,' Pearl said.

She laughed. It was not unpleasant. She was kinder than kindness. Theodora's body bloomed under the kind rain of Pearl. She touched her small purple glass. She loved the glass-eater's purple nose.

'Two ports,' Pearl said. 'No? Well, I shall have another. For me health, dear. Does you good.'

Theodora wondered how the purple world of Pearl, that was so close, eludes other hands. Life is full of alternatives, but no choice.

'When I went from yous,' said Pearl, 'I had a little boy. He died.'

'That was sad, Pearl,' Theodora said.

'No,' said Pearl, 'it was not sad.'

She blew a big white funnel of smoke, and it was logical, but not sad.

'It just happened that way,' said Pearl.

'And Tom Wilcocks?'

'Why Tom?'

'I wondered.'

'Phhh, I never cared for Tom!'

Her breath emphasized.

'I had everything I wanted,' Pearl said. 'I had friends. I had silk gowns and gorgeous lingerie. Nobody hates Pearl. Hey, Dot, give us another port. For the sake of old times.'

Now the port flowed in a powerful purple stream.

'When I was a kid,' said Pearl, 'I used to want an alarm clock. I was scared these was somethink I might miss.'

'Yes,' cried Theodora, 'I know, I know.'

'You!' said Pearl. 'What do you know? Garn, *you*!'

Her mouth tipped. Pearl had descended deeper than the port could reach. Theodora did not suggest that she had perhaps plumbed the same depths. She did not feel capable.

Instead she said in the voice that people were accustomed to accept as hers, 'You are right, of course. I know very little. Still.'

'You poor kid,' cried Pearl in her big white blotting-paper voice that craved for moisture. 'I had a friend who could say off bits of the cyclopaedia. You couldn't ask a question without he knew the answer. You couldn't carry on a conversation. Made me nervous in the end. My bloody word! As bad as your Dad, Cyril was. Remember your Dad, Theo, eh?'

But Theodora would have blocked her ears with wax. She could not bear to face the islands from which Pearl sang. Now her veins ebbed, which had flowed before. Almost overhead hung an almost stationary electric bulb. Pearl saw this too. She huddled. Her white face was streaky grey.

'Sometimes it winks,' Pearl said. 'Sometimes it just looks.'

'Then it is time,' said Theodora. 'I must leave you.'

'What did you expect' said Pearl. 'I got an appointment with a friend. A commercial gentleman from Adelaide.'

Outside the night had ripened. It was big and black. Pearl began to look all ways. Pearl was lost.

But Theodora had the strength of childhood.

'Good-bye, Pearl,' she said, and she kissed the big white face from which the wind was blowing the powder. 'Good-bye, Pearl.'

As poignantly and relentlessly as if the cart were waiting in the back yard.

'So long, dear,' said Pearl.

She began to sway away, glass now, her large flower, but cut glass. She could have broken. Her big white powdered scones moved, but only just, on their stately cut-glass stand.

'Don't tell me I'm shickered,' she said. 'Now where'd that bugger say he'd be?'

Then the night gulped, and she was gone.

Theodora Goodman did not tell her mother that she had seen Pearl Brawne, because it was far too secret.

'Where have you been, Theodora?' Mrs Goodman asked.

'Walking, Mother.'

'And whom did you see?'

Mrs Goodman flung her grammar like a stone.

'I did not see a cat,' said Theodora.

Mrs Goodman looked at her daughter, who giggled before she left the room.

At this point, Theodora sometimes said, I should begin to read Gibbon, or find religion, instead of speaking to myself in my own room. But words, whether written or spoken, were at most frail slat bridges over chasms, and Mrs Goodman had never encouraged religion, as she herself was God. So it will not be by these means, Theodora said, that the great monster Self will be destroyed, and that desirable state achieved, which resembles, one would imagine, nothing more than air or water. She did not doubt that the years would contribute, rubbing and extracting, but never enough. Her body still clanged and rang when the voice struck.

'Theo-*dor*-a!'

I have not the humility, Theodora said.

But on a morning the colour of zinc old Mrs Goodman died.

Theodora took the paper, pushed under the door by the man in braces, and which began all mornings. Her feet were flat in the hall. There had been a murder at Cremorne, and some vehemence about the throwing of a cricket ball, by one cricketer at another, in a match somewhere. On the top stair, which had frayed, Theodora bent to pull the thread. After many years this patch had gone too far. Theodora pulled, but, bending, began to listen to the silence in the house. It was the silence of silence that her heart began to tell. Her fingers ripped the coarse thread from the stair. Holding her breath for a wrench of hiccups that did not come, she went into the room. She is dead, she said, she has died in her sleep. Old Mrs Goodman had died, of course, without her teeth. Her lips had sunk in on her gums, leaving her with a final expression that was gentle, and prim, and uncharacteristically silly. Theodora folded the hands of death. Her breath fell stubbornly, thicker, faster, into the room. She did not cry. On the contrary, she ran downstairs, so fast that she was afraid her body might hurtle ahead. When she stood on the back steps, she was still not sure what she would do, whether it would be something ridiculous and shameful, or tragic and noble.

'Mornin', Miss Goodman,' said Mr Love, who was tying an intervening vine on his side of the common fence.

'Good morning, Mr Love,' said Theodora Goodman.

Mr Love had some kind of pension, and a rupture, and a nephew in New Guinea, and a fawn pug with brown points called Puck.

'There has been a vile murder in Cremorne,' said Mr Love.

Mr Love was quiet, and he almost always wore sandshoes, so that his sympathy, Theodora knew, would be reverent and rubber-soled.

'Yes,' she said, 'I know.'

But she did not know, even now, what next.

She knew that death can destroy, and she had herself died once, at cockrow, in a crumbling of stone and a scattering of ashes. But she could not die again for this old woman who had been her mother, who deserved pity and a few tears, if only for her teeth, suspended in an endless china smile in a glass beside the bed.

Ah, said Theodora, I shall tell Mr Love, and he will know to say the decent and sad-sounding words.

But she hesitated still, with her tongue between her lips. She clenched her hands. She would possess the situation alone, entirely, firmly, a few moments longer. She held her mother in her hand.

6

'But, my darling,' said Theodora Goodman, 'there is very little to tell.'

She felt the pressure of the child, almost as slight as paper on her side, her breath that was almost her own. Her own arm round the child was a formal gesture of protection, scarcely flesh. Now that they approached the hour of the funeral, Theodora was exhausted, as if she had carried more than the burden of the dead.

'Will you really go away, Aunt Theo?' asked Lou.

'Yes,' said Theodora. 'I shall go away.'

'Then there will soon be a lot of other stories to tell.'

'I expect not,' Theodora said.

'Why?' asked Lou.

'Because there are the people who do not have many stories to tell.'

There were the people as empty as a filigree ball, though even these would fill at times with a sudden fire.

'Now you must sit up, Lou,' she said. 'You are heavy.'

'I wish . . .' said Lou.

'What do you wish?'

'I wish I was you, Aunt Theo,'

And now Theodora asked why.

'Because you know things,' said Lou.

'Such as?'

'Oh,' she said, 'things.'

Her eyes were fixed, inwardly, on what she could not yet express.

'Either there is very little to learn, or else we learn very little,' said Theodora. 'You will discover that in time.'

'But perhaps if I live to be very old,' said Lou. 'Like a tortoise, for instance.'

So that Theodora was forced to agree.

The child shivered for the forgotten box, which she had not seen, but knew.

'If I do not die,' she said.

Theodora looked down through the distances that separate, even in love. If I could put out my hand, she said, but I cannot. And already the moment, the moments, the disappearing afternoon, had increased the distance that separates. There is no lifeline to other lives. I shall go, said Theodora, I have already gone. The simplicity of what ultimately happens hollowed her out. She was part of a surprising world in which hands, for reasons no longer obvious, had put tables and chairs.

Part Two   JARDIN EXOTIQUE

*Henceforward we walk split into myriad fragments,
like an insect with a hundred feet, a centipede with
soft-stirring feet that drinks in the atmosphere; we
walk with sensitive filaments that drink avidly of past
and future, and all things melt into music and sorrow;
we walk against a united world, asserting our divided-
ness. All things, as we walk, splitting with us into a
myriad iridescent fragments. The great fragmentation
of maturity.*

HENRY MILLER

7

THEODORA Goodman sat in the hall near the reception desk and waited for somebody to come. She had waited she did not know how long, without caring, among the linoleum squares. These were an old yellow-brown. I can wait here very much longer, Theodora said. Labels were plastered on her luggage, but her face was bare. There are the faces that do not belong particularly anywhere and which, for that reason, can rest unquestioned. Theodora looked at her labels, at all those places to which apparently she had been. In all those places, she realized, people were behaving still, opening umbrellas, switching off the light, singing Wagner, kissing, looking out of open windows for something they had not yet discovered, buying a ticket for the metro, eating salted almonds and feeling a thirst. But now that she sat in the hall of the Hôtel du Midi and waited, none of those acts was what one would call relevant, if it ever had been. She touched the old dark ugly furniture that had a dark and lingering smell of olives, the same sombre glare. There is perhaps no more complete a reality than a chair and a table. Still, there will always also be people, Theodora Goodman said, and she continued to wait with something of the superior acceptance of mahogany for fresh acts.

Somewhere among her things, perhaps in the leather writing case she had been obliged to buy on the Ponte Vecchio, Theodora still had the brochure in which the management of the Hôtel du Midi hinted glossily at *luxe*. Now she was glad that things are rarely as described. Reality reduced the Hôtel du Midi from solitary splendour to a tight fit, between a garage and a *confiserie*. The Hôtel du Midi wore vines and a frill or two of iron. There were the blinds that furled and unfurled still, and the blind that evidently had stuck. Smells came in at the door, petrol and oil, fish, sea, and the white negative smell of dust. A clock ticked, prim and slow, a clock with a fat, yellow, familiar face, removed brutally from somebody's house and exposed to the public hall of a hotel. Somewhere, Theodora remembered, there would also be the *jardin exotique*. She considered its possibility, smiling for her own weakness. It was this, no doubt, that had helped her to decide, why the Hôtel du Midi, and not du Sud, de l'Orient, Belle Vue, or de la Gare, neither Menton, nor Cannes, nor Saint Tropez, but just here. Somewhere at the back, unsuspected, without the assistance of the management's brochure, fantastic forms were aping the gestures of tree and flower. Theodora listened to the silence, to hear it sawn at by the teeth of the *jardin exotique*, but instead feet began to come down the passage.

And a man said, '*Je regrette que vous attendiez, Mademoiselle. Il n'y a rien de plus ennuyeux.*'

'On the contrary,' said Theodora, 'it is sometimes enjoyable just to sit.'

'Perhaps,' said the man, 'but first it is necessary to learn.'

He was not particularly distinguished, but Theodora knew that he would express many just sentiments, putting the apt words in their right order. He would persuade that things exist. He had possibly written the brochure. She confirmed this in time, the author of the brochure was, in fact, Monsieur Durand.

Now he said, 'I can offer you only a small room. *Modeste, mais tout à fait agréable.* With every *confort moderne.* Mademoiselle must understand that many of our guests stay a long time. Even years. It is many years since General Sokolnikov or Madame Rapallo first came.'

Signing her stiff name in the book, Theodora was grateful for her modest but agreeable room. On the desk there were the picture postcards of the *plage.* There was the big penwiper, a dusty black velvet flower, on which the ink had rusted many years previously, possibly on the arrival of the General. Theodora was afraid that she might meet too soon, before she had washed her hands, on the stairs, for instance, Mrs Rapallo, on whose face she had not yet decided, but it wore a purple bloom.

'And where is the *jardin exotique*?' she asked.

'*Ah, vous savez, c'est intéressant, notre jardin exotique.* It is straight through, at the back.'

They smiled in common knowledge.

'But it will keep,' she said.

She was still dazed from the train. Pink rocks had hurtled through the early morning. She was as exhausted, at sudden moments, as if she had been listening to music, some echo of Moraïtis from his country of the bones.

'I have all these bags,' she said hopefully, but in doubt, wondering whether, for the Hôtel du Midi, she had brought too little or too much.

'*Oui. Henriette!*' called Monsieur Durand. '*Sais-tu où est le petit?*'

'*Comme si je savais jamais où est le petit!*' said Henriette.

Taking the bags, because it seemed that in any situation in which *le petit* was involved it was not logical to wait, Henriette shifted with flat feet over the linoleum squares. It was obvious that these had been polished for many years by the feet of Henriette.

'*Mes valises sont assez lourdes,*' suggested Theodora.

'*Elles sont lourdes. Ouaï,*' said Henriette.

Henriette, who was half deflated, the swollen leather of her face, accepted all things, or almost. What the things were that Henriette did not accept Theodora could not decide, as she began to follow. She followed through the dark smell of olives, deeper into the hotel, where green light fell ponderingly through hanging plants and water ran in some hidden cavern. Henriette moved comfortably enough, unconsciously, neither young nor old. She moved as if the toes of her flat feet were splaying over sand. She moved with the friction of calico and brown skin. Her body smelled of nakedness and sun.

Theodora gasped behind the fine ease of nakedness, the superior agility of her porteress in climbing a sudden escarpment of stairs. She looked for now, but did not find, her bags poised on the head of Henriette. I must remember the lay of the land, said Theodora, crossing a small ridge of steps, though without compass she did not expect to accomplish much.

'*Nous voilà,*' said Henriette.

She kicked open with her foot the small but agreeable room, in which *confort moderne* glared from a corner, but dog-eyed from weeping taps.

'*C'est pas mal,*' said Henriette. 'But you cannot bell. *Voyez?* It is broke.'

'Thank you,' said Theodora. 'I am fairly independent.'

She stood holding her practical handbag, which was a travelling present from Fanny, and which had compartments for extraordinary things. Now she held it as if she had just found it, and looked to see what her embarrassment would discover. Somewhere a man's voice, singing a tango, was brick-warm, supple as a cat.

'*Merci,*' said Henriette.

But she listened, distantly, to the singing voice. Henriette's leather face, which would never admit much of what was sewn inside, swallowed a trace of bitterness. Still listening to the voice, she scratched her left armpit and went.

Perhaps it is the implication of the tango, decided Theodora, which Henriette does not accept.

She began to turn in her small room. Maroon roses, the symbols of roses, shouted through megaphones at the brass bed. Remembering the flesh of roses, the roselight snoozing in the veins, she regretted the age of symbols, she regretted the yellow object beside the bed which served the purpose of a chair. She could not love the chair, or rather, she could not love it yet.

Still with a hope for the future of her small room, she continued to turn in it. She snapped the fasteners on her luggage and took out objects of her own, to give the room her identity and justify her large talk of independence to Henriette. She put a darning egg, and a pincushion, and the Pocket Oxford Dictionary. Her damp and melancholy sponge, grey from the journey, was hung in a draught to dry. All these acts, combined, gave to her some feeling of permanence. And she put on her bedside table the leather writing case which she had been obliged to buy on the Ponte Vecchio, and in which, she supposed, she would write letters to relations. Lying on her back, in the dark, in sleeping cars, and the bedrooms of reasonable hotels, she had recalled the features of relations. These did give some indication of continuity, of being. But even though more voluble, they were hardly more explanatory than the darning egg or moist sponge with which she invested each new room.

Now in this one, more formidable because it was the latest, her hopes were faint. Encouraged by the thought of the garden, she could not escape too soon from the closed room, retreating from the jaws of roses, avoiding the brown door, of which the brass teeth bristled to consume the last shreds of personality, when already she was stripped enough. She would go down, at once, hoping her anxiety would not be noticed in the passage, or her sweeping skirt heard. But there were no faces. Only, in the concealed cavern, water could still be heard falling, and the damp hair of ferns trailing from wicker baskets touched her cheeks.

'*Vous cherchez notre jardin exotique.* It is straight through and at the back,' said Monsieur Durand again.

She suspected he had been waiting to repeat just this information, but his smile was blameless as water.

'In the warm evenings,' Monsieur Durand said, and smiled, 'the ladies sometimes take their coffee in the garden. It is agreeable. Our climate is so mild.'

The thin voice of Monsieur Durand hesitated, withdrew, over the pebbles his boots, but the voice still politely dusted down the little once-green iron chairs for the skirts of ladies anxious about the dust or dew.

Theodora Goodman went on. Holding back the sun with her hands as she stepped out, she hoped that the garden would be the goal of a journey. There had been many goals, all of them deceptive. In Paris the metal hats just failed to tinkle. The great soprano in Dresden sang up her soul for love into a wooden cup. In England the beige women, stalking through the rain with long feet and dogs, had the monstrous eye of sewing machines. Throughout the gothic shell of Europe, in which there had never been such a buying and selling, of semi-precious aspirations, bulls' blood, and stuffed doves, the stone arches cracked, the aching wilderness, in which the ghosts of Homer and St Paul and Tolstoy waited for the crash.

Theodora crunched across the sharp gravel, towards a bench, to sit. The air of the *jardin exotique* was very pure and still. Shadows lay with a greater hush across its stones, as if the abstracted forms to which the shadows were attached could only be equalled by silences. The garden was completely static, rigid, the equation of a garden. Slugs linked its symbols with ribbons of silver, their timid life carefully avoiding its spines.

Notre jardin exotique, Monsieur Durand had said, but his

pronoun possessed only diffidently. It was obvious enough now, Theodora knew. This was a world in which there was no question of possession. In its own right it possessed, and rejected, absorbing just so much dew with its pink and yellow mouths, coldly tearing at cloth or drawing blood. The garden was untouchable. In the white sunlight that endured the cactus leaves, Theodora looked at her finger, at the single crimson pinhead of her own blood, which was in the present circumstances as falsely real as a papier mâché joke.

Walking slowly, in her large and unfashionable hat, she began to be afraid she had returned to where she had begun, the paths of the garden were the same labyrinth, the cactus limbs the same aching stone. Only in the *jardin exotique*, because silence had been intensified, and extraneous objects considerably reduced, thoughts would fall more loudly, and the soul, left with little to hide behind, must forsake its queer opaque manner of life and come out into the open.

If, of course, the soul ventured in. Theodora found her bench. She sat beneath a crimson-elbowed thorn. Her hands lay empty in her lap, but waiting to touch. Somewhere there would be people, she knew, reassured by a clatter of forks that came from the rear of the comfortable hotel. So she waited, and watched, and listened to the forks, that must be clattering for lunch.

Through the vines and the window the boy in the tight trousers, who just failed to pirouette, sailed on the smile of his own reflection, contemptuously dropping electroplate on to the little separate chequered tables. Theodora knew that she would fear the tight boy, and that she would be included in the contempt he felt for cutlery. She dreaded her island in the dining room, and the great oceans of dinner and lunch. She never survived the judgement of hotels, because she was not made of scorn. But, in the meantime, the boy sang. He sang like any tango, and his voice smelled of *caporal bleu*. He was smoothed down. She could feel his dark vanity soothed, smoothed at last, to the consistency of discs, as the words of his tango, its *rêves* and *fièvres*, dulled the sound of forks.

Behind the vines, pipes, and plaster patches, under the pressure of its inner life, the rear of the comfortable hotel began to expand. It reassured, like the breathing of eiderdowns in childhood, or the touch of hands. But it was only just tolerated by the sceptical, dry, chemical air of the *jardin exotique* in which Theodora sat. From the garden the hotel was making the best of things. Theodora had the uncomfortable impression that this is all one can expect.

But all the time, inside the hotel, there were the signs of shabby hopefulness, the rushing of water, spit of fat, a square woman at a window who dropped a ball of hair from her comb, the listening face of Henriette. The tight boy, thinking he was unseen, smiled through the vines at a patch of sunlight. For the moment he could ignore the exigencies of love and hate, vanity and self-pity. Even though she had not yet seen them, Theodora could feel that the hotel was full of people, and she waited to touch their hands.

A slight breeze began to play with the cactus fingers. They creaked. The pads of the prickly pear moved in the air as dignified as blotting paper. Age and wisdom, intensified to a point that was unwise, rustled their eyelids, and looked.

But the girl who now ran into the garden, out of the hotel, the girl was young. Unlike General Sokolnikov and Madame Rapallo, who had settled in years ago, the girl had not yet remained anywhere very long.

'I am tired,' she said. 'I am tired of all this. I shall write and tell them I must go away.'

Her white light fell among the cactus roots that she did not see. You did not feel the girl had ever paused long to consider the *jardin exotique*. It was something described by a brochure to entice old women with embroidery.

'This is no way to be'ave,' said the square woman who had thrown her dead hair from the window, and who now followed the girl out. 'To grumble at your Mummy and Dad, who do what they do for the best, and you know they do.'

'Motives are difficult to understand, without faces,' said the girl. 'It is so long since I saw them.'

'That is ungrateful, Katina,' said the square woman, sucking her plate.

'But it is true. Truth is often ungrateful.'

The girl spoke to herself, the words she had saved so long

they were heavy and swollen. Her lips were thoughtful with bitterness and sun. Her hair had been set in a shop. It was very beautiful, and black, but not right. It continued to contradict the authority of fashion, for it is not possible to tie up a bundle of black snakes and then contain their seething. So the girl's hair escaped. She was white and black. Her skin had the bluish undertones of snow and marble. She had run out of the hotel, and Theodora thought of doves, the warm white flight from the cot into the sun. She thought of the one she had held in her hands, both frail and throbbing with impulsion, waiting to burst skywards on release.

'You do not realize, Grigg dear,' said the girl. 'I must go home.'

Her voice died. Each moment of waiting was a death. And Theodora Goodman had become a mirror, held to the girl's experience. Their eyes were interchangeable, like two distant, unrelated lives mingling for a moment in sleep.

Th square woman pawed the ground.

'Your parents will take you,' she said, 'when they think fit.'

'Where?' asked the girl. 'To the next hotel? To suffocate amongst ash trays. To play at islands in a billiard room.'

'And what is wrong with 'otels?' the square woman said. 'Provided there is hot and cold.'

'I must go home,' said the girl. 'Before I have quite forgotten. There was an earthquake, do you remember? And we ran and lay on the beach. There was a black island that shook.'

Theodora trembled for the black island. She looked across at the opposite shore, which was just there, in the sea glaze. The earth was a capsule waiting for some gigantic event to swallow it down. Theodora looked at the island and waited for it to move.

'Miss Theodora,' said Katina, or her small extinct voice, 'I think that the wind has died.'

'Yes,' said Theodora, 'it is most surely dead.'

In fact, it hung, a dead thing, from the twigs of the ragged pine. People came and went, their shrunk faces, their bare feet. Something would happen, they said, but not yet.

' "Then it was that Lord Byron, with a gesture of great

gallantry, put at the disposition of the desperate Greeks his fortune and his life," ' Katina read.

Walls yawned, the walls of the chapel against which the pine stood, and rubbed, not now, but when there was a wind. Now the walls yawned, in anticipation of the event.

'I think we shall not read any more. Dear Miss Theodora, would you mind?' Katina said. 'I would like better to have a talk. About life and things.'

Miss Theodora looked at Katina. She could not often mind, because with Katina, her subtle sleek touch, it was like that. Touching the cheek, Katina melted bones.

'Normally I should mind,' Miss Theodora said. 'But now it it quite definitely far too hot.'

'Dear Miss Theodora, you always find reasons.'

'I am a kind of governess,' Theodora said.

'I would like you,' said Katina, 'to be a kind of aunt. Then we would still come to islands, but without books. We would sit without our dresses, and eat *pistaches*, and do nothing, and talk. And I would kiss you, like this, in the particular way I have for aunts.'

'Go, Katina ! It is far too hot.'

'It is never too hot for kissing. And your skin smells nice.'

In the sun, Katina herself was a small round white flint. That I could pick up and fling, wrapped in my love, Theodora felt, into the deathless, breathless sea.

But instead she said dryly, 'Sometimes, my dear, you say odd things. At least for a little girl.'

'Why odd?' Katina said. 'And why am I always a little girl?'

Exactly, Theodora supposed. She knew they were both of them undeceived. Their shadows mingled in the sand and stones, held hands, waiting for some cataclysm of earth and sea.

When it was dark, and this night in particular, outside the room which had been taken for them in advance, voices just hung in the air, singing of brigands and sudden death.

'Talk to me, Miss Theodora,' the child said. 'The air has stopped. I cannot sleep.'

The air certainly did not advance, and was brittle as guitars.

'Ah,' yawned Theodora, 'it will be morning in time. Then we shall talk'

But they were not convinced.

'Perhaps it will not,' Katina said.

They lay and listened for noises in the walls.

'Miss Theodora, are you sleeping?' asked the child.

'No,' Theodora sighed. 'Why?'

'If we are ever to die,' Katina said, 'I think it will be an island, in which there are many pines, and we shall make a long picnic in a little cart, to the Temple of Athena, and the water will be cold, cold, amongst the stones.'

Ohhh the long night rolled but studded with islands. Then the sudden door-knob stood in the pale morning. Still for a moment. But you knew it was not for long. It would happen soon. Now.

The morning light saw the drawers fly out of the chest. Its tongues lolled. The whole cardboard house rejected reason. Then there was a running. They were calling on the stairs, Yanni the Moustache, and his daughter Science.

'Come,' they called. 'Run. It is the will of God. The earth is going to split open and swallow the houses of the poor.'

Whether the implication of this was moral or economic, Theodora did not discover. Hairpins scattered. There was no time.

'Miss Theodora, what is it. Is it necessary for us to die?'

'No,' said Theodora. 'But there is a serious earthquake. They are telling us to leave the houses. We shall lie on the beach.'

In her arms the child's body, still limp with sleep, was like her own nakedness. Their hearts beat openly and together, in the astonished morning, in which people ran, over the dust, on naked feet. Aie, aie, Science the daughter of Yanni cried, her face quite featureless beneath her skirt. They were thrown out, all of them, out of the functionless houses on to the little strip of sand. Their bodies lay on the live earth. They could feel its heart move against their own.

Theodora held the body of the child. She felt the moment of death and life. Across the water a black island moved, quite distinctly, under a chalky puff of cloud.

'There was an earthquake,' the girl said. 'Do you remember?'

In the *jardin exotique* a wind was creaking through the fingers of the cactus. Their elbows groaned.

'Do I, indeed!' the square woman said. 'It was an 'eavy responsibility for yours truly. Thank 'eavens your parents 'ave better sense than to make their 'ome in a country that is all quakes. Besides, the people are 'airy and uncivilized. Though there are exceptions in this case as any other.'

'I shall die,' cried the girl, holding her head.

And you could see it was a matter of life and death.

'People don't die of affectations,' said the square woman.

People lay on the ground, and heard the shuddering of the earth, and hoped. When the horizon had once more tightened its wire, and it was no longer a matter of life and death, it was difficult to say where one began and the other ended. We like to imagine doors that we can shut, because we are afraid of space, decided Theodora, who lay with her arm protecting the child, with whom she had just experienced the moment of death. Over the opposite island the same small cloud was as ordinary and unmoved, as simple and touching, as a handkerchief.

'Anyway,' said the square woman, grating on the gravel, 'let us go in and 'ave an early lunch. It's always nicer, an early lunch.'

'Look,' said Theodora to the girl, 'you have dropped your handkerchief.'

She bent and touched the body of the cloud.

'Thank you,' said the girl, who had just returned, her eyes almost asked the time.

'Thank you,' said the square woman too. 'She's always losing 'andkerchiefs. Now, come along, Katina, before the General gets at the sardines.'

So they were going in over the gravel, into the hotel, the square woman and the upright, contemplative body of the girl, who questioned Theodora in silence as she went.

To Theodora, who continued to sit in the garden, where black flies collected on the crimson flowers that the limbs of the cactus oozed, the air was no longer altogether dry and hostile. It stroked her. It said: See, we offer this dispensation, endless, more seductive than aspirin, to give an illusion of fleshy nearness and comfort, in what should be apart, armed, twisted, dreamless, admitting at most the echoes of sound, the gothic world.

Theodora unfolded her hands, which had never known exactly what to do, and least of all now. Her hands, she often felt, belonged by accident, though what, of course, does not. She looked at them, noticing their strangeness, and their wandering, ingrained, grimy, gipsy fate, which was the strangest accident of all.

'You have just come from the train.'

'Yes,' said Theodora.

She answered almost without turning to discover whose voice had taken possession of her situation. It was a comfortable statement that it pleased her to accept. Then the woman stood beside her, bending, or rather sagging, to examine through her pince-nez, till you noticed the yellow pores in her large nose.

'I can see it in your hands.'

'I know, and I should wash them,' Theodora said.

'Don't bother,' said the pince-nez. 'It will work in.'

The voice sighed. You felt it would never willingly pass judgement, though the glasses might accuse.

'My name is Bloch,' said the pince-nez. 'And this is my sister Berthe. It is not necessary for me to explain that we are twins.'

It was not. You saw, now, the one was two. But in reverse. It was obvious, subtract one from two and the answer would be nought.

'Like most people, Marthe, she is perplexed,' remarked Mademoiselle Berthe with pleasure. 'The likeness, Miss Goodman – we looked in the book and found your name – the likeness is so striking, we have often, we regret to say, made it the occasion for practical jokes.'

The Demoiselles Bloch giggled, for many past crackers let off under the visitor's chair. But Theodora was less perplexed than thoughtful. In this landscape a familiar rain descended, on to the palms and crossword puzzles. Somewhere in the interior, springs groaned for Sunday afternoon.

'We have been walking,' explained Mademoiselle Marthe, who knew from experience in many hotels that the new or timid guest must be warmed with words. 'In the mornings it is safe, if not always in the afternoons. This part of the coast, you will find, is subject to alarming climatic changes. But in the morning, *l'air est doux*. So we put on our boots, and took our work. On the coast road there is a small round tower which has some connection with Napoleon, though we forget what.'

'It is agreeable to sit there, in the scenery,' said Mademoiselle Berthe, 'and talk about things that happened while the world was still comparatively safe to live in.'

It was a leisurely but melancholy ping-pong that the Demoiselles Bloch had begun to play.

'They say, you know, that Hitler will make a war.'

'Or the Communists will take over.'

'Or perhaps we shall be subjected to both events.'

Doubt continued to express itself. For the Demoiselles Bloch there was much doubt beyond the bounds of their duplicated self. Their consolation lay in worrying wool and cotton into deeper tangles. String reticules, safety-pinned about the level of the navel, spilled trailers of crochetwork or tatting. Under their flat hats cotton repeated itself in thick skeins, wound, and wound, and wound.

'Today we are sad,' said Mademoiselle Marthe. 'I have lost a little stylo, presented to me by the President of the Republic the season we spent in a hotel at Vichy. Sometimes at five o'clock we used to discuss language and food under a potted palm, while eating cucumber sandwiches. So you will understand.'

'Quite often,' said Theodora, 'arm-chairs will disgorge a great variety of objects.'

'We had not thought of that, Marthe,' said Mademoiselle Berthe.

'No,' said Mademoiselle Marthe. 'We shall try. It was an amiable little stylo, though it did not fill. I kept it, of course, for sentimental reasons, and because without possessions one ceases to exist.'

'That,' sighed Mademoiselle Berthe, 'is the terrible, the terrifying possibility.'

'We think,' said Mademoiselle Marthe, 'we ought to tell you we are Jewish.'

The Demoiselles Bloch offered this fact as if it were breakable. They tiptoed tenderly in button boots.

'It is perplexing,' said Mademoiselle Berthe. 'When we were younger we were told to fear the Communists. Now we have learnt it is the Fascists. What are you?'

'I have never really stopped to think,' said Theodora.

And now the sun on her eyelids disposed her to believe that this was the desired state.

'That is dreadful!' said Mademoiselle Berthe.

'It means you are a crypto-something,' sighed Mademoiselle Marthe. 'However. Shall we go in to lunch? There is always food and conversation. The amiable little stylo that I received from the President of the Republic is proof that these can overcome even racial prejudice.'

Now the Demoiselles Bloch began to knit their way between the thorns. They scattered smiles. Because they were grateful, they were grateful for the privilege of living, amongst the ice-plant and the crown-of-thorns. Following them, Theodora felt in her the opening of many old wounds. She could not altogether allow the behinds of elderly Jewesses a monopoly in suffering, though admitting that these have a propensity peculiar to themselves.

'I hope, Marthe,' said Mademoiselle Berthe, 'that there will be sardines to assist your theory. But the General may have finished them.'

'I have gathered the General is fond of sardines,' said Theodora.

'The General is fond of everything that he does not hate.'

Now, licking his large fingers, alone at his inadequate table, for this must be the General, Theodora knew, he belched rather loudly as the Demoiselles Bloch apologized to the *salle à manger* for their presence and their intention of eating food. Released from the Blochs, Theodora sat apart, under the orders of *le petit* who moved between the tables, silent, but with all the insinuation of the many stale tangoes he had sung.

'*Un, deux, trrr-ois,*' called Henriette, the leather voice, through the hatch.

It appeared that she would cry soon. Her tongue had swelled.

'*Il n'y a pas de pâté de fois gras de Strasbourg?*' asked the General.

'*Non, je vous dis, il n'y en a pas. Il n'y en a jamais. Qu'est-ce que vous voulez? A prix fixe!*'

'*Merde!*' said the General.

'I would like to remind you, General Sokolnikov, that there

148

are ladies present,' said the square woman with the girl.

'*Merde, merde, et mille fois merde!*' said the General. 'Shame on Miss Grigg. A lady is a woman's *pis aller.*'

'I don't know about that,' said the square woman. 'But there are some things that are not nice.'

'Even my sister, a reasonable soul, and a spinster, whom I respected, God knows,' sighed the General, 'even my sister Ludmilla was not a lady. She took snuff, and spat in the corners, and wore boots like a Cossack under her long skirts.'

Theodora smiled. Because the General was expecting it. And because her boots rang hollow on the cold yellow grass, and in her armpit she felt the firmness of her little rifle.

'But not all reasonable,' the General said. 'Religious too. She went on a pilgrimage to Kiev. She drank like a man. She said that it brought her face to face with God.'

'Eat your lunch, Katina,' said the square woman to the girl.

Then they began again to sit in the silences of their separate tables, between which *le petit* spun his own resentful, wavy pattern. Many unfinished situations complicated the surface of the dining room, or lay folded, passive, and half recognized amongst the table napkins. They had not yet given Theodora a big white envelope for her napkin, so that for the present she could remain detached, count the fishbones and the sighs of other people.

The General sighed as deeply and as endlessly as cotton wool, but when he smacked his lips, or sucked from his fingers whatever it was, the suction of rubber sprang into the room, out of his face, for this was rubber in the manner of the faces of most Russians. His lips would fan out into a rubber trumpet down which poured the rounded stream of words, which he would pick up sometimes and examine through his little rimless spectacles. Theodora saw all this after the soup. She saw, in particular, the ring, formed by gold claws and a deep, guilty ruby, that held his tie, pushed through like a napkin.

After he had sighed a lot and counted his prawn shells several times, the General wrote Theodora a note:

Madame,
    Physical geography is deceptive. I advise you, therefore, not to explore my face. The others, and particularly Mrs Rapallo, will tell

you I am mad, a charlatan, a boor, a drunkard, a sensualist, and an old man. Admitting to something of all these charges, I throw myself on your sympathy and understanding, which I can sense across the dining-room, and suggest that some time we discuss each other. I would hand you my soul on this plate if it would do either of us good.

Alyosha Sergei Sokolnikov

Le petit brought to Theodora the General's note, which was written distinctly on an envelope, as well as in the eyes of several ladies. *Le petit* dropped this message with considerable graceful scorn. She could see the canker of the rose mouth, the angry blaze of brilliantine. Though not for her alone. Across the distance she could see also the swelling ducts of Henriette, as she gathered prawn shells from other people's plates. The prawn shells rustled and creaked, rustled and creaked. In the hands of Henriette the dream became a purgatory. For choice she would have worn the body of a tango, sleek and supple, violet-scented. She would have sat in chairs of which the flesh returned the pressure of her thighs. But Henriette was the everlasting *vache*. Stung by the example of the General's gadfly note, she breathed, and shifted weight, but she still failed to dissolve *le petit* in the melancholy of her cow eyes.

'*Ah, j'ai mal au cœur,*' lowed Henriette.

'*Tête à claques!*' *le petit* murmured. '*Où sont les bouchées à la reine?*'

Through so much business, of dialogue and forks, the General's note still floated. Its madness shocked the room into an appearance of reality, in which tables and chairs assisted the rite of eating, and the bamboo *étagère* had never stood any nonsense. Tufted with sparse palms, the upright structure of the *étagère* made the reasonable Ludmilla more distinct. Though even she had disappointed, taking God too often from the cupboard, and tramping the roads to Kiev. Theodora felt disconsolate. Under her hand the General's madness was waiting for an answer. She remembered the days, before Ludmilla, when behaviour was more or less predictable. That is, she liked to think she could remember, but she suspected the only certainty is death.

So she took out her fountain pen, which was a travelling present from the boys, and holding it rather upright, wrote:

It should be quite simple. We could meet in the lounge, or the garden, whichever you prefer. I look forward with the greatest pleasure to a chat.

T. Goodman

Mademoiselle Berthe coughed away the silence.

'Comme je suis désolée d'avoir perdu mon petit stylo,' her sister said.

Miss Grigg watched Miss Goodman hand the boy a note, in a manner she would have described as 'without a blush'. Miss Grigg watched Alyosha Sergei Sokolnikov receive a communication from the moon.

It was nothing short of this, the General felt. He trounced Theodora's modest message. To describe anything as simple when everything was desirably vast. Anyone questioning the vastness denied the existence of Sokolnikov. Sensing extinction the General frowned.

'Vous voulez la bouchée à la reine?' le petit asked.

'Je désire tout, tout!' The General frowned.

Theodora sipped her wine. Her veins had begun to flow in great sounding rivers. She heard the cardboard castle of the *bouchée à la reine* crumble and crash beneath the General's fork. It was obvious now that clocks were keeping another time. Swords and braided ancestors hung on the dark walls, and a large landscape of cupolas almost obscured by soot. From the saints' corner she could hear the descant of gold and silver. Holy faces stared with one brown expression above a fluctuating ruby.

'Everything, everything,' said Aloysha Sergei, tracing on the face of the table, in the slops, past the welts of candlewax, his thought. 'When I was a little boy, Ludmilla, I imagined I might some day put it in a box. Then when I was a young man, a youth in my teens, at the Military Academy, to be precise – I can remember my moustache – I discovered that this might not be feasible. Because everything is nothing, I said. For a long time it spoiled my appetite.'

Theodora heard her boots on the bare boards. She sat with her legs apart, like a man, on equal terms with the saints. Sometimes, very late, when the darkness was full of clocks, the world was a little crystal ball that she could hold in her hand, and stroke and stroke.

'Everything is nothing, and nothing is everything.'

As if it were necessary to grumble, at that hour. She could hear his voice falling, and the skeins of smoke, and the intermediate silences, and snow. She held her little crystal comfort in her hand.

'Whereas, if nothing were nothing,' his voice said.

'Go to bed, Alyosha Sergei. It is late. And you begin to repeat yourself. You are drunk,' Theodora said.

'Drunk? In a moment, Ludmilla, you will talk to me about religion.'

'I shall not be so unwise,' she said.

But she knew, and smiled, because the world was a little crystal ball.

'But you believe in God,' said Alyosha Sergei.

'I believe in this table,' she said.

'A vulgar yellow thing that we have because we have nothing else.'

'But convincing,' she said. 'It has such touching legs.'

And because she knew, she smiled.

'Ludmilla,' he said, leaning forward, 'what a beautiful, luminous thing is faith.'

He held his head to prevent it bouncing.

'Do you also believe in the saints?' asked Alyosha Sergei.

'I believe in a pail of milk,' said Theodora, 'with the blue shadow round the rim.'

'And the cow's breath still in it?'

'And the cow's breath still in it.'

'Ludmilla, I love you,' said Alyosha Sergei. 'Even when you are a sour, yellow, reasonable woman, who rumbles after camomile tea. Even when you are yourself. But when you are your two selves among the saints, then Ludmilla, I love you best.'

And he bent forward and touched her moustache, and she noticed there was dirt beneath his fingernails, but it did not revolt her.

'*Vous ne voulez pas de bouchée à la reine?*' le petit asked, weaving willow between the tables.

No, said Theodora, she did not want. At the same time she avoided the General's face, from which he was sweeping pastry crumbs with his enormous rubber hand.

Miss Grigg said you never knew with pastry, it was always something in disguise. The girl looked out of the window, the side the sea was, where men were hauling nets, and the fish were silver as caught water lying in the men's hands.

'*Où est Madame la Comtesse?*' asked the young man who came and stood in the doorway, his face shaped like a scooped bone, though seen flat on it was not unlike a 'cello.

'*Madame la Comtesse,*' replied *le petit, 'est partie, on ne sait jamais où, avec un paquet de sandwiches et sa liberté.*'

'Of course. She told me,' said the scooped bone.

But twice told, it did not mitigate the strain. He went away, leaving a patch of silence by the door.

'*Comme je déteste ce petit maquereau,*' the General said.

'They say 'e's a poet,' said the square woman.

'I cannot help that. I am upset,' the General said. 'Either it is the indigestion, or . . .'

Theodora Goodman read his face. She saw many midnights look into mirrors in doubt, stumble down the corridor, and turn the key.

'It is the indigestion,' the General said.

But soon, she knew, he would unlock his solitude. Soon he would not bear the loneliness. He would look out.

Mademoiselle Marthe said that he should try hot water.

'With a squeeze of lemon,' added Mademoiselle Berthe.

'I shall try nothing,' said the General peevishly. 'And if that woman is a countess I am a cook.'

'Which woman?' asked Theodora.

'You would not know,' said the General. 'It takes a lifetime to unravel the history of such impostors. And you have arrived by the morning train.'

She began to feel this without the telling. But it was something she had suspected all her life. Now she knew. She walked with her hat in her hands, the big straw with the unfortunate sallow ribbons, she walked to where her mother sat, saying in her small, horn, interminable voice: Here is Theodora, we were discussing whether, but of course Theodora would not know, Theodora has just arrived.

'It is often a virtue,' the General said quickly.

As if it were their own problem, and here they had solved it in secret session. The General was glad for something. So that Theodora was also glad.

But now the doors had begun to be thrown open, from some distance, you could hear, many doors. You could hear the opening bars, the rather stiff overture muffled by the velvet through which it played, the heavily encrusted bows just scraping the wreaking gut. Even *le petit* put away his scorn. His body grew softer, listening. He had a child's amazed lips. So that you could hardly bear to wait for the last creaking of the last door.

'*C'est Madame Rapallo*,' said Mademoiselle Marthe.

'*Oui, c'est Madame Rapallo*,' said Mademoiselle Berthe.

'This Mrs Rapallo,' explained the square woman, 'is always one for a late lunch. She's a queer one. You'll see.'

Theodora felt that she almost did not want to.

'Who is Mrs Rapallo?' she asked.

'She is an American adventuress,' said the General. 'Of great ugliness, and great cunning.

'*Non, non*,' protested Mademoiselle Marthe. '*C'est une femme douce, intelligente, spirituelle.*'

'*Et qui souffre*,' said Mademoiselle Berthe. 'She is most cruelly put upon.'

'If you can believe,' said the square woman, 'if you can believe, she is the mother of a princess.'

'Principessa dell' Isola Grande,' said Mademoiselle Marthe.

'Donna Gloria Leontini,' added Mademoiselle Berthe.

To Theodora it was not improbable, hearing the music advance, stiff and brocaded, formal as some flutes.

'I detest Mrs Rapallo,' said Sokolnikov. 'She is an impostor.'

But Theodora, enchanted by the gouty golden music, Theodora forgave.

'Are we not all impostors?' she said. 'To a lesser or greater degree? General, were you never afraid?'

The General blew out his rubber lips. 'I detest all impostors,' he said.

Though without hindering Mrs Rapallo, whom time and history had failed to trip. She continued to advance. Her pomp was the pomp of cathedrals and of circuses. She was put together painfully, rashly, ritually, crimson over purple. Her eye glittered, but her breath was grey. Under her great hat, on

154

which a bird had settled years before, spreading its meteoric tail in a landscape of pansies, mignonette, butterflies, and shells, her face shrieked with the inspired clowns, peered through the branches of mascara at objects she could not see, and sniffed through thin nostrils at many original smells. Though her composition was intended to be static, sometimes Mrs Rapallo advanced, as now. Her stiff magenta picked contemptuously at the fluff on the *salle à manger* carpet. She felt with the ferrule of her parasol for the *billets-doux* that anonymous gentlemen had perhaps let fall. But most marvellous was the nautilus that she half carried in her left hand, half supported on her encrusted bosom. Moored, the shell floated, you might say, in its own opalescent right.

'Well, I do declare. Everybody at an early luncheon. *Comme toujours,*' Mrs Rapallo said.

She said it and you felt she had spent a lifetime convincing the world she was not an Aztec. Now her breath rippled like a dove, her eye barely skimmed her fantastic shell.

'It is lovely, it is lovely, may I look?' asked the girl, rejecting the square woman and the remains of her lunch.

'Surely,' breathed Mrs Rapallo, holding her shell on her hand as if it were some strange bird that she had tamed. 'It is quite elegant. It can't help but float. And that is an advantage. There is so much that is hateful. There is so much that is heavy.'

The girl took in her hands the frail shell. She listened to its sound. She listened to the thick-throated pines fill the room, their clear blue-green water, rising and falling. The music of the nautilus was in her face, Theodora saw, behind the thin membrane that just separates experience from intuition.

Then they began also to hear the General's breath. It swelled the room to bursting point. The walls of the *salle à manger* would either flap open or, from exhaustion, react like rubber, fly back into place.

'Mrs Rapallo,' the General said, and now he advanced too, huge, domed, but never confined, increasing always with the resourcefulness of rubber, pink rubber at that. 'Mrs Rapallo,' said Sokolnikov.

'What is it you wish to express, Alyosha Sergei?' asked Mrs Rapallo.

Meeting somewhere about the centre of the room, you waited for their impact, the hard thick thwack of rubber and the stiff slash of the magenta sword. In moments of contention Mrs Rapallo stood at the head of the stairs. She repelled the un-invited guest with the coldness of inherited diamonds. These she reflected even in their absence.

'Mrs Rapallo,' said the General, 'you have bought the shell.'

'I have not *borrowed* it,' Mrs Rapallo said.

'Mrs Rapallo, may I inform you it is mine?'

Mrs Rapallo's eyelids denied that possibilities existed in the cage. She accepted only sunflower seeds and facts.

'*Je suis allée en ville,*' she said, embarking on what they felt would be a long but necessary piece of recitative. '*Je suis allée en ville.* In a most oppressive bus. There are certain seasons of the year when the plush in the buses of France begin to breathe. *Enfin.* I bought me a spool of thread. *J'ai mangé une glace.* It was a lovely *pistache* green. And I bought, yes, Alyosha Sergei, I *bought* my nautilus. Of course I bought it. There it was. In full sail. I knew I had never seen perfection, never before, not even as a girl. And now it is mine. My beauty, I have waited all my life.'

But Alyosha Sergei Sokolnikov could not utter enough. Words did not fit the passage of his mouth. His hands could not reduce their size.

'You are a thief,' he said. 'It is immensely obvious. If there were any delicacy left in your American handbag, you would not have stolen what it is not possible to buy. Because it is not possible to buy, Mrs Ra-*pall*-o, what is already mine. It is mine from staring at, for many years. It responded through the glass. A tender, a subtle relationship has existed, which now in an instant you destroy. Oh, what an arrogant woman! What a terrible state of affairs! What assassination of the feelings! I do not hesitate to accuse. You are more than a cheeky thief. You are a murderess. You have killed a relationship,' the General cried.

'Alyosha Sergei, you are nuts,' Mrs Rapallo said.

Appalled by such nakedness, the Blochs hung their heads. They scratched patterns with their forks and studied the habits of flies. But what they did not see it was no less horrible to hear.

The General had become quite fragmentary. 'I am breaking,' he screamed.

And the room released him.

'Sometimes the Russians are very Russian,' Mrs Rapallo remarked.

She had a hard American core from which she seldom found relief.

'But I see,' she said, crushing walnuts through her gloves, 'I see that somebody has come.'

'Yes,' said Theodora.

Cast up out of other people's emotions, she felt her features had diminished, she was round, and smooth, and not particularly distinguished.

'Well now, won't that be nice,' Mrs Rapallo said. 'I hope we shall be great friends. I am Elsie Rapallo, formerly of New York City and Newport, Rhode Island, now of this hotel. My father was Cornelius van Tuyl.'

'I am Theodora Goodman,' said Theodora, in case it was expected, though she did not think that she read it in Mrs Rapallo's eye.

'Goodman? There was a young man,' said Mrs Rapallo, 'Lucius, or Grant, I forget which. From Boston. He was an Abbott on his mother's side. A very eligible young man. He had a cleft chin, and sometimes wore a derby hat. In addition to money and relations, he had ideals. I was advised that I could not do better, but somehow, Miss Goodman, it sounded like a tombstone. So this Lucius, or Grant, or maybe Randolph Goodman married a woman who canned meat, and then proceeded to die slowly of Chicago.'

Theodora listened because it was her duty. She had come there for that purpose. Soon she would be told what else would be expected, whether, in her status, she would appear at dinner, or eat in her bedroom off a tray. She doubted whether she would be embarrassed, because Elsie van Tuyl had learnt that it pays to buy even the servants with charm. Standing on the steps, between white columns, she made her welcome both affectionate and quaint.

'It is so dear of you to come to us, Theodora Goodman,' said the white gloves. 'Welcome to our portals. We shall love having you, and in return, we hope that you will love *us*. You and I shall be friends as well as companions. Because my life is almost a perpetual house party, I am particularly in need of friendship. For that reason our rooms have a communicating door, through which we can share secrets, and discuss the proposals that are made to me by rich young men. Soon we shall go up to see if the servants have put soap, towels, writing materials, and books.'

Now she shaded her boater and her smiles. She looked out of the porch towards the water. This, too, overflowed with summer, the blue and white, and the muslin yachts.

'We have a number of interesting personalities I shall be glad for you to meet, Theodora Goodman,' said Elsie van Tuyl. 'But just at present, poor dears, they are out amusing themselves.'

She smiled to cover a pause. She touched her pearls.

'Oh, and this, by the way, is Mr Rapallo,' she said.

Theodora did not turn because she knew that Mr Rapallo would not possess a face. She accepted his dark hand. No one remembered Mr Rapallo's face. He was Niçois perhaps, or even a Corsican. Mr Rapallo, you felt, would disappear.

Everything else in the house was sure, substantial, silver. The buttons strained and kept the upholstery down. Elsie van Tuyl looked a million dollars, in white satin, by Sargent, over the dining-room mantelpiece.

At night when the older women, who had played their cards, sat amongst the whatnots in their diamonds talking of Europe, and the older men, quite grey and gnarled from minting money, minted it still, in their conversation of steel and steam and supernumerary souls, music melted the gardenia trees for the glorious young, who were still hesitating to sell themselves. About this time of night, Theodora Goodman saw, Elsie van Tuyl could never remember which waltz she should save for whom.

'You must help me, Miss Goodman,' said the beautiful young man, creased and laundered, educated just enough, so as not to spoil the effect, of his clothes, of his perfectly shaven, rightly smelling, American cleft chin. 'You must help me,' he said. 'Shall we shake on it? One Goodman with another.'

'I am only a companion, Mr Goodman,' Theodora said.

'Sure,' said Lucius, or Grant, or Randolph. 'Isn't that the

point? Don't you and Elsie write diaries together? And stick on the labels? And pull them off? Don't get me wrong,' said Lucius, or Randolph, or Grant. 'Elsie's the finest gal. She has ideals.'

But Theodora, in spite of adjoining bedrooms and the communicating door, even though she took the ivory brushes to smooth out of Elsie van Tuyl the tiresomeness of the conversations, holding the long, black, intimate, distant, vastly expensive hair in her own hands, always failed to discover just how far companionship went.

'I am tired,' sighed Elsie van Tuyl. 'I have slaved at this season. Let us take our things and go to the shack. Just the two of us. Alone. We shall walk in the lanes, and gather blueberries, and feel the rain on us, and watch the emerald beetles. And, dear Theodora, I need your help and advice.'

Not that Elsie van Tuyl ever took what she asked for.

But they walked in the lanes, the little, sour, sandy lanes, where the emerald beetle staggered, and roots tripped, and the mouth contracted under sour fruit. They walked in the rain, linked, under the sodden trees, past the square white houses. In the morning they washed their faces in a bowl from which the enamel had cracked. In the evening they heard the fire spit, and the dark, sodden branches plastering the eaves.

'I need your advice, Theodora Goodman,' said Elsie van Tuyl. 'I am going to Europe with, well, you know whom. It is wrong. It is crazy. You will tell me to do instead many right and necessary things, because you are stiff as a conscience. Now give me your advice, which I shall not take. I am rich. I can buy my way out. For a very long time. I can even buy off my conscience. Now give me your advice. But, dear Theodora, I have already gone.'

Mrs Elsie Rapallo, *née* van Tuyl, or what remained, and what had been added, contemplated her nautilus, as if this quite luminously justified the hard and bitter facts. The nautilus sailed on the bamboo *étagère*, now past, now present, materialized.

'Incidentally,' said Mrs Rapallo, cracking another walnut in her perpetual gloves, 'incidentally, I have news.'

The wrinkles in her face opened and closed fearfully. You felt that her wounds had failed to heal. But she eyed the *salle à manger* without pain, waiting for someone to contradict.

'News? News?' said Mademoiselle Berthe.

159

'Of course. Can't you guess? It's 'er Gloria,' said Miss Grigg.

'Yes,' said Mrs Rapallo. 'Her letter was waiting at the *poste restante*. Gloria will pay us a visit.'

'When? When?' asked Mademoiselle Marthe.

'That is not yet fixed,' said Mrs Rapallo. 'It depends on her social obligations. They may refuse to part with her in Rome.'

'But of course she will come,' said Mademoiselle Berthe. 'And does she suggest she will stay long?'

Mrs Rapallo fingered salt, reading in it some Arabian mystery that very likely she would not tell.

'She will stay at Monte,' she said at last. 'She will drive over for lunch one day. Gloria, of course, has many friends.'

Le petit had brought a dish of very old *marrons glacés*, that were partly sugar, partly dust.

'Gloria,' said Mrs Rapallo to Theodora Goodman, 'is my daughter. The Principessa. She made a brilliant marriage. My lovely Gloria,' she said.

And she stroked the nautilus, as if she were touching a distance, a more transparent morning, in which she herself stood against the white columns and the yachts.

'*Enfin,*' she said, her basketwork creaking as she got up.

'*Madame ne mangera pas de marrons glacés?*' grinned *le petit*.

'*Oh, ça, c'est dégoûtant,*' said Mrs Rapallo, shaking the dust from a paper frill. 'And besides, *tu sais que je ne mange presque rien. Jamais.* It is dangerous,' she said meditatively.

She looked in the mirror at her own face, the crystallized mauve and crimson, from which time might soon take the final bite.

'But you have your nautilus,' said the girl, whom everybody had forgotten, because she was young.

'Yes, Katina Pavlou, there is always that,' said Mrs Rapallo. 'My lovely shell. But it is very fragile. I am afraid.'

She went now, but without music. There was an opening and a shutting, an opening and a shutting. Then they were all going. Theodora heard. She could hear their skirts. There was a sound of dust.

One was a stranger then, standing in the fragments of walnut shells, which *le petit*, stripping himself of his white apron, would not bother to sweep up. Already, like the others, he was taking out from behind his ear, together with the cigarette, a new and still more secret life.

'*Vous ne sortez pas, Mademoiselle?*' *le petit* said.

'Where?' asked Theodora.

'*Il y a toujours le jardin,*' said *le petit*.

There was. She had forgotten. Possessed by the dusty wax figures, the ritual of biography, Theodora had turned her back. Now she saw it was, in fact, the garden that prevailed, its forms had swelled and multiplied, its dry, paper hands were pressed against the windows of the *salle à manger*, perhaps it had already started to digest the body of the somnolent hotel. There is something to be done, but what, she said. She began to walk across the carpet through the walnut shells and the extinct smiles. Upstairs they had gone to sleep, unconcerned by the growth of the garden. Because it is something that happens and happens, sighed the *bouchées à la reine*. Theodora went outside into the dry, tolerant, motionless, complacent air of the *jardin exotique*. She would in time begin to accept. In the absence of miracles she would worship the stone obelisks with other Europeans. Now also the gravel told her that her shoes needed mending. She would have to ask Monsieur Durand to recommend a *cordonnier* who was both reliable and cheap.

8

SEVERAL times during the afternoon, as the shadows coldly consumed, and the Demoiselles Bloch debated from a window whether woollen shawls would be wiser, Theodora heard the young man whose face when seen full on was a 'cello, walking about the garden, walking and calling a name.

'Lieselotte! Lieselotte!' his voice called.

His shoulders were thin, grey, scarcely more than cloth amongst the fuller, fleshier forms of the garden. Theodora remembered a man whose braces hung down, a man in a window in Pimlico. She had looked down unseen out of her own superior isolation, into the unsuspecting soul of a thin, kneeling man, whose braces hung, swung, in time with his meek prayer, as he prayed and picked his nose. So she had watched the machinery of desperation function desperately. And now the young man, the 'cello or the scooped bone, swung with this same pendulum, calling the obsessive name.

'She has not come yet,' Theodora said.

'How should you know?'

'I know that nobody likely has come,' said Theodora.

'Sometimes she is hideous,' said the young man.

He spoke with an air of having worked this out accurately. He broke off an ear of iceplant, and watched it bleed. But to Theodora the act of destruction was not complete. She still heard the name, to which his voice had given small, quivering, distinct beauty, like a sudden snowdrop, green-veined.

'I suppose I should introduce myself,' said the young man. 'My name is quite ordinary. It is Wetherby. I am from Birmingham, where my widowed mother still lives in a brick house. My father needless to say, was a clergyman. He was a shy, dry man, to whom I never found anything to say. We were happiest when we could close the separating door. But my mother, she is a different matter. She invariably wears blue. At the minor public school to which I was sent, I used to apologize for her protruding teeth. To deny her beauty was exquisite. I used to lie in bed at night and think up methods of torture, and cry as I anticipated their effect on her unsuspecting blue.'

On the trunk of a cactus, flies had discovered a wound. Theodora watched their black invasion of the cactus sore.

'I do hope you won't mind my telling you all this,' said Wetherby. 'It does me good.'

'For a long time now,' smiled Theodora, 'I have been an ointment. I was also an aunt once.'

Her blue hands fingered fairy-tales in braille. She tiptoed in switching off the light.

'I was a schoolmaster,' said Wetherby. 'For a while.'

'And a poet,' said Theodora.

'Yeees.'

In the garden the silence swung backwards and forwards waiting for the moment to strike. When it does, felt Theodora, either he will be destroyed, or perhaps he will stand there whole.

'Yes. A poet,' he said. 'The label was originally stuck on by a Mrs Leese-Leese. She had a country house in Suffolk, and her voice had died. But her suggestive powers were immense. Sitting in her oval drawing room, surrounded by her good taste, she persuaded many of us that we were poets, painters, actors. In this way she hoped she would create her own posterity, although she might ruin us for anything else. Oh, she was very subtle. I can smell her now, the gusts of eau-de-Cologne. Her garden was full of obscure walks, unexpected statuary, and brown leaves. Walking with us, slowly, because she had a hump, or again in the oval drawing-room, she encouraged us to talk on significant subjects, to discuss ourselves, and God. But more particularly ourselves, because in creating our ego by her own will, God became a minor influence, the power was hers. If one rejected her invitations, she wrote letters. These scented out one's vanity. They stroked it from a distance. Even in what one thought was the security of one's own room, with its ugly, haphazard furniture, one was never altogether safe from Muriel Leese-Leese.

Listening to the history of Wetherby, unfolding as logically as a shadow from the root of a cactus, Theodora was not aware that it was meant for her. Rather, she was some haphazard cupboard in his comparatively secure, ugly room, in which he proposed to arrange his thoughts. In the circumstances her shoulders grew angular from expectation. She composed her grain.

'There is a peculiar honesty about the thoughtless kind of furniture,' he said.

She listened to the ticking of the brick house in Birmingham. She listened to the thoughts of Wetherby sluicing the fumed oak.

'I am writing a poem,' he said. 'It is the first time it has been written. It has all the ugliness of truth, going in, and in, and in. It will be praised for its Penetration in the *Sunday Times*.'

'There is a letter, dear,' said the Perennial Blue, with some diffidence of teeth. 'A letter with a Suffolk postmark.'

Lacking the intuition of furniture, she did not grasp that this was more than a letter, the garrotter's handkerchief and the umbilical cord. She held it in her unsuspecting hands, that the close of a century had designed for charitable acts.

'Yes, yes,' he said. 'But I am working. And it will keep.'

As if it really would. He waited painfully, till the door, till he could hide his weakness, but less successfully from the peculiar honesty of furniture. Through her narrow brown face, Theodora watched his hands breaking a letter.

... that Saturday was your day, and we waited, though sensing our defeat. Why are you so cruel, Wetherby, when you can afford to be kind? I can only think that this is the privilege of genius. Now it is Monday, and the others are all gone. The garden is full of absence and burning leaves. I lie here on the terrace, with the old grey shawl covering my knees, and have been reading Proust to steady my nerves. *Mais ça m'énerve plus.* It is a great ball of wool. I have been remembering, in contrast, your poem, the one that I like to think mine, because it was the fruit of that long and trying afternoon when you accused *me* of destruction, and said that you preferred to be smothered by feather pillows. Quite often I speak it to myself, my poem. Today, after Proust, it was a sword. My dear, it is *brutal*, but I am proud. I tempered you ...

After he had read letters Wetherby always tied them in a bundle, so that some day, someone with devotion and tact might fit together the pieces of the puzzle. He put the bundle in a cupboard. Theodora felt her stomach turning and turning to digest.

'I am a poet,' Wetherby said.

In the brick house in Birmingham Theodora heard his mouse picking at ideas.

'Or a sword,' he said, 'hacking at a pylon.'

He rather liked that.

But the *jardin exotique* was all spines. He touched a cactus with repulsion.

'Perhaps you should forget to think,' said Theodora Goodman, whose shoulders were quite stiff.

'You are as bad as Lieselotte,' he said. 'Lieselotte says I am not an artist. But it is Lieselotte's passion to destroy. She says I am not even nothing. If I were nothing I would be magnificent, she says, and then she could love me.'

Now Wetherby began to cough as if he could not breathe the air of the garden, and Theodora could hear his bones. She realized he was all bones, and his breath was spiked. Somewhere inside him fluttered his sick self, trying to break free from the cage of bones.

'No,' she said. 'I meant, rather, that man is not a sewing machine.'

'Are you a Communist?' asked Wetherby.

'That is the second time I have been asked since I arrived,' said Theodora, 'and I do not think I know what it is.'

'I could tell you, but it would take a very long time. And it would not be convincing. Communism is an act of faith. I am a Communist.'

'I am a man, and you are a man,' said Theodora.

'That is emotionalism.'

'It is flesh and blood.'

But Wetherby was walking away.

It should be as simple as doves, felt Theodora, but it was not, but it was not. She looked into her handbag to find some reassuring object, something she had seen before, something all-dimensional. As a child she had resented the indestructibility of objects, before the great millennium of dissolution, the epoch of ideas. I shall know everything, said Theodora in the kitchen. Now at the approach of middle-age and knowledge, she regretted the closed stones, the fossil shells of Meroë.

In the *jardin exotique*, in spite of its impervious forms, of sword, and bulb, and the scarlet, sucking mouths, time continued to disintegrate into a painful, personal music, of which the themes were intertwined. So that it was not possible to withdraw into a comfortable isolation. Theodora sat. Confident her intuition would identify, she waited for Lieselotte to appear.

As she had suspected, Lieselotte was a snowdrop, quivering but green-veined. Depravity had tortured the original wax into lines of purest delicacy. Physical smallness intensified her passion.

'He has been calling you,' said Theodora.

'Oh, he!' said Lieselotte. 'Yes. By nature he is the hero of an operetta. But he chose to be a disinfectant. To disinfect the world.'

'How many of us,' said Theodora, 'lead more than one of our several lives?'

Lieselotte compressed her mauve lips, which were outlined very faintly in black, over her wax skin.

'Perhaps,' she said, 'I should have been born to a circus. To whip the lions through a paper hoop. But I can smell their coats singe, even though I wasn't.'

'Are you also the countess?' Theodora asked.

'My husband was a count. He fell in love a second time, with a myth, but a myth in jackboots. The country where we lived was a country of myths and tapestries and music. The grass beneath the Christmas trees was acid-green. In our forest there was a smell of rot, that was sometimes interesting and sometimes foul.'

In the fairy-tale that Lieselotte told, Theodora expected the candles to be dashed to the ground when doors opened. Wind rushed down the stone passages, swelled beneath the tapestries, till tree and stone and jousting manikins had turned to water, ebbing and flowing where the wall had been.

'Even in summer,' said Lieselotte, 'the valleys were full of mist and orange fungus. Brown, wooden men acted a jolly pantomime of respect to please the *Gesellschaft*. They also came to the castle to hear the music that Rudi ordered as his duty towards *Kunst*. In the summer evenings, by torchlight, in the yard of the castle, we listened to more myths. We caught the sickness of the violins. We accepted the myth of love. Music dripped and coated the walls with a glistening moisture of sound.'

Lieselotte laughed.

'When I painted this music they looked at my pictures and began to suspect my sanity and health.'

Theodora could feel the laughter of Lieselotte, pressed against her body in the cactus cage.

'Finally Rudi sent me away,' said Lieselotte. 'Because I am decadent. Rudi is one of the men with golden skins and mackerel eyes, who see the world through water, or through music, and grow drunk on *Ewigkeit*. Tristan and Siegfried, I think, were this way.'

Winding like a horn through the forest, the leaves ebbed and flowed, cupped sometimes also in the memory, to meditate, stagnate, green-bubbled with scum. Theodora listened to Lieselotte's voice.

'Come with me, please, to my room,' Lieselotte said. 'You shall see my fever. I also want your protection against those who love me.'

She began to lead Theodora through the passages of the hotel, in which people were apparently reviving themselves, shaking off dreams, sprinkling their faces with water, breaking wind, and putting back their teeth.

'Listen,' said Lieselotte. 'They are going to sleep.'

Theodora did not contradict. There were times when she preferred an easy life.

'Here,' said Lieselotte, 'is where I live principally. Here you will find my *raison d'être*.'

Theodora saw that they were in a large room, somewhere high, the light purified by an immensity of surrounding space, the walls pierced by the open windows of pictures. And now she was drawn to the many windows, and the world these contained, the hanging gardens flowering with miraculous questions, the glass pagoda from which her own soul looked out, flaming like a bird of paradise.

'I shall not ask you whether you like my pictures,' Lieselotte said. 'Because there is no more embarrassing question. This is what *I* think.'

And she took a knife, and she smashed the glass pagoda with its flaming bird.

'No!' cried Theodora, holding her hands to her head to protect it from the glass which did not fall.

'Oh, but I am right,' said Lieselotte. 'We have destroyed so much, but we have not destroyed enough. We must destroy everything, everything, even ourselves. Then at last when there is nothing, perhaps we shall live.'

Her voice continued to hack at the screaming canvases, and Theodora, because she knew that this was not yet her crisis, went away. She went to the garden, because there was nowhere else, even though she would sit there uncomfortably upright on a bench, waiting without mirrors for fresh reflections.

'Good evening, Ludmilla,' said the General, who was sitting on a small and complicated iron chair, watching a slow snail.

'I heard that bitch taking you up to her attic.'

'Yes,' said Theodora. 'I saw her pictures.'

'Her *pictures*, did you say?' said Sokolnikov. 'She is mad.'

But Theodora had now found the answer.

'Only chairs and tables,' she said, 'are sane.'

'She is no more an artist than I am a cook,' the General said.

He spat on the leaf of an aloe, where the spittle lay and glittered, distracting him for a moment by its brightness.

'*I* am an artist,' said Alyosha Sergei, in a still, convinced voice. 'Although I cannot produce any material evidence, and it is doubtful whether my sensibility will ever crystallize in just that way. I am the Artist. Very few people have the capacity for creating life, for being. But you cannot deny, Ludmilla, that one moment of my existence is intensely varied, intensely moving. Take that gob of spittle, for instance. A moonstone, a jewel. There is no denying that I am an artist.'

'Or an old clown,' said Theodora, who knew by revelation the way that Alyosha Sergei could somersault through a house, and how she was tired walking up and down, emptying his full ash trays, and mopping up the little damp patches where his thought dripped.

'Dear Ludmilla,' laughed Alyosha Sergei. 'My sister Ludmilla. Varvara was my inspiration, my bright blue cloud, my singing bird. But Ludmilla, my sister, is my reason. She is a good soul, even though her face is yellow and her skirt trails in the mud when there is a thaw.'

But Theodora had no patience. For a long time the close, stovey breath of Alyosha Sergei had exasperated her beyond words. He could fume the ceilings of a whole house. So that when she spoke bitterness yellowed her voice, and her fingers struck at her belt, like keys.

'You ought to be ashamed of yourself, Alyosha Sergei. And I believe you are drunk already.'

'Not yet, Ludmilla,' said Alyosha Sergei. 'Not yet. Or only a little.'

He laughed through his fat red rubber lips, bubbling, and prodding at the snail with his stick.

'I am expecting Varvara,' he said.

'Oh,' said Theodora. 'Varvara.'

'You speak of her with contempt,' said Alyosha Sergei. 'Because I love Varvara. How can I help it? Varvara comes to me in the morning, when I am young. Varvara is a beginning. You don't take over till the small hours, Ludmilla, right at the end. All day you nurse your sense of duty and listen to the clocks.'

Theodora knew that this was true. Other voices had told her so. Varvara swam against the waltz, and they stood in the open doorways, applauding, as she dashed the water from her swan breast.

'Let me tell you something,' said the General, shrinking to normal, as if he remembered for a moment the limitations of his iron chair. 'I do not believe a thing against Varvara. Whatever Anna Stepanovna may say. Anna Stepanovna is a relation, and a vicious woman of a certain age.'

So Varvara was safe in her own morning glaze. She stood in the doorway, with her muff, on which the little crystals of snow had not yet melted. Her breath was still silver in the stovey room.

'Aloysha Sergei,' said Varvara, 'it is morning. Do you not realize? You sit here among the dregs. But we have begun again.'

She flirted the snow off her muff, and looked in the mirror at her brown mole, and laughed, and breathed, because she recognized herself and everything else as so obvious, and at the same time subtle, emotional. Through the window Petersburg was splintering into light.

'Look, Ludmilla,' said Alyosha Sergei. 'She is like a postcard, our Varvara.'

'So prosaic, Alyosha Sergei? On the whole men *are* prosaic. They cannot rise above themselves. Sometimes perhaps in love, but sometimes only.'

'But please tell me I am learning, Varvara. I am learning slowly.'

His face was quite ridiculous in its eagerness, Theodora saw. It had not yet suffered much, except in moments of self-revelation, in drink. But the first blow that would leave the imprint of real suffering was something Varvara still held, clenched tightly inside her muff.

'You are so good, Alyosha Sergei,' Varvara said.

She touched her pale hair in the glass.

'Then you will teach me?' asked Alyosha Sergei.

Outside bells were chiming. They rocked the cupolas. They shook the little particles of cold air. Theodora waited for the clear glaze of morning to split.

'You know, Ludmilla,' said Varvara, raising her voice to rather an obvious pitch, 'you know that I shall go to Staraya Russa, later in the spring, or early summer. Anna Stepanovna has sent for me. It is quite deadly, of course. We shall sit in the little summerhouse by the lake, and drink tea, and sew, and Anna Stepanovna will bring out the sketches and photographs of all the lovers she never had. But there is no choice. Anna Stepanovna is a woman of a certain age, and rich. In other words, a spider.'

Varvara examined in a close, interested way her own gloved hand, which was perfect.

'I try also to think of the advantages,' she said. 'There is a well at the bottom of her orchard of which the water is excellent for the skin. And at night I shall walk in the park, alone, with a shawl over my shoulders, and learn the stars. By heart.'

Theodora dusted with her handkerchief the back of a book, a tactical manual, that had been the property of an uncle.

'Why do you say all this to Ludmilla?' cried Alyosha Sergei.

'Because Ludmilla disapproves,' said Varvara. 'And sometimes it is good to be disapproved of.'

But she smiled for some other reason that she still held inside her muff.

Sitting in the garden with the General, it seemed to Theodora that they had watched the passage of the snail together, their common eye, measuring the inches over many years. More than this. Without stethoscope she heard the heart muttering and ticking under scruffy serge. For the General was a good deal spotted by gravy and *béchamel*.

'If one ever expected to regulate life,' said the General, then Varvara perhaps was in the wrong. But only women like Anna Stepanovna think they can regulate life, and one has to accept a certain amount of what such a woman says, because she is a rich landowner and a distant cousin.'

Anna Stepanovna sat in the little pavilion beside the lake, embroidering a present for someone who would be forced to accept it. Theodora knew that her own skirt was dusty, and she felt ashamed. If they had walked instead of hiring horses, it was because, said Alyosha Sergei, it was less expensive. It also gave to Anna Stepanovna, seeing the dust on Theodora's skirt, the satisfaction of knowing they were poor.

'At K— the peasants have overrun all the big estates,' Anna Stepanovna said. 'They have driven off the cows and horses. They have lost their heads. Ilya Ivanich tells me they broke into Princess Gorchakova's, and brought out the chairs under the trees, and sat on them, and got drunk. They even burned the piano. You could hear the strings ping as far away as the stables, Ilya Ivanich says.'

Alyosha Sergei sighed. 'It is, for all that, a great historical movement,' sighed Alyosha Sergei.

'If that is all the opposition it gets from you men!' said Anna Stepanovna. 'Let them try to make history on *my* estate! But I am told there is a certain general, whose name I am not at liberty to repeat, who will organize resistance and save the situation. If they so much as took a chicken here, I'd string them to my own trees. It is all these so-called liberal ideas.'

Anna Stepanovna wore a black velvet ribbon round her throat, a kind of tourniquet, with a little medallion, the head of a man that she had never loved. Her hair was powdered, because she thought it suited her, and her movements suggested both hungriness and satisfaction.

'Alyosha Sergei,' said Varvara, 'lend me your hands to wind my silk. One there. No, no. So. And the other one here. How clumsy you are, Alyosha Sergei!'

'Then you must teach me, Varvara,' he said.

Soon, Theodora saw, they would walk beside the lake, Varvara and Alyosha Sergei. In fact, they were already preparing, moving things from their laps. Then she could see their feet slowing with words or dead leaves. Wind had feathered the water with a little tender pattern, and faced the trees with silver. She could see Alyosha Sergei opening and closing his large hands beside the lake, his body assuming positions of quite absurd delicacy. And she wanted to look away, because of the emptiness, the hopelessness of his hands. The pavilion, she noticed, had rotted in places through neglect, so that in a high wind she imagined that the lattice must flap.

'Look,' laughed Anna Stepanovna. 'A proposal. Your branch of the family, Ludmilla, never knew what to do with its hands. Alyosha Sergei is too grotesque. And presumptuous. Varvara indeed, a pretty and talented girl, who accepted a young man called Ivanov at a ball last Thursday. He has estates in the Crimea, and is connected with a minister.'

Varvara walked slowly. She stroked her skirt, which was sprigged with little heliotropes, and her eyes were of that brightness which admits and loves its own folly. Varvara was also susceptible to landscape. She would have said : It is too beautiful, and I am not worthy of you, Alyosha Sergei, you must forgive me my weakness, or superior knowledge of myself.

Anna Stepanovna's teeth were quite yellow as she sucked up the dregs out of her glass.

'What, going already, Alyosha Sergei?' she said.

'It is some little walk to the village, as we have not hired horses,' said Alyosha Sergei.

Afterwards, as she felt her long black skirt trailing in the white dust, and the heavy weight of summer lying in the stubble, Theodora regretted that their branch of the family had always been awkward with its hands. She remembered also with longing the weariness of the pilgrimage to Kiev, the exhausted candles, the humble faces of the saints. But now she walked, stiff and upright, beside the steamy rubber body of Alyosha Sergei, and knew that she could not bounce him out of his own path.

'Whatever you may have been told by Anna Stepanovna, Varvara is a good girl,' Alyosha Sergei said. 'Her fault is her humility. And a desire to sacrifice. It is in this spirit, I gather, that she has accepted Federmann. He is a merchant, she says. A Jew. From Königsberg. A reliable though undistinguished man.'

Sitting with the General in the garden of the Hôtel du Midi, it seemed to Theodora that they had watched the passage of the snail together, their common eye, measuring the inches over many years, more than a personal pilgrimage, farther than Kiev.

'You are fidgety, Ludmilla,' the General said. 'You should sit and enjoy the pleasures of existence. But of course you are filled with the mad hopefulness of virtuous and domesticated women. You cannot sit. Here comes Katina Pavlou. She will sit and talk to me. She is still too young to delude herself into thinking she will find anything better.'

Theodora saw the girl who was apparently in the square woman's charge walk out of the hotel. She was nursing a white kitten in her arms. It was also not a bad guess to say she had been crying.

'Good evening, Katina,' said the General.

'Good evening, Alyosha Sergei,' said the girl.

When she spoke, her words came dutifully, as she had been taught, but she was all cloudiness, choked. Theodora knew that she was still dazed by sitting alone in her room, trying to invoke life, and composing the poetry of other poets, which her emotions made her own. There was no doubt at all, she had been copying her warm, disturbing poems into a *cahier* she had bought for that purpose.

Katina Pavlou sat down dutifully and said, 'Did you enjoy your siesta, Alyosha Sergei?'

'You know I never sleep,' said the General, blowing out his cheeks. 'I have not slept passably since '98. I can remember very vividly the last occasion. It was an afternoon. At Nijni Novgorod. There had been a thunderstorm. I woke, and the air smelled of earth, and outside the window some peasants were pulling at a cow by her halter. She refused to move. She had been frightened apparently by the thunder. She had a white star on her forehead. And the peasants were cursing and joking. They swore that in the thunder her milk had turned. I can remember thinking how pleasant it is to wake from sleep, and enjoy lying with one's shirt open, and then to call for tea. I can remember thinking: And this is one of the simple things one can go on doing and doing, endlessly, joyfully. That, my bright Varvara, is the last time I can remember sleeping well.'

'I am sorry,' said Katina Pavlou.

She spoke from her cloud, out of the secret life in her own room.

'Yes,' she said hopelessly, with all the conviction of her age, 'life is full of sadness.'

The white kitten jumped off her lap and advanced to try his nose on a cactus, that Katina Pavlou watched with the agony of what she knew must inevitably happen. But Alyosha Sergei, Theodora saw, had taken on a fresh lease of rubber, was swelling with young hopes, or old. She heard his decorations rustle again and he wiped his whiskers before the *café glacé*. Old men, she decided, should be quietly mopped up before they reach the age of dribble.

'You must let me teach you,' said the General, ignoring Theodora, 'you must let me teach you that abstractions are a great mistake. If I do not always follow my own precept, it is because the concrete often offers itself in a somewhat unattractive form.'

'Ah,' cried Katina Pavlou, 'it has happened.'

Her own white cry followed the kitten through the cactus trunks. She followed with little cries of love, unwinding like a ball of white thread, infinite, but failing.

'Leave her alone, Alyosha Sergei,' said Theodora when the child had gone.

'You were always a conscience, Ludmilla,' the General said. 'A yellow, reasonable woman, whose stomach rumbled after camomile tea. You could never accept fatality. Not even when they showed you the gun.'

'That may be. But leave her alone.'

'Even when they show you the gun. Don't you see, my good Ludmilla, that this is something which has got to happen? Even if she shoots me dead.'

Theodora listened to his voice leading her into a clearing, where they had fixed a little amateur stage, on which the curtain had not yet risen. Looking at the flat surface of the curtain, she was not sure whose corpse had been prepared, but she knew that the *guignol* must not begin.

She felt the General stir beneath her silence.

'I do not intend to talk, Alyosha Sergei.'

'I do,' said the General. 'It is the greatest relief on earth. Greater even than war. Or love. Look, Ludmilla, here she comes, my white kitten. Do you realize I am about to deny my own tragedy? That is why it is so important. Why did I never think of this before?'

Walking with her kitten, which she had retrieved from the dangers of the cactus forest, Katina Pavlou was very young, white, touching. As she walked, she inclined her head to avoid the attentions of the cactus pads, so that her neck was uncovered, and you were conscious of the same sober mystery that is sometimes suddenly revealed in a pan of milk or a nest of secret eggs.

'Alyosha Sergei, you will put on your coat,' Theodora said.

Because, she remembered, it is this way that you deal with a Sokolnikov, with a touch of brass.

'But, Ludmilla,' said the General, and his lips had begun to take a dubious shape, 'do you intend to destroy me?'

His thighs cried, for the aching evenings in which horses pawed under the full plane trees, and the patent leather marked time.

'You will put on your coat, Alyosha Sergei,' said Theodora's voice, yellowed by long proximity to conscience. 'You will take me for a walk. You will point out objects of local interest.'

The General's chair began to squeak.

'But there is never anything to see,' he said. 'Anywhere. The meat is all inside the shell.'

She heard his voice farther, complaining but dutiful, fretting what had been the corner of the almost fluid hotel. Forms were flowing into other moulds. As the light withdrew, Theodora felt that she also had ebbed by several hours.

'Well, Katina,' she said in the accents of an aunt, 'you have found your cat.'

'My Aunt Smaragda, my aunt in Athens, once had a white

kitten, a white kitten with a black tail. A very *charming* kitten,' Katina said.

She used the word timidly, because it was one she had picked up from an older woman, and it was not yet her own. It belonged to the old women who practise social intercourse. As a word it was stale and dusty in her mouth.

'Are you a spinster?' Katina Pavlou asked.

'That is how I am described,' said Theodora Goodman.

'So is my Aunt Smaragda who lives alone in Athens. She had an unfortunate love affair in Smyrna with somebody who went away.'

The shells on the shores of Asia Minor echoed faintly the misfortune of Aunt Smaragda. The air of the *jardin exotique* was full of sad sounds of no distinguishable origin.

'But so far!' said Theodora. 'You make it sound so far.'

'That is something we are not told,' Katina Pavlou said.

And now her voice, white, furred, insinuated itself along the skin. It curled in the saucers of the body like a small white cat.

'I would like to fall in love,' said Katina Pavlou. 'More fortunately, of course. I would like that best of all.'

In the garden of the Athenian aunt, when it was night, when the small white charming cat elongated itself against the lilacs, even marble lost its substance, flowed, and murmured with its lilac throat. The Athenian garden of the Pavlou aunt was thick with white lilac and black trees.

'Oh, I would like to fall in love,' Katina Pavlou said. 'I would like to marry a scientist, and sail with him up the Congo, and do something historical. But Mamma says I shall make a successful match. They are giving me so much to make it with. I shall not tell you how much, because I believe the British consider it vulgar to talk about such things.'

Under the white lilacs and the black trees in the garden of the Athenian aunt, people sat at an iron table discussing Balkan affairs and marriage. Theodora put up her hand to disentangle the big velvety moth whose feet had caught in her hair.

'Say something,' sighed Katina Pavlou.

'I was thinking of Aunt Smaragda who lives alone in Athens,' Theodora said.

'Oh, Aunt Smaragda has the Great Idea. She says that as

Greeks are born to die, then they can die best on the road to Constantinople. She prays for Byzantium. She prays for the day when the saints will blaze with gold.'

Heavy with gold and silver, the icon faces of many aunts smouldered with Ideas. Theodora remembered that she had forgotten to buy aspirin.

'Mamma says it is fortunate that Aunt Smaragda has her Great Idea. Otherwise she'd be buried alone. That is why Mamma married Papa, so she says, so as not to be buried alone. Papa was a colonel once. Now they live in hotels. They follow the season, and Papa plays bridge.'

So that waiting with the child for the door to announce *le lever de Madame Pavlou*, Theodora knew pretty well what to expect.

'*Tes cheveux, chérie, sont à faire rire*,' said the dressing-table voice, smoothing a wrinkle off its own forehead.

Powder had scattered on the imitation buhl at which Europa's Bull, the Colonel with the black eyelids and the moustache, considered the ace of hearts.

'Do you know what, Mamma?' Katina said. 'The waiter at the third table on the left showed me how to squeeze an egg into a bottle.'

The Colonel hummed Meyerbeer and mopped the seltzer off the ace of hearts.

'That may be,' said the phoenix-mouth, flaming for the fifty-seven-thousandth time. 'But normal eggs do not do peculiar things. You are here to learn from Miss Goodman that they are preferable *à la coque, en cocotte*, or beaten into an omelette. At Easter they are also dyed, and make a quaint and pretty present when handed by a young girl.'

'Yes, Mamma,' Katina said.

The Colonel's moustache played Meyerbeer as convincingly as a French horn.

'*C'est ridicule de croire*,' said the voice of the astringent lotion, '*qu'on s'amusera à Deauville ou à Aix*.'

'*Mais alors*,' said the Colonel, throwing down the card preparatory to picking it up again. '*Allons à Baden Baden*.'

It was as logical, of course, as the revolving doors of all large hotels. But it left Katina Pavlou sitting with the kitten in her lap. The kitten's nose, smudged with first blood, sniffed at some fresh dubiousness in a revised universe.

'You are not going?' said Katina Pavlou to Theodora.

She spoke now with less conviction, and her body assumed the immobility of the leaves of the *jardin exotique*, which, from association, she had begun to imitate.

'You will not leave me,' Katina said.

'No,' said Theodora.

It was a cold stone, which she would have warmed if it had been possible, but her hands were as watery as promises.

'No,' her voice said, speaking the code language of human intercourse.

But even Katina Pavlou had begun to know that people are generally forced to do the opposite of what they say. She knew that the weather had changed, and that a wind which had started up from the sea was threading the grey paths. You could also hear the stairs protest beneath Sokolnikov.

'Ludmilla,' he called, 'are you coming?'

So Katina Pavlou took the fact for granted.

'I suppose I shall go and darn my stockings,' she said. 'Or I shall write a reply to a letter, in reply to a reply.'

And as it was more or less arranged, Theodora went towards the General's voice.

'Let us make this walk that will give no pleasure to anyone,' said Alyosha Sergei. 'Let us at least explore your perversity.'

In the hall he was huge, in his overcoat and scarves, and a flapped fur cap that he had fastened over his ears.

'So that you will have to shout,' he said, 'and will think twice for the truth of what you say.'

Remembering Katina Pavlou, Theodora did not reply.

They began to walk along the street, along the asphalt promenade, on one side of which, protected by brick and stucco, glass and iron, life was being led. But the other side, the sea side, flowed. They had put an iron railing between the asphalt and the sea. But this did not deter any latent desire. It was as much a protection as theory is from fact. This was the evening air damply stroking, wind fingering the bones, the opening and closing of violet and black on its oyster-bellied self, the sound of distance which is closer than thought. The iron railing spindled and dwindled in the evening landscape. Sometimes faces looked through the openings in brick and stucco, from their pursuits behind glass, or under the blunt planes, or in the elaborate bandstand, looked out to wonder at the extent of their own charade.

But only to wonder at, Theodora Goodman noticed. The most one can expect from the led life is for it to be lit occasionally by a flash of wonder, which does not bear questioning, it is its own light.

'You see, Ludmilla,' said Alyosha Sergei, 'it is the same as anywhere else, the same. In the window above the *quincaillerie* there is a woman who will have a child in December. I have watched her adding it up. When the post-office clerk from Marseille, who has seen his future in a mirror, cuts his throat in the bathroom of his wife's father, who has invited him for fifteen days to tell him his faults, they will stitch silver tears on *crêpe* and pretend that it was insanity, so that they can give him a tombstone and curse his grave.'

'But it will not affect the calendar of the woman who is having a child in December,' said Theodora Goodman.

'No,' said Alyosha Sergei. 'Unfortunately, no. She will have her child, some eventually spotty boy, who will hate algebra, and marry the daughter of Madame Le Bœuf, and be killed in a war. This Madame Le Bœuf, who is at the moment wrapping a stiff fish in a sheet of the *Petit Marseillais* for the curé's supper, is chiefly obsessed by eternity. She would like to know that her soul will be wrapped stiffly in a sheet of paper and not expected to swim.'

'Through eternity,' added Theodora Goodman.

'Alas,' sighed Sokolnikov.

But Theodora did not reject the word. It flowed, violet, and black, and momentarily oyster-bellied through the evening landscape, fingering the faces of the houses. Soon the sea would merge with the houses, and the almost empty asphalt promenade, and the dissolving lavender hills behind the town. So that there was no break in the continuity of being. The landscape was a state of interminable being, hope and despair devouring and disgorging endlessly, and the faces, whether Katina Pavlou, or

Sokolnikov, or Mrs Rapallo, or Wetherby, only slightly different aspects of the same state.

'How beautiful it all is,' said Theodora Goodman as she watched the motion of the lavender hills.

She could breathe the soft light. She could touch the morning, already flowering heliotrope and pink, through which the leather men dragged brown nets bellying with luminous fish.

'Beautiful!' cried the General, grinding his ferrule on the asphalt. 'It is as beautiful as a Sunday newspaper. It is an enormous crime.'

He spoke to the air, which, in its evening detachment, remained serene.

'You remind me of my ex-wife Edith, of whom I have not yet spoken,' the General said. 'She made many such remarks, without thinking. Frequently she said: You'll be the death of me. But my wife Edith is still alive. A cheeky, arrogant woman. A retired cook. I married her for her income, and for years ate mince. Yes,' sighed the General. 'In Kensington. Ah, Ludmilla, why is suffering so intensely personal?'

He paused, but not for an answer, more as if resting on the stairs to feel his heart. He looked back to accuse, Theodora saw, the figure of Edith, who stood deliberately buttoning her brown kid gloves.

'If that is a dirty look, you can save it,' Edith said. 'Let me tell you from the start, Alyosha Sergei, all you suffer from is inflation. Wind, wind, wind, whatever the fancy name. Now I am going out to chapel. If you're hungry, there's mutton in the larder, and a prune shape.'

'She was a practical but insensitive creature,' the General said. 'I hated her extravagantly. She slammed doors. Her bust was decorated with a cairngorm, which she inherited with her fortune and many hideous objects in bronze from Mrs Arbuthnot, an old lady whom she tyrannized. Edith was most herself when dusting bronze. She had a clock in the shape of the Houses of Parliament that she loved with passion. Her week begun and ended with the winding of her clock, which was protected by a glass dome. You should have seen, Ludmilla, the love and agility with which she removed the dome, as if she were baring her own bronze soul. The ritual was timed to take place just before the stroke of one. Afterwards, listening to her clock, in the middle of Sunday, on Mrs Arbuthnot's Wilton carpet, Edith shone.'

Edith also snorted. Theodora saw that she had been poured right up to the lips of her kid gloves. Her cairngorm eye was fringed with pebbles, slate, and fawn, that never closed.

'What you needed was a statue, Sokolnikov. To be married to a statue,' Edith said. 'But a statue with 'oles for eyes, that would cry and cry and cry. Never flesh and blood, and roast mutton on Sundays. Oh, no, no! Nor for Sokolnikov!'

Theodora heard the General swell.

'You are an insolent woman, Edith,' he said. 'I don't wonder Mrs Arbuthnot died.'

'She was an asthmatic subject,' said Edith. 'In the end it got at 'er heart, I 'ave it in writing, Alyosha Sergei, if you are suggesting, if you are suggesting.'

'I am not suggesting that you used a knife.'

'You are mad, mad, mad!' shouted Edith, who was pouring her gloves together in the hall.

'Whenever the answer is not in bronze, that is the cry of the middle classes. Fortunately, Edith, you have got your clock. When you return to it after chapel, after singing your satisfactory hymns, you will find the duplicate key to your stained-glass door underneath the mat.'

The General ground the ferrule of his stick into the asphalt promenade.

'And yet you say that all is beautiful, Ludmilla, speaking like a clockwork thing, or a Methodist hymn.'

'Poor Alyosha Sergei,' said Theodora Goodman, because his arm had asked for pity. 'I suppose there was always the Victoria and Albert.'

'I had mislaid my galoshes,' he said, but more distracted by the present moment, as if this were focusing.

It was obvious the iron railing and the tamarisks surprised him, the way external landscape does surprise on returning to position. The deepening hills were less solid than Sokolnikov. Even Theodora could not accept spontaneously the wire baskets which had been put by public spirit as receptacles for old newspapers, banana skins, embarrassing letters, and melancholy flowers. The wire baskets, she saw, were as surprisingly full as other people's lives. But these did not convince as, side by side, she walked with the General in almost Siamese attachment.

This oneness made the moment of collision far more desperate, when Sokolnikov, gripping the rail, heaving like the sea, shouted, 'Look!'

'Is it an accident?' Theodora asked.

'No,' replied Sokolnikov. 'I suspect it to be part of a deliberate and peculiar plan.'

Theodora peered out of their common emotion, and began to see, commanding the distance, a flashing, dashing, crimson cape.

'Why,' she said, 'it is Mrs Rapallo. How magnificent! But how strange!'

'Everything is expected, nothing is strange,' corrected the General wearily.

The same great nesting bird which had presided over lunch now flew through the evening, ruffling the pansies and the mignonette with its enormous wings. With beautiful glissando the crimson was advancing, flurrying, slashing, flirting with the wind. It moved outside the rigid Mrs Rapallo. The cloak was leading a life of its own. Sometimes it toppled, not so much from weakness as from pleasure. To test the strength of the wind, to toy, to flatter.

'She will blow away,' Theodora cried.

'Never,' said the General feelingly.

'Oh, but she is a beauty,' Theodora said.

And she clasped her hands for all that is gold, and crimson plush, and publicly magnificent.

'Have you not heard her clatter? She is the soul of aluminium,' the General sighed.

But contempt did not enlarge him. He had diminished sadly. He was half himself.

'Ludmilla, I beg you. You will turn away. You will send this purple arrogance to hell.'

'Now, now,' called Mrs Rapallo, out of her crimson careering cape, over the wind. 'I kind of guess, Alyosha Sergei, you are at it again. You are telling me off.' Her crimson consumed a tamarisk, and flatly demolished the sea rail.

'But at times I am buoyant, Miss Goodman,' she insisted. 'On some evenings I refuse to sink.'

Then they were all caught up, the three of them, in Mrs Rapallo's cape, tulipped in crimson that the wind waved.

'There now, you see, I will have you,' Mrs Rapallo said. 'There is no escape for some of us.'

Theodora laughed. Warmed by her own pleasure, she was also afraid that a piece of Mrs Rapallo might break. The motion of her limbs was audible.

'You will please release me from your idiocy,' the General said, serious now as compressed rubber.

'If we choose to sing "Jingle Bells", we choose,' said Mrs Rapallo. 'Some evenings, Sokolnikov, are quite definitely mine.'

But the General detached himself from the cape. Midway in the gesture Theodora heard with anxiety something tear.

'I have had enough of enough,' said Sokolnikov.

Discomfort was increased by grey grit which whirled in spirals off the asphalt and scratched at the eyes.

'Even one's own tenderest thoughts,' he complained, 'are not above suspicion. *You*, Ludmilla!'

It was very miserable. It was as sad as one bassoon. But also dignified.

'Mrs Rapallo, I forbid you to persecute me further.'

Then his back was going, furred and flabby, returning along the asphalt promenade.

'Oh, but you must not leave us,' Theodora called, coaxed. 'Alyosha Sergei! This is where we *talk*.'

Mrs Rapallo laughed, or rather she set in motion the mechanism of her laughter, letting fall a shower of serious teaspoons on to the pavement.

'*We* talk? My, my! You are ambitious, Miss Goodman,' Mrs Rapallo mocked. 'With Alyosha Sergei it is a question of who winds the phonograph.'

'Even so,' Theodora said, 'we were playing a tragedy of which I have not yet heard the end.'

'The end?' Mrs Rapallo screamed.

So that Theodora laughed too. Her voice cut. It was quite horrible, rending. In betraying the General, she had laid bare many gaping moments of her own. If she could, she would have made some gesture asking for forgiveness. She would have touched his receding back, but already he was a footfall. Even the wind had died. Mrs Rapallo's cape hung.

'Well,' said Mrs Rapallo, chewing the word in her once more careful mouth, 'now we are sober.'

She sighed. Across the empty asphalt the crimson trailed its flat rag. Her glove fingered a tatter that her mind was attempting to explain.

'I have been on my evening walk,' Mrs Rapallo said. 'Most evenings I walk as far as the *poste restante*. Just in case. Though tonight, of course, after this morning's bounty, I hardly expected more. Gloria is so good.'

Theodora could not contradict, because Gloria was still a blur. Whether her nails tore flesh as well as bread, she did not yet know.

'Does she write often?' she asked.

'One must expect women of rank to make certain sacrifices. One accepts to be the sacrifice. Willingly,' Mrs Rapallo said.

At moments when she was composed, resigned, Elsie Rapallo, *née* van Tuyl, had the stiff and formal look of something on an occasional table, but an Edwardian occasional table, something in enamel or cloisonné, commissioned by a Grand Duke in order to show his patronage, and then forgotten.

'Gloria had a vocation for the world,' Mrs Rapallo explained. 'I mean, even as a kid Gloria was *distinguée*. She had poise. You would have been surprised, Miss Goodman, at her grasp of current affairs. Her touch on the pianoforte was quite lovely. At fifteen she had a smattering of several languages. She had even begun to master Rumanian, with the help of a gentleman we met in Cairo. And most important, she could wear clothes. So it was only to be expected that Nino – that is my son-in-law, the Principe – should be impressed. Naturally it also cost a little. Almost the last of what I could afford. But I pulled it off with the help of Nana Trumpett. And everyone agreed that no mother had ever bought such brilliant prospects for her child.'

When Mrs Rapallo made up her mind it was not possible to disagree. Her face had the metal of conviction underneath the skin. She smiled too, graciously, just as far as breaking point.

She smiled and nodded her great hat for all the brilliant moments she had lived.

'If we stand right here, we shall see,' Mrs Rapallo said.

'We shall see?' asked Theodora, for whom the transition from asphalt to marble was too abrupt.

'Don't be absurd,' Mrs Rapallo smiled.

And it was. It was obvious that cardinals would pass. Discreet flutes, a gloved Corelli, prepared the way through the cinerarias and conversation. Faces are magnified by music, Theodora realized, and hoped that the cardinals would not delay.

'Is it not brilliant?' whispered Mrs Rapallo.

Her smile was not less mauve than the cinerarias in which she was embedded, as she parted the strips of music and counted pearls.

'Brilliant,' Mrs Rapallo breathed.

'It is also painful,' Theodora said, now firmly grafted on to marble.

'Physical suffering is a social obligation,' Mrs Rapallo decreed. 'Always remember, Theodora, there's nothing like stairs. They command such a vista. They lend importance. Everyone passes sooner or later. And sometimes one notices disgraceful things one wasn't meant to see.'

Mrs Rapallo peered. But Theodora parried the blows of marble, and prayed for the cardinals who failed to pass. Under a Veronese, the ices had begun to melt.

'There is Nino – my son-in-law, the Principe,' Mrs Rapallo explained.

She waved her fan, of which the lace had come unstuck from the skeleton of bone. Emotion had also pared her face. The words were frantic in her teeth, as there was the possibility, just, that Nino might not see.

'Is he not beautiful?' Mrs Rapallo said. 'As beautiful as a chauffeur. In fact, on one or two occasions there have been mistakes.'

But where is Gloria?' asked Theodora, shocking the silence in a hush of flutes.

'You may well ask,' whispered Mrs Rapallo out of the sticks of her fan. 'Gloria is in audience with a most important personage, behind the Canova group, in the gallery on the right.

Her opinion is frequently sought, my dear, *sub rosa* of course, on matters of state. Gloria has intellect. She could have been a man.'

But Canova just failed to disclose the body of Gloria. Her mind remained obscure, together with the problem of her thighs, though her shadow fell velvetly across the marble floor.

'My enchanting child was always generous,' Mrs Rapallo said. 'Always give, give, that was my Gloria. Up to a point of exhaustion. But soon she will leave for the Côte d'Azur. She will enjoy a few weeks' relaxation in a small but expensively appointed villa, living exclusively on strawberries and champagne, practically naked in the sun.'

In the grey friable landscape, between the sea and what remained of the hills, on the now damp asphalt, old women had come down to rummage through the metal baskets for scraps of bread. The aching letters and the brown roses turned to water in their sieve-hands. Sea sounds came from their throats, as they picked at words, and swallowed. Canova sank.

Theodora Goodman shivered.

'You have gotten a chill, dear. It is the mistral,' Mrs Rapallo said.

But Theodora could not explain it was still the touch of marble.

'I am feeling indifferent myself,' said Mrs Rapallo. 'I am a victim of regurgitation. I guess it is that now.'

Placing a glove on her bosom, which decades of social history had built, she held it there as protection from all and what. Her eyes rolled, showing their blue-white china and the small red veins. They rolled so violently that Theodora was afraid they might become detached from their wires.

'Let us go in, Mrs Rapallo,' she said rather too quickly. 'Let us go in.'

She persuaded the damp crimson with her hand.

'Go in? Where?' Mrs Rapallo asked.

'Into the hotel.'

'Oh,' said Mrs Rapallo, 'we shall go in all right. We shall go in *there*. I believe you have taken fright, Theodora Goodman, at something you have seen. But you must never take fright, whatever the others may tell you. If my eyes appear a little strained, it is only because so much has happened. '

Under a shade which had once been pink, but which was now the colour of dust, somebody they did not see was playing a gavotte. Theodora heard the stir of beads hanging from the deathless lamp. She heard with some sadness the gavotte, which had, she thought, the tight, frilled appearance of the music that Fanny used to toss into a room. Whether Fanny survived in more than a phrase or two of a bright, tight, mechanical gavotte, Theodora was inclined to doubt, in spite of the letters that she wrote home, regularly, from places of interest, the gothic, or baroque, or landscape letters that relations do not read.

Mrs Rapallo's crimson cape trailed violet on the frayed stairs.

'A penny for them, dear,' she said.

'I have a sister,' said Theodora.

'What is she like?' Mrs Rapallo asked.

'She is a wife and a mother. She puts down eggs in water-glass. And twice she has had the Governor to lunch.'

'It all fortifies,' Mrs Rapallo said.

Though the motion of Mrs Rapallo herself, and the stiff music of her flowered hat, cast a slur on substance. She half confirmed Theodora's doubt.

'It is most important to believe that relations do exist,' said Theodora desperately.

'Oh, but they do. Always,' Mrs Rapallo said. 'Don't their letters tell us so?'

But Theodora was uncomforted. Mirrors also expressed doubt. We like to believe that we believe was multiplied in glass.

'Theodora Goodman, I sense that you are melancholy,' accused Mrs Rapallo on the threshold of her own room. 'When I was a girl we took champagne. The gentlemen expected it.'

'That is the difference,' Theodora said.

'Yes,' sighed Mrs Rapallo, her finger on the light.

She hesitated before some final act of sincerity or nakedness. Then the light shone. It began to penetrate the jungle, the triumphs and disasters of Elsie Rapallo's reckless room. This was quite full. Theodora edged. Although she was uninvited, she knew she was expected. She could see the magenta mouth pursing to confess. She could feel the tangle of the undergrowth, feathered, musky, tarnished, putting out tendrils of regret and hope, twitching at her skirt. Most distinctly, and with a shudder, she felt the touch of plush.

'These are my things,' Mrs Rapallo said.

'Then I am a nun,' said Theodora Goodman.

Because it seemed as if her own life had narrowed to a cell.

'It all depends what you need,' said Mrs Rapallo.

She exhaled, as deeply as red plush, so that dust flew, spiralled, and resettled. Theodora edged farther, avoiding as much as she could avoid the music boxes she might set off, the peacock feathers, and the tremulous fern. In Mrs Rapallo's room the moment apparently lay where it fell. She walked, she saw, on the upturned faces of received envelopes, sly, animal switches of hair, and the crumbs of a rubber sponge. There was no hope in the stiff smiles of photographs that they might eventually be released. These had become resigned to smile or frown away their vanities, yellow as autographs, whether Mussolini, or Edgar Wallace, or Queen Marie of Rumania. They stared and stared, out of the haphazard and rococo growth of spoons, bells, *bonbonnières,* baby's coral, china eggs, biscuit figurines, and silver toys encrusting several occasional tables, Moorish, Second Empire, and *Art Nouveau.* This then, was Mrs Rapallo's room. Corners confessed physical secrets. And a great crimson chair, *alter ego* of the cape, offered with its lap not so much rest as the restlessness that rushed, hesitated, coiled and uncoiled among the bric-à-brac.

'*Pourquoi tu te caches? Viens, mon cœur,*' Mrs Rapallo called.

As the shadow fell, she braced her arm, reinforced by her will, to catch. There formed, first, fur and eyes, then a slightly shabby monkey.

'*Embrasse Maman,*' Mrs Rapallo coaxed. '*Tu as froid. Je te chaufferai. Fais-moi la bibize, fais la bibize a ta mé-mère.*'

Whether it was cold or not, she warmed the shabby fur, trying to revive in it her own ghost of passion.

'*Elle s'appelle Mignon,*' she said. '*C'est un être doux, qui mourra, quand même.*'

Theodora did not deny that this was a possibility, breathing the stale air, that smelt of dust, and eau-de-Cologne, and animal excrement. She retreated from the monkey's paper hands.

'That is not kind,' said Mrs Rapallo.

'One is not always kind. Once I almost did a murder.' Theodora said.

'That is different,' said Mrs Rapallo. 'That is also different.'

She stroked the monkey's hood with her gloves. It was a matter of solemnity.

'*Mignon, dis, c'est autre chose,*' she said, not altogether asking. 'Either courage or inspiration is required for murder. But for kindness ... Although *he* was kind. He was as kind as silence, and as unkind. Silence is slow, soft, kind, sometimes also terrifying. For instance, eating a boiled egg.'

Theodora saw that this was true. She saw the back of his neck. She saw the dark hairs above the dressing gown, the hairs of his neck, still and dark. She saw the neck bend, as the face approached the mouthful of egg. The face she did not see. She had never seen the face.

When Mr Rapallo came into the room, motion reached the point where it becomes a still. Theodora was invariably caught with one absurd hand stretched above her head, or she was raised on her toes in pursuit of some goal that she no longer dared pursue. Mr Rapallo made the humbler gestures ridiculous. He wore a dressing gown of black brocade, on which silver parrots were dimly embroidered. There was also a hole that had been burnt once by a cigar. Watching his cigar poised, you waited for the next ash to drop, from the hand that almost did not tremble. He had a persistent habit of contracting the gristle on the back of his dark neck, but the movement never reached convulsion. In Mr Rapallo the tension remained tension, and unexplained.

'Soon he will go,' whispered Elsie Rapallo. 'This is just a formality. It's always brief.'

Elsie Rapallo was at her creamiest in morning gowns, deep, white, heavy as magnolias, beneath the thick black heavy hair from which Theodora had brushed the confidences. Raising her arm at the window in the face of silence, to part the curtains, to invoke a morning caller, sighs fell steamily from her lace, back from the elbows and the moss-green knots. There was a richness, an overpowering richness about the morning gestures, and in the afternoon, horses would paw at the gravel, bringing the Duchess or Nana Trumpett to tea. The visible details of Elsie Rapallo's life were scattered like the visiting cards of important persons, on a silver salver, to be noticed. But there were also the private regrets, by which she was devoured. Silence ate at the magnolia flesh. Elsie Rapallo was half spent.

'He has gone,' said Theodora Goodman.

'He has gone,' said Elsie Rapallo. 'Then we can rattle. We can fill our lives. We shall forget our debts and our failures.'

She held out her hands to receive something immaterial and childish.

'But, above all, our debts. He says that the pearl collar will meet the bill. It was always hateful, anyway. That pearl collar cut. Look, Theodora, look, and you will see the scar.'

But Theodora did not look long. She knew from experience those occasions when banality is balm.

So she said instead, 'You shall tell me the cute, sweet things that Gloria says and does.'

'Gloria,' said Elsie Rapallo, 'has gone to the Champs-Élysées with her *bonne*.'

But in her absence the light was full, soft, yellow, filling the lap. The cheek was rounder. The chair was softer to the body.

'Yes, my cute, sweet Gloria,' Elsie Rapallo settled, sighed. 'My little Gloria says: Give me your diamonds, *Maman chérie,* I shall put them on and pretend that the President has asked me to breakfast; I shall go as a shower of diamonds, *chère petite Maman.* Gloria says, she says: I am my second-best in diamonds, and a third in sapphires, but emeralds is unlucky so I can't say that they suit at all. So I say to Gloria, I say: Why, Gloria, now why, if diamonds is only second, whatever is first? She says. Now wait, Theodora, this will kill you. You must admit that Gloria is cute. She says: Why, *Maman chérie,* if Gloria wants to look her best she'll go in her own white skin. There, Theodora! There! Can you beat Gloria?'

'No,' Theodora said.

'But wait, Theodora, wait. Gloria's learning about religion. It's time, I thought, and you've got to somehow bring in God. Jesus loves Gloria? she says. Of course, I say, of course, gentle

Jesus loves us all. And *Maman* loves Gloria? Well, I kind of guess she does. Oh, says my Gloria. Why, I say, isn't that enough? Oh, she says, it all helps, but if no one does, it don't matter, Gloria can love herself. Can you believe it, Theodora? All as serious as pie.'

But now, in the shabby night, in her encrusted room, Mrs Rapallo hugged her monkey.

'Mignon is cute and sweet,' she said, ruffling the fur hood with her glove. 'But we are disenchanted, Miss Goodman. Our daughter, the Principessa, tells us we stink. I have always encouraged honesty.'

In the shabby night the photographs of royalty protested. Up to her waist in objects of virtu, Theodora longed to escape, but she was not sure it was possible. She had become involved. Old teeth in an empty jam-jar grinned at her helplessness. She heard the snigger of the tremulous fern.

'You should relax, dear. You are tired,' said Mrs Rapallo. 'Or read a book. A book where things happen.'

Though you knew she did not believe that they do, outside the *Almanach de Gotha*.

Her dead, underwater eyes looked distantly at the nautilus, which Theodora now noticed in the room for the first time. Static and not, beside the *compotier* with the wax fruit, the nautilus flowered. You could almost touch it. But you did not touch. Because you cannot touch a music, a flowering of water, the white smile on the sleeper's mouth. The nautilus flowered and flowed, as pervasive but evasive as experience. The walls of the Hôtel du Midi almost opened out.

'It is strange, and why are we here?' said the voice of Theodora Goodman, parting the water.

'I guess we have to be somewhere,' replied Mrs Rapallo.

9

In the Hôtel du Midi the night slowly solidified. From the brown lounge Theodora listened to the doors closing, which was a quite definite closing, on other lives. As usually happens, and not less impressively each time, she was left to her own devices, like a mouse in a piano picking at the bones of a gavotte. Under the once-pink shade the light still burned, that somebody had forgotten, and the beads were still there to tell. On such occasions the soul will have faded a good deal. It jumps beneath its attempted composure. This was apparent to Theodora. She heard the exhausted springs of the arm-chairs. She saw the ash trays, which had brimmed almost over, with ash, and the exasperated gnawings of pale nails.

If Theodora continued to sit, it was for no great reason. She did not wait, or expect. She sat in a state of suspended will. She sat and heard in time the voice of Mademoiselle Berthe.

'*Ma sœur a perdu sa brosse à dents,*' she heard.

And the voice of Mademoiselle Berthe was disarranged.

'She will hardly have left it on the piano,' suggested Theodora.

'*Je sais. Je sais. Je suis tellement nerveuse.* First the amiable little stylo, and now the *brosse à dents.* I am walking for my own distraction,' Mademoiselle Berthe explained.

She was disarranged. The hair of Mademoiselle Berthe had been prepared for the secret act of sleeping. Her hair was less wound. It hung in long white cotton ropes, down and down, the long white ropes of sleep. But she was not yet *narcotisée.* The black silk that she held wrapped to her bust palpitated still.

'My sister is upstairs sipping a *tisane,*' said Mademoiselle Berthe.

To explain the absence of herself. For she was really only half there.

Theodora remembered, or had been told, that sometimes the conscience will rumble after camomile tea.

Mademoiselle Berthe continued to fret, groping over surfaces and rummaging in pockets. She looked out of the window.

'There have been bombs,' she said, 'in Spain.'

As if she expected to see them flower, sudden and scarlet, in the still world of the *jardin exotique*. As if it were already the season of events. But the garden continued to wear the colourless expression of glass. There was a moon up. Its light ate at, but failed to consume, the ridge of flat metallic hills. These were a corroded acid-green. The garden was intact.

'You see, there are no ruins,' Theodora said.

She was comfortable with momentary wisdom. Soon she knew she would yawn.

'No, but there are other indications. Do you realize, Miss Goodman, that walls are no longer walls? Walls are at most curtains. The least wind and they will blow and blow. Now I must go to my sister. We count the remainder of our possessions before we sleep.'

Theodora listened to the departure of Mademoiselle Berthe. She went on felt feet. The long cotton ropes unravelled into passages and silence.

'Then I am also smug,' said Theodora. 'It is time I walked. For my own distraction.'

She walked through the hotel, choosing to lose herself, or not choosing, in the Hôtel du Midi there was no alternative. And especially at night. At night there was the space of darkness, a direction of corridors, stairs which neither raised nor lowered the traveller on to a different plane. In this rather circular state, Theodora walked with her hands outstretched, to ward off flesh or furniture if the occasion should arise.

'*Vous désirez quelque chose, Mademoiselle?*'

She saw in time that this was Monsieur Durand. He still spoke professionally, but his voice, his face, were drained. Monsieur Durand, Theodora saw, could not have produced even a glass of water, if she had asked for it. Because Monsieur Durand himself was asking. He was drained by asking for what he would not be given.

'No,' said Theodora. 'Thank you. I think I have, more or less, everything I want.'

'Ah,' breathed Monsieur Durand, as if not quite convinced.

'And you, Monsieur Durand? What is the matter?' Theodora asked.

'*Rien,*' said Monsieur Durand.

Though quite obviously he meant *tout*.

Braces gave him an exposed look. Theodora knew that he must have varicose veins, and perhaps a collection of colonial stamps. More certain than his circulation, flowed, under the stubble, some great subterranean despair, of which he would have told now, if his voice had not grown stiff describing *confort moderne* to arriving guests. So Monsieur Durand remained a face on braces in the dark.

'*Eh bien. Mademoiselle, je vous souhaite une bonne nuit,*' he said.

'Thank you,' Theodora replied.

Her gratitude was formal, but it was what Monsieur Durand, in spite of his braces, would expect.

Then he was a detached cough, as Theodora continued to circulate. Sometimes a blade of light, between a carpet and a door, slit the darkness. She saw the boots in duplicate, of the Demoiselles Bloch of course, their long dark tongues perplexed and lolling on the mat. But these fragments of identity and the regular appearance of a china knob, designed apparently for turning, did not convince her of the importance either of feet or hands. The act of darkness demolished personality.

Guided by a corner of darkness, a kink in endlessness, just after she had touched with surprise and hope the bones of her own face, Theodora passed an open doorway that blinded by its audacity, or rather an unconscious insolence of solid light. The audacious doorway had the same contemptuousness as certain flesh, which does not interpret dreams, nor see beyond its own reflection.

Looking through the lit doorway, Theodora saw that *le petit* stood in the mirror. He stroked his vanity through the glass, and his vanity was golden, more convincing than darkness, the sullen, golden face of flesh. *Le petit* loved his reflection endlessly, his back turned on any irrelevance, whether it was the cough of Monsieur Durand, Theodora was not sure, or the sigh of Henriette. Because *le petit* did not acknowledge desires, except his own. He was his own solid, golden flesh. He blew the smoke from his straight nose and watched for his glass face to clear.

Theodora trod quietly so as not to disturb any exposed dream. She would have asked which way, if it had been decent to inquire, but it was not. When the darkness settled down again, she began to feel that she was lost. She touched the darkness for a sign. She touched a face that was soft and tough as chamois leather.

'*Ah, c'est vous*,' sighed the voice of Henriette. '*Personne ne dort plus.*'

'I think I am lost,' said Theodora. '*Je cherche ma chambre.*'

In the darkness the disapproval of Henriette was implied. It was dry and unexpressed. Her feet chafed. Theodora followed the direction that was taking shape. She was again a child. It was soft as sighs yielding to the superior wisdom of Henriette.

'*Elle dort, Quand même*,' said her loud voice.

'Who?' Theodora asked.

Before she saw. She saw the propped head of Mrs Rapallo lolling in sleep.

'*Elle dort. Elle rêve*,' said Henriette, with a touch of dry bitterness. '*Elle prend ses rêves d'un petit paquet sur la commode en marbre à côté de son lit.*'

Taking it for granted as part of Henriette's superior knowledge, because these were details that the light did not explain, Theodora glanced through the doorway at Mrs Rapallo's sleep. Now, disguised by nature, the lips were pale. The eyes were inward-looking things of china. Overhead, on the great branching brass of the bed, hung Mrs Rapallo's hair, against which a shabby Mignon dozed, and huddled for warmth. It was a cold tree.

Henriette laughed. '*Vous voyez?*'

She had a gold tooth that gashed. It is quite hateful, decided Theodora, the gold tooth of Henriette. And the eyes, cavernous from long looking, at a distance, through doorways at night.

'*Ce vieux cadavre vit encore. Quand même*,' laughed Henriette. '*Elle rêve.*'

'Thank you. I have seen enough,' said Theodora.

And it was not so much Mrs Rapallo as the cavernousness of Henriette.

'*On y va, on y va,*' said Henriette, also a servant who sensed very quickly the whims of guests.

They had, in fact, arrived. Henriette threw open again Theodora's *chambre modeste.*

It was perhaps *plus modeste,* but recognizable, from the objects she had put there in the morning as a safeguard, the darning egg, the dictionary, and the superfluous leather writing case. Hearing the fainter slippers of Henriette, listening to her own silence form in the small room, Theodora loved her sponge. There are moments, she admitted, when it is necessary to return to the boxes for which we were made. And now the small room was a box with paper roses pasted on the sides. Theodora walked across the carpet, frayed by similar feet in modest circumstances, with arches that have a tendency to fall, in shoes that soon must be mended. She took off a garnet ring which had been her mother's, but which had changed its expression, like most inherited things. She put it on the dressing table, inside the handkerchief sachet, which was the garnet's place. I am preparing for bed, she saw. But in performing this act for the first time, she knew she did not really control her bones, and that the curtain of her flesh must blow, like walls which are no longer walls. She took off one shoe, with its steel buckle and its rather long vamp. Standing with it in her hand, her identity became uncertain. She looked with sadness at the little hitherto safe microcosm of the darning egg and waited for the rose wall to fall.

It began to palpitate, the paper mouths of roses wetting their lips, either voice or wall putting on flesh. She was almost indecently close to what was happening, but sometimes one is. Sometimes the paper rose has arms and thighs.

Theodora realized she must accept the tactile voices of the voluble wall.

'When I look into your eye I can see myself,' said the voice. 'That is why you are so necessary to my existence.'

It was the voice of Wetherby, Theodora heard, the breath so close it touched the bones of her cheek.

'But small,' said Lieselotte. 'The eye reduces as well as intensifies. That is why you hate. Because it shows an amoeba, or anyway, some small, squirming thing.'

Hot hands twisted paper roses. Sweat had begun to penetrate

the paper wall. It spread, larger than Africa, lapping the dry surface with thick, swollen, African lips.

'If I put my hands like this,' Wetherby said.

'You would not dare,' said Lieselotte. 'You would remove the source of all your despair and satisfaction. If I were to die of just this extra pressure, which your hands have not the courage to give my death would mean your suicide. You must continue to suffer, slowly, by any and every dreary means, to feel the numbness and desperation of what you choose to call love.'

The hands were making a cage, Theodora felt, the hand in hand, from which temporarily the bird had flown.

'And yet you have loved me. You have told me so,' Wetherby said.

'I have given you what I have been given,' Lieselotte sighed. 'Surely by this time you must understand we have entered the age of *Ersatz*.'

'But I have felt something stronger in your arms.'

'That,' said Lieselotte, 'is pity.'

'But it is also love.'

'Have it your own way. It is also contempt. It is also power.'

'But you love your power. I can feel it in your mouth, in your moments of greatest revulsion.'

'Of course I love power. Who doesn't? And best of all I love the power that pity gives. Once the object of pity accepts, he is lost. The rot has set in. You should know, shouldn't you? You! You! You!'

'I know because I love you.'

'Because you love pity. You crave for it. There! Take it. There!'

Whether blows or kisses it was not clear.

'And you crave to give.'

'Well?'

'You have confessed your weakness. You are dependent on me.'

'Oh, God, yes, I am dependent on you all right. If you put it that way. To the end. To the end.'

So that it is no longer possible, sighed Theodora Goodman, to distinguish which is which.

Love is undoubtedly an acrostic, and that is why I have failed, she decided as she listened to the teeth on teeth grinding out words, and silences give clues. She saw a great stillness replace the frenzy of the paper curtain. She sat with a Testament in her lap, and read the Acts, to prepare herself for sleep, relaxing as Mrs Rapallo had recommended, with a book in which people come and go. But in this book the people came and went with a directness and simplicity that amazed. People no longer come and go, said Theodora, people are brought and sent.

'Ah,' cried Lieselotte, her sigh turning on the pillow. 'Where were we, my *love?*'

'Why, we were where we left off,' Wetherby replied.

'I supposed so. Do you know that once I was a little girl with plaits no thicker than cats' tails? I walked beside the Baltic in a blue dress and looked for the midnight sun.'

'Do you know, Lieselotte, you have never stopped being a little girl, except that you have learnt to look at objects through a glass eye and then to describe their antics?'

'The antics of objects are indescribable,' Lieselotte sighed. 'I never expect to make more than an attempt.'

'That is our hope,' said Wetherby.

'Hope?'

It was a bubble on her lips in some smooth sea in which she already swam.

Swimming too, somewhere off the shores of an island, Theodora hitched her trousers under the green water and prepared to touch land. Fire was coming towards her, and voices, and finally heads, along the banks of a little creek.

'Who are you?' they asked, holding their fire close to the water.

'My name is Epaphroditos,' said Theodora, rising shakily on sudden stones.

Wind twanged in her moustache, which was thick with salt.

'That is strange,' they said. 'You are unexpected, to say the least.'

'Well, I cannot tell you any more,' said Theodora. 'Because I am waiting to be told.'

Before her stone rolled. She retrieved her head from above her lap in the strict space of her *chambre modeste*.

'You are sleeping, Ludmilla?' asked Alyosha Sergei.

'I was,' said Theodora. 'And you?'

'Never.'

'It must be sometimes a great bore.'

'Everything is boring,' said Alyosha Sergei. 'Boredom is a motive force which we are apt to overlook.'

Theodora began to have a suspicion that Sokolnikov was a great man. He was the greatest bore. She closed her Testament, which had been given to her by a clergyman in a train near Bournemouth, and prepared to listen to words.

"All things spring from boredom,' said Sokolnikov.

He patted each statement like a balloon, not the gay globe of carnival, but a turgid gas balloon, determined to escape from its moorings in a slow wind. Theodora yawned.

'Do we not work from boredom? Or would, if necessity did not exist. We sing from boredom. We fornicate from boredom. Out of the loneliness of boredom, we marry. Then, as a sop to our bored vanities, we proceed to reproduce. It is even probable that God created Adam on a rainy day.'

'I cannot confirm that,' Theodora said.

'But you can save me, Ludmilla, I beseech you, please. Let us make conversation and debauch ourselves interestingly for many hours. It is most stimulating.'

'Go, Alyosha Sergei!' she cried. 'You are a bore.'

But she came, as she had always come to Alyosha Sergei, her man's boots on a board floor. They were, in fact, that complementary curse and blessing, a relationship.

'Yes,' she sighed, 'I shall come. If it will settle anything.'

'Nothing settles,' belched Sokolnikov. 'It always rises, again and again.'

Theodora followed him down the passage, and the whole darkness lunged and plunged as if it might soon tear free. The passage was full of wind. But the room into which they walked, after a last lurch and a last righting, the room at least was moored.

'I shall pour out a little one for the saints,' said Alyosha Sergei. 'Do not accuse me, Ludmilla. It is far too late.'

It was too late for clocks. It was the hour for rubber words.

She watched the glass under his hand become solid as he poured, glitter, quiver solemnly for a moment, and dissolve into shapelessness.

'There, Ludmilla,' the General said.

Together they watched the lovely lake, which was most necessary and natural. Theodora knew now that it could not have been otherwise, the endless, brimming, shivering glass, and the little, passive, touching lake. There were other things as well. There was the carcass of a duck. There were the smoked sprats that came from somewhere else in wooden boxes. The sprats were stiff and glazed in their wooden boxes on the table in the General's room.

'I have been making a small meal,' said Alyosha Sergei, and, even now, he broke the heads off several sprats and stuffed them into his mouth.

'You are an odious and repulsive glutton, Alyosha Sergei.'

But her words were worn by much use and had a certain shabby tenderness.

'Now you speak like Anna Stepanovna,' said Aylosha Sergei.

His mouth quivered, rejecting the tails of several sprats, and an enormous bitterness that he had not bargained for.

'They say they tore down the little pavilion beside the lake. They used it for firewood the following winter. Anna Stepanovna protested, but her argument was ineffectual.'

'And the pavilion was rotten,' said Theodora remorselessly. 'On one side the lattice had broken loose. When there was a wind it flapped.'

'Yes,' said Alyosha Sergei. 'The pavilion was rotten.'

So the pavilion was reduced to smoke. Theodora's eyes smarted. She remembered the silver bellies of the trees that the wind tumbled beside the lake in summer. It was not possible to reduce the melancholy ripple of the leaves.

'It was, of course, right, Ludmilla. And they strung up Anna Stepanovna to her own trees for eating her own chickens. And they wiped the frozen snot off their faces with pieces of embroidery that she had spent years pricking and torturing out of canvas. And they burned the house, which certainly had patches of damp on the ceilings, and worm in much of the wood. But none the less, one must admit, the rightness of certain acts is a melancholy fact.'

Emptying his mouth of all this, Alyosha Sergei began to feel the need for putting something inside. He fished in the carcass of the duck for its liver and placed it carefully on his tongue. Theodora bent forward, because it was time she also did something to dissolve her own hard shape. She bent and took the glass which had stood waiting amongst the skeleton fish, on the edges of the lake. She took the glass and it trembled clearly in her hand. The little glass had a clear and innocent beauty, before which she could not humble herself enough.

'How right it is,' she said.

'What is?'

'Finally, almost everything,' Theodora said.

'You are a fool or a saint, Ludmilla,' said Alyosha Sergei.

She was nothing that she knew. She drank the glass of vodka and the room sprang closer. These walls, too, had naked swords, but the blades jagged from attacking the heads of bottles, and the wires from which they hung had rusted in the sea air. He had arranged his boots against the skirting, where they glared, toeing the line. On the bed there was a cotton bedspread, of large, open, though intricate pattern, which Theodora felt she must eventually unravel.

'A fool or a saint,' said Alyosha Sergei. 'And I, I have so much food inside my belly it has begun to ache.'

He laid his head sideways on the table amongst the skeletons of fish. He began to snore, releasing a great deal of wind through endless ramifications of rubber.

Alyosha Sergei is a pig, a pig, breathed Theodora, who at times could not contain disgust, and particularly now, watching the motion of pig's bristles on the smooth pink rubber skin. Littered with squalor, she said, brushing from her skirt the wishbone of the duck.

It irritated her more to remember his pig's chest, that he had bared for greater comfort, and it was white and flabby as the scraped carcass of a pig, on which meandered two or three grey, ridiculous, forgotten hairs. Now that he lay with his head in the trough, his chest was covered, but it remained a grudge to be jealously nursed. The bile came in her mouth. She could feel that her face was leathern and yellow, and she realized that she had not taken her camomile tea.

Wake up, you swine, she would have shouted, at any moment, she would have banged her flat hands on a gap in the table, or kicked him with her boot.

'Ludmilla, you are going to accuse me,' said Alyosha Sergei.

He sat up, or half, and the backbone of a sprat trembled fatuously on a whisker.

'I should say so,' she said. 'You were snoring like a pig.'

She could not make it pointed enough, her hateful bodkin.

'You, who never sleep,' she said.

'I was thinking,' said Alyosha Sergei.

'Then it is a great blessing,' she said, 'that the majority of mankind does not.'

But it was unequal, her voice knew.

'It is time we were going,' she said more gently.

It was unequal, because the room, with the ceiling which had been fumed over by Alyosha Sergei's voice, and the black portraits, and the golden saints, and the other rooms, which creaked with emptiness and mice, the whole empty, expectant house was full of that desperate affection which she had never quite been able to give. So that now, on the point of leaving, her mouth trembled, and expressed something shapeless that was neither hatred nor love.

'Of course, we are going,' said Alyosha Sergei.

Now that the streets were quiet all emotion was unconvincing. It was several hours since the breath had come and gone in spasms, and that astonishing scene of men turning to wax in the gutters. But you could no longer hear the cries gush from paving stones. Now the silence lay in pools. It had quite congealed.

'In three hours we shall reach P—, if we are fortunate,' said Alyosha Sergei. 'There we should meet Tomokin and Michael Ivanich.'

'You have said that seven times.'

'Conversation, Ludmilla, is one indiction of reality.'

But she could not convince herself that she was not about to attempt to cross the mysteriously open space which separates beginning from end. And here was Alyosha Sergei, who looked into the street, as if he expected a bear with a hand-organ, or dancing girls with streaming ribbons.

Here was Alyosha Sergei, who said, 'I remember once meeting an old landowner from the Ukraine who had a cure for most things. He boiled nettles with a little *kvass* and took a soup night and morning. That amiable old imbecile, Ludmilla, was thrown from a piebald horse and dragged for several *versts*. When finally he was picked up by some peasant women who were gathering mushrooms in a wood, for all they knew he was offering his recipe of nettles to God.'

She turned her back, inside the big serge cloak which she had fished out of an attic for the journey, and which smelled of time, of childhood, nettles, rain, and the slow smell of dung, so that the act of turning was as much avoidance as exasperation.

She turned her back and said, 'Have you got the money?'

'Money? You should know, Ludmilla, that it is not possible to buy off God.'

'Then, let us go,' said Theodora. 'There is nothing to wait for.'

She put up her hand to arrange her hair, which she found, of course, that she had cut off. She was a thin man in a cloak, with the trousers stuffed inside her boots, like a Cossack or a peasant.

Alyosha Sergei began to laugh.

'You are the Pale Horse,' he laughed. 'The Pale Horse with his ears back.'

She would have laughed too, but sometimes she could not. And the whole house was aching with the laughter of Alyosha Sergei. So that Alyosha Sergei's laughter was enough.

'You are drunk,' said General Sokolnikov, looking for the bottle in the debris of sprats, in the glare of light in which they sat, under a severe arrangement of suspended swords, in a mediocre bedroom. 'You are drunk, but not yet drunk enough.'

'No, but I am warm,' said Theodora.

She was. She was enough. She had not yet unravelled the large, open pattern of the cotton quilt on the General's bed.

'You are intoxicated by your own melancholy,' said Sokolnikov. 'You expect too much of life.'

'I have seen extraordinary things,' Theodora said.

'Everything is extraordinary,' said Alyosha Sergei.

She looked at the cotton quilt on the bed. She arched her eyebrows, because at this moment the vodka leapt inside her. She looked at the cotton quilt, which was after all only a honeycomb.

It was both simple and extraordinary. It was a honeycomb, but without bees. There was no brown buzz. There was only the imprint which Alyosha Sergei's body had left on it that afternoon.

'Everything is so extraordinary,' he said, 'that there is some question of whether we can withstand the impact, whether we can survive.'

Theodora took the glass, which had begun to quiver and glow again amongst the stiff, salt spars of the little glittering sprats. She drank, and her head was electric, it was full of silver wires.

'I have survived,' she said.

She put down the glass on its small but heavy base.

'You? You are an illusion.'

'I beg to contradict. I can show you my passport,' Theodora said.

But he had got up. He had gone to listen, scattering the fragments of food that hung, fastening his ear on the door as if he expected to suck up sounds. Then he came back and put his finger on her arm. He touched the strange and thoughtful substance of Theodora Goodman, which was not apparently flesh.

'You, Ludmilla,' he said, 'are dead.'

So that she ebbed with the greatness of it.

'It is difficult to believe,' said Alyosha Sergei. 'None of us could. Neither Tomokin, nor Michael Ivanich, and there was also a gentleman who had not yet made your acquaintance, and who had studied the toll system of Germany at Göttingen. This gentleman, whose name I have forgotten suggested that at the moment of death the soul chooses freely, which naturally removes much of the melancholy from the occasion. Michael Ivanich and I were considerably interested in this hypothesis, and were anxious to hold a little discussion. It was also unpleasant walking in the dark. But Tomokin, who was greatly moved, he kept mopping his face with a red cotton handkerchief which had been given him for the journey by his old nurse, Tomokin said it was our sacred duty to make for the frontier and join Yudenich. So it was decided we should walk, and the difficulty of this operation, and the pain from the wound in my left buttock, prevented me from explaining adequately to the gentleman from Göttingen that you had protested, Ludmilla, when they showed you the gun.'

It was moving towards her darkly across the clearing. Her feet were rooted now in mute needles. She stood close against the tree, which smelled strongly of resin, the tree which was rough and so close that it had ceased to be a comfort or protection, as she could feel its heart beating painfully, erratically in its side. Released by the lusty, palpitating gold and red of firelight, trees leapt skyward in sudden puffs of branch and crest. Across the clearing trees had begun to move. It was these that frightened. She smelled the fire. She smelled the voices, their smell of sweat, and dark hair, approaching out of the darkness, this was thick with hair. In the general disintegration of firelight, and darkness, and burning resin, and sailing trees, the belt round her waist was no great guarantee of personality.

'Ah, here it is. I was right,' said a voice. 'It is a *barin*.'

Fire gave a face to the darkness, big and round, snub, with humorous nostrils.

'You were right twice, Petya. There are two.'

'Fetch them out, the bears. Into the light. Where we can see them. We'll make them dance at least.'

Theodora heard the many voices, that were also one, and the faces one, the big, dappled, half-genial, half-hostile face of firelight with the gaping nose.

'Yes, fetch them out, Petya,' said a woman who smelled of excitement.

She wore a sailor's cap on her head, but only just. She was as firm and pretty as polished apples.

'There is no system to all this,' said a precise fellow with a small beard. 'Revolution means system.'

'Long live the Republic!'

'Long live Kerensky!'

'No! Down with Kerensky! Long live Lenin!'

'Long live Lenin! Kerensky is a windbag.'

'I would like to agree,' said Alyosha Sergei, who had begun to feel the weight of silence. 'Kerensky is a brilliant fellow, all fire and feeling. A man of warmth and enlightened ideas.

Kerensky is a movement in himself. But, paradoxically enough, a movement requires more than movement. A movement requires a rock.'

Silence spat resin. The faces were quite flat in the wonderment of silence.

'Friends, we have an orator in our midst,' said the precise beard at last.

A dark face, a kind of gipsy horse-dealer, who wore a brass ring with a stone too flash for a diamond, and who had been enjoying himself for days, began to laugh. He could not laugh too much. He passed it on. Other faces flashed. A sailor. And the polished apples of the fresh woman heaved.

'Who are you?' asked the precise fellow.

'My name is Lukich,' said Alyosha Sergei. 'And this is my younger brother Pavel.'

'Occupation?'

'We have a business in the city. We are timber merchants in a small way,' said Alyosha Sergei.

'I am tired of all this nonsense,' sighed an old man. 'Let us sit down. My feet hurt.'

'And no doubt Comrade Lukich was walking in this forest at midnight with a view to trees,' said the beard.

'With his younger brother Pavel, don't forget,' said the horse-dealer.

'On the contrary,' said Alyosha Sergei, 'I suffer from insomnia, and find that the night air under trees has a certain soporific effect. We came here also when we were boys, to gather mushrooms after rain.'

Somebody cleared his throat heavily and spat. It was rather tame.

'There is something here, comrades, that only men would swallow,' said the woman in the sailor's cap. 'If my younger brother Pavel can explain his trousers, I am a fish.'

'What has Anfisa found? What is the younger merchant hiding in his trousers?'

'I say what is he not hiding,' Anfisa said.

'It is quite true,' said Theodora. 'Anfisa is, of course, right. My brother is among other things a buffoon. But let us at least follow the old man's example and sit down.'

She longed for the good warmth of fire, to sit on the rough, resin-smelling log with her knees somewhere near her chin. Whether the others followed suit was immaterial, because there are certain moments of consoled physical exhaustion where others stay or go.

'No, you don't,' said the beard. 'You are answerable to the people.'

'Am I not a person?' asked Theodora.

'That is not for you to decide.'

'Who are you, anyway?' somebody else asked.

'I am Ludmilla Sokolnikov, and I keep house for my brother in St Petersburg. We come of a reasonably good but impoverished military family. We have a house which is almost empty, because we have sold most of what was in it. Sometimes we go on short visits to richer relatives who have estates in the country. Only sometimes, though. For my brother is a bore, and as you see, I am yellow and thin, with a slight moustache. I am single, for the same reason, because I am ugly, and because I have never been in a position to buy a husband.'

'Listen to this!' the horse-dealer said.

Then for a moment there was a thick wall of silence, over which even the beard failed to climb. Theodora, who had sat down in spite of opposition, looked at her knees. She was greatly consoled by the simplicity of things.

'They're all right,' sighed the old man, who sat opposite, nursing a bottle near the blaze of fire. 'A revolution's all very well. But you must breathe. Leave them alone. They're all right.'

Theodora did not care. She listened to Alyosha Sergei. The truth had made him gasp. He had a moist eye.

'My sister Ludmilla has put things in a nutshell,' he said. 'Our story has a touching simplicity of its own, which I had not realized before.'

'It is a complete fabrication,' said the beard.

'A what?' asked Petya.

'A lie.'

'Yes, yes,' said the woman. 'All this Pavel nonsense first. I agree. How do we know they are not spies?'

'You would talk your mouth off, Anfisa,' the horse-dealer said.

'Is it not free speech, gipsy, that we're fighting for?'

'Yes, yes,' said Alyosha Sergei. 'If it is a lie, let us at least discuss the lie.'

'That is fair enough,' said the old man. 'But give me vodka any time. Vodka's the poor man's friend.'

The beard was almost ready to make a decision, which had been maturing some time now behind his face. He had been forming the words that he had read in pamphlets, and it was only a matter of choosing those that sounded best.

'The revolution,' he said, 'calls for action, and the liquidation of the bourgeoisie.'

'It does, it does! Long live the Republic!'

'Well?'

Then Theodora realized that this game had pistols.

'It is absurd,' she said. 'We are ridiculous, all of us, standing here among the trees, playing a ridiculous game, when we should be in our beds.'

But she was not sure that the ridiculousness of this game which is called life, whether it is played in a *salon*, or on a battle-field, or in a forest clearing, does not invariably prevail.

'I protest,' she said, and this too sounded ridiculous.

The horse-dealer's face had seen something, something that was strange, but only for a moment, as if it were too great to accept, the face promptly closed. Now it was sullen, sweating flesh. Theodora remembered the face somewhere on the road to Kiev, and Anfisa, who smelled of her own excitement, and the carved Petya. Her life was moving round her. She heard a burst of pigeons released from the silver bellies of the trees beside the lake. She bit her mouth for the loveliness of many heavy, breaking summers. Then she began to ebb with the greatness and paleness, the thin, watery lightness, of the event in which she was taking part. It was a mystery which even the hand on the trigger now admitted.

'Then I am dead,' said Theodora.

'You are quite dead,' said Alyosha Sergei.

The breath came glugging up in him from somewhere deeper down, because almost always early in the morning he was overcome by emotion. His stomach was sad with sprats. He was a victim of something undefined.

'And you?' Theodora asked, because she had lost him amongst the trees.

'My end was far less apocalyptical,' he said. 'After a short pause to consider the ethics of it, naturally and regrettably I ran. In the course of this operation I received a slight flesh wound in the left buttock. There was also something soft which hit my face in the dark. Possibly a frightened owl. But I continued to run. It was not so much a physical act as an emotional state. I ran till I reached the village where I met Tomokin, Michael Ivanich, and the unknown gentleman from Göttingen.'

'The gentleman who hypothesized,' said Theodora.

She had not noticed before the grave and reasonable face of the wardrobe in Alyosha Sergei's room.

'Exactly,' said Sokolnikov. 'But the gentleman from Göttingen did not console. I was a wreck of my previous self, Ludmilla. It was as if experience had wrenched out my conscience by the roots, with a pair of tongs, and after a short bleeding space I sensed that it was dead.'

'Death is far less emotional,' Theodora said.

The General vibrated steamily.

'It is as simple as a bottle,' said Theodora. 'And as clear.'

It had pared down to this.

'And as empty,' she said.

'Then let us remove the bottle,' said the General.

Which he took, and pitched, over his shoulder, at the wall.

'Now there is nothing,' he said.

As if he were almost afraid to accept the responsibility, now that it was done.

'But there must be something,' he said. 'Or an illusion of something. Ludmilla, if you love me . . .'

'Yes?'

Her head lolled.

'If you love me, there is still one beautiful act to be done. In the room of this American adventuress, this mother-in-law of pomposities and insolence, there is a nautilus that she stole. I do not wish to repeat the act. But let us look, just once, together, at this lovely shell. Ludmilla, if you love me, you will fetch it. You are less resonant than I. You do not bounce at inconvenient moments. Bring, bring the nautilus.'

Theodora saw no reason why she should not. She was herself by now as vibrant and transparent as a shell. And at the same time she began to be obsessed by the same obsession as Sokolnikov, to hold the nautilus, to hold, if it is ever possible, to hold.

'I shall most certainly try,' she said as she got up, propping herself with two wooden fingers on the surface of the table that was thick with carcasses. 'I shall most certainly try.'

'My excellent Ludmilla,' cried the General. 'I have every reason to believe that you will execute this mission.'

But she did not bother to consider whether the room contained certainty of action, or just a steamy Slav. On the whole, she thought, certainty did not inhabit the rooms of small hotels. But she began to cross the floor. She observed a row of empty boots. She observed a door, waiting miraculously to receive her exit.

Then the passage was darkness. Darkness flowed, whether up or down she did not know, but soft as dandelions to blow. If I have not blown out the darkness before noon I shall have reached Mrs Rapallo, said Theodora Goodman. She watched the darkness for a monkey combing hair. Mignon, she mumbled, recoiling from the paper hands of darkness, but at least it did not examine its dandruff in public, or had not done so yet.

A light stood in a saucer in Mrs Rapallo's room.

Elsie Rapallo is afraid of the dark, said Theodora Goodman.

Though why, she did not know, for the light fingered unmercifully. It exposed the considerable mineral deposits in Elsie Rapallo's abandoned skull.

Theodora stood in the doorway and considered which path to pick. They all wound. Sometimes it was the perplexed objects of darkness which obstructed, sometimes a dream stirred and threatened to form. Walking at random, she heard her feet bruising the faces of old letters. Tactical foresight made her avoid Queen Marie of Rumania, whose autograph had hands.

It is an exceedingly long way, Theodora sighed.

'It is an aquamarine,' said Mrs Rapallo, in quite a distinct voice.

Her cheek rubbed against some greater depth of sleep. And there was *le petit paquet sur la commode en marbre*. Of course.

As Henriette had said. Mrs Rapallo had finally dissolved the marble groups that waited beneath the Veronese, spoons poised above the ices, for cardinals to pass.

Theodora advanced. She was somewhere near the little table in marquetry which threatened to erupt music if she touched. She held her skirt. She dreaded the stiff music that Mrs Rapallo's boxes must contain.

I have come here, she said, for the nautilus.

Though now she had begun to doubt whether she could reach. Whether the pampas of the darkness would allow, and its great clouds of grass, heavy as breath, that she parted with her ineffectual hands. She also doubted whether the nautilus was substance enough, or whether it would blow.

Just then Theodora slipped on satin.

'Nous avons pris le thé chez Dodo,' Mrs Rapallo said.

Many agonies righted themselves on many tables. There was a gingerbread heart on which Theodora read *Ich liebe dich,* in dust or sugar.

But she was there also, she saw. Her hands could just touch an article of furniture, ugly and involved with carved game, on which the nautilus stood.

Above the bed, on its brass branch, Mrs Rapallo's hair had begun to chatter.

This is a possibility that I had forgotten, Theodora said.

She had forgotten also the feel of monkey, the kind of orphan intimacy of monkeys' hands. Launching out of the darkness with one purpose, the monkey sat against her neck. The monkey touched a pulse, and touched, and touched. A terrible nostalgia for skin to inspire its monkey finger.

'Mignon, I am touched,' Theodora said. 'But now I am in no mood, in no mood at all, for monkeys.'

As if Mignon were prepared to hear. Mignon was all sadness. Mignon held her ear close to Theodora's skin, counting the murmurs, as if for monkeys the promised land is flesh.

Mrs Rapallo stirred, and scratched her scalp.

'Mignon. Pretty Mignon. *Va-t'en*!' Theodora said.

But she could not shake the monkey's heavy sadness. Mignon clung.

Something desperate must happen, Theodora felt.

In the semi-darkness of Mrs Rapallo's room, furred and clammy as monkey skin, with the same distinctive smell, she looked for some event. But in Mrs Rapallo's room events were past. They hung from hooks, or littered the chairs with discarded whalebone. Nothing would ever disturb the dust, except a finger aimlessly writing a name. *Gloria Leontini*, the finger had written, on the small undecorated space of oak on which the nautilus stood. *Principessa dell' Isola Grande,* garlanding the foot of the *compotier*.

But the *compotier* was hope, the wax oranges and nectarines, from which a mouth had already taken bites. Theodora seized with love this child's game of fruit. She took the small, pocked orange, with its sallow bite. She rubbed it on her sleeve.

'Look, Mignon, my love. You will go and fetch the orange, or stay, whichever you wish.'

She heard the orange bump, thump, dangerously into darkness. She heard the monkey's feet scratching, spattering the faces of old letters. Somewhere in darkness Mignon transferred her melancholy to a wax orange. At least she did not return.

Theodora took the nautilus. Spikes pricked her breast. Her hands were water.

'Ahhhh,' sighed the mouth of Mrs Rapallo, its slack skin opening far too close to the surface of sleep.

Then Theodora made the darkness move. It was released. Her skirt flowed. Ferns shook. The dull and usually unresponsive tails of pampas grass flumped against her fixed eyes. She was walking down the passage with the nautilus.

Somebody, who was it, flew downstairs, Theodora remembered. She was not surprised.

'It is not surprising at all, Alyosha Sergei,' she said.

'On the contrary, it is fantastic,' said Sokolnikov.

Impatience had made him swell. He filled the door. She could not see his detail, but there was no mistaking his bulk.

'My lovely shell,' he said, out of a long distance and a congested throat.

'That is all very well,' said Theodora. '*Your* lovely shell. But who will put it back?'

His face drained the nautilus.

'You have the irritating vice of practical and virtuous women, Ludmilla. You think too far ahead. Anything may happen,' he said.

It might, of course, it might. And now she knew that it must. It had as good as happened. She heard her own cry through her still closed mouth. Her heart turned in her side, because, she knew, the nautilus is made to break.

'Will you not look, Ludmilla?'

Soloknikov was holding it in his hands. His faced oozed long opalescent tears.

'Do you remember, when we were children, the moon was transparent? You could watch it pulse like the skin on an unhatched egg. Then it began to solidify. It became as opaque as a *dragée* at a christening.'

Alyosha Sergei, you foolish child, Theodora could not say, this is a crisis in which even I cannot protect you, and as for your moon, it is lost.

'Somebody is a thief,' Mrs Rapallo said.

She stood in the passage without her hair. Her words were blunted by her gums.

'Sokolnikov we knew. But you, Theodora Goodman! And intoxicated too.'

Her hands explored without design the tatters of an old lace gown. Out of magenta she was pale.

'Of course I am all that you say, Mrs Rapallo,' Theodora replied.

She could not explain. She could explain nothing, least of all her several lives. She could not explain that where there is more than one it is inevitable always to betray.

'Do not let her deny you, Ludmilla,' the General fumed. 'It is not possible to steal what is not her own.'

'But it is,' Theodora said.

'It is mine,' said Sokolnikov.

'I know,' Theodora cried.

Silence fell solider than wax.

'You are drunk, Ludmilla,' said the General.

'I have never seen more clearly,' said Theodora slowly. 'But what I see remains involved.'

Mrs Rapallo had begun to move.

'I have my shell,' she said. 'General Sokolnikov, it is all I have got.'

And the nautilus became a desperate thing of hands. Theodora heard the crack of bones. Hands were knotting the air. Then, hands were hands.

'Then it has happened,' Theodora said.

She looked at the shivered shell. Mrs Rapallo had turned.

'I guessed that it would,' she said.

'A murder has been committed,' the General cried.

'Go, hang out your soul to dry. You Russians were always damp,' replied Mrs Rapallo.

Theodora did not know if the General slammed his door then or later, or where the retreat of Mrs Rapallo began, grating on the darkness her slow and solemn rags. Now the night was denser. Emotions had trodden into the carpet the slight white rime which was what remained of the nautilus. Theodora herself felt considerably reduced.

10

THEODORA Goodman began in time to knit a garment in grey wool.

'What is your great work, Miss Goodman?' asked Mademoiselle Marthe. 'We should be interested to know.'

'Perhaps it will be a jumper,' said Theodora Goodman. 'But I have not yet made up my mind.'

'How right you are,' Mademoiselle Berthe sighed.

Because the Demoiselles Bloch were quite determined in their projects, which often failed.

Doilies, for example, doilies, they said, sometimes have intentions of their own.

The Demoiselles Bloch stirred their hair with crochet hooks. They were perplexed.

But Theodora Goodman continued to knit her grey wool, in the angle of a kind of little wintergarden, on one side of which pressed the *jardin exotique,* and on the other the sea. The corner of the little wintergarden in which she sat was transparent, but it was not dangerous. Flies died frequently, but on the whole it was *sympathique.*

'*Oui, il est tout à fait sympathique, votre petit coin,*' said Monsieur Durand to the *Anglaise* who stayed.

Because this was one of the gifts of Monsieur Durand, to fit the landscape to the guest.

Theodora Goodman did not protest. Just as she had not chosen, particularly, that particular *petit coin.* But it suited. And she watched her hands knit. She listened to the stiff palms. The forms of the *jardin exotique* pushed upward endlessly. And on the sea side, the waves folded and unfolded, also endlessly, their receiving and rejecting hands.

Theodora Goodman drew out a long grey stream of wool, out of an undistinguished bag.

It is easy and contenting, she confessed, to be a chair.

But she was not altogether deceived. She counted the bodies of the dead flies. She waited to be pushed around.

She began to hear the approach of Katina Pavlou into the little conservatory. The approach of Katina Pavlou cut through the long grey strands of sleep that knit together the Hôtel du Midi after *déjeuner*. For after *déjeuner* the Hôtel du Midi was only held together by sleep. Into the grey woollen fuzz and buzz of afternoon sleep fell the first white phrase of Katina Pavlou's approach.

Now Katina Pavlou walked without direction. Her eyes were dark. She had written, Theodora knew, in the blue *cahier* that she had bought from the *papeterie* beside the post office, she had most certainly written:

> *Your voice is the first velvet violin*
> *that my heart beats against*
> *in so much sadness wrapped*
> *waiting for you my love to take.*

Almost certainly Katina Pavlou had written in purple ink. Her hands were stained. Her eyes were cloudy with the words, and with the emotions that still welled up.

Theodora Goodman sat and knitted the long grey soothing strands of wool that did not altogether soothe. Theodora loved Katina Pavlou. She waited to be pushed around. She could feel Katina laying the hot palms of her hands on the window pane, as she looked not particularly at the sea, waiting for what. It was a grey day. Mist hung about the sea, tatters of mist on the hills and the sharp spikes of the *jardin exotique*. Theodora felt Katina lay her hot cheek against the mist. Her skin drank the moisture which did not satisfy. She waited. Outside in the garden the aloe had not yet shrivelled into its legend of death.

Oh, the afternoons, the afternoons, Katina Pavlou would have sighed.

In the useful pocket of her dress Theodora Goodman had the letter from Lou. Lou was writing in purple ink. Lou's letter was heavy with other afternoons.

... algebra, Aunt Theo, is my chiefest torture. I cannot think in x and y. It is doubtful whether I shall ever learn. But whatever Father says, the nuns are nice. He says that Mother is wrong to send a girl to a convent with a lot of micks. But I cannot see, from experience, that there is anything wrong with nuns. In fact, I love Sister Mary Perpetua. She has the loveliest, saddest face. On my birthday she gave me a bag of aniseed balls and a little wooden cross. Sometimes in the afternoon we sit together, and watch the boats, and then I feel that I shall *never ever* have such a friendship ever again.

When I leave here and go to Audley, it is different. I think parents are difficult. Last holidays the MacKenzies came to stay. Mr MacKenzie is now quite red, and once fell down. Mrs MacKenzie told Mother I would be better if I lost my sallowness, and filled out, though thin and ugly women wear their clothes more easily. Sometimes the holidays at Audley are rather long. It is not the mornings, but the afternoons. Then I can only hope I shall be free ...

Theodora felt the letter from Lou crumpled hot and electric in her pocket. She remembered the violet sparks from trams in the late, grey, heavy afternoons.

Now she heard Katina Pavlou, round another corner in the wintergarden, and several palms, she heard her turning magazines. She heard the leaves of magazines hesitate and stick in the thick and steamy afternoon. She heard also the other presence begin to swell.

'Ah, there you are, my dabchick,' Theodora heard.

'Here I am and nowhere else,' Katina Pavlou sighed.

'A little pale, but not less interesting.'

'I am nothing,' Katina Pavlou said quite firmly. 'I know exactly what I am, General Sokolnikov. I know myself. I know.'

She turned the pages of the magazine. Theodora knew that the General was about to bounce. There were all the first indications of elasticity.

'I doubt,' he said, 'whether my moorhen knows the shape of her own ear.'

'My ear? Now you are being ridiculous, Alyosha Sergei,' Katina Pavlou said.

She laughed. It fell light and white into the afternoon.

'It is most earnest. See? Now you are touching it, you are touching your ignorance, but you cannot touch it away.'

'My ear is an ear,' Katina Pavlou said.

'Your ear is a fascinating organ. It is far more interesting than that stupid American magazine.'

'How funny you are, Alyosha Sergei,' Katina Pavlou said. 'This magazine is full of people doing things, in factories, aeroplanes, and diving suits.'

'Alas, you are still impressed by the age of motion. You are a child, Katina Pavlou. And I am old.'

'I am sixteen,' Katina Pavlou said.

But it fell with no less melancholy, its small bell. Theodora Goodman counted the bodies of dead flies.

'You are sixteen,' the General murmured.

Theodora realized that his sigh was scented. Without seeing, she knew that the smile of Sokolnikov had been embalmed.

'If I were to give you my life, child?'

'Your – your *life*!'

'You laugh?'

'But dear Alyosha Sergei, you say such funny things.'

Theodora Goodman, under the dry spasmodic palms, knew that her own laughter, which she held inside her, hurt.

'This is disastrous,' said Sokolnikov, all steam, because he wanted still to show himself something that perhaps he could not show.

'It is the unseasonable weather,' he said. 'This morning in the bathroom my own voice cannoned off the wall. The glass from which I was about to gargle shattered in my hand.'

'It is lovely weather, but sad,' said Katina Pavlou.

Theodora knew that she had laid her face against the window and was speaking into glass.

'I like the garden best when it is still and cool.'

'The garden is always detestable,' the General said.

'Look, Alyosha Sergei, what is this plant with the big damp leaves that are full of holes?'

'That is *Monstera deliciosa*. Its fruit is eaten when black, and one would say, almost putrid.'

'How peculiar.'

'You will find, my popinjay, that much that happens comes as a surprise, and much that doesn't happen is still possible.'

A chair creaked. The General's chair, perhaps, had aching thighs.

'Come here, my sweetheart, my Varvara. I have a present for you. A prize for prettiness.'

'A present! Let us open it, Alyosha Sergei, and see.'

'Oh, it is nothing. Let me assure you in advance. It is a small box of marshmallows that seems to have become a little crushed in transit.'

'But, Alyosha Sergei, how kind.'

'Knowing the sweet tooth of all young ladies . . .'

'One Easter they gave me a box of marshmallows. When I was thirteen. And I ate them all. I ate till I was sick. It was quite lovely, I remember, but I was thirteen.'

'Now you are sixteen,' the General said. 'And I shall help you eat these. You shall pop one carefully in my mouth.'

Theodora was glad that she did not see the great rubber lips reach forward, tremble, and close. But at least she heard the smack.

'There,' said Katina Pavlou. 'Now your face is powdered.'

She laughed.

'Alyosha Sergei,' she laughed, 'now your face is the face of a clown.'

'Let us at least eat the sweetmeats,' the General said. 'Until we are sick.'

'I have not hurt you, have I, Alyosha Sergei?'

'I have not been hurt since I was shot in my left buttock running away in the dark.'

'How ridiculous you are!'

'Then you do not love me? A little?'

Theodora heard the rubber silence lean over steamily to touch.

'Of course, I adore you. If I did not, I would not kiss you. There!'

'It is usual also, I believe, to call one's lover by endearing names.'

But Katina Pavlou laughed. It bared Sokolnikov, it bared him to the soul.

'I shall call you,' she laughed, 'I shall call you . . .'

'Yes?'

'I shall call you my *Monstera deliciosa*. But you are not yet putrid enough.'

Theodora heard Sokolnikov contract.

'Oh, dear!' Katina Pavlou laughed. 'How ridiculous we are.

I must dry my eyes. But now we shall be solemn. We shall sit, and you shall tell me, General Sokolnikov, about some campaign.'

'I do not think, after all, I am in any mood for conversation,' said Sokolnikov.

'You are sad, Alyosha Sergei? I was sad before you made me laugh.'

'Are you in love, Katina Pavlou?'

'No,' she said. 'I am not in love. I have not yet been in love.'

And Theodora Goodman knew that Katina Pavlou had stood against the window, beyond which, in the still greyness of the afternoon, the waves folded and unfolded, endlessly, their receiving and rejecting hands.

Theodora put the indeterminate garment she was knitting into its appropriate bag. She coughed the cough that never does deceive. In the little transparent wintergarden she felt that they were all three considerably exposed.

'Oh, it is you,' the General said.

He was cold. Since the evening of the nautilus both Mrs Rapallo and Sokolnikov had avoided her, as if mirrors tell.

'Yes,' said Theodora, 'it is I.'

Sometimes even grammar is unavoidably exposed. She looked outside, the garden side, at the big damp leaves of the *Monstera deliciosa* which were full of holes.

'This room is quite horribly naked,' Sokolnikov complained.

Katina Pavlou held her face against the window. She was closed now, opaque. She sang her own song, in her own language, whether of love or death, it had its own to and fro.

'I would like one day to make a picnic beside the sea,' Katina Pavlou said. 'Let us make a picnic, Miss Goodman. And you shall come, Alyosha Sergei. And we shall ask . . .'

'Child, I am too old for rocks.'

And cold, Sokolnikov was cold.

'So I have been informed,' he said. 'Now I shall go and clean my spurs. It is Thursday afternoon.'

'But you shall come,' Katina Pavlou called. 'We shall talk.'

'Oh, yes, we shall talk,' the General said. 'It is a small hotel. You shall have many opportunities to tell me things.'

But his feet marked some slow rubber repugnance on the stairs.

'There. He has gone, poor thing. And I have hurt him,' Katina Pavlou said.

'He will rebound,' said Theodora. 'He will even sit on rocks.'

'Then we shall make this picnic, Miss Goodman?'

'I dare say it will be made,' Theodora Goodman said wryly, remembering another stiff group beside the church.

'I am so glad,' Katina Pavlou sighed.

She turned her face against the glass, and then, unaccountably, began to cry. For Katina Pavlou had become the amazed and frightened instrument recording some climatic disturbance, still too sudden to accept or understand.

'Dearest Katina,' Theodora said, 'it would be easier if you would tell.'

'It is nothing,' cried Katina Pavlou.

The windows of the little wintergarden, blurred by the action of the salt air, did not disclose. There was no guide. There was only a general and continuous, consuming sea sound.

'Dear Miss Goodman, I wish that I could tell. I wish that I knew,' Katina Pavlou cried. 'But it is nothing. Nothing. Nothing at all.'

So it is to take place then, Theodora knew. The picnic will disclose. There will be stuffed eggs, and conversation, and silences, and swords. But the picnic will be made. Already the little wintergarden could not contain the event. It pressed, it brimmed, rustling with the barely suppressed wind of excitement the brown bodies of dead flies.

'A picnic?' Mrs Rapallo said. 'How queer. And how uncomfortable.'

She propelled her words outward like deliberate amethysts, which she then observed, with some pleasure and some distaste, from beneath bluish skin.

'I was never one for the alfresco,' said Mrs Rapallo. 'Life was intended to be lived indoors. At its most intense it smells of gardenias.'

Since the night of the nautilus she had shrunk. But she came. She came to the picnic, still dubious whether grass offered much beyond moisture, and whether the elaborate machinery of the waves would soothe.

'I shall put myself here,' she said, patting an orange rock with scorn.

Mrs Rapallo had to settle her magenta, compose her crimson, tilt her great jaundiced hat, before she could suffer the sun, if only obliquely, from under her parasol.

'There,' she said. 'There is now some design in nature.'

And she sniffed at the red trunk of an offending pine.

Soon the landscape had begun to fit. The air withdrew its obliviousness. It stroked. The sea moulded the human form into tolerant shapes. How far the sun condescended was seen in the face of Katina Pavlou, its open, golden petals, with the dark seeds for eyes. Theodora waited for Katina's eyes to germinate. She watched for the expanding of some mystery that she had already guessed at and rejected.

'If you open your hand I shall tell you a fortune,' said Wetherby as he reached forward and took the fingers of Katina Pavlou.

'No,' she said. 'There is still eating to be done.'

She withdrew her hand. She could not answer for the behaviour of her bones.

'How right you are,' Lieselotte laughed.

She lay on her back, chewing with her small teeth the sweetness from a piece of grass.

'Wetherby cannot resist the telling of fortunes,' Lieselotte said. 'To tell his own fortune in other hands. He is the original interpreter of mirrors. Am I not right?' she said, turned.

'You are always right,' said Wetherby.

But he did not propose to investigate the degrees of hate. Sun destroys self. For the moment he could accept his nothing. He wondered also, a little, at the hot skin, purple-stained, which had just escaped from his own hand.

'Katina! Come on, Katina!' Miss Grigg commanded. 'It is your duty to see that guests are supplied with paper napkins and cardboard plates.'

'Of course,' Katina said.

She took from her skirt the hand that she had held clenched to contain her secret, and which, spread for a fortune, would have palpitated like a leaf.

Theodora put stones, one at each corner, to hold the table-cloth. It was a neat, solemn duty that she liked. There was a bounty hinted at, and a shape, even if ultimately unachieved by human intercourse. Man's machinery fails, she suspected, beside the more sinuous reasoning of the waves. She heard the crimson protest of Mrs Rapallo's parasol drowning in blue, and blue, and still deeper blue.

'My eyes are not made for this,' complained Mrs Rapallo. 'I cannot see. What do you suppose has happened, Theodora Good-man? When I was a girl I could see the gum oozing out of bark. I could watch the red cabbage bugs playing at love. The sun was a ball of fire, at which I could stare without fear or discomfort.'

It is from long looking at a wall, Mrs Rapallo, Theodora would have said, but refrained.

So Mrs Rapallo sulked, and her eyelids oozed, and she tilted her parasol at the sun.

'Let me press you to a sandwidge, Mrs Rapallo,' coaxed Miss Grigg. 'Or a *croaky de poison*. There's nothing like food. And sea adds salt.'

Miss Grigg's enthusiasm ran red under her white twill.

'Picnics,' she said, 'are nice. When I was with the family of the late Colonel de Saumarez, M.B.E., at Winchester, picnics were the order of the day. We used to take our lunch into the forest, to Lymington. The late Colonel was a jolly man. 'E could tell a tale like nobody's business. No one had shot so many tigers, or stuck such pigs, or 'ooked such wopping sharks. I was devoted to 'is kids, Lilian and little 'Enry, though 'Enry went to the pack.'

Miss Grigg fanned a fly away from the niceness over which she presided by right and nature, the egg sandwiches and sausage rolls, the chicken wings and pale aspic prawns. But nastiness always dares. So she frowned, and shooed, and protected the cloth, where her soul lay sliced and open on a cardboard plate.

'Yes. Poor little 'Enry. 'Enry was a love. Used to like to chase the pigs. 'E said the pigs wore combinations. Would you believe it! At Lymington, of course, the wild pigs were tame, not like the ones the Colonel stuck abroad. And Lilian sat beneath the trees, as nice as nice. Lilian was lovely. She took a lord, and turned stout in the end. But what 'appened to 'Enry is something we shall never know. First 'e blows 'is fortune, then 'is brains, in a bedroom in Bayswater. All 'e left was a note on the washstand to say 'e was in 'is right mind. Tt-tt-ttt,' sighed Miss Grigg. 'Countess, can't I tempt you to an egg?'

'Thank you,' said Lieselotte, 'I have eaten.'

'Lord!' said Miss Grigg squarely. 'I 'aven't begun.'

But Lieselotte, Theodora saw, was engulfed in some personal disaster, that was also perhaps little 'Enry's. Lieselotte read the letter on the washstand written in her own familiar writing.

'The castle in which we lived was full of such events,' said Lieselotte. 'They were called a sacred German *Pflicht*.'

'And what is this German *Flick*?' asked Miss Grigg.

'It is something that cannot be explained in any other language. It is a kind of upsurging of the German bowels.'

'Well I never!' said Miss Grigg.

'But I failed to upsurge. Although Rudi handed me the gun himself. He called it the benefit of honour. I couldn't. Even when he dictated the letter I should write.'

'Your 'usband was a wrong 'un. Downright bad,' said Miss Grigg.

Lieselotte fingered bread.

'Only bread is good, Katina Pavlou,' said Lieselotte.

Katina Pavlou did not hear. There was no reason why she should. Sun had undone her bones. Her body had learnt a suppleness of water. Suddenly she bent and mingled.

'You are not eating,' she said. 'You are bored. But the best part is still to come. We have wild strawberries and sour cream.'

She blushed. She would have called him by some intimate name, touching without hands. But since discovering in a book that he was called Lionel Aloysius, she blushed. She was ashamed for him.

'I?' Wetherby asked.

He was not altogether sure. He turned his face. Now the sun was suspect.

Theodora Goodman smiled, knowing that for Wetherby the truth resided in Birmingham. She also heard the squirming of the paper rose. If I am to take and break this child, Wetherby would have said, the suffering will not be mine.

'I was thinking,' Wetherby said.

'Of what?' Katina Pavlou asked.

Oh, well, he supposed, if it was to happen.

'I was thinking,' he said, 'that I had not noticed the two brown moles on the lobe of one of your ears.'

This is so easy, he said. He smiled at the sea. But it was not Wetherby. He smiled for the clerks in parks who expose themselves regularly, in words, on benches.

Katina Pavlou touched the crumbs. 'I hate my moles,' she said.

'But they are so right, Katina Pavlou.'

Wetherby, speaking the right words, could read the smile on Lieselotte's face. It was his own scar, his own hatefulness.

'I hate my moles,' Katina Pavlou said.

As if she could not love enough all that lived and breathed. Theodora knew Katina Pavlou's smile. Trees sprang suddenly from rocks and sand, the first trees. Her arms parted the waves. Katina's face had opened, Theodora saw.

Mrs Rapallo cleared her throat, from a long way down. She stirred. She touched her orange rock, groping for the plush that was not there.

'Moles can be removed,' Mrs Rapallo announced. 'With an electric needle. Painlessly. I remember Maxine Bosanquet had one in an awkward place. Otherwise she was perfect. Maxine was famous for her skin. And pearls. Pearls seemed to feast off her. Many of us lent her our necklaces to be refreshed. What a glow they returned with! I was always death to pearls,' Mrs Rapallo said.

She shook her shoulders for some unpleasantness, both far and close. She felt, and turned. Painfully prizing open her eyelids, she looked and said, 'I guessed as much. The monster is approaching. After all.'

'Why, yes, it is the General,' said Katina Pavlou.

Under a handkerchief that he had knotted into a cap, the General flamed. The air was full of displeasure, Theodora heard, as he sweated closer through the trees. Twigs were snapping. Sand slurred. The rock suggested great gurglings of subterranean water, as if the sea were protesting in the belly of the earth. Over his waistcoat he wore, to contain himself, or to celebrate the occasion, an enormous gold chain.

'General, you are on fire,' Lieselotte called. 'Come, and we shall put you out with crushed strawberries.'

'I am in no condition,' wheezed Sokolnikov, as he pressed between the last trees.

'At your age you should take care,' said Lieselotte, quietly squeezing the head off an ant.

He heard. He stood on the edge of the clearing, handling himself tenderly. He was conscious of his ridiculousness. For a moment Theodora feared that, possessed by some demon of jollity, Sokolnikov might crow. If he had lost his paper nose, the cap was still knotted on his glistening fat.

'Oh, I shall do nothing to shame you,' said Alyosha Sergei. 'I shall not die.'

No, remarked Mrs Rapallo, obliquely under her parasol, no, she said, he was not the kind.

'Come,' Alyosha Sergei,' Katina Pavlou said, and went, 'you shall sit beside me, because I love you.'

And she did. Now Katina Pavlou loved the world. She reached upward like the black and serious branches of the pines, outward like the all-embracing sea, she was self-contained as rock. See, I can see, her eyes said, as she touched the ridiculous arm of Sokolnikov. She could afford to love his ridiculousness, but he recognized the touch of charity.

'Thank you, Varvara, you are kind,' said Alyosha Sergei solemnly. 'I think also you have grown.'

'I am wearing higher heels,' Katina said.

Even if it only half explained, it was necessary to say. Dry words can nourish.

It was as necessary as food. Theodora knew, pushing towards Sokolnikov the hard-boiled eggs. It was necessary that Sokolnikov should feel the final twinge. It was necessary that Katina Pavlou should discover fire. And Theodora Goodman, watching the charade move with all the hopes and hesitations of the human mechanism, knew that because she loved and pitied, the humiliation and the pain were also necessarily hers.

'Thank you, Ludmilla, for your kindness,' said Sokolnikov, accepting eggs.

Today his voice was old, and he looked with surprise to see in his hands eggs. He would beat together in his hands, to crack, two of the hard-boiled eggs, but it was no less strange. The cap cocked to listen. He could not have been more amazed if the sound had come from billiard balls.

'On the estate of a female relative, Anna Stepanovna, who died in what may have been the necessary revolution, who shall say, there was an old man called Grishka, who had a little hen,' said the voice of Sokolnikov.

But it was not the hour of much attention, so nobody listened to Alyosha Sergei. Sea lulled the bodies into fresh attitudes of anticipation, sleep, and melancholy. Directly under the sun the rocks, orange and stubborn, were painfully oblivious. Mrs Rapallo, clawing through kid, felt the prick of limpets. Sun fell through the slats of the pines, or revolved in catherine wheels on the inner flaps of the eyelids. Lieselotte counted many such revolving planets. Contentment was close, and coloured, and hot as sand.

'I believe you are going to dislike me, Miss Goodman,' Wetherby said.

He turned on her, on his elbows, his full face that was reminiscent of a pale 'cello.

'I have reached the age of tolerance,' said Theodora. 'It is agreeably compact. Everything fits in, in time.'

'This little hen was loved by Grishka,' said Alyosha Sergei, who was already making mountains out of eggshells. 'She had a cunning eye. She would sit on his chest, and pick grains of corn from out of his beard.'

'I would still accuse you of disliking me, Miss Goodman,' said Wetherby, 'if I did not dislike myself.'

'Then, if it is that way,' Theodora said.

But because she did not lay on his forehead the cool hand of sympathy, which was his due, he went among the trees. She could hear him breaking twigs.

'And when they held her up without her feathers, ready for the pot, as Anna Stepanovna insisted, although she was only a stringy little hen, old Grishka cried.'

'Oh, chook, chook, chook! Dearest General, you have been telling a story,' said Lieselotte, 'and we have lost the thread.'

'I flattered myself I was entertaining the company with a few reminiscences, however humble,' the General said.

Mrs Rapallo held her glove to shield her face, of which the skin was stretched tighter than a drum.

Theodora watched Katina Pavlou go among the trees. She could see her white, crushed skirt. She could not hear, but in her own throat Theodora felt the words.

'Why have you gone away from us?' Katina Pavlou asked. 'You are hurt, or irritated.'

Theodora felt the words. She saw the face of Katina Pavlou, where the sun fell between the trunks of the serious pines, the face waiting to give some token of love, or even to receive hurt.

'I went, Katina, because I did not like myself,' Wetherby said.

Theodora knew the words. She watched him take Katina Pavlou's fingers, and read his own mind into the purple stains.

'I shall like you,' said Katina Pavlou. 'If you will let me.'

'I should love you, Katina,' Wetherby said.

He watched her fingers tremble in his hand.

'There is no need,' said Katina Pavlou. 'If you will let me, I shall love you enough. If you will let me show you.'

'I don't think you understand,' he said, 'all that it implies.'

'Why should I understand?' Katina Pavlou said. 'I *know*!'

She could not love him enough. Theodora could not bear the beating in her throat. She was oppressed by a heavy music, a secret darkness of the trees, in which the sun just failed to glisten. Theodora watched Katina Pavlou's face in Wetherby's hands.

'There,' said Wetherby. 'If you cannot see.'

'But I see! Why should I not? Oh, but it is good to kiss. The world is good.'

'Oh, but the world is sick,' Wetherby said.

He began to cough for some afterthought.

'You shall see as I do. Now it will be different. Because I shall love you,' said Katina Pavlou.

'Yes, you shall love me,' said Wetherby.

But he began to walk away among the trees.

'What's got into Wetherby? 'E's a queer one,' said Miss Grigg. 'And thin. Wetherby wants feedin' up. Look at 'im goin' off. A regular scarecrow. Perhaps 'e's remembered or forgotten something.'

Lieselotte laughed. 'Wetherby has forgotten what he wants. He has gone to look for it,' she said.

Miss Grigg sucked her teeth. 'Some people never know,' she said. 'Some people never know there's nothing like food. Now, Mrs Rapallo, won't you pick a wing of chicken? It's a pity your girl Gloria couldn't come.'

Theodora heard the stiff flutes miss, as Mrs Rapallo moved her parasol, dragging the crimson shadow across her face.

'Donna Gloria,' said Lieselotte, behind her eyelids and their fierce stars, 'was otherwise engaged in Rome.'

'In Monte,' Mrs Rapallo corrected.

'Mrs Rapallo, you say, in Monte!'

'The Principessa arrived on the coast three or four days ago,' said Mrs Rapallo. 'She will drive over one day for lunch.'

'In the blue Delage,' said Lieselotte.

'With the lacquered woodwork and the monograms,' added Miss Grigg with mounting rapture. 'And the electric lighter, and the vase for roses.'

'And her mother's monstrous egotism,' said the General, who was crushing eggs.

But Mrs Rapallo, who had in her day withstood the blows of marble and the eyes of children, Mrs Rapallo did not hear.

'My daughter's rank,' she said, 'requires certain appurtenances.'

'My daughter's ice,' said the General, whose humility had begun to glitter.

'Let us pick up the pieces, Miss Goodman,' suggested Lieselotte.

She began, with her small deft hands, which at times could appear innocent of motive, to gather the sodden cardboard, the fragments of food, and the emotional shreds of the paper napkins.

Then the picnic is finished, Theodora realized, rolling the hot napkins into a neat ball.

But not the sea. The sea had stretched out into the flat serenity of afternoon. The sea no longer folded and unfolded, offering between spasms the possibility of a drowned face. Blue opened and opened, fetched up the distance, quenched thought and metal. Feebly resisting the moment of transparence, a paper napkin that someone had let float stroked the noses of fish.

'Let us go now,' they said.

'Yes,' they sighed. 'Let us go.'

They took the baskets. It was a long stretch of sand, and between trees.

'Katina, Katina, we are going,' called Miss Grigg.

'Yes, I am coming,' Katina Pavlou said.

She followed the flat figures, but at a distance, because other lives are flat and external. Katina Pavlou trailed her hand against the trunks of trees.

'What is it, Katina?' Theodora Goodman asked.

Though fingers told that questions were superfluous. The hands held the answer. The hands were hot.

'It is nothing, Miss Goodman,' Katina Pavlou smiled. 'Look at this blue. I am blind.'

Then they walked. Theodora knew that they had reached perfection. She felt Katina Pavlou, who was heavy and warm with some inner perfection of her own. But perfection, alas, is breakable, whether it is marble, or terracotta, or the more fragile groups of human statuary.

'How far is Africa, do you suppose?' Katina Pavlou asked.

'Far enough,' Theodora Goodman said.

II

OFTEN enough Theodora wondered whether it was time for her to go. There were days when faces did not open. She heard the hedge of knitting needles in the lounge. In the strict space of her *chambre modeste*, where *confort moderne* refused at times to flow, she opened the suitcase and smelled its emptiness. There was also the sheets of the *Corriere della Sera* she had used after losing her shoe-bag in Siena. But Theodora did not leave. The melancholy fact of emptiness was not enough. She waited for some act that still had to be performed.

Au mois d'avril il est gai, au mois de juin on mène une vie assez tranquille, au mois d'octobre l'air fait du bien, Monsieur Durand used to say, to meet emergencies.

Monsieur Durand suggested seasons with the bland conviction of his own brochure. Because there are certain conventions of expression and behaviour to be observed, even by those guests who look out of windows, or yawn, or thoughtfully trace the veins of a plant.

That is all very well, and true, Monsieur Durand, Theodora would have said, but you forget how you bared your teeth one morning in the glass, and wondered whether their desperation would bite, or whether your tongue, branching suddenly and peculiarly from your mouth, might not be uprooted by the hand like any other fungus, all this you forget, Monsieur Durand, and that I saw, and how we agreed, in silence, that it was too insignificant to remember.

But Theodora did not say. She folded her receipt, for another week, gravely, edge to edge, and went outside, because it was inevitable, into the *jardin exotique*.

Pervading the stiff, and at the same time fleshy, forms of the garden, the morning was bright, cheerful, tinkling. The garden gave up no secrets, if it had secrets to give. Brooms had made correct patterns on the gravel, and the natural occurrences of dew and mist had sponged the pig's face and washed the aloe down. There was no visible disorder, except that on the benches the occasional droppings of birds blinded with their whiteness, and from a cactus sword hung what was either a spider's web or an unfinished doily.

Theodora looked closer to discover which.

'You are quite right, Miss Goodman,' Wetherby said. 'It is six afternoons from the life of the Demoiselles Bloch. Doilies do escape.'

'Oh,' said Theodora. 'Yes.'

She was neither prepared nor altogether pleased. She picked the doily off the cactus, as if it were her duty to hide the meeker weaknesses of others. Reddening a little, she put it in her bag, to return later in the morning to its rightful reticule.

'The Demoiselles Bloch,' she said, 'often have trouble with their things.'

'How right, how right,' said Wetherby.

He was reading the Continental *Daily Mail*. This morning he was a thin young man in a tweed coat, of which the elbows had leather patches. Under the thick forelock of nondescript hair, which gave him the expression of a goat that prefers to consume tins, his face absorbed news, while remaining superior to events. Wetherby was immune.

'What is the news?' asked Theodora, because it was the least she could do to cover her dislike.

'The body of a dancer has been discovered, in a parcel, in a cloakroom of the London tube,' Wetherby said. 'The Führer is annexing somewhere else, and half America has turned to dust. Now, Miss Goodman, shall you go or stay?'

'Then you do sometimes relate the personal to the universal,' Theodora said.

'I am sometimes forced to, by the people who disapprove,' Wetherby replied. 'But oh Lord, it is early. It is too early to plunge. My stomach is full of breakfast. Let us observe instead the advantages of our zinc surroundings. It is all that a garden ought to be, neat and not native, resourcefully planned, as opposed to dankly imaginative. Preserve me from the swish of dead leaves and urns full of torn letters.'

He was pleased by his own facetiousness, Theodora heard. Its bright metal cannoned down the paths.

'But you are not pleased, Miss Goodman,' Wetherby said. 'You will not be pleased while I am I.'

His squamous hands were increasing her disgust.

'I could not be more indifferent,' Theodora said, 'if you chose to be *x* or *y*.'

Algebra, she felt, with Lou, would remain her chiefest torture.

'Tell me something, Miss Goodman. Tell me the truth. If I could have loved Katina Pavlou just as she leapt from your imagination, clothed in white, and all the nostalgia of what has never happened, then it might have been different.'

But now Theodora trembled for the dark. Now the garden raised its swords. She avoided Wetherby, but Wetherby pursued.

'Perhaps in different circumstances I would have lain with my head in your lap, and discussed Tennyson and Morris. But the escalators have carried us apart. And now, Miss Goodman, the times have turned sour. I think I am right in saying of love that the most one can expect is the logical conclusion.'

Theodora laughed. Now she could not control her dark moustache. It was a fierce and hateful thing. But the eyes of Wetherby were clear as mirrors.

'Not that one does not continue to hope,' he said. 'I am obsessed.'

'Yes, you will continue,' Theodora laughed. 'You will love your obsession. You will love the faces of mirrors. You will love your own anxiety.'

Sitting on the bench in the *jardin exotique*, Theodora Goodman and Wetherby looked at each other, like two people coming out of a tunnel, rediscovering each other's features, as if there had been no exchange of darkness. He was a pale young man in a tweed coat. She was a sallow spinster of forty-five.

Wetherby looked at his wrist.

'Soon it will be time for the postman,' he said. 'I am expecting a letter from Muriel Leese-Leese. She keeps me here, you know, ostensibly for my health, though actually so that she may enjoy the pleasure of torturing herself by correspondence. She is lost without her daily twinge.'

'And after that,' said Theodora, 'you will find it is time for lunch. How the morning passes.'

Wetherby folded the *Daily Mail*.

'I shall not be here for lunch,' he said. 'I am going to walk along the coast with Katina Pavlou, to the round tower which has some connection with Napoleon.'

'It has, they say,' Theodora said.

The tower to which the Demoiselles Bloch walked occasionally, in strong boots and overcoats. Theodora herself had never been as far as the tower, but she suspected it. Especially now. She suspected the dark smell of damp stone and possibly a dead bird. She loathed the folded body of the dead bird, and the maggots in its eyes.

Disgust knotted her hands.

'All right. It was no choice of mine,' Wetherby said. 'None of it.'

As if he had noticed the twitching of her dark moustache.

Alone, Theodora listened to the morning pass. She walked in the garden. She would have chosen an acacia, of which the green shade covers with superior benevolence, but the garden did not cater for emotional states, least of all desperation. The garden encouraged exposure, and then contained it, with all the indifference of zinc.

There were greater commotions too. There was the commotion of the electric current. Miss Grigg stood in the hall. She held the electric iron. She held it for Monsieur Durand to see, as if it might explain something of which exasperation was incapable. Miss Grigg said that in no hotel of any standing, in no hotel in which she had ever stayed, had the electric current been cut off quite so frequently. Miss Goodman would bear her out, that such things did not happen in hotels. It was not possible for ladies to press their slips.

Monsieur Durand looked sadly at Miss Grigg's iron, which did not after all explain, any more than words.

'It is the municipal power,' said Monsieur Durand, 'that does not for the moment circulate, but which will circulate again.'

In the lounge, under the pink lampshade, a hand was practising a gavotte, each note white and separate that it picked up.

Do you know, Miss Grigg, Theodora wanted to say, the music has not begun yet?

But it was not possible, just as it is not possible to convince certain faces that a murder is being done in the next room.

So instead she said, 'Yes, Miss Grigg. It is just as Monsieur Durand says. He is not the municipal power. And the current will circulate again.'

So that Miss Grigg was cut. She was left holding her inarticulate iron. Her face was flat and functionless.

'But all the same, one expects,' she said, 'to find what the prospectus puts in words. In the best 'otels. In the 'Otel Excelsior, at Chamonix, they even 'ad an electric device for pushin' the snow off the window sills.'

Theodora listened to the hand, round the corner in the lounge, pick up each white, separate note of the gavotte. Each note trembled tentatively, fell, was gathered again, to glisten. The music flowed into a purer music, whiter and lighter.

'Katina,' called Miss Grigg. 'You remember the 'Otel Excelsior? And the little trouts? Trouts with their tails in their mouths.'

'No, Grigg, it was the Hôtel des Alpes,' said Katina Pavlou round the corner in the lounge.

The voice blurred, as the music doubled on its underwater self, with the glistening surety of snow water, a bluish white, joyful and perpetual as mountain water. Katina Pavlou lifted her hands and the music fell, sure, and pure, and painfully transparent. So that any possible disaster of age or experience must drown in music. Disasters, the music implied, are reserved for observers, the drowning drown. Caught in this iciness of music, Theodora felt the breath stop in her throat. She went inside the little wintergarden and closed the door.

'It is difficult to escape from music. Music pursues.'

It was General Sokolnikov, of course, who sat beneath a palm. In the steamy atmosphere of the little wintergarden the palm relaxed in rubber strips, as the General ponderously licked a postage stamp.

'You must realize, Ludmilla, that you cannot close doors.'

It was true. Even in the little wintergarden music sluiced leaf and frond. It trembled in distinct drops on the pots of maidenhair.

'*You* must realize, General,' said Theodora, 'that something has happened, or will.'

She held her front, afraid that her dress might not ultimately contain her agitation.

'As if I didn't,' said Sokolnikov. 'The municipal authorities have cut the municipal current. It is a habit that they have.'

Then it is not possible, Theodora knew, it is not possible to tell.

And now the General was engaged in the act of extraction. He was easing the stamp from his tongue.

'I was writing to my ex-wife, Edith,' he said.

Not without some distaste for his tongue, some suspicion of fish. Carefully parting the leaves of a begonia, Alyosha Sergei Sokolnikov spat.

'We have adopted this peculiar convention of two people exchanging letters,' the General said, past an excess of tongue. 'We describe our digestions and the weather. In this way we cherish what remains of an unfortunate relationship. In this way it is easier to impose the reality one chooses.'

'Then, there are many?' said Theodora.

'What questions you ask! Though you, of course, are different.'

His voice hesitated to disperse air. He made her thin, though she was, she realized. Her dress stirred only in a wind of music and words.

'Yes,' said the General softly. 'You, Ludmilla, you are an illusion. You died years ago in the forests of Russia.'

She was almost ready to agree.

'Then, thank you, Alyosha Sergei,' she said, 'thank you for accepting this illusion.'

'Oh, illusions are necessary. It is necessary to accept. I shall tell you a secret. Incidentally. I was a major once. Also a colonel. Perhaps.'

'Then you have deceived us, *Major*?' Theodora said.

'Deceit, Ludmilla, is a wincing word. I was a general in spirit, always. If I was not in fact, it was due to misfortune, and the superior connections of my subordinate officers. But how I have lived, in spirit. Such bugles!'

There was no further note in the Hôtel du Midi. It was quite

236

still. How long this might continue seemed to Theodora to depend on Sokolnikov and the furniture.

'In time it will be time for lunch,' he sighed, examining the envelope as if he doubted the address.

'I do not expect to be here for lunch,' Theodora said. 'I am going out. I am going to put on my hat.'

'Why?' asked Sokolnikov, 'why put on your hat if your haste is so indecent?'

'Alyosha Sergei,' Theodora said, 'you do not know.'

So that the windows quivered, and a grey cloud, blowing out of Corsica.

'Oh, but I do,' said Alyosha Sergei.

He sat in a deflated heap.

'They have taken the coast road,' he said. 'They are walking towards the tower which has some connection with Napoleon. He has taken her hand because she expects him to. And although his hand is dead, she is moved, because the music is still moving in her own. It does not much matter whether it is he. Because she has chosen. She has chosen this as the moment of experience. And experience has a glaze. It has not yet *cracked*,' the General almost shouted.

Theodora Goodman began to circumnavigate the furniture.

'At least my feet can move,' Theodora said.

'Yes,' said Sokolnikov. 'And I do not wish to deter you. You can also create the illusion of other people, but once created, they choose their own realities.'

All that afternoon Theodora Goodman, walking hatless between houses, past trees, near the fragments of stone walls from which lizards looked, heard the words of Sokolnikov. Like rubber they departed and returned. Now her motives were equally elastic, because Sokolnikov had made her doubt. So she could not take the direct road. Roads did not lead through the infinite landscape in which she hesitated, least of all the obvious red coast road. As the town thinned out into advertisements and tins, she wandered higher, where the needle turrets of signorial villas were strangled by roses, and the night club still wore its daylight tarnish. She walked on the edge of the lavender hills.

Here the air had begun to rub. Mist strayed along the skin, dissolved the substance of rock and tree, and confused the intentions still further. Many little anxious paths dispersed through the stiff heather. Goats sprang, scattering their dung. If I were to cross this ridge, she said, suddenly abrupt with purpose in the afternoon, I shall see the stone tower, if this also has not dispersed.

From the pink house beside the poplars the woman in the periwinkle dress watched some *Anglaise* making a walk without a hat. Outside the house the rosemary bushes were spread with shirts. The woman in the periwinkle dress had come outside to inspect her washing. Now she felt it carefully for damp. She twitched a sheet that twigs had made mountainous.

Was it this way to the tower? Theodora asked.

She stood by the gate of the pink house. She waited to hear words. The woman's arms were white with flour. Theodora waited for one word, out of a lost epoch, shaped and baked in kitchens.

Yes, said the periwinkle woman, it was this way to the tower, it was past the olive field and the well, though it was the habit of people to make this walk by road.

The woman pointed with her white arm. There was no doubt that the strayed *Anglaise* would find the tower. But strange, the strange *Anglaise*. The woman gathered up her washing. She carried the armful of stiff white sheets into her square pink house, out of the mist.

Theodora walked straight. A smell of soap and baking had lessened the influence of Sokolnikov. She would hedge the olive field, as the woman had advised. She walked almost joyfully. Beside the field she heard the great, sounding depth of the open well, of which the stone lip had sucked moisture from the air. The tower too would have filled with mist, and the intolerable, pervasive smell of crushed nettles.

From the spine of the hill Theodora saw the tower. It was strong and solitary and white. But whether its thick walls enclosed, in addition to damp, the smell of nettles, and possibly a dead bird, some personal exaltation or despair, was as obscure as the alleged moment in which Napoleon split the historical darkness of that part of the coast.

But I have come here for a purpose, Theodora said, if only to be confronted with my own inadequacy. At a distance her mouth contracted under the coldly sensual lips of stone. She began to go down.

She went quickly, quicker, now that she saw. She saw the solitary figure, moving among rocks, away from the tower, out of her line of vision. She could not identify, but she could hope, but she could run. A bird whirred out of the heather. She was hardly conscious of the intervening stones, or the ankles in which she trusted, though these were thick as sticks. Some animal, rabbit or hare, cowered and leapt away in terror hearing her torn breath.

Then she began to call with what was left.

'Katina! Katina! Katina Pavlou!' Theodora called.

Out of the blur of wind and running, on the now settled shoulder of the hill, the face of Katina Pavlou turned.

'Why, Miss Goodman, it is you,' Katina Pavlou said.

Touching with her feet the obvious red coast road, Theodora Goodman gathered her awkwardness.

'Yes,' she said. 'I came.'

'How funny you look. And without a hat,' Katina Pavlou said.

Her voice was cold. Her voice was as cold as stone.

'I left on the spur of the moment. And I walked farther than I thought. Now I am out of breath,' Theodora Goodman said.

They began to walk along the coast road which would lead eventually to houses.

'The mist is unexpected, I believe,' Theodora said, 'for this time of year.'

'The mist?' said Katina Pavlou coldly.

Her head was turned, so that she was looking at the sea. Her hair hung, in some fresh way it had been done, Theodora Goodman saw, for some purpose. The hair, the body of Katina Pavlou, were conscious and intent.

'Oh, let us walk. Let us get it over quickly,' Katina Pavlou said. 'This is a hateful road.'

She walked quicker. She walked too quickly. Katina Pavlou was going over, Theodora saw, she was going over all the time on the new high heels that she had begun to wear.

'Katina dear,' Theodora Goodman said.

She took the cold, dead hand, that she would begin to warm.

Her face began to fumble with words, and a rather stupid kind of happiness, that was also painful.

'Yes, Katina,' she said, 'this is always a long and intolerable stretch of road, but it is not interminable.'

I am quite, quite stupid, Theodora felt, I can feel it on my face.

But Katina Pavlou looked at the sea. And along the red coast road the enclosed automobiles pressed towards expensive pleasures. Faces eyed for a moment people who walk.

'Have you ever been inside the tower, Miss Goodman?' Katina Pavlou asked.

And now Theodora felt inside her hand the hand coming alive. She felt the impervious lips of stone forming cold words. She dreaded, in anticipation, the scream of nettles.

'No,' said Theodora, 'I have not been inside the tower. I imagine there is very little to see.'

'There is nothing, nothing,' Katina said. 'There is a smell of rot and emptiness.'

But no less painful in its emptiness, Theodora felt.

'Still, I am glad,' said Katina Pavlou, speaking through her white face. 'You know, Miss Goodman, when one is glad for something that has happened, something nauseating and painful, that one did not suspect. It is better finally to know.'

Under the still skin of Katina Pavlou's face the blood had not yet begun again to flow. Since yesterday, Theodora saw, the bones had come.

'And what has happened in the meantime?' Katina Pavlou asked, as they re-entered the territory of Dubonnet and Suze.

'I doubt whether I am better informed than you,' Theodora replied. 'There was, of course, the failure of the municipal power. Here is Miss Grigg. Judging from her appearance darkness will reign.'

'Yes, imagine, Katina,' said Miss Grigg, who was standing squarely on the step. 'How we shall manage to fork our food into our mouths is something only the Almighty knows.'

But Monsieur Durand said, 'There shall be lamps and candles.' And there were.

There were lamps and candles. There was the legendary light

of oil and wax. There was the light of light. Now that Theodora had stitched her skirt, which had torn on a bush somewhere on a hillside, and washed away the dust, and the water had tightened round the edges of her face, she watched with pleasure the renewed objects of the dining-room. She did not eat much. She watched Katina Pavlou scooping the avocado. By lamplight, movement was smooth, the flesh as suave as avocados. The eyelids on Katina Pavlou's face were still and golden, but uncommunicative. Tonight the faces at their separate tables did not communicate, and Theodora was relieved that they should remain contained, whether by exhaustion or some instinct for secrecy.

Only Mrs Rapallo's table had not flowered. Here the light shrivelled into shadow and the upright box of Ryvita, with which normally Mrs Rapallo made havoc of silences.

'Where is Mrs Rapallo?' Theodora asked.

'*Elle n'est pas descendue,*' replied *le petit*. '*Elle ne mange guère. Enfin, ça ne vaut pas la peine de descendre, et quand on risque de se casser la figure.*'

Scarcely pausing in his saraband of plates, his body moved with the smoothness of contempt and custom. *Le petit* had pinched off a cigarette and stuck it behind his ear. He had a merciless continuity. And Mrs Rapallo's Ryvita stood still.

'Thank you. Yes, I shall take coffee,' Theodora agreed.

Because to refuse *le petit* required daring. Or to dare the stairs, she considered, after the wry, medicinal coffee, the inhabited undergrowth of Mrs Rapallo's room.

On the whole, she knew, there was less daring than duty in her knuckle.

'Mrs Rapallo?' she knocked. 'It is Theodora Goodman. May I come in?'

Through some distance and the flat door she heard the sounds of revival.

'Theodora who?' said Mrs Rapallo. 'Oh. Yes. You. Come inside, Theodora Goodman. I shall, of course, be glad.'

'What is the matter, Mrs Rapallo?' asked Theodora as her feet slid across the faces of old envelopes.

'I am sick, Theodora Goodman,' Mrs Rapallo said.

'Oh,' said Theodora. 'Where?'

'Nowhere in particular,' Mrs Rapallo said. 'That is to say, *je suis ennuyée, je suis ennuyée un tout petit peu de tout.*'

'That is not fatal,' said Theodora.

'Well,' replied Mrs Rapallo, 'I am not sure.'

Mrs Rapallo lolled, both her head and voice. It is unusual, Theodora Goodman felt, for Mrs Rapallo, whose words are as stiff as biscuits. But it was not possible to deny the sinuous expression of floating in Mrs Rapallo's eyes.

'There are ways and means, of course,' said Mrs Rapallo with a smooth smile, arranging her scalp where the hair had been.

Then Theodora remembered *le petit paquet sur la commode en marbre*.

'There are ways and means,' said Mrs Rapallo, 'just as there are variegated tulips and facial surgery.'

Without looking on the *commode en marbre*, behind the silver *bonbonnière*, Theodora expected to hear the *petit paquet* rustle. Instinct suggested she should rescue, if the tulip-coloured stream had not already carried Mrs Rapallo out of reach. So she stood straight, and wrenched from her head a platitude once the property of Fanny Parrott.

'Oh, but Mrs Rapallo, you have so much to look forward to,' Theodora said. 'And now that your daughter has arrived. Surely the Principessa will drive over one day soon in the blue Delage?'

Mrs Rapallo composed her skin.

'It is time, Theodora Goodman, that you and I agreed that the Principessa does not exist.'

And Theodora remembered how the Canova group had intervened.

'It is a pity,' said Mrs Rapallo, 'because Gloria had poise, and an epistolary style. Her use of words was almost plastic. After dropping the letters in the box, I could not bear to take away my hand. I was jealous of the iron flap that swallowed Gloria's letters down. How I longed for them to return to me, as they did, of course, almost at once. On such occasions I would hide behind a tamarisk, between the post office and the *papeterie*, so that the trembling of my gloves would not be noticed. Gloria was lovelier then, far more brilliant than even I had conceived, in creating her. And unlike any child of the bowels, entirely mine.'

'I cannot believe,' said Theodora.

She had begun to doubt, in fact, whether Queen Marie of Rumania.

'What do you believe?' Mrs Rapallo asked.

'I do not know.'

Because now that she swam in Mrs Rapallo's tulip-coloured stream, reason and motive were rinsed out.

'You must relax, Theodora Goodman,' said Mrs Rapallo. 'You must relax and float. You will find that figures will evolve, squares, chains, and galops. Sometimes you will place one hand on your hip, sometimes you will feel the hand of your partner in the small of the back. But believe me, the essential is to relax.'

'Yes, yes,' Theodora cried, made anxious by such gyrations in a full room. 'But does Rapallo come in?'

'Oh, yes, he does. Very definitely, yes. On a Thursday morning. They opened the door of the hall. He was selling a patent medicine. He undressed me with his eyes. I was not unwilling. I had fallen for his boots and his sadness. I fell. I fell.'

Mrs Rapallo's teeth bit the pieces.

'I came to ten years later,' she said, 'on an iron bedstead, in a cheap hotel in Munich. All he had left behind was a pair of yellow gloves, of which he had been proud, rolled in a ball on the carpet. It was a naked moment, Theodora Goodman, naked as hell.'

In self-preservation Theodora looked for some other object, stuffed bird or *compotier*, on which to concentrate till Elsie Rapallo was once more clothed.

'However,' Mrs Rapallo said, 'as I had been endowed with physical agility and mental whalebone, I continued to appear *dans le monde*. I kidded this same *monde* into accepting me for my wealth and wit, though the one had disappeared, and the other had been damaged. In return I was allowed to suffer the knout in all the best drawing-rooms in Europe.'

She touched her bones under the sheet, as if she were surprised not to find them broken.

'At a pinch I wrote my own invitations,' Mrs Rapallo said, 'and passed through many doors of which I should never have had the entrée. In this way I have heard the smiles open on the faces of royalty, and stood so close to the making of history that I have been suffocated by the stink.'

Elsie Rapallo dipped on her tulip-coloured stream that did not respect substance as it flowed. Theodora trod the sodden faces of old letters and the yellow smiles of photographs. Grazed by a random amethyst, dazed by the bobbing of a wax apple that would not drown, she accepted the cardboard collapse of Mrs Rapallo's room. Since it was the natural thing to flow, she flowed.

'It is lovely, Mrs Rapallo,' Theodora said.

'But it is not always like this. Sometimes it is a nothing. I hate its paper.'

For a moment of terror she was afraid she might have lost her passport, and groped across the *commode en marbre* to hear the rustle of the *petit paquet*.

'Sometimes,' Mrs Rapallo smiled, now that she was reassured.

'Sometimes also you sleep,' Theodora soothed.

'She does by fits and starts,' said Mrs Rapallo, her same slack smile.

She settled the sheet, that seemed to stir with a separate will.

'*Dors, mon cœur,*' she coaxed. '*Dors, Mignon.*'

She held herself tenderly, smoothing the invisible recalcitrance.

'The hands of monkeys, Theodora Goodman, are what you would call inquisitive,' Mrs Rapallo said.

Theodora Goodman finally left what remained of Mrs Rapallo. She herself felt the monkeying of sleep. Her face was drawn out. She could not lie too soon on her own narrow bed, stretched thin and straight as a dead saint.

Sleep stretched the thin grey passages of the Hôtel du Midi, or rounded them into grottoes, of which the walls lapped elastically. Skin is after all no protection against communicating bedrooms. *Ouai, Mademoiselle, c'est la peau qui m'échappe, la peau que je ne touche jamais. Ouai, Henriette, et qui n'existe plus,* because, *chère vache,* it is a tango pure and not so simple. Monsieur Durand has also discovered this. It is a tango that whips with its braces as required, the meeker shoulders, waiting whole mornings to wince. *Non, non, non, je n'en peux plus, mais, si, si.* In this way muscular candles sweat. Not the poreless skins of paper. *Vous voyez, Mademoiselle, comme je souffre, comme je suis lié à mon propre brochure, que toutes les saisons ont le même air d'enfer*. They also offer plates.

Theodora Goodman's feet touched the brass bar at the bottom of her bed at approximately 11:35. She confirmed this by the oddly familiar face of a little travelling clock she had inherited from her mother.

There are still whole slabs of sleep, said her dry mouth, whole slabs to be consumed.

She lay and listened to the stirring of the wallpaper, the mouths of paper roses open and close.

'Lamplight changes you,' he said. 'I can watch your heart beat.'

'Like the *ingénue* in the tower?'

Lieselotte's laugh stripped the silence.

'No, Wetherby, no,' Lieselotte laughed. 'Let us accept our bodies as they are.'

'She, at least, had the decency to be impressed.'

'She does not yet know herself. She has not explored her own depths.'

'Your trouble, Lieselotte, is that you hanker continually after a lost innocence you will never find. I have watched you paint a picture. I have seen you grope after some original shape that you have almost forgotten. Don't go. Why should you be afraid?'

'I am afraid,' said Lieselotte, 'that I may do you violence if I stay.'

Hell has its words, Theodora heard, as she trod deeper water beneath her brass bar. But it is too late to hate, she sighed, it is far too late. Far away a mouth of glass bit the darkness. This way words finally shatter, or the envelope that protects human personality.

'Miss Goodman, oh, Miss Goodman,' Theodora heard.

Words sucking her back to the surface struck her with a dry gust. She sat up straight in bed. She was oblong and straight. Suddenness had made her function on a hinge.

'Miss Goodman, something has happened,' said Lieselotte. 'You must come.'

But she was still hinged.

'You must come at once. Something terrible,' Lieselotte said. 'You must come quick.'

How beautiful she is now, Theodora saw. As if some terror has melted wax. Fear flowed in Lieselotte's transparent face. Her gestures and her hair streamed. But her eyes were a dark, fixed terror. Then it is, said Theodora, something terrible and strange. And the air is branching, she saw.

'Yes, do please come quickly,' Lieselotte cried. 'Do not you understand? I tell you, I tell you there is a fire.'

Now, in fact, you could touch the grey branches of the air. Paper roses were dying on their stems. Theodora felt for conviction and her slippers.

'Can't you see?' Lieselotte cried. 'The fire!'

Terror was streaming on her wax hair. But Theodora's gestures were wood. She watched the revival of roses, how they glowed, glowing and blowing like great clusters of garnets on the live hedge.

'Oh, please, please, let us do something,' Lieselotte said.

'Have you informed the *pompiers*?'

Because Theodora Goodman had not yet caught. She was filled with a solid purpose. Her handkerchief sachet must be reached. Whether or not the *pompiers*, and Lieselotte's recitative.

'I have never seen fire run,' Lieselotte cried. 'It ran across the carpet. If I could find him. After the lamp broke. If I could see his face. After the words smashed, in a moment of glass. After the fire. And now, Wetherby, Miss Goodman, Wetherby is dead. I have killed him.'

Theodora Goodman had to reach the handkerchief sachet.

'There is a garnet ring,' she said, 'that was left me by my mother.'

She took in her hand the small cool stone.

'Then we can do nothing?' asked the dead voice of Lieselotte.

Her voice was grey smoke.

'Do? Yes, we shall do. Lieselotte?' Theodora called.

We shall do, Theodora heard her own thin voice promising smoke. But where and who was Lieselotte was also problematical.

Theodora trod through smoke.

'Lieselotte?' she called.

But she was calling fire.

She was alone now, in the passage of a hotel, of which wall-paper rejected a long imposed flatness. Walls whipped. All the violence of fire was contained in the hotel. It tossed, whether hatefully or joyfully, it tossed restraint to smoke. Theodora ran, breathing the joy or hatred of fire. She was not certain where. She heard the desperate cockroach pop under foot. Her own report, she supposed, would not be so round or, authorities said, final.

Then the night was thick with quiet stars.

'Ahhhhh,' said the voices. *'En voilà encore un.'*

Theodora suspected regret.

She saw the white faces, or the crowd face, breathing the fire. There are moments when faces are interchangeable. It was one of those. Sparks shot and fell. The flat, flower faces bent on their emotions, swaying to receive some strange pollen of fire.

'Il n'y a pas d'enfants là-dedans?' asked the crowd.

Because children are best.

'Il n'y a pas de mères?'

When the wind ran, they shivered with regret or fear.

Theodora Goodman put the garnet ring on its usual finger, below the joint which showed signs of stiffening with arthritis. It was rather an ugly little ring, but part of the flesh. In the presence of the secret, leaping emotions of the fire she was glad to have her garnet.

'Mademoiselle Good-man! Mademoiselle Good-man!' she heard.

Then the crowd still had its personal moments. It was the Demoiselles Bloch. They were wearing identical raincoats, and their hair.

'We have lost everything, everything,' said Mademoiselle Marthe, as if she took a pleasure in confirming what had always been bound to happen.

'But you have yourselves,' suggested Theodora.

'Oui, c'est vrai,' Mademoiselle Berthe said, perplexed. *'Mais vous savez, quand on perd ses affaires ...'*

The Demoiselles Bloch were sure that even fire conspires.

When the roof falls, said the crowd, then it will be something. The falling of the roof is always the best.

'But where are the *pompiers*?' Theodora asked.

'It appears that they are having some difficulty with the carburettor,' said Mademoiselle Berthe. 'It is often like this, the people say.'

Yes, exactly, Theodora realized, exactly this fire, but which does not always burst skywards so triumphantly.

She craned her neck to watch the stars of sparks. Much sawdust would burn in this fire, and combed hair, and the black beetle in the wood, and the cockroach in the cold *consommé*.

'Katina! Katina Pavlou!' the voice called.

Theodora Goodman had not heard this old ewe since lambing time, its solitary bleat separated by frost.

'I have lost Katina Pavlou,' said Miss Grigg. 'I was asleep. Then, people are shouting fire. 'Ow can a woman keep 'er wits amongst a lot of bloody French? And now I 'ave lost Katina. I shall never answer to 'er parents.'

'Miss Grigg, it cannot, you will see, it cannot happen,' Theodora called, before the exasperated bell.

'*Ah, voilà les pompiers!*'

Nothing can happen, she promised glibly, when everything did.

But the bell will save, they said. *Voilà les pompiers.*

'*Vite! Vite! Il y a des hommes dans la maison,*' said Theodora, salving with difficulty a few words.

Her tongue was as effectual as the stiff clapper of a bell.

'*Ouai, ils sont perdus là-dedans, les gens,*' said the *pompier*.

He began with tact to unfold a hose, which neither he nor Theodora expected to function. They brought a thin ladder to prop against an incandescence.

'*Regardez. Voyez,*' they said. '*Ahhh! La vieille!*'

Theodora watched the window, on which the crowd now focused. The window had become quite encrusted with fire. It had a considerable, stiff jewelled splendour of its own, that ignored the elaborate ritual of the flames. Everything else, the whole night, was subsidiary to this ritual of fire, into which it was proposed that the thin ladder should intrude.

'Mais ils n'approcheront jamais de cette fenêtre,' said the hopeful crowd.

The window remained aloof, apparently determined to resist. For a moment Mrs Rapallo looked out, as if she were not watched, but watching something that was taking place. She was wearing her hair, for the occasion, but her eyes had floated out of reach. How the *petit paquet* will flare, Theodora regretted, and the *commode en marbre* crack. But it was obvious that Mrs Rapallo was gratified by such magnificence. From the window she contemplated, only vaguely, the vague evidence of faces. Fire is fiercer. Fire is more triumphant. Then, she turned and withdrew, and there was the windowful of smoke, and Mignon pressing her hands on hot glass.

'Ah, la pauvre!' they called. *'La pauvre bête! La vieille!'*

'But where is Katina Pavlou?' cried Miss Grigg.

'And the Countess, and Wetherby?' said the Demoiselles Bloch. 'And General Sokolnikov? It is a tragedy of which one reads in the papers.'

'I doubt whether Wetherby and Lieselotte are alive,' Theodora said.

Because fevers consume, or are consumed. Nor did she expect Monsieur Durand, *le petit*, or Henriette. They too must have destroyed each other. But Sokolnikov, she said, there are some lives.

'Yes, I am here, Ludmilla,' said Sokolnikov, blowing like the sprays of several hoses. 'I have escaped. That is, a few minutes earlier I was delivered by a miracle from a horrible and tragic death. Let us praise your saints. It reminds me a little of the occasion at Dvinsk when the barracks caught fire. Afterwards, at an inquiry, it was established that it was arson. The occasion at Dvinsk was as impressive, if also more emotional, on account of the number of horses which were roasted alive. The screaming of burning horses was heard by the peasants of a village several *versts* away. It even became the source of a local proverb : When horses scream at night, look to your *kvass*.'

Sokolnikov mopped his head. His spectacles were brilliant with excitement.

'It was no miracle, Alyosha Sergei,' said Theodora, 'that you failed to burn.' Her affection could not have allowed it.

'What is it you are muttering, Ludmilla?' shouted Sokolni-kov. 'I wish you would explain.'

At most, he would evaporate in a great, hot cloud.

'It is nothing,' she said.

Not even a cloud. Sokolnikov was deathless. She could not explain.

She could not explain the certainties, even in the fierce mouths of fire.

'*Mais dites*,' the crowd said, '*il n'y a pas d'amants là-dedans, qui meurent enlacés sur un grand lit de fer?*'

'There is still Katina Pavlou,' whimpered Miss Grigg.

'But here she is,' said Theodora, with the certainty of certainty that fire will open.

'*Ahhh, regardez*,' sighed the crowd. '*Une jeune fille! Elle a perdu son fiancé? Où est sa mère?*'

'The Lord be praised!' cried Miss Grigg. 'What are they saying about 'er mother? Madame Pavlou is at Evian les Bains.'

They were watching Katina Pavlou walk out of the burning house. She walked with her hands outstretched, protecting herself with her hands, not so much from substance, as some other fire. She could not yet accept the faces. As if these had read a reported incident, of which, she knew, the details had been inevitably falsified. But Katina Pavlou had seen the face of fire.

'Thank you, Grigg,' she said, receiving the shawl, because it was easier to.

Miss Grigg was all psalms and angora. She put, and touched. She touched again.

It was essential to wrap up tight, the Demoiselles Bloch advised, on account of the night air, it was essential for the *poitrine*.

But for the crowd it was essential that the roof should fall. It waited for this intensification of its lives.

'Miss Goodman,' said Katina Pavlou, 'have you ever seen a burning piano?'

Theodora had not, but she had watched other moments writhe, distorted by less than fire.

'Let us go somewhere else,' she said because it was exhausting.

The Hôtel du Midi was now a set piece of fire. Theodora Goodman and Katina Pavlou went round to the back, pressing close to the wall of the *confiserie*. They sat on a bench in the *jardin exotique,* where a slight dew had fallen, in spite of events. Katina Pavlou took Theodora Goodman's hand.

'I shall go away,' Katina Pavlou said, touching the bones in Theodora's hand. 'I shall go to my own country. Now I know. I shall go.'

'But how?' Theodora asked, remembering the revolving doors of many-starred hotels.

'Why, but I am at liberty,' said Katina Pavlou. 'Aren't I?'

Theodora considered the phases of the fire.

'Why, yes, I suppose,' Theodora smiled.

'I shall take some money and some food,' Katina Pavlou said. 'Tomorrow you shall come with me to the station, Miss Goodman, and I shall buy the ticket.'

It was easy as this. Already Katina Pavlou sat in the train, eating the chocolate and the *petits pains.* The mountains flowed.

'Yes, my dear Katina,' Theodora sighed.

Already, from her corner, Katina Pavlou watched the slow smoke rise from white houses and sleepily finger the dawn. She sat upright, to arrive, to recover the lost reality of childhood. Her eyes were strained by sleeplessness.

'Yes, Katina,' Theodora said.

There was no reason to suppose that this was not the sequence of events. Theodora contemplated the fire eating the feeble fretwork of a gable, turning it to fierce lace.

Then the crowd began to call. The roof would fall, called the crowd. It was time, time, time. The voice thickened.

'*Ahhhh,*' cried the crowd in a last desperate spasm of consummation.

Theodora was glad that she did not see the faces flame.

'I shall not look any more,' Katina Pavlou said.

There was blood on her face. It had dried. It glittered, rather like new paint, or a murder on the stage.

'And what shall you do, Miss Goodman?' Katina Pavlou shivered.

'I? I shall go now,' Theodora said. 'I shall go too.'

She touched the smooth, cold skin of a leaf of aloe.

'Where?' Katina Pavlou asked.

'I have not thought yet,' Theodora said.

The forms of the *jardin exotique* remained stiff and still, though on one edge, where they had pressed against the side of the Hôtel du Midi, they were black and withered. Their zinc had run into a fresh hatefulness.

'But I shall go,' Theodora said, indifferent to any pricking pressure, any dictatorship of the *jardin exotique*

Katina Pavlou yawned. Her face was rounding into sleep.

'I may even return to Abyssinia,' Theodora said.

After the metal hieroglyphs she felt an immeasurable longing to read the expression on the flat yellow face of stone. If the biscuit houses still existed.

'You will go *where*?' Katina Pavlou asked.

'Come, Katina, you are almost asleep,' Theodora Goodman said. 'We must join the others. Listen. They are calling us.'

Part Three HOLSTIUS

When your life is most real, to me you are mad.

OLIVE SCHREINER

ALL through the middle of America there was a trumpeting of corn. Its full, yellow, tremendous notes pressed close to the swelling sky. There were whole acres of time in which the yellow corn blared as if for a judgement. It had taken up and swallowed all other themes, whether belting iron, or subtler, insinuating steel, or the frail human reed. Inside the movement of corn the train complained. The train complained of the frustration of distance, that resists, that resists. Distance trumpeted with corn.

Theodora Goodman sat beside the window in the train. Her hands were open. She had been carrying a weight, and now she was exhausted, slack, from receiving full measure, a measure of corn. Against her head the white mat gave her face a longer, paler, yellow shape. Like a corn cob. But in spite of outer appearances, Theodora Goodman suggested that she had retreated into her own distance and did not intend to come out.

This distressed the man in the laundered shirt, who wished to tell about his home, his mother, his cocktail cabinet, the vacation he had taken in Bermuda, and how he had sold papers as a boy. He sat in a corner, opposite Theodora Goodman, and felt and looked nervous, and fingered his mentholed chin, and rustled cellophane.

Or he talked, and heard his own voice made small.

Because all this time the corn song destroyed the frailer human reed. It destroyed the tons of pork the man's firm had canned. It dumped the man's cans beside the railroad track. It consumed the man's plans for better pork. The well-laundered, closely-shaven man scratched his slack white muscles through his beautiful, hygienic shirt, and could not understand. He could not understand why, beside the strong yellow notes of corn, his voice should fall short. He chewed popcorn, chewing for confidence, the white and pappy stuff that is a decadence of corn.

Theodora heard the difference between doing and being. The corn could not help itself. It was. But the man scrabbled on the surface of life, working himself into a lather of importance under his laundered shirt. She heard the man's words, which were as significant and sad as the desperate hum of telephone wires, that tell of mortgages, and pie, and phosphates, and love, and movie contracts, and indigestion, and real estate, and loneliness. The man said that the population of Chicago had risen from 2,701,705 in 1920 to 3,376,438 in 1930. The population was being raised all the time. But in Chicago also, Theodora had seen the nun who danced along the sidewalk, unconsciously, for joy, and the un-naturally natural face of the dancing nun had sung some song she had just remembered. The nun's feet touched grass. So that Theodora smiled now. And the man in the perfect shirt was encouraged. He leaned forward to tell the populations of Kansas City, St Louis, Buffalo, and Detroit.

So they were getting somewhat at last.

In her turn, Theodora tried to remember some population of her own. But she could not. She tried to remember some unusual game that is played after adolescence. Because it was time, she saw, that she contributed to ease the expression on the man's face, that was an expression of expectation, and sympathy, and pain. But she could not. And the man, sitting back, said that, anyway, it would be fine for her folks to have her back home after so much travelling around. It would be safe. The man had read his papers, it seemed. Europe, he said, was a powder maga-zine, all hell was waiting to be let loose. Then he sat back. He had done his duty. He had composed life into a small, white, placid heap.

Theodora remembered she was in America and going home. She remembered the letter to Fanny in which she had written:

My dear Fanny,
   I am writing to say that I have seen and done, and the time has come at last to return to Abyssinia. Because I like to allow for events, I cannot say when I shall be with you, but probably some time in the spring, that is, of course, your Abyssinian spring . . .

'Theo is coming home,' announced Fanny Parrott. 'What is more, she appears to be quite mad.'

Fanny dug at her cup, to sweeten her annoyance with the dregs of sugar. With the tips of her teeth she bit the half-melted sugar and looked apprehensively at her safe room. A room is safest at breakfast. At Audley the mail arrived in the afternoon, but Fanny had deferred Theodora's letter, waiting for the safer moment of stiff, sweet porridge, and the consoling complacency of bacon fat, when she too was stronger. Though even so.

'Well?' said Frank, who was fitting bacon, lean, fat, lean, half a kidney, a square of toast, and a little gravy, on to his fork.

Thought was slow and comfortable as breakfast. No one should destroy Frank Parrott. He was stronger than Theodora. He wiped the gravy from his mouth.

'We are not committed to Theo,' he said. 'Theo has always led her own life.'

If guilt stirred, and impinged on Frank Parrott's conscience, it quickly congealed. He swallowed down a mouthful of fat meat, and felt personally absolved.

'But she is *my* sister,' Fanny said.

'Well?'

'I have my conscience,' said Fanny.

As if this wistful thing might break.

'And I cannot bear it if you sit there saying *well*. I would rather you made no comment.'

Because she had begun to enjoy nerves. It was one of the many peculiarities which made her superior to Frank, and which a man accepted. Besides, his financial status and social position justified a wife who had nerves, and could pronounce French, and knew what to say to an Honourable.

But there were moments, too, when Frank Parrott was the Lord, when Fanny watched, and Frank Parrott was thick and red, and Fanny was glad. Fanny watched Frank push away his plate, both to assert his authority and because he was finished. Frank Parrott went and stood against the fire. To roast his rump. He was thick and red. His thick, polished leather legs were stood apart and striped with fire. When he had cleared the phlegm, Frank would speak, but not before. Now he was choosing words, like a fat sheep out of a pen. Fanny watched, her breath just thicker than porridge. There is a time in life when there are pretty long stretches of contempt, broken by the bubbling moments of lust, which are also called love. So Fanny loved Frank. He was the father of her complacency.

'There is no reason why we should put ourselves out for Theodora,' said Frank. 'Theo has never put herself out for us.'

'No, Frank,' said Fanny. 'It is true.'

She was struck by the sudden loveliness of truth.

'And Theo will be happier in some good solid boarding house,' said Frank. 'With a mob of similar old girls.'

'Yes,' said Fanny. 'We can take a nice room for her.'

'Somewhere where she can show her postcards after dinner to the other old girls.'

Warmed by fire, his great acreage could dispose of more than souls, the bodies of sisters-in-law.

'There is no need,' said Fanny, 'to be unkind.'

But she smiled. Now she touched the envelope of Theodora's distasteful letter with less care. Fanny loved letters, but the comfortable narrative of wives and mothers, or some harmless appeal by charity, which she would allow to stroke her vanity before tearing up. Not the dark, the mad letters of Theodora. Before Fanny could destroy these, they had torn her.

'And Theo is not so old,' she corrected. 'She can't be more than forty-five.'

'Old enough to have learnt sense,' said Frank.

'Mother,' said Lou, 'why is Aunt Theo mad?'

Outside the window the world had not yet thawed. Lou waited for the aching shapes of winter to dissolve into a more familiar fence and tree. Cutting toast, her hands were still miserable from Brahms.

'What a thing to ask!' said Fanny. 'As if . . . It is difficult to say. But it is none of your business.'

Lou would not ask more.

'It is a manner of speaking,' said her father.

'No,' said Fanny, raising her voice to the bright confident pitch that parents adopt for the presence of children. 'Theodora is not so old.'

'But stringy,' said Frank. 'The type that does not die.'

'Oh, Frank!' laughed Fanny.

Her labours to establish respect were wasted.

'Poor Theo!' she laughed. 'How cruel!'

Then Fanny took a knife and slashed the butter. She owed

this for something that continued to rankle, under her laughter, unexplained, for Abyssinia perhaps.

The sun was still a manageable ball above the ringing hills as Lou went outside. She walked through this stiff landscape, carrying her cold and awkward hands. She thought about the cardboard aunt, Aunt Theodora Goodman, who was both a kindness and a darkness. Lou touched the sundial, on which the time had remained frozen. She was afraid and sad, because there was some great intolerable pressure from which it is not possible to escape.

Lou looked back over her shoulder, and ran.

Sometimes against the full golden theme of corn and the whiter pizzicato of the telephone wires there was a counter-point of houses Theodora Goodman sat. The other side of the incessant train she could read the music off. There were the single notes of houses, that gathered into gravely structural phrases. There was a smooth passage of ponds and trees. There was a big bass barn. All the square faces of the wooden houses, as they came, overflowed with solemnity, that was a solemnity of living, a passage of days. Where children played with tins, or a girl waited at a window, or calves lolloped in long grass, it was a frill of flutes twisted round a higher theme, to grace, but only grace, the solemnity of living and of days. There were now the two coiled themes. There was the flowing corn song, and the deliberate accompaniment of houses, which did not impede, however structural, because it was part of the same integrity of purpose and of being.

Now that the man in the laundered shirt slept, Theodora Goodman could search her own purpose, her own contentment. I am going home, she said. It had a lovely abstraction to which she tried to fit the act. She tried the door of a house and went in. There were the stairs, and the cotton quilt on which she threw her jaded hat. She waited for the familiar sounds of furniture. She looked for her own reflection, in mirrors, but more especially in the faces of the people who lived in this house.

The train rocked the track. The man in the laundered shirt stirred. He was having trouble with his groin.

Then, in a gust, Theodora knew that her abstraction also did not fit. She did not fit the houses. Although she had in her practical handbag her destination in writing, she was not sure that paper might not tear. Although she was insured against several acts of violence, there was ultimately no safeguard against the violence of personality. This was less controllable than fire. In the bland corn song, in the theme of days, Theodora Goodman was a discord. Those mouths which attempted her black note rejected it wryly. They glossed over something that had strayed out of some other piece, or slow fire.

The train rocked the track.

Lying on her shelf at night, listening to the dying wind of many sleepers, Theodora was afraid that this movement might end in an intolerable clash of cymbals. So she compelled her stockings. So she unfolded herself from the narrow shelf. Her hat, with its large black gauze rose, more a sop to convention than an attempt at beauty, was easy to manage. It knew her head. She was soon ready.

There were bells in the night, wheels, and a long gush of steam.

Theodora trod down, out of the high, stationary train, on to the little siding.

A Negro with white eyes suggested that this was not the sort of thing that people did.

'No,' said Theodora. 'But you will not tell.'

The Negro had a kind face. And he was sleepy.

And presently the train had gone, with all its magnificence of purpose, towards California. She heard in the distance its meek, flannel cough absorbing darkness.

There were several small streets of a small town, in which Theodora walked. The town lay wide open, between darkness and light. Soon the colour would drench back. But for the moment Theodora and the sleeping town were pale. Sitting on a step, her head against a tree, she waited for shapes to gather, or sleep. The drifting silence, and the broken sounds of sleep, and the watery colourlessness of early morning were all one.

Finally bark began to bite. She lifted her cheek from where it had been grained by the friendly tree. Sunflowers had appeared over a fence, though their big suns had not yet begun to flame. They were still bemused by dew. The town was pink, mostly, of baked mud, an earth pink. A bronze cock on a wall shook his feathers into shape. There were the frame houses too. The old sagging house, for instance, on the step of which Theodora sat. This house was still comfortable with sleep. But the bronze cock flaunted his metal throat and crowed. Somewhere a voice tore itself from a sheet. A thin, dark, perhaps an Indian woman, or a Mexican, lifted her head and looked, rising out of deep darkness Theodora saw. Theodora looked away, thinking that she recognized her own soul in the woman's deep face.

The bronze cock was screaming. Voices came from kitchens, prominent voices, because they were still feeling their way, and cold, because every morning is the first.

Theodora looked up and saw the small white-haired woman, very white, floury white, who looked out of the house against which she was sitting. This woman had the young face of an old bright child. She had the appearance of looking for something at which to complain, but not in anger, for company. Then she saw Theodora Goodman and was so surprised she withdrew.

Recovering from her surprise, she soon came out again. The woman could not resist. She had a lot to tell. She would not ask much, but she would tell. And Theodora was glad of this, as she could not have answered. She did say that she had come by train. But the woman could not pause. She had to tell about her younger daughter Frances, who was multiplying on the coast, and her elder daughter, Myra, at Topeka, who had the hand for cheese cake. Then the woman remembered, and brought Theodora a cup of milk and a piece of sweet, fluffy bread. The bread was not real, but there was a blue shadow round the rim of milk, that she knew from childhood. She sank her mouth in the cool milk, and it became warm from her suddenly hot, protesting mouth.

'Are you sick?' the woman asked.

Theodora said that she was not.

Then it occurred to the small woman that she should start to arrange this stranger's life, who had come by train, and did not know much.

'Because you gotta go *some*where,' the woman replied, when Theodora said she had not thought.

'I do not particularly want to go anywhere,' Theodora said. 'Though I have money in my bag.'

There was not, fortunately, a great deal the woman wanted to know. So long as she could arrange a life she was content.

So she said there was a guest house farther up that was fine, with individual cabins, where people went, and artists, where Theodora should go, and there was a canyon, and an Indian pueblo, and an Indian that was petrified, from falling down a cliff and lying upside down in the right kind of water for many years. This is where Theodora should go. To rest. The woman's son was going that way with a load of apples, presently, and Jake would run her up.

'Jake!' the small woman called. 'Jake!'

The son raised his head from a dark window. He laughed, because he was still half-asleep, and because he did not know what else to do. Jake's neck was muscular and golden. He rose, and he was a statue, but he would not reflect much, Theodora saw.

So it was arranged, while Jake threw water at his body.

Theodora sat in Jake's truck. She waved good-bye to the small old child. She saw that by the middle of the day the fierce sunflowers would be oozing dust. Already the bronze cock brooded and drooped.

Then they went. The stiff road began to move. It became more sinuous. It swerved and dipped. The wind was quite serpentine at each curve of road, and before the hollows of white, flumping dust. They dived. Theodora Goodman and Jake sat high. It was grave, and dignified, and beautiful to fly like this through the empty landscape, but an emptiness that did not matter. The emptiness of this landscape was a fullness, of pink earth, and chalk-blue for sky. And the rim of the world was white. It burned.

Jake held the wheel. Driving, Jake was good. But they stopped too, and he was the same statue of hard, golden wax, that conveyed one or two ideas. From the back of the truck there was a smell of hot apples, the apples that they stopped for Jake to deliver, beside the road, or just off. Then Theodora sat in the smell of hot apples and dust. Once there was a bus pulled in at a gas station, and a dwarf was singing of eternity, as if he knew, and meant it.

They went on. Jake did not speak much. He laughed. They went on across the world, which Jake took for granted. Or they stopped. And Jake got down to juggle apples. Finally, Theodora was tired of Jake. She looked back once to see, but Jake did not, before she took the road that opened.

Theodora walked up the small side road, which went up the mountain, steep enough, and full of rocks. The sandy, rocky road wound up the mountain, for no set purpose, you would have imagined, except there was evidence occasionally that this must exist. The sand in softer parts between the rocks was bruised by tyres. Theodora was determined to follow this road. She was rigid with determination and purpose as she walked. Sometimes she bent to the greater incline of the road. Sometimes her dry mouth gulped. Sometimes the brown leathery flaps of her nostrils fastened with desperation on the air. She was walking between pines, or firs, anyway some kind of small coniferous tree, stunted and dark, which possessed that part of the earth. Animal life was moving in the undergrowth of dark, dead twigs and needles, and stiff, thistly things, and yellow grass. Small clearings were covered wholly with dead grass, which made a queer stiff sound of moving when there was wind. Theodora could smell the dust. She could smell the expanding odour of her own body, which was no longer the sour, mean smell of the human body in enclosed spaces, but the unashamed flesh on which dust and sun have lain. She walked. She smiled for this discovery of freedom.

In her hand she still held, she realized, the practical handbag, that last link with the external Theodora Goodman. Out of the undergrowth a small furred animal raised its head to examine her surprise. She stood, tall and black, making a shadow, at the bend in the road. She rummaged in the handbag, amongst the startling objects that people carry in such receptacles, and found aspirin and eau-de-Cologne, the snapshot of children in a row, nickels and bills and a sticky lozenge. There were also, she saw, the strips and sheaves of tickets, railroad and steamship, which Theodora Goodman had bought in New York for the purpose of prolonging herself through many fresh phases of what was accepted as Theodora Goodman. Now she took these and tore them into small pieces which fell frivolously at the side of the road. The shock of this disturbed the furred thing in the undergrowth. It ran. She heard it over sticks. Even the undergrowth, she reflected, rejects the acts of honesty. But she personally was gladder. After dawdling away quite a lot of what was now afternoon, she continued with longer strides up the rough road.

Presently this eased out. Soon we shall come to something, she knew. In a rut there was an empty can that had not yet filled with dust and stones, the wrapper still pink with an unnatural formation of Vienna sausages. Later she began to smell cool sand, soaked apparently by the trickle from a hidden spring. She noticed initials carved in the scaly bark of a tree, an uneven *AJ*, from which resin oozed. This last clue made her debate whether she was prepared. She touched the face which soon other faces would perhaps attempt fumblingly to read, but after hesitating a moment with her feet in the consoling sand, she went on towards the words and silences of human intercourse.

Trees thinned out in front of her, leaving an open space, a patch of ragged, ripened corn, a house that had been built purposely for living, the clutter of sheds, hutches, corral, cans, hessian tatters, and broken toys that such houses accumulate. Theodora was glad of all this. The prospect warmed many past failures. She gathered her humility and approached the wood gate, beyond which a scruffy red dog bristled and barked. At what point after she had lifted the latch the dog stopped tearing at her skirt she was not sensibly aware. Only that she looked down into his red eye, and found that he was regretting anything that might have occurred. He ran, whined, quivered, and slobbered at her hand with a large tongue.

'Hi, Red! Down Red!' a woman called from the house.

Although there was no need, although the dog was now abject in his puzzled friendliness, the woman called and protested until she could see her way closer to contact with the stranger.

'You darned idiot dog!' the woman shouted in a kind of pleasant and confused exasperation.

She was sandy as her own mountain road. Her skin was rough, freckled, unequivocal stuff.

'It is all right,' Theodora said. 'We are friends.'

Children had come now. They were grouped about the mother, waiting for something to happen, to which they themselves would not immediately contribute. The children stood in the silences of expectation.

'Come far?' the mother asked.

'Yes,' said Theodora. 'Very far.'

She hoped the woman would not make any awkwardness. She hoped this very much. The great awkwardness of questions that people ask, though they content themselves with half-answers.

'What can we do for you?' the woman asked.

She had screwed up her eyes in their sandy skin, but not in hostility. The children had turned to look, not at the stranger, but at their mother, as if the clue would come from her.

'Well,' said Theodora, 'I don't know that there is anything in particular.'

She could not ask to be allowed to stand, unpersecuted, there in the yard, or to sit on the edge of the porch and look at her own hands, or the children's faces, and back to her own hands.

'You're miles from anywhere, you know,' the sandy woman said. 'Are you lost?'

'No,' Theodora said.

The woman quickly brushed back her sandy hair away from her eyes. She turned her face sideways and said to the corner of the porch, 'Guess you'd better eat. Joe'll be back soon. Then we'll see. Eunice, quit picking your nose.'

She slapped the hand of a thin child, who put the hand behind her back and frowned.

'Our name's Johnson,' the mother said.

She waited for some such contribution from Theodora, who did not make the move. So the woman immediately shifted away into deliberate activity.

'Better come and get that dust off of you,' she said. 'You look a sight. It hasn't rained here in months. We're lucky to have our spring.'

Theodora followed Mrs Johnson into the dark confusion of the house. She avoided a celluloid doll, upturned on boards. She knocked against a sewing machine. There was a smell of boiled potatoes.

'You must be happy to live in this house,' Theodora said.

'Are you crazy?' said Mrs Johnson.

'I mean,' said Theodora, 'everything is so clear. I mean . . .'

But she could not explain the rightness of objects to someone who already knew those objects by heart.

'We're well enough,' Mrs Johnson said. 'Though we'll die poor. Joe ain't got the touch.'

She pushed through into what appeared to be a wash-house, and Theodora followed behind. Then Mrs Johnson kicked some shape into chaos. The children stood around.

'You won't mind this,' Mrs Johnson said, indicating with her shoulders the haphazard nature of the wash-house, its old frayed baskets, sticks, bottles, and faded cretonne.

'You won't mind,' she said.

But it did not matter whether Theodora did.

While Mrs Johnson went for water, which she said was on the boil, Theodora was left to withstand the impact of the glances of children, not so much boys and girls as inquiring silences. There were four of these. Three were sandy, but one was dark. His lips were full, and red, and dark. There was a great space between the dark one and the shadowless, sandy three, the difference between depths and surface. Mrs Johnson would accept the depths, and love the depths fearfully, but she would not understand. At the moment of his birth, or moments in the arms of her husband, she had come closer to her rich dark child. But she preferred to sun her sandy self, to cover doubt with humorous exasperation. She preferred life to be unequivocal and freckled. Eunice was her mother's child.

'Why do you wear a hat?' Eunice asked finally.

'I got into the habit,' Theodora said. 'Like most other people, I suppose.'

'Mother don't wear a hat,' Eunice said. 'None of us don't wear hats.'

'Don't you listen to her, ma'am,' said a long boy. 'She's fresh.'

Theodora removed her large and shameful hat.

'I ain't,' Eunice said. 'You quit pushin' me around, Arty. I'll tell Mom.'

'I like you,' said a girl whose voice touched.

She fingered Theodora's garnet ring.

'What's your name?' the child asked.

'Theodora.'

266

'*Theerdora*? I never heard that before.'

'What sort of name is that?' Eunice said. 'Hi, quit, Arty, Lily!'

Because there was a need to express shame, and they had begun to push, kick, cuff. And Eunice screamed, more out of convention than from pain.

'Don't you listen to her,' they all cried.

All except the dark boy, who said nothing. He picked with a knife at the wicker of an old basket and smiled.

'Eh, you kids, what's all this?' said Mrs Johnson, returning with a black kettle. 'Kids are a pest,' she said.

The water fell with a warm hiss into an old enamel bowl.

'There's soap an' all,' she said. 'Now come on, you kids. Leave the lady alone.'

Theodora began in the agreeable silence of the wash-house to wash her hands. She folded them one over the other. She folded them over the smooth and comfortable yellow soap. Her heart was steady. If all this were touchable, she sighed, bowing her head beneath the balm of silence contained in the deserted iron room.

Then she heard the pick, pick. She turned and saw the serene closed lips of the silent boy.

'Oh,' she said. 'I thought you had all gone.'

He compressed his lips and picked.

'And *your* name is what?' she asked.

'Zack,' he said firmly, as if it could not have been anything else.

She could not read him, but she knew him.

'Are you visiting with us?' he asked.

Because she was a blank, he added, 'Are you going to be here some?'

'No,' she said.

She shook her head, but it was the finality of sadness.

'Why?' he asked.

'You will know in time,' she said, 'that it is not possible to stay.'

He looked at her queerly, with his mouth as much as his eyes, as she cupped her hands and spread her face with water from the enamel bowl.

'What is that?' he asked, touching the flattened gauze rose on her discarded hat.

She turned to see what, so that he saw her face, soft and shiny with water.

'That,' she said, 'is supposed to be a rose.'

'A rose?' he said. 'A black rose?'

Then he went quietly, and she watched him through the window walking alone through the stunted pines at the bottom of the dirt yard.

Although Zack had gone, Theodora continued to experience all the triumph of the rare alliances. And because the wash-house had contained the mystery of their pact, its darkness glowed. There was no form, whether of abandoned furniture or discarded clothing, that had not grown. Theodora wiped the water from her face. The rough, scorched towel was all virtue. She was touched by the touching shapes of the hugger-mugger room, but while admitted into their world, it was with no sense of permanence. She noticed from a distance an old distorted pair of women's shoes that had sunk in mud once when there had been rain. To live with these, she knew, required a greater degree of indifference or else humility.

Outside, the sound, the sound of a car had begun to increase. Then the car itself drove through a scattering of speckled pullets into the yard. It creaked, the old Ford, steaming with distance, and white with dust. The man got down from out of the old car.

This, Theodora supposed, would be Joe.

He walked across the yard with the nonchalance of owner-ship. There was the banging of a wire door. Then a silence, as if something great and extraordinary were being explained.

Now Theodora could not bear to go out. She was isolated in a small room, but it was not desirable to leave it.

'Guess you're pretty hungry,' said Mrs Johnson, breaking in.

Theodora had not thought, but she supposed she was.

'We got noodles,' said Mrs Johnson. 'There's no meat,' she added, to flatten expectation.

Theodora did not expect. Not in the short passage. She expected nothing. The passage was not long enough. Brushing past several old coats, hanging stiffly from pegs, she was ejected brutally into comparative light.

'Joe, this is Miss ... ? It *is* Miss?' asked Mrs Johnson.

Theodora's throat was tight with some new terror, that she could not swallow, in a new room. Her hands searched.

'Yes,' she said, bringing it out of her throat. 'Yes,' she said, but her hands could not find.

They waited. Her forehead pricked with sweat.

'Pilkington,' she said.

'Glad to know you, Miss Pilkington,' said Mr Johnson.

The room loosened. She felt Mr Johnson's hand.

Theodora could have cried for her own behaviour, which had sprung out of some depth she could not fathom. But now her name was torn out by the roots, just as she had torn the tickets, rail and steamship, on the mountain road. This way perhaps she came a little closer to humility, to anonymity, to pureness of being. Though for the moment she stood under a prim pseudonym in the Johnson's kitchen, waiting for the next move.

'You just sit down and make yourself at home, Miss Pilkington,' Mr Johnson said.

It should have been so easy, but she sat carefully on the edge of a rocker. At least Mr Johnson had decided to take much for granted, she felt, and for this she was relieved. Probably there was a great deal, anyway, that Mr Johnson took for granted. It was in his body, a casualness of stance inside the shabby dungarees. He was dark and physical. There was not much connection between Mr Johnson and his children, though they did match his casualness, standing in positions of half-attention in different quarters of the room, each with his own personal occupation, whether whittling wood, turning the leaves of a catalogue, or pulling the wings of a fly. If there was a subtler link, it was with the dark boy. Mr Johnson had the same habit of stressing with his full dark mouth the expression of his eyes. Only the child was already older than the father would ever allow himself to be.

'Queenie says you come a long way,' Mr Johnson said.

'I have come from Europe,' said Theodora.

'We been to San Francisco once,' Eunice said.

Nor could Mr Johnson quite visualize so far. He smiled, but it was for more familiar wonders. He shifted his position easily in the chance surroundings of his own room. Theodora knew how there must have been times when Mr Johnson threw himself in long grass, and chewed the fleshy grass with his strong teeth, and half closed his eyes. He had that ease in his body. Mr Johnson's eyes were still full and blind.

'Well, now, that's interesting,' he said. 'They say there'll be a war.'

It would happen, Theodora saw, to the ants at the roots of the long suave stalks of grass.

'Probably,' Theodora said, 'unless God is kinder to the ants.'

She felt the eyes fix. On the mantelpiece there was an orange marble clock, which also had begun to stare.

At this point Mrs Johnson, her head held back, her sandy hair flying, in protest at the steam, brought a big white dish of noodles from the outer kitchen.

'We're gonna eat now,' said the child Lily, who had touched Theodora's garnet in the wash-house, and who now took her hand.

'You shall sit by me,' Lily said.

Then there was a great scramble, in which Theodora was caught up, whirled, and again isolated. It all revolved round the immense dish of steaming noodles, above which Mrs Johnson stood, wiping her freckled hands masterfully on her cotton skirt. When Theodora settled, she noticed that she was sitting opposite Mr Johnson and Zack. In the midst of so much sandy sediment, they were still and dark, like two dark, polished stones.

'Gee, I do like noodles,' Arty sighed, holding his head on one side and looking along the table.

But Eunice said, 'I like cornbeef hash best.'

Mrs Johnson dolloped the clumsy noodles with great agility on to Theodora's plate.

'Guests first,' Mrs Johnson said.

Mr Johnson broke bread. He ignored the masterful ritual of his sandy wife. But she bent towards him. The gesture of her arms was gentler as she passed the plate, poured coffee, pushed across a knife. Once the back of her dry hand brushed the skin of his arm. Then she bent her head and touched her hair. There was something quite humble about the masterful Mrs Johnson in the presence of her husband, or even before her children when they became a family.

Theodora swallowed the food. Very palpably she felt the presence of the Johnsons, their noise and silence. Their sphere was round and firm, but however often it was offered, in friend-liness or even love, she could not hold it in her hand. So that she swallowed with difficulty the mouthfuls of warm smooth noodles, which to the Johnsons were just food. Everyone else ate the noodles, and, later, a pie, with dark sweet fruit.

'Tell us something about your travels, Miss Pilkington,' Eunice said, as if you could tell all things always in words.

Eunice would.

'You speak when you're spoken to,' said the mother. 'Miss Pilkington is tired.'

'Why don't Miss Pilkington visit with us, Mom?' said Zack, with the slowness of difficulty, counting the stones of fruit on the edge of his plate.

His mouth was stained.

Theodora heard her own spoon beating on the plate.

'We can fix you a bed, anyways, for the night. Can't we, Joe?' Mrs Johnson said. 'Then you can run Miss Pilkington into town in the morning in the Ford.'

'Sure,' Mr Johnson said.

'It is a trouble,' said Theodora.

She looked desperately at the marble clock, and at a long white feather that trembled in a vase at its side, in a slight breeze.

'Why?' Mr Johnson laughed.

He showed his white teeth, on which a piece of the dark fruit skin had stuck.

'No trouble at all,' he said.

There was no trouble when you sat easy in your clothes. Mr Johnson leaned back. Life had sluiced his casual, muscular body, leaving it smooth.

'It is very kind,' said Theodora, out of her conflicting throat.

She heard her own spoon rattle. Mrs Johnson looked quite disturbed. She, after all, had more knowledge of anxieties.

So it was settled, at least in theory.

'Miss Pilkington will stay,' they cried, beating with their spoons.

And then the plates were cleared.

Theodora sat, experiencing the superfluity, the slight imbecility of the stranger in a large family, in the face of the things that normally happen in the house.

'Just you sit, Miss Pilkington,' Mrs Johnson called. ' 'Tain't no trouble at all.'

Theodora heard dishes plunged in water. She heard Arty flicking the legs of Eunice with a wet towel. Mr Johnson had slammed the wire door and gone across the yard on some mission of cows or chickens. In his absence she could see his hands plunged in moist bran or pollard, his contained and rather animal eyes intent above the tin.

So that Miss Pilkington sat alone.

She began slowly to rock in the old and ugly rocker, rocking to a more intimate relationship with the objects in the room. These were ugly too, but right, up to a point. They had grown purposefully out of the room, just as the four children, three sandy and one dark, had grown out of the mother's womb. Even as a skinny cavernous girl in a walnut frame, Mrs Johnson eyed the world with confidence, seeming to take for granted the logic of growth and continuity.

Why then, said Theodora Goodman, is this world which is so tangible in appearance so difficult to hold? Because she herself, in contradiction to the confidence of Mrs Johnson's photograph, could not answer for the substance of the marble clock. She went nervously and touched the clock. Her hands slid over the surface, not of objects, but of appearances.

'That clock was a wedding present from somebody rich,' Zack said.

He had come and stood behind, and his face had opened, she noticed, to communicate.

'It is a handsome clock,' said Theodora, who was ashamed that her secret gesture had been observed.

'I never liked the clock,' said Zack.

'Why?' Theodora asked.

He stuck out his dark lower lip.

'I never liked it,' he said.

She went and sat on an ottoman, which obviously was not used much, both because it was hard and because it was covered in a stuff that was proud and formal, something for occasions.

Zack came and looked at her. Now he was very close.

'You don't want to stay with us,' he said, looking at her straight.

She was close to his fringed eyes, which had approached, till his forehead touched hers, and she could feel the soft questioning of the lashes of his eyes.

'Oh, Zack,' she said, 'you must not make it difficult.'

Because he had rubbed his cheek against her cheek. Their blood flowed together. Her desperate words, ordinarily dry, had grown quite suddenly fleshy and ripe. Their locked hands lay in solid silence.

'If I go,' she asked, 'will you sometimes remember me, Zack?'

He hung his dark head.

'Nothing much happens here,' he said.

'I shall remember this house,' said Theodora.

She got up, ostensibly to escape the aching position on the ottoman, and went and pushed the wire door that opened on to the front porch. Zack was following, she heard, but he would remain on the steps. One of these moved slightly beneath her feet.

'You have forgotten your hat in the wash-house. With that black thing,' he said, 'the black rose.'

'So I have,' said Theodora.

But she continued to walk on, away from the house in which she might not be able to make the necessary answers. She knew by this time that there was often a kind of surprise in people's eyes, and this she was anxious to avoid. So she walked. Zack was taking it for granted. He bent and turned up a stone on a fresh phase of strange, slow life.

Theodora walked beyond the yard, beyond the dry flags of corn, and the gate upon which the red dog was stiffly lifting his leg. She walked to that point in the road where she had left off. She continued, climbing higher, where the road led, though this was less determinate. It wandered over rocks and sand, almost obliterated, or else its ruts cut deep where floods of rain had run, giving these scars the appearance of natural formation. Trees encroached too, the same stunted pine, bluish in sunlight or where dust lay, black in shadow. Although the Johnsons had already eaten, it was not yet late. The light had reached that metallic stage, of yellow metal, before the final softening. In its present phase it gave a greater tension. Theodora heard the crackle of the undergrowth. Sudden glimpses of the black trees struck cold. Then, there was a small plateau and a house, which she imagined must formerly have been the final objective of the faint road.

Theodora did not stop to investigate for signs of life. Her feet led deliberately. She went towards the house. It was a thin house, with elongated windows, like a lantern. The lower part was black slabs of logs with paler clay or adobe slapped into the interstices, but higher up the house became frailer frame, with the elongated windows, through which nothing showed of course, on account of the height. But the windows had also the blank look of the windows of deserted houses. Because there is nothing inside, they do not reflect. The glass coats up with dust.

This, then, was the blank house that Theodora found. But it did not deter. She went towards the house door, which was frame like the upper part, and a natural colour, darkened by the weather. All through the clearing where the house stood, the grass was yellow, dead. Fire would have run here. But the house itself in no way suggested that it might be carried away by the passions of fire.

Theodora found the padlock that the owners had left, presumptuously protecting their house with a seal of iron. Another time she might have been deterred, but not now. It was obvious that this must break. She had never been more confident. She picked at the screws of the hasp with her fingernails, and the screws came out easily, out of the old soft wood. The token padlock fell away from the house, so that she was able to walk in, into the smell of dust and animals.

The rough and awkward sounds of her motion yawned up through the house. The exterior had not deceived. There was not much inside. The objects that people had not valued. The things that were old or broken. And dust. The world was dim with dust through the coated windows, the glass of which normally would have had the amethyst tinge which is noticeable in certain light.

Theodora Goodman walked through her house with pleasure.

She walked up the narrow, railed stairs to the upper part. There was the same space of emptiness, but the larger windows gave more light, the windows that she threw open now, and there the valleys flowed. In this light the valleys did flow. At the foot of mountains they moved in the soft and moving light, the amethyst and grey. They flowed at the roots of the black sonorous islands. All the time the light seeped deeper into the craters of the earth.

Seen from the solitude of the house the process of disintegration that was taking place at the foot of the mountains should have been frightening and tragic, but it was not. The shapes of disintegrating light protested less than the illusions of solidity with which men surround themselves. Theodora now remembered with distaste the ugly and unnatural face of the Johnsons' orange marble clock. Because the death rattle of time is far more acute, and painful, and prolonged, when its impermanence is disguised as permanence. Here there were no clocks. There was a time of light and darkness. A time of crumbling hills. A time of leaf, still, trembling, fallen.

In the house above the disintegrating world, light and silence ate into the hard, resisting barriers of reason, hinting at some ultimate moment of clear vision. Theodora experienced a fresh anxiety. She doubted whether flesh was humble enough. She was afraid that the ticking of her eyelid might distort. She was ashamed of the inadequacy of the intermediate furniture. So that she went quickly downstairs, her feet and heart, to do the things she had seen women do in houses. She swept back white ashes from the hearth with an old broom that was still lying in a corner. Unbolting doors and windows she opened the house to the air. With some love she arranged a chair and table which at least were the essential of chair and table. Then she laid sticks and after breaking several matches, which she had in an emergency box in her practical handbag, she made the little tender tongue of fire that would soon consume a great deal of doubt.

Afterwards she sat back on her heels and looked towards the door, where she saw that a man had come, without coughing.

'Evening,' the man said. 'It's a steep climb up.'

He came and sat in the chair which Theodora had put.

'I did not notice,' she said.

'It's still a stiff climb.'

She heard his breathing, and saw the attitude of his body, both of which suggested he would stay. The man with the relaxed body might even have prior claim to the house.

'And this chair was always uncomfortable,' he said. 'It has a little rail with two carved knobs which eat into the back. But perhaps you have not yet experienced this.'

'Then I am an intruder in your house,' said Theodora.

She sat meekly on her heels beside the fire, which had grown, it had begun to complicate.

'It is yours,' said the man.

He had not two thoughts on the matter, it appeared. Or else the decisiveness of his words was accentuated by his changing position, to extricate from his pocket a pipe, which he began to fill.

Theodora did not know what to do now, whether she should thank, or whether it was not expected. Whether even the man's largeness of gesture might not be an instance of inverse imposture. But she got up off her heels, as her toes had grown numb. Outside, darkness was thickening, under the black pines, which would soon be solid with darkness, and in the shifting valleys. The little fire possessed the room of the house. It recreated the faces of Theodora Goodman and the man. She sensed her own, but she saw the face of the man, whose skin was ruddy fire.

'My name is Holstius,' he said, watching the fiery particles of his pipe, which he had lit with a stick.

Theodora touched the table for greater precision.

'I have seen you somewhere perhaps,' she said. 'Somewhere on a railway station, or in a hotel.'

'Possibly,' he said.

But it was a possibility, it seemed, into which he did not intend to go. He drew deeply on his pipe, and the bowl flowered. He was greatly interested in this.

In spite of his detachment Theodora was not conscious of isolation. Looking at Holstius, she remembered the morning on the bridge at Meroë, watching the cold brown water flow, at the shaggy side of the Man who was Given his Dinner, and how at the time she had been infused with a warmth of love that was most thinly separated from expectation of sorrow.

'They are very thinly divided indeed,' Holstius said. 'In fact, you might say that expectation of happiness is expectation of sorrow. The separating membrane is negligible.'

Theodora held the edge of the common table with her fingers. His voice moved her with a deep sadness. He was both detached and close. Because, although he spoke in abstractions, these answered the depths of her being. And what made these sensations of love and sorrow more poignant, actual, wonderful, was that she could have touched the body of Holstius, his thick and muscular, but quiet and soothing, hands, the ruddy skin, the indication of bones, the coarse greyish hair, the eyes, of which the expression was not determined by passion. Walking with her father on the frost at Meroë, or sitting with him in his room, in which the pines were never quite still, she had been impressed in the same way at times by a congruity, a continuity of man. But at times, at times, when expectation exceeded fact. Death had taken George Goodman and put him under marble. Fact corrected expectation. Just as the mind used and disposed of the figments of Mrs Rapallo, and Katina Pavlou, and Sokolnikov. And now Holstius. She watched the rough texture of his coat for the first indications of decay.

'You suspect me,' Holstius said.

He spat into the fire. She heard the strong hiss of spittle.

'I suspect myself,' Theodora said, feeling with her fingers for the grain in the table.

'Yes,' he said, 'you have been groping that table like a blind thing for the last ten minutes.'

Then she began to hate the revealing honesty of his face. She dug her nails into the wood.

'Why,' she asked, 'am I to be subjected to these tortures? I have reached a stage where they are not bearable.'

Her breath beat. The walls were bending outward under the pressure of the hateful fire. Then, when the table screamed under her nails, he said quietly, 'Ah, Theodora Goodman, you are torn in two.'

'What is it,' she asked agony, 'you expect me to do or say?'

'I expect you to accept the two irreconcilable halves. Come,' he said, holding out his hand with the unperturbed veins.

She huddled on the boards, beyond hope of protection by convention or personality, but the cloth on the legs of Holstius had the familiar texture of childhood, and smelled of horses, and leather, and guns. She rested her head against his knees.

'You cannot reconcile joy and sorrow,' Holstius said. 'Or flesh and marble, or illusion and reality, or life and death. For this reason, Theodora Goodman, you must accept. And you have already found that one constantly deludes the other into taking fresh shapes, so that there is sometimes little to choose between the reality of illusion and the illusion of reality. Each of your several lives is evidence of this.'

Resistance had gone out of her as she lay, her head against the knees of Holstius, receiving peace, whether it was from his words, and she was not altogether sure that he spoke, or from his hands. His hands touched the bones of her head under the damp hair. They soothed the wounds.

Later it seemed to be morning where her head lay. There was a weal on her cheek where the chair had eaten, numb but not painful, for she was in no such inferior state to experience pain. Light was beginning. It was already yellow, but not yet strong. Theodora turned her head and saw the brown bird with the velvet eye. Even at close quarters it was not critical, and might even have perched on the rail of the chair, of whose inanimacy Theodora Goodman was still a mere extension. Only when she drew her legs across the boards to restore her body to its working shape, the bird lifted its immaculate feet, bunched, trod the air, still undecided whether to settle, drooped, gathered, flirted its wings, opened out, and flew through the door. Then Theodora made the additional effort and stood on her feet. The numbness of her whole body left her with intensely clear vision. The almost empty daylit room had a pleasing innocence of detail and shape.

Walking through the back door, which, she remembered, was the way Holstius had come, she went amongst the trees. They were of a deciduous variety on that side of the house, still green, but washed out, exhausted by the summer. Her feet sank in the soil before water, which trickled out of tufted grass, to fill and overflow from a rusted tin. She took the brown water, burying her face in hands and water, till it ran down, and afterwards, in rivulets, in devious directions, under her dress, against her skin. The water made her laugh. She looked at the world with eyes blurred by water, but a world curiously pure, expectant, undistorted. She could almost have read a writing on the bark of any given tree.

Later Theodora returned to the house, and in a fit of comfortable conscience brought an old iron bowl that she had seen on a shelf, to fill, to clean the floor of her house. Because Holstius would return some time during the day. She knew. In this she was positive. In fact, she shaded her eyes already against the blue smoke, rising from the valleys and creating a distance. She looked through the trees for the tree walking, which in time would become Holstius. She smiled to herself as she anticipated the recognition of his kind eyes.

But in the meantime she made a widening lake on the board floor of the house, spilling the water generously from the iron basin at her waist. Then without soap, she began to scrub the boards with an old brush. This way she had a certain affinity with the women in houses. She approached close, but respectfully, to the wood, so that she might appreciate its ingrained humility and painful knots. If Holstius had returned at that moment he would have approved, to see her as simple and impervious as a scrubbed board.

Instead, a car came, groaning over stones. Theodora sat on her heels, raising her arm and the scrubbing brush for protection. The car stopped. She heard its abrupt door. She could not sense that this was in any way connected with Holstius. There was anger and exasperation in the dead grass, also a slight diffidence, almost fear, as feet covered the distance to the house. Theodora sat with the scrubbing brush upraised, and her thin mouth. If they intended to break open her peace of mind, from curiosity, or out of malice, she was prepared to defend.

'Well, for goodness' sakes!'

It was Mrs Johnson. Her sandy hair, hatless, blew at the window sill. Her colourless but anxiously friendly eyes shifted a little to avoid what she might have to see.

'Oh, it is you,' said Theodora, lowering the brush.

She could not help but love the practical face of Mrs Johnson, which for the moment, at least, was practically helpless. This was not a situation which Mrs Johnson could touch, or to which she could apply a poultice.

Then Mrs Johnson jerked her head, and laughed, and grasped

the window sill, and said, 'That was a nice thing you did, Miss Pilkington. Walking out on us. I'd got the sheets out, ready to fix your bed. You left your hat too.'

'It was not very polite,' Theodora admitted.

The sky was intensely blue and majestic behind Mrs Johnson's pathetic head.

'I should say,' said Mrs Johnson without malice.

She took a breath and came round so that she stood in the doorway.

'Lucky the kids spotted your tracks this morning. She's gone further up the road, they said. So I said I'd run on up an' see. Before I took the milk.'

Theodora got on her feet to match Mrs Johnson in an attitude of neighbourly intercourse.

'That was kind of you,' said Theodora. 'But . . .'

'Joe had a hunch you might have looked in here,' Mrs Johnson said. 'We *hoped*. For your *own* sake.'

She began to look round the room for something to tell her husband.

'My, though,' she said. 'I guess you were lonesome.'

Theodora touched the gentle ash with her toe.

'I made a fire,' she said. 'I am very happy in this house.'

Mrs Johnson frowned resentfully. She resented Theodora's state of mind, because it was something that she could not understand. Now she shifted round for words, to resist the slow silence of the dead grass.

'Maybe for a vacation,' said Mrs Johnson with a tight bright laugh. 'If your tastes lie this way.'

She looked round again at the exasperating house. She looked for some object, from out of the circle of her own life, with which to make an alliance, but all she found was the old iron bowl. This, in connection with Theodora Goodman's obsessive act of scrubbing, was so obscene that her eyes retreated.

'Well, now, Miss Pilkington,' she said, 'what are we gonna do? I got the milk to run to Martins'. Then I am at your service. I suggest you come on down to our place. It's brighter there. And comfortable. I'll fix some dinner for you. We got steak for dinner,' she said.

All this was said and said, Theodora realized, because Mrs

Johnson dared not stop. Mrs Johnson would not know the great superiority of stationary objects.

'Oh, no,' said Theodora flatly and kindly, and because she was touched by the suffering face of Mrs Johnson, she added, 'Thank you.'

'But you can't stay *here*!' said Mrs Johnson. 'Alone. In this darned old shack.'

Theodora saw how Mrs Johnson's soul would have winced and contracted in a similar situation. This was why Mrs Johnson had to protest, why she stood firm, with her bare, sandy legs slightly apart, and tried to wrench the soul of Theodora Goodman into her freckled hands.

'I can,' Theodora said. 'I can stay here perfectly well.'

Because she firmly intended that this game for the soul of Theodora Goodman should be finally hers.

'Besides,' she said, 'I expect that Holstius will come back, if not this morning, some time during the afternoon.'

'Holstius? Who the hell?' Mrs Johnson said. 'Why, his name was Kilvert!'

'I don't know about that,' said Theodora.

And it was unimportant.

'Yes, Kilvert went out to the coast eighteen months ago. Shut up the place. Didn't say when he was comin' back. Folks in town heard that Kilvert died.'

Then Mrs Johnson stopped and turned something over in her mind.

'We don't seem to be gettin' nowhere at all,' she said at last.

Theodora lifted her eyes to see whether Mrs Johnson's face was being sly. It had adopted that fatal flatness which is never quite a disguise.

'Well,' it said, 'I got work to do.'

And Mrs Johnson was going out of the door. She walked with long steps over the grass towards the car, of which the bonnet still shimmered, its metal surface broken by a haze of heat. So that Theodora was alone. She embraced with love the silence of her own room. And soon Holstius would come.

'Miss Pilkington?'

It was Mrs Johnson again. She came back. She was carrying a loaf of bread and a small iron can.

'Guess you'll need these,' she said. 'Whatever else.'

Theodora took the things, because it made Mrs Johnson better to give. She had a talent for freckled children. But some, it seems, turn out dark.

'How is Zack, Mrs Johnson?' Theodora asked.

'Zack? Why, Zack's okay. He's a slow boy, but good.'

She had some difficulty with the door of the car, so that she had to raise her voice.

'Not so quick by half as the other kids. Not so intelligent,' she said.

Something occurred to her that never before. She turned on Theodora Goodman a look of dubious dismay, of sudden helplessness. Then she gathered her long legs into the car and drove off.

The mountain began to relax after Mrs Johnson had gone. It pricked with insects. A cone fell. You could hear the wings of birds parting the heat.

Theodora stood by the window. The struggle to preserve her own instrument for some final, if also fatal, music that Holstius must play, had been at times difficult and unpleasant, but at least it was preserved. She looked out. She was conscious of the immensity of her own possessions, her blaze of blue. Now she could eat the bread, as a concession to Mrs Johnson. She put the pieces in her mouth, wiped the crumbs off, drank the milk from the lip of the little can. But in performing these acts, she continued to look out of the window, at the secretive pines and the disappearing road. If she had had a watch she would have looked at it, to measure her anxiety. Because she was afraid that Holstius. She was afraid. She was afraid of something that Mrs Johnson had begun.

Presently she went down through the trees to the place where the spring ran. She sat beside the brown water which welled out of the rusty tin, full of frog spawn and the skeletons of leaves. She decided that she would wait here for Holstius, where the formation of the land gave her a certain amount of protection, where the light and shade, tree and grass broke her body into less obvious shapes. Anyway, out of the house. Now she suspected the house. Man would be very admirable within his own freckled limits, if it were not for his native slynesses, and, more particularly, his desire to strain perpetually after truth. It was this which had led him to fix the roof of the house, propped like a lid on a stick. Twitched from a distance by a cord, the stick would fall, and the lid imprison the unsuspecting victim. So Theodora avoided the house and the subtlety that Mrs Johnson had prepared.

She stirred the water, squinting through the light at her hand, which still wore its flesh.

'Ah,' she breathed sharply, shading her eyes, and the water ran startlingly over the surface of her hot skin.

She had heard the boots squeak among the trees. She saw the flash of the hat, because today he was wearing a Panama which still disguised his face. His clothes were the same stiff daguerreotype. His expression had not yet evolved out of the shadow of the hat.

'Why are you sitting here?' he asked.

'Because I was afraid, I suppose,' she said humbly.

She turned her face aside, to minimize its foolishness. But she did not expect censure. She was too calm.

Holstius sat down. He looked at his hands, which were calloused from driving horses.

'You will go back up to the house,' he said. 'Did you know?'

'Yes,' she said, or mumbled. 'I suppose I knew.'

There was nothing that she did not know, only this had to be laid bare painfully. Holstius laid his hands on, and she was a world of love and compassion that she had only vaguely apprehended. Leaves glistened down to the least important vein.

'They will come for you soon, with every sign of the greatest kindness,' Holstius said. 'They will give you warm drinks, simple, nourishing food, and encourage you to relax in a white room and tell your life. Of course you will not be taken in by any of this, do you hear? But you will submit. It is part of the deference one pays to those who prescribe the reasonable life. They are admirable people really, though limited.'

Theodora nodded her head to each point she must remember.

'If we know better,' Holstius said, 'we must keep it under our hats.'

She would pin on it the big black rose, of which only Zack, of all the Johnsons, had sensed the significance.

Then Theodora sighed.

'It has been interesting,' she said, 'and at times lovely.'

'It has been? It *is*,' Holstius said. 'Your sense of permanence is perverted, as it is in most people. We are too inclined to consider the shapes of flesh that loom up at us out of mirrors, and because they do not continue to fit like gloves, we take fright and assume that permanence is a property of pyramids and suffering. But true permanence is a state of multiplication and division. As you should know, Theodora Goodman. Faces inherit features. Thought and experience are bequeathed.'

In the peace that Holstius spread throughout her body and the speckled shade of surrounding trees, there was no end to the lives of Theodora Goodman. These met and parted, met and parted, movingly. They entered into each other, so that the impulse for music in Katina Pavlou's hands, and the steamy exasperation of Sokolnikov, and Mrs Rapallo's baroque and narcotized despair were the same and understandable. And in the same way that the created lives of Theodora Goodman were interchangeable, the lives into which she had entered, making them momently dependent for love or hate, owing her this portion of their fluctuating personalities, whether George or Julia Goodman, only apparently deceased, or Huntly Clarkson, or Moraïtis, or Lou, or Zack, these were the lives of Theodora Goodman, these too.

'So you understand?' asked Holstius, looking down from the shade and calm of his Panama hat, for there was no wind to stir it.

'Yes,' said Theodora Goodman. 'I understand.'

She had worked it out, mathematically, in stones, spread on the ground at the toes of her long shoes.

'So that it will not be so irksome,' Holstius said.

'No,' she agreed.

She could accept the pathetic presumption of the white room.

'I should go then,' he said. 'Up to the house. Because they will arrive soon.'

Theodora stood up and hitched round her skirt, which had slipped askew. This way we abandon the dangerous state of music and achieve the less distracting positions of sculpture.

'I shall go then,' she said.

She swept back a dark shadow from her face with her quite solid hand. Out of the rusted tin welled the brown circles of perpetual water, stirring with great gentleness the eternal complement of skeleton and spawn.

For this reason Theodora Goodman did not thank, or think much more about Holstius. In the act that she was performing, walking up the slow hill towards the house, his moral support was assured. Now his presence was superfluous.

At the corner of the house she stopped to finger tentatively the spikes of a thistle. Because she had heard the car again. So she looked from beneath her eyelids, like a child, and waited, and touched the cruel spikes.

The car stopped in the clearing in front of the house. From round the corner she could just see. She could see the car, boiling over from the hill, and the last spasms of its self importance. There were three people in the car, she could see. There was Mrs Johnson. Of course. There was Mr Johnson. Less expected. And there was a mild man in spectacles. His skin was exceptionally mild as he got down out of the car. Theodora knew that his eyes would be full of subtle sympathy. But she could not see these yet. The sun was striking the metal rims of his spectacles.

'Here we are then, Doc,' said Mr Johnson, who showed no great inclination to leave the car.

It was obvious that Mr. Johnson had been brought there against his will, to share in something that he did not care to share, that it was unmanly to avoid, but which he would, if given a chance. So he sat sideways and laughed shortly, to halve his share, as it were, and to reveal his manliness. At the same time Theodora realized that the withdrawn and muscular Mr Johnson, who had his own dark moments, as he had shown her by his silences and certain positions of his body, and who had even reproduced his shadow in one dark child, this same Mr Johnson would not be her ally.

Still, she sighed, and touched the thistle, it is often like that.

'So this is where Kilvert lived,' said the mild man, for something to say.

Mrs Johnson, who had been having trouble with the door, her side of the car, now tore it open.

'That's it,' said Mrs Johnson. 'And where this crazy Annie has chosen to live now.'

Mrs Johnson's words hurt her. Sometimes she had to make her own words hurt, until she felt the smarting of her eyes. Because Mrs Johnson suffered, excessively, from an excess of tenderness. For this reason she was hard.

'She's not crazy all the time,' her husband said.

'Lucidity,' said the mild man, 'isn't necessarily a perpetual ailment.'

Johnson, who might have protested, forced himself to wonder whether he had driven home the bar in the corral gate before leaving. He grunted at the other man, and chewed grass.

Mrs Johnson had come forward. With determination she crossed the clearing. She came and stood in the lower room of the house. She called.

'Miss Pilkington?' she called.

She went upstairs. And down. She stood at the back door, and her voice had a frail sound of disguised ineffectuality as she called at the trees of a deciduous variety that grew on that side of the house.

'Darned if she ain't . . .' Mrs Johnson wavered into silence. 'Kept on talking, she did, of some guy called Holstius. Not that I fell for that.'

'But perhaps you fell for Miss Pilkington. Perhaps you ain't seen her,' her husband said.

Because Mr Johnson and the mild man were by this time also in the house. Mr Johnson had sat, to isolate himself from those who stood, and who were conducting this unpleasantness. He sat on the chair with the two carved knobs. His wife continued to stand at the door. She screwed up her eyes. She decided she had not heard her husband's remark.

Theodora, who had come round to the front window, could both see and hear. It was a strange and interesting situation. As if she were dead.

'An interesting supposition,' smiled the mild man.

His voice carefully decontaminated words. There would never be accusation in anything he said. But Theodora knew that she must not shiver.

'I am afraid that I have set you a problem,' she said now. 'Actually I do exist.'

She left the window, and came at once, quietly and decently into the room.

'Why,' said Mrs Johnson, 'for a moment I sure thought you'd walked out on us again. This is . . .' she continued, 'that is, I'd like you to meet . . .'

'My name is Rafferty,' said the mild man, coming forward with considerable bland confidence. 'I've come to take you down with me to town, where there are folks who'll make you comfortable.'

He looked at Theodora, sharing a secret and not.

She laughed.

'You Americans,' she said, 'make life positively pneumatic. But how agreeable.'

And she held her head on one side as she had seen ladies do on receiving and thanking for a cup of tea.

Then they all laughed.

'Shall we be getting along then?' Rafferty asked.

'Yes, Doctor,' Theodora agreed.

They went outside towards the hot car.

'Here,' said Mrs Johnson. 'I brought your hat, that you forgot.'

So Theodora Goodman took her hat and put it on her head, as it was suggested she should do. Her face was long and yellow under the great black hat. The hat sat straight, but the doubtful rose trembled and glittered, leading a life of its own.